Stephen Pett's
SIRENS

"In this beautifully written novel, Stephen Pett proves himself to be a master of language. But he also tells a story that has the pure and dangerous voltage of honest rage—it jolts you upright in your chair."
—Rick DeMarinis, author of
Year of the Zinc Penny

"This is brilliant writing—remarkable as that blue moon we are meant to yearn for, unique as that oft-cited cold day in hell. *Sirens* is a novel to holler long and hard about—seductive and alarming, beguiling and urgent, as terrific and terrifying as a week in Wonderland. Pett has the word 'master' written all over him."
—Lee K. Abbott, author of
Strangers in Paradise

"A furious voice and vision. *Sirens* is relentlessly American, and Carlos Cade takes his place among the mitigating heroes of our literature, torn between the ecstatic forces of nature and the loneliness of civilization."
—Michael Martone, author of
Alive and Dead in Indiana

"A compelling novel. I was pulled through each page by the driving narrative and at the same time dazzled by the lyricism of Pett's language. Here's a novel to sink and settle into, a delight in its richness, and a book to place up on the shelf with Flannery O'Connor's *Wise Blood* or Thomas Wolfe's *Look Homeward Angel*."
—Mary Swander, author of
Driving the Body Back

ALSO BY STEPHEN PETT

Pulpit of Bones (poetry)

SIRENS

VINTAGE CONTEMPORARIES

VINTAGE BOOKS

A DIVISION OF RANDOM HOUSE, INC.   NEW YORK

SIRENS

Stephen Pett

Thank you for your confidence and help,
Sam, Jane, Molly, Pat, and Robin.

A VINTAGE ORIGINAL, FIRST EDITION
JUNE 1990

Copyright © 1990 by Stephen Pett

Library of Congress Cataloging-in-Publication Data
Pett, Stephen Willard, 1949–
Sirens / Stephen Pett. — 1st ed.
p.   cm. — (Vintage contemporaries)
ISBN 0-394-75712-2
I. Title.
PS3566.E884S5   1990
813'.54—dc20   89-39322
CIP

Book design by Chris Welch
Manufactured in the United States of America
10 9 8 7 6 5 4 3 2 1

for Clare

SIRENS

1 —— THE GREAT SALT LAKE

They swung onto the gravel shoulder behind me just out-side of Rawlins—a '66 Impala rusted halfway up the doors. "Salt Lake," I said. A big Indian took a leak by the passenger side while I squeezed in back. His black shirt hung from the door. In the middle of one of his soft tits was a scar, orange and ragged, like a mouth, where a nipple should have been. He pushed his pink-tinted glasses onto his head as he climbed back in. The bleached-out bumper sticker on the glove compartment said RED POWER.

With the transmission whining somewhere up around ninety, the driver—long braids, big smile—poked his part-ner and grabbed a cassette off the dash. He flipped a butt out the window. A bird dove into the radiator. The driver said, "Shit." His partner punched on the tape, this eerie goddamn flute music, and they both lit up Chesterfield Kings, and sparks swirled all over hell, and the faster we went the smaller all the bushes and hills got and the hotter the sun.

"You guys got any grass or anything?" I hollered.

Neither turned—with the engine, the wind, the flute like goddamn sirens. I probably dreamed the sonsofbitches.

Rain.

The driver's wiper worked but only smeared things

around. They pulled up outside the Overniter on West Temple. The rain drummed the roof. Lightning. The swamp-stale stink of the lake. Drops streaked the window where I could barely see myself staring out, needing a shave and a drink. The driver had been running at the mouth in some damn lost language. He and his buddy were laughing now. The buddy said, "This joint don't charge much."

"Peace," the driver said. "Some of us're gonna get where we're goin'."

This bony guy with buck teeth leaned out on the counter by the register, the register's drawer open, empty. Not even midnight. "Hey, Jude" in violins in the ceiling speakers. Everything about him's just right: His tie is right, his shirt is clean, each oily hair on his head is in place. But next to the mints between his hands are black horn-rimmed glasses, one lens cracked, one lens gone.

I said, "Hey." This wide-eyed Mickey Mouse phone was on the floor by the paper racks, missing its cord.

He said, "Hey," but stared at his hands. Thunder shook the windows.

"I'd like a room. Cheap."

"They broke my glasses."

"Who?"

"Took my wallet."

"Call the cops."

"The fourth time in three weeks."

"Call the governor."

I unwrapped a mint and popped it in my mouth. I used a pay phone in the kitchen.

While he leaned there, waiting for the police, each breath so deep it squealed, I lifted a key off the board behind him. "Just forget it," he said. "To hell with this place. Without my glasses, what am I supposed to do?"

A free room. A slug or two of Old Crow out of my duffel. HBO and Cinemax. Crusty shag carpet the color of Pepto-Bismol. Michael Caine shot Superman on the TV chained to the wall.

Welcome back, Carlos Cade, dumb shit. You should have waded to the Greyhound station and boogied out of there. But that would have been smart. Smart's for your next life.

And for college professors.

"Dr. Downes is on another line."

I held. A hot sun. A clear sky, blue splashes down the sidewalk, shrinking puddles from the night before. Worms.

"Hello." At least eighteen years and I would have known that voice, shy, deep.

"Matt." Two semi's roared by my booth. I liked the threat, the size of that sound.

"Who is this?"

"Carlos."

After a wait of air brakes, a jet rising over North Temple toward me, a robin busy at a puddle, Matt said, "Let me close my door." Then he said, "I thought you'd call some day."

"You get a lot of attention in the papers."

"For keeping a cow alive on a machine."

"That's something."

"It's something. So ask me."

"Ask you what?" I slowly lowered my shoe on a night crawler. I fake smiled at my reflection, at two sea gulls sitting on a billboard for Ringling Brothers at the Salt Palace, at how quickly we had come so far. "Ask you what?"

"I'm going to hang up."

"We should tell," I said. "We need to . . . to pay back . . . to erase a lot, a lot of shit."

He took so long I lit a smoke. "Where's the good?"

"The good? Hell, the good is getting out from under it."

"That's not how it would be. What do you *really* want?"

"To get even."

"With whom?"

"You know."

"I don't know. Cade, I'm sorry. That's the sum of it. I'm sorry. And if you talk, I'll deny all of it."

A click then seashell quiet. A taxi lost its hub cap, a silver disc that clanged and bounced and rolled behind a Gulf station. I breathed and heard a rush like fire through the phone.

2 —— DRY CANYON

Start with one blink of the eye way the hell up Dry Canyon.

I remember long shadows when it happened, dark, deep spiders of shadow in every corner of the mountains. And dust, a steam of it.

Lots of days we laced on sneakers, grabbed a couple of the canvas-covered canteens Matt's old man left on their porch, and hiked the few blocks to the dusty foothills, trailing a dog or two. Goddamn, the sun hollowed you like a gourd, shined so hot you couldn't sweat. You stepped from the green, clear, sprinklered edge of the Shriners' Hospital lawn onto desert and liked it, the heat, the dry, the emptiness. The dogs went home.

We followed this rutted-out old mining road up under the U on the first big mountain. The slope rose forever, loose red dirt and rock, thin grass and sage, cactus and

burned-out sego lilies. We carried sticks. Gerry had a sling-
shot. He fired at the charred pile of mattresses and tin cans,
at the magpies always posted there, where the road ended.
We all shouted.

The Six Shooters, older, taller, loped now in long, muffled strides this August before fifth grade. Gerry Olds and
Matt Downes went off nine months to Catholic school.
Lance's money bought him loose of the ragged likes of me
and Skink on the Wasatch playground the rest of the year.
Lance Arthur, Utah's famous young governor. Fall, winter,
spring, Pep, Ryan Peppers, stayed scrubbed and right with
God: Mormon see, Mormon do. Who gave a shit? Summer
was still summer and this scuffed-up gang, pals trimmed
back to size.

This was an honest-to-goddamn adventure cutting
around onto that steep north wall of Dry Canyon, the hot,
huge sky shrunk suddenly between two ridges. We ran
along a deer trail, a smooth, even track through the rubble
of that mountainside at least two hundred feet above the
bottom. Hooves scraping that ground for centuries. Sometimes we'd leap a pile of fresh pellets. Sometimes we'd see
four or five vanish far ahead in shadow or a stand of scrub
oak.

We flew. We flew along that narrow strip of trail, raced
above that dust-hazy chasm, one black hawk gliding below,
blue jays shrieking. My God. We stiffened our arms like
wings and dove through the sky, through a seam between
the dry, white heat flaming off the ground and the canyon's
cool wind.

"I'm a bald eagle," one of us hollered.

"Condors are bigger."

"Nothing can catch a falcon."

Shouting back and forth, we flew, faster, smelling the
sage, hearing only the wild throbbing of our shoes. Some-

times a lizard sliced the trail, slipped over the edge, slid down and down and down, to catch a root. Or disappear.

Once as we cut through a boulder's black shadow, Skink screamed. "A rattler. Didn't you hear it?" Rocks flew off our feet like shooting stars.

The trail held level on the slope. The twisting notch of canyon floor slowly rose to meet us, slowly widened to more than a black scratch of creek and a tinsel strand of green. We flew *there*, to that jigsaw corner in that desert puzzle of heat-stroked mountains. The city was gone—off in our pasts somewhere before this brown rock and tough-bunched scrub oak.

Cicadas screech and all the stones you see turn against each other. But the smell . . . the smell is damp, muddy. In a narrow, grassy channel trickles clear, icy water. Pep says the green stuff in the pools is cress, and we eat it. We drink. Water spills over my lip and down my neck. I lift my head in this first shade in hours, in the grinding, in a soft movement of hornets and bees sharing cool ground with sweating, harmless, beat-to-shit boys.

The shade stretched from a limekiln—at least that's what we called it because Gerry or Lance said that's what it was. They said that two-story block of crumbly yellow bricks set in the mountainside was where some pioneers got lime— for whitewash, plaster, lots of things. A wide hole at the top funneled to a little hole at the bottom, into what was like a big, arched fireplace. I never did figure the thing out. Seemed to me maybe the hollow in the middle filled with rain water they boiled down with a hefty fire underneath, but that was as far as I got. I didn't care. It was a mysterious goddamn piece of the old days. You could climb the slope beside it and stare into the dark deep hole. I could see Gandy, my grandmother, in a bonnet tending the fire. I could see cavemen. I could see myself—and like what I saw.

We were cavemen. Ape-men. Animals. Egyptians. Explorers. Cavalry men. Cowboys. But most often Indians, chest-pounding, war-whooping, earth-loving, wild-child Indians. That's what we were that day. We played Indian. We fought to see who would be Chief.

You've heard them. Kids' voices smooth as sand: "WOO-woo-woo-woo, WOO-woo-woo-woo." Owls wail and coyotes howl above the shrieking insect sound. Through dead leaves, over boulders, splashing through that tiny stream, we wore buckskin and rode spotted ponies loyal and smart and strong as buffalo bulls. Then scratched and wet and black in the mouth, eyes, and nostrils, one of us climbed the loose, dry slope and stepped onto the kiln.

He shouted over the edge, "Chief! You can't get me. Chief! You can't get me." Whooping louder than ever, the others scrambled and wrestled up toward him. The point was to tag the Chief, but by the time one of us started onto the kiln, he had usually slipped over the side and slid down the slope. No one stayed Chief long. The new Chief shouted. The rest began at the bottom again.

We were tired, dragging long shadows, tired as kids get, not aching, just empty: no muscles, no weight, nothing. Kids can lose themselves like that. To the game. The noise. The dirt. The grabbing hands. Laughter that couldn't stop. Lance knew that. The game was nearly over.

And there was Skink, with his big, round face, on top of the kiln, shouting at us climbing toward him slowly now but still climbing. Lance dragged us aside. As Skink jumped past him, Lance grabbed his arm and threw him down the slope. "You'll have to pull me off."

We lunged for Lance, sure, but we didn't give a shit about getting him. He stood at the back, swung at us, yelled, and shoved us away. His birthmark darkened under his arm. And that small red scar beneath his eye. Soon enough, Pep and Matt and I parked below in the spreading shade. Who needed a side ache? Gerry wobbled above Lance, made a few half-hearted charges, then lay hot and pink in a clump of scrub oak. Magpies laughed down the canyon. The rocks turned against each other.

Skink kept on. Just Lance, then, crouched dark and loud—"Chief! You can't get me"—and dirty, moon-faced Skink charging up and sliding down. Skink almost had Lance the last time. He got his hand, but Lance yanked loose, lifted a foot, and kicked out so that Skink tumbled head over heels through red dust to the bottom. Finally, as if his back hurt, Skink pushed onto his knees, blinking, his mouth open and empty until he stood: "I hate you, you rich fairy bastard." Then tears. He said, "I'll make ya. I'm gonna be Chief." He lowered his chin, took one step, and stopped, eyes frozen wide, fists unfolding. Skink fell forward. A lizard scurried through the sage.

Gerry got there first, jumped down the slope, shouting, "Hey, you guys! Hey!" Lance stood still up top, arms stiff and thin. Pep laughed. We three laughed in the shade. But bent over Skink, Gerry called, "Lance threw a rock. Come on. Hurry." I saw it again then, a red rock round as a cherry spinning up off Skink's surprised face. I saw it. Just above his eye. Matt and Pep ran too.

Gerry and I rolled Skink over, knowing he was dead. Crying, Gerry said, "Lance killed him. Lance killed him." I didn't cry. Just barely there, just a set of hands reaching in, holding an arm, I turned a dirty boy the same size as me onto his back.

"He ain't dead," Pep said. "He's breathing."

But Matt said, "Look," and we saw the red button of blood among the freckles.

I said, "Jesus."

Then Lance called down, "Throw some water on him." So we did, handfuls from the stream, cold, real water. Nothing. Skink wouldn't move. But he breathed. And I heard something like the flicker of flame when I listened at his chest.

"He must be in a coma," Matt said.

"He's dying," Gerry said.

Pep said, "No, a coma. He's not blue or anything."

Kneeling in leaves, I tried to figure what a rock like that could do. I thought Skink would soon enough cough or something, sit up, rub his eyes, and smile, and we could go home. We waited, Lance still overhead. A shadow spread to Skink's feet. Pep asked, "When do comas end?"

Matt said, "Hardly ever." He looked at Lance. "You put him in a coma."

Finally Lance whispered, "He had it coming." Two dark magpies drifted slow circles around his head, out and back, out and always back, with no effort of wings.

3 —— NAMES

June 21, two years earlier, 1958. THE LONGEST DAY, the caption said. We didn't know that.

The lady photographer drove a pink Delray. The photograph would turn yellow, how newspaper gets, like dead skin. And the faces, blurred to start with, would almost fade away. Her camera used black plates. Lance said, "What's she up to?" Her black hair stayed still in the breeze. We stood dripping, all six of us in cutoffs, the sprinklers sizzling at our backs.

"Just do what you've been doing," she said. "That's what I want."

So we held each other's waists and ran through the cold spray in that blinded line the length of the island. She slipped off her red heels and trotted beside us, clacking the plates in and out of her camera. "I'll be sure to send you copies," she said, and she took our addresses.

That Sunday Hickler or somebody dropped the front page of the *Salt Lake Tribune*'s local section through the mail slot. My old man got to it first. "Goddamn," he said. "Here's Carlos in the paper. Good goddamn."

I run third from the end. Lance leads, fists tight against his chest, the pink birthmark on his side gray here, like the shadow of his heart. Gerry and Matt come next. Gerry the fastest of all, the tallest, grins to the side, both feet off the ground; Matt, head down, stocky, pushes instead of being pulled, his shorts slipped so low a white line divides him in two. Believe it or not, I'm holding on to Matt with just one hand so I can wave. Wave! Jesus. Skink's forehead presses my back, his round little body tucked, his hands tight around my stomach. Pep follows last, nearly straight out, feet curled like wings. All of us are slippery, glisten. Pep's old man called us the Six Shooters.

Pep's father fixed pin-setting machines at the Pal-D-Mar Lanes. Old man Skink butchered part-time at Crystal Palace Market two blocks away. Gerry's dad did something halfway important out at Kennecott. Six of one, half dozen of almost any other, mine was a border neighborhood, where east side met west side and just about everything in between.

One Saturday Matt drew a treasure map of our block of Twelfth East. While we slurped cocoa on his playroom couch, watching *Sky King* and *Roy Rogers*, he lay on white linoleum with crayons and paper. We kept the map in a

Hills Brothers can in the Downeses' garage. It showed our major trail, down behind Hickler's Market, past the Skinks' roofless tool shed, the Skinks' siding house bulging all around, the flaking, gray Plymouth on blocks in the yard. Then the path snaked over fences, under a hairdresser's redwood deck, and crossed the street to Pep's. Pep's blue corner place was huge, but other people lived in most of it, students from the university and older ladies with orange hair and miniature dogs.

The line circled Pep's apple trees, avoided the widow bitch's yard altogether, crossed a doctor's porch roof, and cut under an upside-down motor boat to Matt's, drawn a little large but still nothing fancy, just another one of the shoulder-to-shoulder row of mostly brick houses. A bigshot at the *Tribune*, Matt's old man drove a creamy yellow Jaguar, and his mother wore fur coats that sparked at night when she climbed in and out of the car. The track curved around Gerry's next door, Gerry's like the rest except for a lamp out by the sidewalk that turned on automatically at sunset.

Then as it swerved away from three flower beds, the trail line became arrows that led to a big X and a treasure chest back of the Arthurs' garage. The Arthurs' place fit the pattern, but it had pillars, white pillars too big to get your arms around. A two-briefcase lawyer heavy in the face and dead dark around the eyes, Lance's old man kept to himself. With no Mama Arthur. A tall, stooping black lady climbed the hill of steps up to their door in the morning and strained back down again at night. Lance called her Auntie.

We didn't have a treasure. Lance said, "That's where we'll bury it when we do."

Arrows came at the X from the other direction, too, from a line that crossed the street at this end of the block, after cutting up from Hickler's back of some garbage cans and my house, my house bigger than I ever thought of it. Matt drew a palm tree by my window.

In the middle of our trail, that circle, of everything on the map, set off in a gravelly, rough river of road, three green city-owned islands were splotched with yellow, for the dogs I guess. Our islands. Big yellow mutts dragged raw bones out there from behind Hickler's. Sometimes in a race to kick the can or tag or tackle somebody, you'd fall on one of those maggoty bones and damn near die. Fat men in jungle helmets came with riding mowers and these long metal rods for turning on sprinklers. And on hot days we sat and wrestled and ran in the spray.

My sister, Hilda, said, "That's you waving. 'Carlos Cade.' Look."

The radio sang, "God Gave Noah the Rainbow Sign."

You got a home in that rock
Just beyond the mountain top.

Papa said, "We ain't been to the park this season. It's about time."

Mama said, "How did the paper know your name?"

Don't think I'm a Mex, an Indian, or anything. Hell, I have red hair. My folks tagged me Carlos after this guy my old man hopped freights with during the Depression, a crippled guy who slipped jumping aboard outside of Albuquerque—period. My namesake. Goddamn. Papa ended up with his gold pocket watch. Can you beat that? A Mex hobo with a gold pocket watch. And this thick book with a hand-tooled cover.

My old man couldn't read, but he held onto that book, too, *The San Francisco Earthquake*, with lots of drawings of pigtailed Chinese running from fires and black cracks in the ground. He'd show it to us sometimes and say, "There's worse things than dying." The back was Scotch-taped. With Mama damn near dead one time, he got out that precious book—wrapped in brown paper—wiped the wet hair from his forehead, opened to one of the pictures, and cried without sound.

I never cried.

Two doors up from Hickler's, our one-story frame excuse for a home squatted behind a tidy pink brick place, down a cramped alley loose with white gravel the size of walnuts. We made do with three rooms, not counting the bathroom, with concrete floors, so help me—the only part that never got hot. In the bathroom, under the leaking steel sink, you could see where somebody named Lincoln put his hands in the wet (still wet) cement. A dog had zigzagged through the kitchen, like maybe it detoured to lift its leg on the stove. And just behind my sister Hilda's bed was the print of one of those big ladies' combs. Jesus.

Imagine lying naked on a mattress that smells like fire in a room all dark greenish with a Coke-bottle sort of moonlight. Flies hum past and pop their heads against the walls. Heat drips down your face and neck and sides. Two windows in the tight room are open, but air so dry and dusty only powders your tongue. Somewhere off in that green darkness your sister whines quietly whenever she breathes. She is naked, too, in the goddamn heat, waiting for morning. You like her whining because it's not yours. "Faraway, faraway, faraway," chant the crickets or katydids or whatever the hell they are.

If you can't stand it, if you loosen your tongue enough to talk and squeal the door open on your parents, they send you back. They are naked too. Their room is filled with stiff ribbons of cigarette smoke. In bloodless yellow light they look like the empty wax bottles you buy to bite the tops off and suck dry. If you bother them twice, your father beats you with an old car antenna, and sometimes it is better than the heat.

That's summertime. Winters just flicker with school and snow. And once or twice the *Tribune* Christmas tree downtown. A star flashed on top.

Our landlady kept the front house, charging my folks I-don't-know-what chickenshit amount for our sweat palace. Bottoms, MRS. I. C. BOTTOMS, her mailbox said, honest to God. As old as she had to be—she looked two hundred—she lived alone, except for a green parrot named Rudy, my old man said. I only saw her twice. Once when Gerry Olds broke her side window throwing one of those walnut rocks at me, this chalky, rutted face opened a round, black mouth in the ragged hole of glass: "You spineless bastards." A voice so high it almost wasn't there.

The other time, I was mowing the front grass, her squealing, antique push mower, my old man's orders. In the shade after just one turn, I pulled off my T-shirt. How did I know she was there? She could have been empty threaded in the spidery web of her rusty screen door right then. Empty eyed. Jesus. Finally she said—I'm sure she said—"You're a fine-looking young man, Tommy."

Christ.

In the alley once I heard Rudy cackle, "I love you, Tommy. I love you, Tommy." I don't know who the hell Tommy was, but, odd as God, I've had days where I caught myself saying, in that tiny language of hers, "You're a fine-looking young man, Tommy."

So that Sunday we went to Reservoir Park with a long bag of bread and bunches of thick green garden onions somebody always left us. While young couples in white clothes, serious rich kids with dark tans, loped and swung rackets on the tennis courts, we wandered the base of a hill of pine trees and through the tall grass alongside the fence, looking for balls. Mama carried a deep paper sack with string handles. We almost filled it. "We" was me and Mama and Hilda. My old man, his forehead shining, short breaths ending in short rattles, a cough now and then, slouched on ahead of us, "scouting," he said, and then sat in the shade somewhere and smoked Old Golds. A cigarette fit right there where the scar under his nose puckered his lip. We sat by him and ate.

After the onions rolled in bread slices and long luke-warm gulps from the water fountain, we trudged up to the University Golf Course and scavenged for balls in the roughs alongside the fairways. Mama doubled back and forth like a bird dog. You'd be surprised how many we found. The pro shop paid right now for what we got, a nickel for every one without cuts. My old man pocketed the money. We took our time going home, Papa breathing louder and louder, Mama dragging the bag full of tennis balls.

I'd had my picture waving in the paper. Who cared what the ignorant assholes shouted?

Family outings.

Hilda's the one painted CADE over the mail slot in red fingernail polish. My parents could hardly count, let alone write. We got by on "relief," a crackpot name for it, you ask me. Could that have been enough? We always had something, a warm meal, okay with ketchup, scrounged out of canned and greasy odds and ends. With lots of squashed, soft white bread.

I think a few days' worth of groceries every month came from the Mormons, believe it or not. I remember clean teenage boys in baseball hats unloading brown bags from a station wagon outside our door. My old man strung the

Mormon block teachers along until they looked, sweating
big circles in those starched, white shirts, eyes spread, like
they thought he'd sprout wings. If he believed a word, he
never told us.

I'm not sure how we got anything else those years. Once
Mama sent me and Hilda down a wide street to wait behind
some trees. In brightest daylight she took a hose and a jug
up alongside a blue Buick. Afterward I thought the sharp-
breathing gold stuff sloshing in the jug was cider or a new
kind of soda pop. What she did that for I don't know. We
never had a car. They didn't drink it, I'm sure. See, my
old man blamed all his gut problems on the gasoline and
Sterno he put away in his hobo days. Who knows?

On my birthdays and most Christmases, I got tennis balls,
tennis balls painted different colors. My old man shook his
head and said, "Lookee there." One I remember in my
stocking even had a face drawn on, a grinning face with
yellow buck teeth. The same for Hilda. Sub-for-Santa
brought our only store-bought toys in cardboard boxes on
Christmas Eve. Mama and Papa never lied about Santa
Claus. My old man made us thank the men who delivered
those toys. Then while we eyeballed the packages, he said,
"There's Saint Nick for ya. Grown folks acting like children.
Heads full of jelly." We never did go to church.

Sundays, with chipped, stained, white cups full of coffee
that a long time ago stopped steaming, Mama and Papa sat
across from each other at the kitchen table, my old man in
his underwear, and smoked. Instead of loose-stringed hill-
billy garbage, radio those mornings boomed with southern
voices threatening us with Gawd: "Eternal dayumnation."
God songs. The house trembled. Hilda laughed at the ser-
mons. I pushed outside—never mind my old man's mumbled "Stick around."

One Thanksgiving the Shorters, this model Mormon

family from a model siding house three doors the other side of Hickler's, brought us a whole turkey dinner, right down to whipped cream for the pumpkin pie. They portered in at least a dozen full, flowered dishes without so much as a whatdyathink. "Don't say a word," a grinning Mr. Shorter said, his tie tacked with a gold star, his station wagon humming in the drive. "You've something to be thankful for tonight." The light shivered. My folks' white breath trailed through the cold shadows outside while the Shorters laid our table.

Dinner tasted good, all right, but I skipped seconds and passed on pumpkin pie. My folks ate empty-faced just like every other meal, only taking longer. Then the next day, with Hilda and me in tow, they hauled the Shorters a shopping bag full of tennis balls, along with the dirty platter and plates. I don't know where Mama found the grimy greeting card she stuck in the sack. Mrs. Shorter cried.

Mama whistled with her cheeks puffed out all the way home.

The photographer with the black hair never did send those pictures, unless maybe Matt's old man had them and never passed them out.

4 —— IMPOSTORS

So Matt won't talk.

The sea gulls fly. A man dressed like a boy—baseball hat, rolled jeans, sneakers—rides a bike loaded with papers past, hitting each puddle. Heat. I smoke. Initials are scratched on every surface of the telephone booth. I know what I am doing.

I'll try Danny Ingus, another ghost from the past. Danny's old man's the only Ingus in the book—Ingus Salvage. No thanks.

I call my mother. They say she is resting and is not to be disturbed.

I walk downtown. Two new skyscrapers. Motorized trolleys. The Pioneer Limited, a street train all on rubber wheels, hauls out-of-towners past the shrines. Everyone's ironed. Everybody's squeaky clean. Small trees bud in their pots on Main. I still look for the *Tribune* thermometer.

I drink an Orange Julius before I head for Yellow Cab. The bars have their doors open, the soaps on TV's inside. A couple of bums snore on the wet sidewalk. The Union Pacific Station is right there, but where to? A train calls.

This stocky guy with a gray Santa beard carries a clipboard to a cab. The cabs are dirty. He doesn't smile. A phone rings out a window. The dispatcher has bat-wing glasses with fake diamonds in the corners hanging at her neck.

She takes a call. Another. Then she says, "We don't need no drivers." She is too old for the red of her lipstick.

"A guy named Ingus worked in the garage. Danny Ingus. He still around?"

"No," she says, looking at the clock. She works the switchboard and touches a wet finger to a curl on her forehead.

This little bald mechanic's got grease up to his armpits. "Hey," he shouts into the row of raised taxis. "Guy here looking for Danny Ingus."

This old guy finally wanders from the gloom. His hearing aid is blue. His shirt says JIMMY. He carries a wrench. "Whatchou want with Ingus?"

"He's a friend."

"He ain't my friend," the man says. He touches the wrench to his cheek. "He stole lots of stuff from us. We caught him with nothing but some tires. All he got was fired. He should have got shot. His friends steer clear of me."

Santa honked and pulled over two blocks down. He left the cab idling and took his time walking up. He smoked a meerschaum stained yellow. He tamped it with a bullet casing. "I hear you want Ingus. A friend would know he split."

"It's been a couple of years. We go way back."

His eyes small, he checked both directions, tamped again. "He needs friends, I'll tell you," the man said and puffed. "Ingus is okay. Saved my ass a couple of times upstairs. Now they're sticking him with everything. He's got a new name. Castro." He shook his head. "Seemed smart. He's a steady after ten at Tricky Mick's down on State. What're you called? I'll phone him."

No Castro in the book either. Big surprise.

The blond pushed it right up into the fat guy's face. The fat guy wolf howled, laughed to his fat buddies in their black Harley shirts, and then—one fat hand around her ass—wadded a bill into her G-string. She pulled away. His buddies held him back. She smiled, her teeth too long. Lifted her eyes, stepped farther in her tall red heels. Held her tits, swung them slowly, spun her gold hair in smoky specks of light flying off the mirrored ball burning, turning up high. Herb Alpert. Scratchy. From the speaker lid of the red plastic record player she'd started up behind her on the box-top stage. The Tijuana Brass. She pranced. RITA MENU, the sign said. Her eyes flashed when Fat Boy lunged again and hooked her leg. She yanked free. His buddies had his arms. The crowd whistled and clapped. She turned, shimmied with her back to the noise. They threw coins. Hooted.

"Hey, brother," he said, "or is your official handle

Brother-in-Law?" He laughed, one tooth black. He squeezed my shoulder. Danny Ingus, all right, his hair slicked straight back—wiry, nervous Danny. He'd had his nose fixed or something, no more twist to the left. And he had this thick mustache, a crucifix earring, and a dog's head belt buckle. When we were both around, I'd seen him two or three times a year since junior high. A few beers, a handful of pills. He rubbed one eye, the eye with the funny pupil, his eyes older in the creases stretched damn near to his ears. Still, acne shadowed his cheeks, still the tattoo. "I might be able to set you up with a working friend of Rita's."

"Nah," I said, and I stood, tipped the last beer from my glass, and spoke to his earringed ear. "I'm back on business. Serious business. Let's go outside."

Rita's record stuck on a low roll of trombone. She stomped the stage and it started again. Swinging his phony leg across the gravel lot, Danny took off his straw cowboy hat. "Look," he said. Alongside the pheasant feather band, Johnny Rodriguez had autographed the brim: TO FREDDY—KEEP THE FAITH . . . "I'm Castro now. Fred L. Castro. Remember that? Shit." He pulled the hat back on and shook out a cigarette. We leaned on a pickup bumper. The hot grease of traffic. A breeze cooled my neck. "Where the hell you been?"

"Good question," I said. "Where haven't I? You owe me some bread. I need it." Fresh from rehab, way back, Danny'd hit me up for $275. Moaned in my barber chair one time. "You look flush," I said.

"Flush I ain't," he said. "Yet. Two weeks I'm rolling in it. I'll cut you in. Triple your money. No risk."

"I've got business."

"Any for me?"

"Personal business."

"Mine's with big boys," he said. "Cake." He shook his head. The lake drifted in, the salt sour breath of the Great Salt Lake, dead water, dead beaches. Air turned inside out.

He lit a jay. We passed it.

"I'm talking *right now*," I said. "I need a place. Work."

"Hey, I'm your man," he said, exhaling, grinning. "Where I punch in, boss pays shit but he pays. The ends meet. And the guy don't ask nothin'." He laughed and shifted his weight, twisted the boot on the fake leg. I caught his arm before he fell. He sat back on the bumper. "The roost is harder. We got a Hide-a-Bed, but hell, my place's a fucking closet. Rose'd shit if I put you up."

"How's the kid?"

"Older. Every damn minute." He squinted over the last hit. "Hey, remember old lady Shiftlet, the one took me in when my folks bombed out? She's got this boarding place. We'll call her. Trust me. I'm your man."

"I need cash."

"She'll float you. A deposit, whatever. No worries. I've got this fucking gold mine, I'm saying."

"Right." The cars ground by in dirty clouds of exhaust.

"Hey," he said. "I seen this poster at Safeway for a revival meeting. So your old man got religion. 'Father of the First Lady,' it said. He found *his* gold mine. Lester Cade, born again."

"Once was plenty for him," I said. My ribs cinched up, and my hands wouldn't open. "For me, too."

"So where *have* you been? You was in barber school, what, three years ago. Arthur owned it, right, your buddy Lance Arthur?"

"I clipped some big shot's earlobe." I laughed. He lit another number. Two guys pulled in four cars down. They passed a bottle and listened to Tanya Tucker. "Then Arthur fixed me up at his ranch. But that got old, using the bastard. I'm finished with him, just about anyway. Shit, I busted out of there with a carnival."

"No kiddin'?"

"Now I'm bustin' in."

"Good for you," Danny said. "Me, too. In a big way."

5 —— *THE OLD WEST*

Four years before, I'd gotten loose of Salt Lake as a gen-u-ine cowboy on Arthur's King Peak Ranch: strays, ditches, fence, three square, and a roof at night.

Here I was this guy who'd burned some big bridges, done time in the State School, never set foot in a college, missed Nam—here I was as good as looked after for life. I should have liked that. No matter how badly I screwed up, Lance would come through. First, there was the time I got arrested in the desert. Then I left the ponies' gate open at Beehive Amusement and two of them drowned in the swimming pool. No problem. Some oily rags I didn't soak combusted in a wooden maintenance building fifty yards from the roller coaster. The park fire team won an award for that. Lance got me on at a buddy's barber school. That ended the day I snipped this city commissioner's ear. On the sixth floor of St. Joseph's Villa, a nursing home for healthy bank accounts, I said so long to my mother, who couldn't remember who the hell I was. And one week later Lance had me punching cattle between two rows of still-snowy mountains in eastern Utah, this Cartwright kind of spread, mostly a family getaway he'd picked up cheap.

Sometimes I saw my sister riding with her kids. Her long hair sailed behind her. Her spotted horse would prance and run, and she always worked the reins with just one hand. I got along all right. I'd earned my keep way back when. Nobody at the ranch knew any of that. Even liquored up, I kept my story to myself—hidden away.

The storm heaved against the log walls, hissed. The wind rattled down the chimney pipe. Lance Arthur waved from the TV set. The old-guard state senator running against him had conceded. Checkers, our foreman, handed out Dutch Masters cigars. I smoked a cigarette, popped a beer.

Only four of us were left to stay on from October till spring—Checkers, Moon, Cook, and I—to stay bored mostly, except for Checkers, who made this twisty kind of furniture out of willows. "Arthur'll be the youngest governor in the whole blamed country," Checkers said from the corner, branches all over the place. "Could be a hell of a president some day."

Moon flicked his cigar on the floor. He said, "Sure. Of the Power-Hungry Dip Shits maybe."

Cook was from L.A., via Korea, and Moon started out in Phoenix. They weren't lifers like Checkers. Over whiskey sometimes, Cook talked about humping it up to the pipe in Alaska. Cook liked cold. Moon said he'd paddle his own homemade dugout down the Amazon. "I'll stay," I said. "Marry one of them tan flag girls on the highway out of Coalville. Buy my own ranch." They laughed.

The hail started up again, shaking the windows. None of us had voted. Too damn far. Too damn muddy. Too damn tired from moving hay. Too damn pointless. Cook flipped to *Hawaii Five-O*. "Poker?"

"You guys," I said.

I threw on my parka and sat out of the wind on the porch. The cigar sailed ghosts of smoke over the white yard, above the barn. A thin moon dropped down when the storm moved past. I shook, but the goddamn cigar still burned, and this was the world I was looking at, just as much mine as anybody's. I pulled up my hood and I heard them.

Geese. Wailing over. I splashed out through the slush, out to where the only light was just that moon. Flapping. Gray bodies in a long, slow, noisy line squeezing through the stars.

July.

Moon jumped on the brakes. Way the hell out in the nowhere middle of Summit County, his damn Datsun truck squealed sideways. We'd hit something. My head bounced off the passenger window. The headlights blinked and then flared over sage and rock and wire. Cook said, "Jesus Christ, Moon."

Moon push-buttoned an end to Hank Williams, Jr., and threw us into reverse. He straightened his hat. He clicked in his cheek like he did for waitresses and green horses. We were loaded. "Road killed," he said.

"Damn near," I said. "Fix your brain on getting our asses home in one piece."

But the big, round-faced son of a bitch kept her rolling the wrong way, using his mirrors since the Plexiglas windows of his camper top were covered with bumper stickers and decals of elk and ducks and trout. "Jesus Christ," Moon said. "How 'bout that?"

Cook shook out a match halfway to his cigarette. He coughed and whispered, "Them mothers is supposed to be gone."

The headlights swirled way off into the darkness. Right in front of us on the loose shoulder of that two-lane, no-where-gray run of asphalt was humped this big mound of black fur. Moon hustled through the buggy light, the motor idling. Six six, long and smiling all lit up like his likeness pounded out of tin, he tilted his straw hat back and crouched down. He lifted a black hairy head big as a TV— and grinned.

Cook popped another Pabst and said, "A fucking bear."

For a guy tattooed up one arm and down the other, Cook sure was slow to get a kick out of anything.

"Come on," Moon said, leaning in to cut the engine. The crickets picked up. "A goddamn bear rug. And bear steaks, Cook. He's still warm."

Moon drained his last one. He crushed the can and laughed under a million goddamn stars. I was out now. I smelled bear, like onions and cinnamon combined.

As Moon opened the camper top and dropped the tailgate, Cook shouted, "They got laws, kid. You gotta tell the wildlife cops. They weigh 'em, measure their teeth. You can't just up and butcher one."

"We can lift it. Who's gonna know? Give them cowpokes at the ranch a surprise."

"Suppose Arthur gets wind of it?" Cook asked.

Moon bent in real close to Cook. "You gonna break wind?"

"To that asshole?" Cook patted Moon's shoulder. "What have we been moanin' about all night?"

"Keep your moaning in the bars."

"Arthur's not coming up till he brings those Jap cattle guys this weekend," I said. "By then what's to see?"

Moon said, "Damn right. Come on."

I squinted into the glare of the headlights and hefted a warm, thick front leg, slippery almost in deep fur. Heavy. A thick smell like bailed hay. No blood. No cuts. Jesus. "Pull," Moon said. He held up the head and carried the other half of the front end.

We'd hoisted the fat back end onto one of Moon's shag floor mats. As it scraped over the pavement, Cook pretended to tow it along from one side. "A girl bear," Cook grunted. "Not even a growed woman."

"Heavier than any two growed women I ever had," Moon said, but it was Moon got her up in back of the truck. The springs squeaked. The Datsun sagged. Then he crawled in there with her and got her head straight, propped up on the silver-horned saddle he'd sneak off the ranch to brag about as his whenever he took off for Evanston on a drinking spree. In the dim light of a washed-out moon, he slammed the tailgate and slapped his hands. "Who'd fucking believe it?"

Cook sat in the middle again and he laughed too, now. Cruising through the ghosts of mountains, we passed a pipe of Mary Jane, the King Peak Ranch still a valley and a bridge away. I was holding this big toke down, feeling sad, when the truck tilted and Moon pulled hard left to hold it on the road. Then it rocked. And we heard this long, strange, high, whining growl, like the noises the monster snarled in *Frankenstein*, only louder.

When I looked back I couldn't see a goddamn thing, but I knew what it was, and there was a banging now, the truck bouncing from side to side, damn near off the ground.

"Stop," Cook shouted. "Stop."

Moon laughed. "And do what? Do you believe this? Hell no, I'm going home to shoot the son of a bitch. Flashlight's in the glove box. See what's up." The crazy bastard accelerated down the hill toward the river. And the banging and the bouncing.

When I finally got the beam around, sure enough, there was a goddamn, red-eyed live bear back there tossing that fancy saddle from one wall of the truck to the other. Whining. Who knew when the hell it would get bored with that game? And we rocked along, raced along, and, Jesus, maybe it was brain damaged from whatever hit and stunned it. I was laughing too, Cook's cigarette throwing embers everywhere. I ate the rest of what was in the pipe.

Nothing but a few rabbits on the road when we came flying down, the Henry's Fork sparkling for just that long before—boom!—we hit the bridge, tires whumping, Moon hardly in control, the banging behind us, the camper windows cracking now. The bear didn't give a damn about the light. Her mouth locked onto a stirrup, she threw her front end back and forth like a bull. Snorted like one, too. And goddamn, for all the decals and shit, not one of the busted windows was all the way out. Hell, that bear couldn't have fit through those little windows anyway. Cook said, "You crazy fuckers."

We took the gate turn on two wheels, the headlights blinking off again but coming on. The bear didn't like something, the bumps in that half-assed gravel road, the rocks rattling underneath, something—and roared. The flashlight bounced, but there she was slamming her head against the roof now, blood on her yellow teeth.

"Moon," I said.

"I'll drop you then swing down back of the barn," he said. "Get Shifty's rifle and meet us."

"I ain't goin'," Cook said.

Moon worked the wheel, the veins popping off his hands, his hat cocked over one eye, his lower lip tucked inside. "Moon," I said.

"Damn but we made it," Moon said. Lance's big "weekend" house rose up in its nest of pines. Alps, his Saint Bernard, stood white on the porch. And clawing. A wild clawing. The bear stared back now, clawing at the bed, trying to dig us out.

Moon swung south toward the bunkhouses and the mess hall. "In the chest's the best spot," he said. "You think so?"

"Moon?"

"Yeah. Get ready to bail."

"Moon," I said, "you don't want to shoot the bear, not yet."

"The hell I don't. Why not?"

"I've got a better idea," I said. Moon laughed louder than that other noise when I told him.

"Goddamn it," Cook said. "Let me out. He'll lynch your asses."

Moon said, "How the hell's he gonna know?"

Cook dove past me when I opened the door. The Saint Bernard bellowed and loped beside the truck.

Moon yelled, "Gotta make it fast." The goddamn noise.

He eased the Datsun through the trees back of the house and around the pony corral just out from the rear stoop. The Bernard kept his distance while I got the key from under the brick by the bottom step. The bear groaned and poked its angry nose out a hole next to a goddamn decal of a bear. I opened the dead bolt on the door. Then I hand-signaled Moon back up snug against the stoop. When he cut the engine, the bear calmed down, sniffed out that hole now, moved its tongue through the air.

"Perfect," Moon said, and it was, the truck bed dead level with the top step. "But how do we know that bear's goin' in?"

I hurried inside and came back out with a loaf of Roman Meal bread. I laid a trail through the door. "It'll work." Then I lobbed a slice through a camper window hole. That brought old black bear back to life.

"I'll get my rifle," Moon said, "be ready when she finally busts loose."

"Plenty of time," I said. "I left the fridge open. She won't hurry. Question is, how do we open the topper?" The Bernard came growling up but eased back when I yelled.

" 'At's easy," Moon said. "Come on."

I followed him up across the hood to the topper roof. Rocking. Like a damn freight car. Moon gave me his hat. He flattened out and leaned over the back. I balanced above him with the light. He leaned farther. I stood on his leg, and goddamn, he unlatched it. "Easy," he said.

She didn't burst out. Didn't do anything at first except sniff and groan. Finally she squeezed through, first with the goddamn leg I'd carried. Slow. And what if she *was* brain damaged? But her nose stayed aimed at the bread, to hell with the barking dog. She'd just put her head inside the door when a window squealed open next to us.

"What're you assholes doing?" Checkers screamed, Checkers, half-blind, half-crippled, half-dressed.

"How 'bout you?" Moon asked. "Arthur know you're usin' his house?" A lamp burst on behind Checkers. Holding a Levi jacket to her chest, a fat girl stepped into the light.

"Better lock your door, darlin'," I said. "You've got company."

Checkers said, "You two sonsofbitches are fired. I'm gonna call . . . I'm gonna call . . ."

The bear was in, and now old Alps bolted up the steps and charged inside. I jumped down and closed the door.

Goddamn the dog screamed. Pretty soon it barked from another part of the house, though, so I figure the bear just chased it off. But, Jesus, did it bark.

Now the fat girl's feet came through the window. She dropped down, pretty agile for a fat girl. She had jeans on, but her blouse was open. Her bra was black. "You cowboys think you're funny, huh?"

"Yup," I said.

But here came Checkers out, hat on cockeyed, pants inside his boots. The girl buttoned her blouse. Checkers grunted when he landed, straightened his glasses, tucked in his shirt, and jumped for Moon. Moon knocked him down and said, "Come on, Checkers. Just a joke."

His shirt dirty and untucked again, Checkers stood slowly, like his back hurt. His glasses hadn't budged. "Assholes," he said. He went hobbling off screaming through the trees about how he'd call the sheriff and get his goddamn Winchester to "ventilate you shit brains."

"We'd best beat it," I said. Then it sounded like the whole

damn fridge fell over, this big kaboom with bottles breaking and dishes rattling. The bear moaned. "Yup," I said.

"Give me a ride," the fat girl said. "Please."

After she let us each do her down by the river, we heard the siren. The red light twirled across the bridge. "You guys are wild," the fat girl said. The dark air was damp.

Toward dawn, headed east out of Cheyenne, Moon said, "Je-sus. Not my night. My bear up and attacked my prize saddle. You reckon Arthur'll send anybody after us?"

"I know he won't."

"Hey, that big girl was nice, wasn't she?"

"Okay."

"She yacked in my ear the whole damn time. Said she loved me the second I touched her."

"Me, too."

"God, she was nice."

Moon pushed Hank Williams, Jr., back into the eight track. I tapped my foot and smoked Lucky Strikes. Nothing died.

6 —— THE CHAIR

Then, okay, a year and a half later the pressure comes again.

"That never killed nobody," this farm kid calls out.

Four o'clock show, April 1, Lincoln, Nebraska. Lust Brothers' Carnival. First day of a new season. The tent smells like something needs to be buried longer. When that midwestern wind cries out over that godforsaken prairie, the tent trembles right down the king poles. Sparks climb the coil in the glass bubble behind me. Hell, I'm shivering in just red leotards and a damn silver swimsuit. But I'm big time, and I know it. I'm strapped in the electric chair that killed Bruno Richard Hauptmann. Princess Electra touches a light bulb to my nose. The bulb glows. A woman says, "Lands." The rain wants to wash us all away.

Now Electra puts the bulb in her mouth and holds my hand. Again, the bulb jumps on. She throws the bulb to the stage. It explodes in chips that tick my feet. "Just an ordinary bulb," she says, "an extraordinary man." She bends to kiss me, her lips puckering, her chest ready to spring out of her skimpy costume. Then zingo, sparks leap between our mouths, orange bolts that run back and forth in her eyes. Our lips never touch. Our skin crawls with electricity. The spark dischargers sizzle. She pouts. She struts away, picks up a cigarette in a long holder, and touches it to my cheek. It smolders. "Durn," an old man mumbles. She pulls smoke deep and blows it at the crowd.

"And now," I call, "the feat you have all been waiting for. Across this glorious nation men of evil intentions were regularly removed from this life through use of a device such as the one in which I am seated." Electra points to the canvas mural hanging over us, a skinny man in this chair, wearing a white shirt and tie, face wide with fear, watching as a huge shadowy figure reaches for the switch. Over them from left to right in thick paint, the *Spirit of St. Louis* flies through black clouds, a man carries a baby down a ladder against the wall of a white mansion, and a small angel floats from a muddy grave. "This very mechanism ended the life of the diabolical kidnapper of the Lindbergh baby and over one hundred and fifty master criminals."

Electra says, "This is not a trick. This is a natural wonder. No one should play with power. It can kill."

And it has. This is the honest-to-God chair. But wired with static electricity now, safer electricity. I laugh. "When I say the word, the princess will boost me to six thousand volts, enough to destroy ten men. Ready!" Electra stands by a huge dial, her feet just so. And the voltage will rise, and my muscles will tighten.

"Wouldn't toast bread!" that same farm kid in the back calls out.

"Set."

"Chair's as phony as you are."

"Let that boy through," I say in my deep, dark show voice.

Twenty or thirty of those gawking, cattle-headed no-accounts shuffle a step or two to the side. The kid hikes on up. This too-big seed company hat makes his ears stick out. And goddamn if when he smiles wide at everybody he doesn't have fangs. The locals laugh. The kid takes them out and says, "These is about as real as you." And the crowd's tickled.

I lift my lip to show *my* teeth, sparks crawling over them, copper-lined caps hard as coral, specially made by this retired circus dentist in Orlando. The rain pounding the canvas sounds like the ocean.

On his shoulder, the kid's got one of those Florida chameleons—$2.50 from Old White Beard down the midway—strung to a safety pin on his chest. It tilts its green head. Blinks. Shit, lightning bursts over us just ahead of thunder, and I say, "Put your lizard on me."

A couple of beer bellies up front say, "Go ahead." The rain steadies out, crackles.

I say to Electra, "Up the juice." She turns the dial and the overheads flicker and fade.

And the boy grins, unpins this blinking, green lizard, holds it up for the crowd, and then sets it on my arm. Just like that the lizard freezes, stiffens. The kid cries. Like the goddamn wind. His open, whitening, freckled face. A guy in the back shouts, "All right," and everybody claps. Right then's when I made up my mind.

After the show I sent word down for the kid to get another chameleon. His old man said, "Boy sure does have a mouth, dudn't he?"

From then on Ray Lust all the time egged me to zap
frogs or toads or snakes. No thanks. I stuck with light bulbs,
cigarettes, and sometimes a radio or toys—bombers with
headlights, drum playing bears, like that. Of course my
finale stayed the electric chair. I squirmed and moaned and
flopped my head over. Then when Electra cut the current
and slapped me, I came around and laughed, my teeth
bursting one last time. Sometimes I felt it, like my blood
had heated up. Sometimes I remembered something way
back. The crowds swarmed down for signed postcards:

STRANGEST WONDER OF ALL!
STRUCK BY LIGHTNING!
AS A CHILD!
BATTERY MAN!
INVINCIBLE!
EVEN THE ELECTRIC CHAIR!
HAS NO POWER OVER HIM!

I packed the yahoos in two shows a day, seven days a
week. It had taken me going on a year, including one long,
dirt-wage, equipment-repair winter in Florida—I couldn't
believe the ocean—to get inside a tent.

Moon and I'd signed on with the carnival outside Hayes.
Hal Lust said a man could work up fast through the rides
and the games and make big money. " 'Sides all the travel.
And farm chicks'll squeeze your balls off."

Moon said, "We been there."

We wore these mustard-yellow coats with LUST SHOWS
on the pockets. Moon ran the Wild Mouse. I got bumper
cars. I'd spent half my life next to Ferris wheels, listening
to goddamn calliope music. We had a bunk in the back of
a semi trailer. Mattresses thin as socks. Hit plenty of bars.
Hit plenty of bozos. At the end of August in Amarillo,
Moon took off for Nashville with a country singer he picked
up at a honky tonk. She smiled like Marie Osmond and

carried melons like Dolly Parton's. She sang like Junior
Wells. But hell, Moon had it bad: "We'll get her on the
Opry and go from there."

"I'll pass," I said. "There's Betty. And the Lusts're
headed for Florida, remember."

"It's your funeral."

Moon caught my Battery Man routine that next summer
in Louisville. I'd lifted most of it. Guy before me, in the
same tent, same get up, same spiel, damn near—who stumbled over one too many bottles of gin and fell off a railroad
bridge—was Electron. "Well, I hope they're payin' you,"
Moon said.

Moon's girl, Melody Lord, sang backup for Ed Bruce at
the Kentucky State Fair. "Ed says she's got the ingredients."
Moon wore a gold neck chain and smoked-lens glasses. He
had a new Trail Duster—red. "Image's important." He
waved out the sunroof as he drove off.

Molly Cord—Princess Electra—would frizz my hair. She'd
powder me pink. I'd put these orangy contacts in my eyes.
The teeth. The outfit covered with lightning bolts. Shit. I'll
bet half the yokels thought I'd explode. I pulled $150 a
week. I had a roost and a girl. I had it licked. Ray Lust
said in front of everybody that I was the best ever. Who
knows?

Florida made me nervous. No seasons. Too many waves.
Then that last spring—well, there was that kid with the
lizard. After that when the current hit, I could feel my
pulse pick up. Three times a day I sat in the damn thing.
"Men of evil intentions" hardly ever had, not this hot seat,
not any. I was headed nowhere. Strangers packed the tent
and stared. With every farm's fields just barely stubbled
green, with every road wet and black, with clouds half purple over everything, I couldn't sleep. Maybe five hours max
a night.

Betty Reekle and I shared a trailer, had since Moon split. She loved me. She was a weight guesser. If she missed yours by more than five pounds, you won a stuffed animal. "I just feel it by looking," she said. Near the middle of the afternoon she'd up and cry. Bang. Then she'd throw off all her clothes and ball up behind a pile of pillows in the corner. I'd shoot the shit with the guys around the rigs until the evening shows. One day Al Shale—he'd been Betty's steady boarder before me—pulled me off away from the others and said, "She's still crying, I guess."

"Yeah."

"You know why?"

"She won't say." A jet passed over the empty plains— Kansas again.

"She saw her parents die," he said. "Chicago. She was eleven or twelve. Some loony shot a store full of nobodies."

A dog barked. A pony whinnied. A donkey opened its wide voice. Clouds. I ground a cigarette into the muddy sawdust. Jesus.

I called my mother because—because I wanted to know if she still hung on. "I'm her son."

"Just a minute," the woman at St. Joseph's Villa said. From the booth, I watched two bikers shoot pool in the smokey light. I sipped my beer. "Mr. Cade?" the woman said. "I'm sorry to say your mother is not doing well."

"What's the problem?"

"Let me get the floor nurse for you."

"No, that's all right." I was out of change. And what did it matter?

While Betty sobbed in the corner the rest of that afternoon, I perched backward on one of her ragged steel dinette chairs and watched. Every now and again she stopped, lost, her head trembling, her yellow hair wet and matted around her cheeks, mascara murky beneath her empty eyes.

I found a powdery sheet of pink paper in Betty's dressing-table drawer. While she groaned like the ghosts in the god-damn Haunted House, I printed a note with her eyebrow pencil:

Honey—
I did something once I never said a word about to you. I'm going back to Salt Lake to think it out, to get it out of my system somehow. To get even. Someday maybe you'll get over your own lousy history. I hope so. Someday maybe I'll help you.

So long,
Carlos

I rolled up my spare shirt and pants and tucked the bundle under my arm. I had $187 in an envelope behind the tub. I left two fifties on the floor. I doubt she heard me go.

7 —— *THE BLACK DOOR*

Scotch-taped on cardboard and wrapped in the clear plastic of a bread sack, the newsprint photo hung under the rusty horseshoe over the stove. Mama still scratched her head, staring at it sometimes, a whole year since the lady took it, and said, "Yup."

And Mama whispered and purred as she combed Hilda's hair those days. "Darling little Jill," she'd say. "That girl is a little queen." Hilda's face soured at that stuff, but I'd lay odds she believed it too. Across those dandelioned islands all haloed with lawn sprinklers, there they lived up on a weedless, landscaped rise in their golden yellow house with those tall, white pillars (that sounded empty, like watermelons, when you thumped them), Jill, the lady of the manor, Lance's big sister. Her childhood shined: her curls, her purses, her shoes. I remember her socks: thin pink things turned at the top to tiny sewn flowers.

I remember Jill clean, round, just so, like one of those ribboned Kodak-picture girls in camera store windows— except for her ears. She tried to hide them, or whoever did her hair tried to. Once you saw those ears, though, they stayed with you. Dollar-size welts around cold blue holes. You wouldn't expect a girl with ears as awful as those to smile much, and she didn't. I never heard her laugh either, but then I wasn't around Jill all that often. Even later, when she'd outgrown the socks, she wore her hair tight and low— her mouth, too. Most of the time.

Anyway, Mama feathered Hilda's brown hair like wings, patted her back, and kissed her cheek. Then Hilda, holding her head steady, fluttered up the alley.

All combed up in the white afternoon sun of the island, she spun, pranced in small circles too carefully for play. After half an hour or more, if nothing happened, she slowly stopped, like a music box running down, and wandered home. Often enough, though, the Arthurs' black door opened while she twirled, and Jill's silverplated small voice called, "Come in here, Hildy. Come on." That's all it took. My sister leaped across the hot pavement and up those empty stairs.

At first I'm sure I felt a little jealous of her going into that house. But she and Jill *were* the only girls in the neighborhood. Lance had lots of other guys to hang around with.

Hardly ever frilled up like his sister back then, Lance usually wore cutoffs, dirty sneakers, and a ragged Yankees hat.

Except for his eyes, set deep, always cool, he was a kid. Just a kid. Sure we knew they had real money. We knew his old man had a hand in The Beehive, the amusement park across town. Lance'd own it someday and give us free tickets. That's where he took his birthday party every June 1. Neighborhood kids weren't invited, just the sons of his father's "business buddies."

Pep, Skink, and I circled up the Downeses' drive and around behind the Oldses' fence. A baby could have climbed through the ivy onto the Arthurs' garage. We lay on the hot tar paper and peered into that cool, barbered, laughing yard where we wanted to be. The black lady served pink ice cream from a wide silver bowl to pale, noisy boys with hair so slick the sun flashed off it. She sliced thick wedges of dark cake. In a white shirt, Lance sat at the head of a picnic table, quieter than the others. I think he knew we watched. We stayed until they left for the park, until the black lady ferried their messy plates away.

Only Gerry and Matt, whose own places came in a close second and third anyway, ever went inside the Arthurs'— until we all rushed in from the limekiln the next summer.

And really, up till then everyone mattered. Neighbors nodded and cut their grass and fetched another sack of groceries.

Take a guy fifty, fifty-five, with one of those Mormon, age-resistant, soft-boiled bodies—plump and soft and smooth as a marshmallow. Put black plastic glasses wrapped at a joint with a Bandaid on his round, pale face. Add an apron—blood spattered. Give him a smile that won't go away but never quite arrives either. You've got Hickler. And if you change the glasses to little, gold, horn-rimmed things, you've got his wife too. Salt and pepper.

Hickler spent six of every seven days beside the noisy National cash register in that long musty little room he called his market. Mrs. Downes, Matt's mother minus her mink, shopped beside Mrs. Shorter, a Mormon bishop's paunchy better half, beside Mama, the three in line in order of arrival in front of Hickler's flaking, pea-green counter. They didn't gossip, never got past pleasantries. They waited to charge, to pay, to beg. They waited. Do you see?

Kids liked Hickler. He stocked his one big case with candy—penny, nickel, dime—fifty different kinds I'll bet. We gawked in groups and streaked our filthy hands across the glass. He never said a word. He never shooed us off the front stoop. I'm sure he kept an eye open, though, as often as I caught him glancing out.

Grimy, scabbed, and crew-cut to the scalp, all six of us are there. A bike is on its side in the dirt by the street. With us in the hot shade, two dogs pant and collect flies. Matt and Pep sit on the curb, feet in the water, the gutter wet and slimy brown whenever sprinklers run. Lying on their stomachs on the gray, gum-wadded cement, Gerry and Lance use rocks to draw fanged monsters and V-winged birds. Lance twists the outside dial of the diver's watch he got for his birthday two weeks before. Under the empty, dark windows of the store, Skink and I chew red licorice on the stoop, arms touching, freckled backs cool against those green tiles.

I feel the sweat itching at my eyes, smell the dust, and see us clear as the stamped-tin Coke scenes rusty-nailed at each corner of Hickler's, as the red line stuck at 95 in the 7-Up thermometer by the door.

Hilda went to the Arthurs' just after the meat man carried in two sides of beef. You could smell it. A dog wagged its tail. I watched Hilda dance just past the sprinklers more like sparklers in the sun. I don't know if anybody else saw her skip off to the stairs, through the white pillars and the black door. Nobody said anything. The meat man drove away. The dog rattled in its throat. That was the sound of that afternoon. And green flies. And the crackle of gum.

Then Matt said, "Get a load of that."

"She don't have any clothes on," Pep said, "no shoes or nothin'."

Lance? He laughed, I'm sure of it, these deep dimples.

Across the island, Hilda raced through burning sprinklers with wild arms. Hollow and black and wide, her mouth. Her body, almost gone it is so pale in the center of those dark and frightened arms and legs, barely balances the mouth, the head, the leaking hair. I don't know what I say. I run.

Eyes, wet, quiver. Painted fingers whiten tighter on her arms. Tears, like beads of ice, melt into black spots on the kitchen floor. My sister's shoulders rise to her ears and fall. She shivers with the words: "She stole my clothes, Papa. Stole 'em."

Hilda tries for breath, my old man hunched around his belly, leaning out over the table at her, his hair all messy and wax eyes. I don't know where Mama is. And more of Hilda's noise, Hilda stripped, still pink from every neighbor staring, those son-of-a-bitching wide-eyed windows, the sun like nettle.

She shivers. The sound.

Like a muscle, the scar under my old man's nose tightened. The corners of his mouth rose. I thought sure he'd laugh. I took hold of Hilda's shoulders. I said, "Help her, Papa. Help her."

The smile bunched the stubble of his face. And finally Hilda said, "Oh, Papa."

Jesus. His eyes. His lips straightened. He sat back. The chair grunted. He said, "So what're you poor babies gonna do about it?"

One deep breath at a time, Hilda quieted—like a train. She wiped her nose. "Cut her heart out. I am." She staggered across the room and pulled the rusty bread knife from the drawer. Big as a sword. Papa just sat there, belly and all.

All of a sudden, though, she drops the knife and runs through the house to our room, shrieking once, again. My old man sniffs, locks those eyes on me, and doesn't blink. "Well?"

The guys still stand at the head of my alley. Lance swells and shakes his head. I smash the smile with a fist so wrong I almost break my thumb. We fight. We bite and pinch and twist through gravel. Lance jolts my stomach with an elbow. Then he underhands a spray of Bottoms's flower bed at my eyes. But I grab him, grab his hair and his cheek and pull and squeeze, and when I am damn near so cramped I'll have to quit, he says, "Stop. Stop. My ear." And I stop as soon as I am sure his fight is gone, as soon as I can see. He bleeds from a line on his right cheek wide as his eye, the cut so bad a scar will last forever. His earlobe is torn.

"Get her clothes."

"No."

"Come on, Lance. You lost." Matt stepped between us. "You wouldn't want his old man in on this."

Lance opened his mouth but said nothing.

My nose dripped onto the Arthurs' porch in small red explosions while I waited. Lance didn't bring that paper bag—so light, the dress, the shoes. The big black woman did. She stayed, hands on her hips. and stared. Jesus, I finally said, "Thank you."

"You're welcome," she said. And with a small click somewhere deep inside everything, she became a broad black door that would never open.

8——*LATTER DAY SAINTS*

Jill hardly ever came outside anymore. Because of what happened with Hilda the first of the summer? Everyone knew things must have changed, but Hilda still pranced, Jill still called. I mean, Lance had his scar, like a little red caterpillar. Once he said, "Look. You gave me this." He laughed. We got along okay.

Sunday mornings. A neighborhood of trees then, trees so thick with leaves you'd think they'd die.

I liked lying on my stomach in the matted grass on the middle island, forgetting who I was or where. Families, packed like dolls into clean cars, slid out of driveways: the Oldses and the Downeses and the Pepperses off to the Cathedral, the Shorters and the Skinks to their wardhouse. The kids never waved.

Then most Sundays Old Man Arthur's long, blue Continental groaned shining down their drive. I tried to see more than his black eyes and purple cheeks through the tinted windshield. Lance said Hank—he called his father by his first name—liked to "shoot nine." Lance blinked into the light when he came out. He said, "Hey, what's cookin'?"

Sometimes we played a lazy game of catch or wandered a few alleys. Mostly we just sat. Watched the old guys. Fish-faced men with spooky smiles. They filed out of nursing homes, group houses up side streets, glided slow as shadows. This one fat black guy's collared chins bulged smooth as water balloons. His eyes were candle wax. A bony, drooling midget led him by the hand. Sometimes I laughed at the poor sonsofbitches. Sometimes they laughed back. One, short, hollowed out, and bald, talked to trees. He never wore shoes. Just socks. Bright socks, deer-hunter red.

Last always came Captain, named for his square-billed straw hat. And his straight back. Captain had been beefy, you could tell, the spread of his shoulders, the size of his hands. Now he was bones. Bones and blue skin. Heavy, gray eyebrows. Fingers twisted around an ivory-white bamboo cane layered with rubber bands of every color—like beadwork.

Captain fell short a few cents upstairs. If you held your arm out, huffed and tugged as if maybe you had a pit bull on a leash, and said, "Hey, Cap, look at this new mutt I got," he'd squint right through that empty air. Spit to the side, wink, lift his lips around yellow teeth, and shake his head.

"Damn, boy," he'd say, "that's fine."

Captain had explored Africa. He'd been a pirate. He was Babe Ruth. He was a ghost. He'd been someone important once, you could see that.

Lance said, "Captain." Burning up on the middle island, we lay on our stomachs on dry grass, some idiot damn stray black collie panting between us, a few million gnats trying for our eyes.

Sure enough, here came Captain dragging his heavy shoes home from the Twilight Zone. Just a little lead man far off at the end of the block, a statue, stiff back, stiff cane, clothes washed out in sunshine. If you watched long enough, you knew he moved because you knew. He pulled a shadow. Blues and yellows and pinks—a bright shirt, his strange cane. Forever. Always just out there, that upright, empty son of a bitch never arrived.

"C'mon," Lance said. "C'mon."

Like I said, the rutted, dusty alley by the Downeses' looped around back of the Oldses'. The dog barked. Sweat itched my eyes, then burned. Dirt smoked from Lance's heels as we ran.

"I know that dope'll do it," he said. In his garage, kneeling by two lawn mowers and some rakes, he reached behind a stack of doors. He opened a small plastic treasure chest. Rubber bands. Red. Blue. Yellow. Green. He winked. "I bought 'em offa Timmy Shorter. He gets 'em for his paper route."

The collie was gone. I squeezed the milk out of dandelion stems and looked up sometimes to watch Lance spreading the rubber bands from Hickler's to the corner. Captain, his eyes hidden by the blue bill on his straw hat, still stood fifty yards away.

It seemed like three Sundays, five Sundays, a lifetime of silent Sundays that we waited, chewing grass, squinting, itching. Lance chewed at his nails too, until his thumbs bled.

Finally . . . Captain got there. He bent faster than he walked, but even so it took years for him to pick them up, sometimes in sloppy fistfuls, and wrap them around his cane. Lance laughed for a while, through his nose. He stopped when Captain stooped and started up when Captain stood again. "Can you believe that dumb ass?" His eyes ran. His arms were beet-juice red.

My shoulders hurt. Captain leaned in shadow now. Lance's father honked as he pulled into the drive. Nearly dinner-time. I wanted to be indoors, despite the goddamn heat.

My mother was sick then. She smelled in a filmy sort of nightgown, propped up in bed. She smiled when I touched her leg, eyes dry, her teeth all caked with food. I fought hard not to cry. The dark heat of my room felt cooler. But my stomach hurt and Captain would never finish with all those rubber bands.

Sundays were Gandy.

My grandmother—we called her Gandy, don't ask me

why—was just a sack of knobby bones. But she had eyes the white blue of birds' eggs, gentle eyes. Gandy lived in those eyes. Those eyes loved me.

I knew she couldn't see, the way her chin stayed up when she hobbled through her little place, the way her caramel-colored hands tickled over things. But "blind" wasn't Gandy. My old man told me, "What Gandy don't see ain't discovered yet." She always knew when I was into something. She screeched up through her nose until I stopped. Same for Hilda, only Hilda made faces at her.

Once a month or so when it was warm, some Mormon all scrubbed and sanctified hauled us to Gandy's on a Sunday afternoon. A few times it was Mr. Shorter. Gandy never visited us. Once I heard my mother hot with my old man: "She coulda made me want her. She didn't. And that old thing idn't hurtin' anyway. I know what hurtin' is." My old man grunted. Whenever we went, my folks sat outside on a stone bench under Gandy's one tree, a cherry, which she called a "cheery." With cigarettes going they drooped over thin crossed knees until our ride came back.

Gandy stirred in her deep purple chair when we got there—and as we left. Moved her eyes, never much more. She smelled like soap, but Papa once said she stank of whiskey. I think that was just his screwed-up notion of the only way somebody nudging ninety and that different could be happy. If I had to say, I'd guess she *was* happy then. She was tough, always staring down the world, daring life to *really* hurt her. Son of a bitch. I remember the big mountains in her eyes.

Gandy's house sat up high on the last street but one against the foothills behind the Capitol building. It was a pretty decent neighborhood really, a lot like ours, and I don't think anybody bothered her, for good or bad. The only visitor I ever saw she had was the Salvation Army. Her house—or whatever the hell you call one room and a bathroom that didn't deserve the name since it didn't have a bath—had been a garage. One wall was two big doors bolted shut and caulked up tight. Most of the facing wall had been chopped out for a huge window. You could see the whole Wasatch range.

She sat up there above it all, smelling like soap. And now and again, after shifting her jaw from side to side and sucking in those loose, thin cheeks, she talked. Her lips. Her tongue touched the air. Words came. Little ones. High, soft ones. Words from the edge of hearing. The edge of seeing, like Papa said. The valley she saw was big as God, empty, and dry, the city a desert camp. Believe it or not, her parents—just the two, before her old man took four more wives—pulled their lives across the plains on hand-carts. "Papa wore a blue coat with two deer ears on the collar, so's he could hear twiced as good, he said. He was a butcher, with hands like cleavers they was so hard and sharp. A grocer man. When we come up this hill, it could have been the climb to heaven, so steep. Nothin' but stickers and snakes. Says he likes the view. We had cattle all over this slope." Hilda saw it too. You could tell by her face.

A camp in the desert. "A desert garden," Gandy said. And I turned from the mountains to her tiny yard, and the bench, and my parents smoking cigarettes.

Gandy's father quarried and carted rock and built a mansion on that hill. Looking at that sorry building next door, you hardly knew. But in its day, so Gandy swore, that was *the* house. In its day.

The roof was barely slated before all the wives but Gandy's mother lit out to dodge the polygamy law. "Like gettin' torn to pieces," she said. Lonely. Gandy was the youngest of three by her mama. Her father wrote pamphlets and gave speeches. The roof leaked. Then, his beard gone white, the old man got shot in Nevada over checking on his wives.

The church saw to Gandy's mother for a while, until she stopped going to meetings because church, she said, meant nothing but pain. Gandy's brother took two wives himself and went to Mexico. In the desert garden, Gandy and her sister and her mother stayed put. When the mother choked to death on rhubarb pie, the sister, Louise, got *the* house and quick found a man without a dime to live in it with her.

Gandy gave herself—gave up—to a no-account son of a bitch named Locksaw, an upstart of a banker who knew as much about banking as she did. When Emmet Locksaw died at forty-five in his sleep—his one piece of luck—Gandy found herself—in debt with three kids and one (my mother) coming—forgotten in the middle of a settlement become a city. The war was on. Her sister gave her the garage, which way back when had been a storage shed or a stable or something. On Sundays Gandy took her children into the big house for supper. "Quiet and dark as death." When the sister was run over by an ice truck, the suppers stopped. I'm still related to the people in that big, shitty thing, but I don't know how. Gandy's place, her little room full of soap and mountains, keeps cars dry at night again.

9 —— GETTING EVEN

Now I was back. To stay. To stay real for once, I thought.

Afternoons I manned bay number three at Spud's Suds. I pushed down antennas, checked for open windows, and signaled the dirty cars through. I toweled them off on the other side. I grinned into their blue exhaust. I vacuumed under mats and behind seats. I found rubbers, money, dope, a hamster, and, once, a stick of dynamite. My hands cracked. Not Spud's. Spud also owned the used-car lot next door—Spud's Wonders, so called—and Spud himself sat in a tight, tiny booth in between. Usually he "read" magazines, *Hustler*, *Penthouse*. Usually he sat on his butt, which was big enough for a baseball team. The job barely covered my two crummy bread-box rooms in the Samson Apartments on Third South—the Shiftlet place—and three square.

Danny said, "Two weeks. Your money back and then some."

Mornings I would write my story. I could. I cut down on the drink and smoke and all that. Matt would only have to sign. Hell, he could rewrite it if he wanted.

And I had the note.

I would not watch TV news, listen to the radio, or read the paper. Screw the governor's phony, famous life. I knew him.

I wrote with a fountain pen in a black notebook that said The Spiral on the front. The first part came fast:

This is the truth, every last word of it. I am getting something off my chest because it will do many people a lot of good to know what happened. I am sorry I have waited so long.

We lived a few blocks from the foothills. A bunch of us boys would hike there. We played games and spent a lot of time in Dry Canyon. We felt very far from everything there. Six of us went there. Lance Arthur was one of us. He killed a boy named Greg Skink in Dry Canyon. The rest of us kept quiet. This is exactly how it happened.

———

At two I clocked in at Spud's. By ten I was soaked and sore, my mouth full of soap. Jesus. After stumbling home in the hot dark, I usually changed my shirt and spent time with Ginny, a woman with a nice chest two doors down the hall. Who taught driving. No kidding. My second night I'd just hiked the stairs when her door gushed open to this bright yellow light. This curvy silhouette called, "Can I bum a smoke? I'm quitting, but well, I'm cutting down. I'll buy you a pack." She wore this white gauzy dress—low up top— with this wide snakeskin belt that held the works in place.

I didn't tell her much. She thought I went to college part-time. "I want to counsel delinquents," I said. That I worked at the U library some and on the grounds crew. She liked me to rub her back, she liked old movies. Fine.

To help furnish my place, Danny left a lamp, a radio, and a couple of chairs by the mailboxes inside the front door. He never came up.

Danny worked the early shift. As I walked in he drove off, two times hollering he'd be back to get me for a beer. We'd split a pitcher at Tricky Mick's, him all the time check- ing his watch, picking the scabs on his face, twisting his mustache. He'd say, "You keep that Friday open. You're going to get a show with your money. You can help out, nothin' heavy duty." He'd say, "Only a week, Cade," then, "Three more days, *amigo*. You're gonna get a show." He dropped me off in a squeal of outsized Goodyears. I popped in on my hot little driving instructor.

But the beer or something—my job, the late-night work- outs, Danny so fucking private about his goddamn business, who knows?—fuzzed me up, brain wool, and the parts about my sister and the fight didn't read like they should. My writing hand hurt. The fountain pen leaked.

Ginny begged me, "Please stay over," kept us up even later talking about it.

"I flunked out once before," I told her. "This time it's do or die."

"I want you in me till the crack of dawn," she said. And she squirmed and breathed long, slow breaths, her tits shiny with these rum-colored nipples.

Ginny surprised me twice in one night. First, this lonely driving teacher with the virgin smile and the *Penthouse* headlights, whose parents farmed outside Paul, Idaho, who nagged me that alcohol pickled "the brain" (as if that mattered), opened her purse, after she'd fed me homemade ravioli with this German beer from the liquor store, and lifted out a tiny pipe, dark wood with silver bands, and a Baggie of green rocket fuel. I broke training. When she toked, she closed her eyes. She held the smoke and hummed. She undid her blouse. We held each other, pulled each other half off her couch, laughing at some movie about a high-class detective with a wire-haired terrier. She rose and fell like a goddamn mermaid in the sweaty waves of blue light. I said, "You're blue."

She sang, "I'm so blue," and her back curved. Her ass tightened in my hands, and her tongue stiffened. "Blooooo." She squirmed away. "Close your eyes," she said.

I'm all wet on the throw rug, cooling down, down down, movie traffic fizzing like flies, when something falls on my stomach. I reach to slap it off but look and stop and lock eyes with a cat, this Ivory Snow—white kitten that blinks and licks at my salty damn dampness and tickles. Ginny laughs. "She's yours."

"The hell."

"I found her roped to a tire in a parking terrace. Who'd do a thing like that? Poor kitty. If you won't stay with *me* at night, you need something to cuddle."

"One pussy or another."

"Ha ha."

I lifted the kitten to the floor. Ginny leaned down. I switched off the set with my left foot as she kissed me.

I got at it early, hunched above my notebook, smearing ink all over my hand. On the counter behind me, my new kitten tapped its tongue against a saucer of milk, a small sound like a combination lock. I named him Mr. Cat. Hardeeharhar. Ginny said he was a girl. I looked. In a while, I'd tell her he ran off down the fire escape or something. Shit. I'd dump him in a nice mousey field up a canyon. When he knocked the catfood can of cigarette butts off the window sill, I kenneled him in the oven. So I'm not Mr. Rogers. You think anybody is?

I hid The Spiral over a ceiling tile in the closet.

A man on the bus wouldn't stop laughing. He drooled.

"Your father come to call," Mama said, so puny she hardly shaped her yellow robe. I helped her from her bed, her arms just bones. A woman with a walker hobbled past her door. "He held my hand." The veiny, shiny, thin hand Mama lifted pressed my face. "Now you." Muzak. Carnations in a glass vase. Her washed-out eyes drifted to the window, where a sparrow hopped along the sill.

"In the middle of his stripy tie was a pearl." She circled her thumb and forefinger. Dishes clattered far away. She licked the five teeth left in front. "He kissed my ear." She tilted her head. One of her canaries whistled in the corner.

A big lady with red glasses leaned into the room. "Lunch in twenty minutes."

"Lunch?" Mama said. Her eyes tightened down. She looked at the present in her lap. "Did you run off from school? Where's your lunch?"

I pulled my chair closer, could smell the toothpaste on her breath, her skin rotting. "Mama. Mama."

"Mama," she said. She teetered to her feet. The heart-shaped box of chocolates I brought dropped from her lap. "Mama's coming for lunch."

"It's okay." Her elbow would snap if I squeezed. I could lift her with a finger, a thought, kill her with a breath. She scraped her slippers to the bed and sat. A silver Jesus slept on his cross above her head.

"Light me a cigarette, Carlos."

"They said not to."

"Light me a cigarette." Sweat glistened on her neck. I struck the match. "Your sister never smoked in her life," Mama said. "How do you reckon that happened?"

"Mama," I said when the lady with red glasses returned. "I'm going now."

"What a man oughta do," she said. She pulled the smoke down and closed her eyes.

10 ——— HEARING NOTHING AT THE LIMEKILN

Skink's pale head. Red dirt. Flies. Cicadas grinding. Gerry's voice whimpering somewhere underground. Matt and Pep beside Skink, kneeling. Tears. White lines track their dirty chests. Skink is going to open his eyes and laugh his ass off. Lance stands in the sky, staring out of two black holes. His shadow grows onto Skink. Lance doesn't move. Skink doesn't move. The sage smells charred, stinks. The shadow moves, barely.

"Bring him up here."

Gerry says, "It's no act."

"Who says it is? C'mon. Bring him up here. You have to."

Pep says, "He needs somebody, Lance. No joke."

The shadow leaps at the limekiln. Skink is hurt now for the first time, hurt in that sour, milky sunlight. We look up when the dirt sighs down the slope, when a few small rocks collide beside us, a sharp ticking above the cicadas and the pressure in our ears. Lance slides down, rides the slide like a skier in red powder, in red clouds, in dusty flames, his eyes hard and flat as quarters tucked inside thin, squinty lids.

We watch him. Gerry smiles. Pep and Matt stop breathing. Lance folds his lips between his teeth for just that long and steps past me with a new shadow. One fist opens above his head. He bends. He leans into us and grunts. The sound is like a board breaking. Lance nods and says, "See?"

I look at a blue monster horsefly on the bony ridge of Lance's back and wonder why he doesn't reach for it. Then the noise is real again against the empty white flesh of Skink's face where a red handprint darkens. Skink's closed eyelids are calm and smooth. His mouth gives up a clear strand of spit. His chest rises, and falls slowly. "See?"

I wonder where Skink has gone all turned in on himself like that. I try to feel nothing myself right then, but the fingers sting through, burn, tighten—my face branded, not Skink's. My face. The man in the moon. The boy in the moon. The moon leaking that watery light out of that boy.

It took years to thicken this skin. Right then I wanted it toughened, like Lance's, and the four of us, kneeling over Skink, looked up at him brittle as scrub oak against the sun.

"Leave him alone," Gerry finally said. "What'd you do that for?"

Lance's voice dropped like stones: "To show you he's not coming back. So you'd pee your pants."

Blinking too much for the light, Pep stood up. "I'm going down, going for help. Geez, somebody'll bring him back."

"Get my dad," Matt said.

"Call the cops," Lance said. "Be sure'n tell 'em I did it."

"It was a accident," Pep said.

Lance laughed. "And when Mama Skink says we did it on purpose, what do you say? 'No, ma'am. We were playing Indians and one little pebble came loose and hit him just right.' What can you say?"

Gerry cried again.

"That we were playing," Pep said. "The truth. A game. You threw a rock. It hit him and—"

"And if you do, I'll tell 'em you guys held him down and told me to thump him right there on the head. It was your game, too. I'm not going to jail or reform school or . . . My old man says kids are never the same they go there. You want to go? Do you?"

The cicadas were the rhythm then, breathing.

Pep looked at me. So did Matt and Gerry. Why? How come right then they waited on me? One last breath pulled deep into the canyon, and I said, "Yeah, so what ya want us to do?" Somebody had to.

We were covered with flies. The air hatched, the heat hatched, the rock hatched with grasshoppers, moths, butterflies, hornets, wasps, bees, green beetles, pinching, itchy, shit-eating gnats. No one moved. Gerry's cheeks, varnished, scabbed with snot he'd wiped, would crack, split, and show his bones. Matt and Pep stared. Lance took root in dust. Two hawks circled, swirled like ash. On the ridge, the sun sat ready for the great fall into blackness. Nobody looked at Skink.

The roller coaster. The Screamer. One car comes in, empty this time, nobody getting off, no faces to read, just this quiet, blue car that you will be the first to ride. And you can see the track steep into darkness, but there's no fucking way you can know what comes after.

Here you are. You. "Hurry up, please. Hurry up, please. Hurry up, please." A gate has closed.

I want to shout "Don't jump" to the goddamn sun. Our shadows, like whipsnakes then, twist off into the sage. No one looks at Skink. Skink just is, or was. We don't want to go to jail. We want to go home. We can't. Lance's eyes won't move.

I say, "What do you want?"

"We," Lance says. "What *we* want. There's only one thing." Lance kicks the dust at Skink. "Him. We have to make it right, like it just . . . happened."

"And hurt him worse?" Pep asks.

"Look at him," Lance says. "Can we?"

Gerry stands, then Matt—slowly. Pep whispers, "Why?"

Lance says, "I didn't mean to. You know I didn't. C'mon." He points to the top of the kiln. "*Come* on."

Sobbing. Crazy sobbing. That's all Gerry did as we dragged Skink by the legs backwards up the slope. That's mostly what I remember, that and the smell. I guess Skink shit his pants, which made it easier somehow. To hell with bugs. The shadows were deep. My chest hurt, the only part of me really there. Lance and I tugged at the cool ankles, Pep and Gerry the knees. Matt crawled ahead, tore up any rocks and roots he could. Slow and hot and Jesus Christ, we finally made it, got the filthy, stinking boy's body in the green shorts onto the dirt, the crumbly yellow bricks up top. The breeze or something, but I smelled water, just water, the freshest smell ever. Some bird sang a long, smooth somersault. Skink's eyes were cold. The sun was ready. Lance hardly spread his mouth: "Move him in a little. Yeah. Here. More. Easy. Okay."

The hole inside began gently enough, rounded in for

maybe five feet before the sudden, funneled plunge to darkness. A spider crossed the darkness on a white thread. On his stomach, Skink lay head down, face hidden, shadowed, arms out straight from his sides, feet together—somehow familiar again. I wanted to hold those feet, those shoes. I swear I did. Red Ball Jets. I smelled water. You could hardly tell at first he moved, just barely sliding, the faintest sound of pebbles silting down the hole, the thin, smooth trails behind his Red Ball Jets on the brick, a tightening in us all. When he went it was nothing, just a sigh. A dive. The cicadas stopped, though, and Gerry stopped, until an empty, muffled, slumping from below.

No one looked in underneath. We knew. We only stood up top a second more before Gerry took off, ran slipping down to the trail and into the canyon. And we followed. And honest to God, as I dodged my way over the clear, cold creek, over and around the oldest rocks that ever were, I didn't believe it ever happened.

We weren't halfway when I heard Lance—it could have been Pep—yelping like a coyote up ahead. I know I laughed. I want to laugh now.

11 —— *WHAT IT COMES DOWN TO*

Lance's eyes that summer, shiny smooth, like greased bearings; and their eyes, closed, stuck—empty.

The police, with special dogs and big flashlights, brought Skink out. The darkness hated me. I led the way. My old man didn't give a shit if his son went back. He said, "Course you'll show 'em where your buddy fell." He aimed his cigarette at the cop outside the screen. "Count on my kid." I tied my sneakers, wishing I'd eaten, knowing it wouldn't have been possible. I was tired, sure, but tighter than bed springs. My stomach hurt. I wanted to go. I wanted to forget. I wanted to know.

In a light white as smoke, the five of us finally got back. Without a word, we raced mostly, huffed out of the foothills and then through two quiet-as-the-moon neighborhoods on a lime-white trail of sidewalk.

Lance said, "My place," and we followed because it was the first, because he was once and for all Lance. Lance's house: the flying carpets, the cake-top paintings on blue walls, the dark carved furniture, the cool, cigar-stale silence deep as the den in the rear. Jill stepped from their kitchen with a glass dish of white ice cream. She wore a nightgown, and it was pretty, but this was hardly goddamn dinnertime.

"Is Hank here?"

"What's wrong? What?"

"Where is he?"

Jill turned her eyes toward two doors wide with yellow light.

"Go eat your treat upstairs, huh?"

She left us just like that, and we moved without sound— except a sort of wheezing deep inside Gerry—through that doorway to the den. Boneless in a leather chair, his feet in leather slippers on a leather stool, Old Man Arthur nursed a soggy stogy and squinted at the news. Huntley and Brinkley. I could hear them in that shit-of-the-world way of theirs telling the entire goddamn country about a boy in Utah whose playmates sent him headfirst down a hole.

Old Arthur had a dog's face, a Saint Bernard's, all open and kind, but I got the feeling that under those whiskers, behind the mustache and those sloppy lips, were the flesh-tested teeth of something lots wilder. He guarded his teeth, spoke to the side through a small slit, his voice low and clear. Once Lance told him, he took a long, wet pull on the cigar, dropped his feet to the floor, switched the TV to darkness, and said, "Hand me the phone." After he hung up, the cigar cold, Old Arthur said, "Lance, son, see them to the door. I'm sure their parents wonder where they are."

"I was just gettin' ready to come look for you," Papa said. I slumped through the screen door. Without a shirt he looked lots older, a scar stitched across his round belly, all of him sagging and damp. He had the radio tuned to a talk show, people whining out their lives. My lower lip quivered. He sucked a Pall Mall and studied a speckled yellow fishing lure up tight beneath his eyes. "Got a razor up your butt?"

"Where's Mama?"

"Took to bed. One of her head pains." Now he found whatever he knew he'd find in my face. "If you're sorry for somethin', all you got's two choices, boy. Forget, that's one. Or slap-patch it over. Sorry's for dying. Hear?"

"Greg Skink, the kid from that saggy place the other side of the Hicklers', *he's* dead. His body's up in the hills dead, and Mr. Arthur's called the cops."

"So?" He lighted up another smoke and somehow got the hook of that lure stuck fast in his thumb. With a quick twitch of his tongue, that's all, he snapped it out and then blotted the bright tiny globe of blood onto the white paper of the cigarette. "Was it your doing?"

"I couldn't of stopped it."

"You got two choices." His eyes watered and he reddened as he coughed.

The head of the cops' rescue team told me to set the pace in that dusty, dark canyon not two hours later. I walked as fast as two damn-near ruined legs would let me. I didn't talk.

That night didn't want to sleep—ever. When we finally

bunched beside the kiln, yellow suction cups of light fastened on the blackness, the goddamn dust, the bastard creek, the rocks, the sage, I sat in dead leaves. The awful whining of the dogs could have been me with that hot taste in my stomach and the mountains like ghosts whispering on my neck. Could have been Skink's old man stooped there, his face empty eyed, a paper mask. The dogs got quiet when this small policeman with glinting glasses worked Skink out. Just crickets and breeze. Skink was gone. Even his smell. The happy mouth smiled hard and dirty to the side. His legs were tucked against his chest, his arms out stiff behind. The shape of him knelt on the stretcher, head down, arms lifted like wings. Just crickets and breeze. Until the sack. The cops took turns carrying him. When we walked, Skink, so rigid, bounced inside the black plastic of his bag.

You wouldn't have recognized the guy all scrubbed and smooth and suited up in that satiny casket. I rode to the mortuary with Mr. and Mrs. Hickler. Hickler said I should be there. Like I told you, Hickler had it, what you hope you'll have some day, faith or something. He believed he made a difference, that everybody could. I believed he was a fool, even then, and maybe what I envied was he didn't seem to give a shit what I thought, what anyone thought. He didn't mind lugging boxes of groceries to old farts' back doors without so much as a thank you, buddy. He didn't mind dragging a cracker-assed kid to a funeral. It was my first. I thought I'd watch men in black with ropes lower a box into the ground. Instead family and neighbors and everybody sat in a narrow, purple room, and listened to organ music, and stared over the imitation Skink—and cried.

Hickler spoke with smooth, low words. The oily-haired grandfather who prayed first called him Bishop Hickler. I couldn't listen.

Hilda had gotten me all dressed up in a clean, striped

shirt and stiff pants, but still I was the only boy without a coat and tie—Pep and Matt weren't there—and I sort of felt like I was in a casket too. While Hickler stretched his voice just so, I looked away from the white-faced Skinks at Lance and Gerry. Lance winked, barely nodded. Gerry, head down, didn't even blink, his mouth thin, open, dark. Then we stood. "Dust to dust," Hickler said with a tremble, and I didn't believe that—not really. The organ wailed. And Skink's lost, closed eyes—shells from the bottom of the sea.

Hers too, only her eyes, those shells, were rough as walnuts. And knowing she'd been blind didn't make seeing them sealed up like that any easier. The girl inside was gone. This was the rock—of Ages. Gandy looked like some mummy yanked from a tomb, like petrified wood in a Sunday dress.

It was eleven days later. Old Man Shorter drove this time, but they had her laid out in the same damn mortuary. You know, it's still true: When I picture death, there's no heaven or hell, just me in clean clothes, me stiff and buttoned and empty as Christmas, me on my back in a tight box in that low, purple room with organ music like trees creaking.

Hilda and I were the only ones who cried at Gandy's funeral. With a wiry red veil over her face, moving her tongue across her lips as though she could taste it all, Mama looked at the oval paintings, the flowers, the casket, the curtains, but not at the ten or so people in the pews. Papa wore a tie. He used it to blot beads of sweat off his lip. Who were the others? Damned if I know. They were easy to forget they were so ordinary, a couple of ladies, a couple of men—maybe the staff of the funeral home. They sat, they stood, they left. The room smelled of new shoes.

Papa always said death comes in threes, "like railroad cops." Not in my experience. More like new shoes that'll never leave the box. For me death comes in twos: lightning and thunder; JFK, Lee Harvey Asshole, that sort of thing. Skink and Gandy were the first. A kid round as the moon, an old lady carved out of it. I didn't want to, but in some goddamn place deep down I knew the connection. Gandy died nine days after Skink—from life, I guess. This time I saw the casket closed. This time I saw the box in its hole. This time I heard the dirt, like dogs' feet, and smelled it. Hilda squeezed my hand and squeezed and squeezed.

I kissed the rock, and I said to myself, So that's what it comes down to.

12 —— PIT 'EM!

The power wagon shivered up high on its springs, over heavy-lug, waist-high tires and aluminum mags. Two yellow halogens glowed up top. A familiar blond winked down from the passenger window, chewing gum. This big guy with Hitler hair reached a paw out the back window to shake my hand. "L.G.," he said, Danny's younger brother. "I'm grown. The army done it. Lookin' good, Cade."

"Climb up," Danny called.

The rear windows were painted with desert scenes—a moon over cactuses, a coyote on a mesa, a red sun and silver sage—too tame, like movie shots. The wagon's body was primed, flat gray metal. "This is some goddamned machine," I said, swinging in off the running board, behind Danny—Castro—next to L.G. Johnny Cash rumbled gospel on the radio. I put my bundled work clothes by my feet on the beer cans on the floor. Spud nodded from his booth as we pulled away.

"Our old man put it together," L.G. said. "Got his*self* put back together, too. It's for sale."

The ceiling had been ripped out to a fringe of thread above the windows, replaced with an American flag hung in even tucks that shivered with speed. Springs popped.

"You remember Rita," Danny said, "minus the clothes, from Tricky Mick's." Over her bare arm across the torn front seat back, the blond glanced at me, her ringed fingers playing with Danny's collar. "Her real name's Florida." He laughed. "No shit. Florida Sands. Florida, meet Carlos Cade."

"I used to live in Florida," I said.

"Do tell," she said. "I'd like to breathe them orange groves at blossom time. Man down there offered me a job once."

"You're good at what you do," I said.

"It keeps me in lipstick," she said. Her false eyelashes damn near brushed my face. Her gold hair was braided up the back of her head. Inside all that makeup, she could have been nineteen, she could have been fifty. Before Danny lit up, I smelled her, a sweet smell from a bottle.

"So this is it," Danny said. He took off his hat and pushed back his hair. We rolled out on State, hot rod heaven, cars scoping cars scoping cars, a neon fence of stunted signs for pizza, burgers, and beer.

L.G. chewed bubble gum. A bubble snapped in the dark. L.G. said, "Stop and let me grab a pint."

"Tonight we're clean," Danny said.

L.G. said, "I ain't worried."

I said, "Should I be?"

Danny shook his head. "Faith in you old pal, Cade. Faith."

Somewhere past Ninetieth South, we turned east through Sandy, "a development," ten thousand identical aluminum lifetimes full of pregarage sale, La-Z-Boy macho, real-live beer jocks. "Take a peek over your shoulder," Danny said.

In the shifting black back of the wagon, in a cage that gleamed whenever headlights shot in, a hairless, stumpy log of a dog lay on its side. It looked paper thin in the flashing light, the shed shell of a dog.

"We going hunting?" I asked.

Florida said, "Do you hunt?" She put a cigarette between her lips. I lit it, then my own. Her nose was freckled. "I went deer hunting with a man in Wisconsin once. He shot himself, and I stopped the bleeding and saved his life. He bought me this one." She held up the index finger on her right hand, a ring with a square, heavy stone.

"Cade," Danny said. "What we're doing tonight is one hundred percent business. Big bucks is the deal, big, big bucks. Don't let nothing about this fool you. I've got this little pistol here. Put it in your coat." He reached a silver automatic back.

"You said you needed a hand was all."

"That's all."

"I'm not partial to guns—with good reason." I pushed it away. "I've got a knife. What is this shit anyway, big-time dognapping?" I tried to laugh.

"Dog fighting," Danny said slowly. "Real as you please dog fighting. That mutt back of you's gonna be the best."

"Quicksand," Florida said. "He named him after me."

"Tonight Quicky's got a match. This win and he goes for grand champ. The Vice is the other corner, a goddamn terror, no rollover. But hey, that's the game. Risk pays. Quicky, though, ain't a risk. Shit, he's on the treadmill twice a day. Eats better'n Ray Leonard. The risk is the people gonna lose their money. I need you to cover things."

"Not at two hundred and seventy-five dollars."

"For a friend. For triple, make that four times your money." The lines of streetlights disappeared. At the mountains, we swung into a green canyon, a two-lane following a stream. I smelled water.

"My knife doesn't mess around," I said.

"Give *me* the pistol," L.G. said. "Put him in the corner."

Florida said, "Jesus, let's get jumpy or something."

"This is it," Danny said. A log gate. Crickets blasted when we stopped. L.G. hobbled through the mothy headlights. Lights flared up behind us, but I couldn't see the car for the desert pictures. With a hand over his eyes, L.G. held the gate. "It's put-up time," he shouted past us. He laughed. The driver in back gunned his engine.

Danny said, "Business, Cade, remember." Florida lit her own cigarette.

We thumped over a timber bridge. The stream sounded like fire. The dog just lay there. Two red tracks took us and our tail through tall grass up a winding slope.

L.G. said, "Shiftlet's along. He's alone."

"His pals are ahead of him, you can bet." Over the wheel, Danny pressed the side of his watch, and the face glowed. "He's bringing up the rear. Ours. A half hour and counting."

"Shiftlet?" I leaned forward next to Danny.

"Yeah. Bobby Bull. We still get along. He's the one turned me on to dogs. Give me Quicky as a pup cause he run from a cat or some shit. 'Sposed to kill it. Otherwise son of a bitch's done right well for himself. Knows who it pays to know. Slips a few bills to his mama, too. Problem is he's in the other corner. Problem is business is business. You can bet his boss is ticked about Quicky. Rolly Musk is the one threw Quicky out. Bobby's business is kissing the big boys' butts. We're gonna bite 'em."

"We're okay," L.G. said.

Danny lit a cigar. "We're okay. This'll put us in the clear."

Florida did her lips and kissed down on a Kleenex. Another car joined the lineup on the hill. A rabbit zigzagged in and out of the light.

Jammed into rubble at the crest, like a chunk dropped

from Mars, this monster sandstone slab had chiseled into
it the coiled mound of an old-time beehive—the state sym-
bol. Bees, for God's sake. Who the hell would want to see
themselves as bees? Lance's old man called his park Beehive
Amusement. Shit. Hives without queens? You figure it out.

The road leveled. The trees turned to aspens to ever-
greens. The air chilled down. Florida said, "Brrr."

L.G. said, "Quicky smells it." The dog sat in the back,
leaning into its cage, its mouth cracked to make way for its
tongue.

"The Ledge, this place is called, Cade. A pioneer built
it."

In the glow of a fishhook moon, a white cliff leaned tall
as an iceberg over an old-timer stone house—flood-lit at
all four corners—and a silver-roofed, weathered barn, one
door wide and orange. The Jag back of us joined a few
hot-shit foreign jobs parked by the door. Two Harleys. We
found a spot in the field alongside the barn, among twenty
or so Rent-a-Wreck contenders and maybe half a dozen
pickups, most packing dog boxes. Goons leaned on fenders
here and there. A mutt barked. Still Quicksand sat. And
Elvis sang "Hound Dog" inside. The guitars twanged off
the cliff. Florida said, "Yipes," looking up. She touched my
hand.

I said, "That's rock." She giggled. I squeezed her back
before Danny limped around. Her bones were deep. If this
was such a goddamn serious business, what was she doing
there? L.G. stepped between us. Florida stood apart. She
said, "Brrr," and put on a vest as skimpy as her skirt. I
flipped my cigarette at the moon. Two guys talked three
trucks away.

Danny said, "Here's the deal, Carlos." He spoke with the
cigar tucked in the side of his mouth. "On the card is us.
Period. Fifty pounders. For a shot at the crown. A lot of
dollars. We don't want to fuck up, do we, L.G.? This win

and the one more, I cash Quicky in. Thirty g's, give or take. Buyers is lined up. Thirty g's. Or I hold him for stud. Steady money. A grand a shot. This is real."

Roy Acuff or some other Opry drawl let go with "Old Shep" now. Someone called, "Yahoo," in the barn. Smoke moved through the light.

A guy stepped up. He shook his arms out longer in his stiff denim three-piece. He leaked cologne. Under a flat rack of curly hair his eyes and mouth were too close to his fighter's flat nose. He dropped a hairy hand on Danny's shoulder. He said, "That pup's come pretty far."

"Bobby Bull," Danny said, swinging his cigar at me. "My old buddy, Carlos Cade. The governor's brother-in-law, no less."

I said, "Danny."

"You remember Carlos. He's boarded at your old lady's."

Bobby Bull Shiftlet nodded, mostly watching Florida hug herself up against the wagon. We didn't shake. A forest sharpened the air. So quietly I almost missed it, he said, "You're pushin' your luck, Dan." He wiggled his tie and straightened a school ring. "I'll take a hundred."

"All I got's taken."

"Jesus," Bobby Bull said. "Later." He stomped off.

The cliff rose like a drive-in screen.

"All right," Danny said. He wore the hat. He gestured Florida over, blew a long rope of smoke. He held my sleeve. "Before is no trouble. My money's down. They want a fight. So, L.G. stays out here with Quicky while we go in. Here's the deal. There's this fenced ring, this pit. Right? The dogs go at it in there. Florida will sit just back of the fence on this side. I want you to park with her, blade handy." His cigar was stubby now. He chewed it. He puffed, the tip hot orange between his teeth. His earring glittered. "Through a gate across the way is where Vice comes in, the Great Rolly Musk's pride and joy. You'll see Shiftlet there.

Quicky's gate's by you. Only one person goes in with each
dog. I work Quicky, only me. Musk's got a hired hand."

Florida laughed. When Danny blinked at her and spit
hard to the side, she said, "Sorry."

"Musk's got this retired pro wrestler name of Nicks handles his dog. When Quicky wins, we've got two worries—
our money and our dog. L.G. stands by to help me when
they break at the end. Then he covers *us* from the door.
Cade, you just make sure of Quicky, see no one grabs him,
goes after him. Simple. Just walk me out."

"This is the gold mine, huh?" I asked, but, shit, he was
already swinging with his long shadow to the door, Florida
teetering along on her heels beside him. How much money
would change hands? Too much from the looks of things.

"Evening," a sawed-off, muscled guy said. He yawned.
He wore a pistol in a new, tooled holster. He lifted a wide
fist of dollars. "Ten bucks each. Worth every dime."

Danny said, "He's with us."

Some bluegrass group yodeled "Old Blue" through black
speakers mounted under the loft. Three wagon-wheel
chandeliers hung in smoke above the white-fenced pit. Guts
buttoned into seersucker and madras, tucked into designer
jeans, seven or eight well-heeled, double-chin types
hunched in padded, captain's chairs to the side, two slinky
women along. Behind a bar of scratched black wood in the
corner—a bar with a brass rail, and a spittoon at each end
in sawdust—the bartender smoked a corncob pipe. The
rest were mostly noisy stiffs, loudmouth working guys
who'd bet on anything outlawed in the dark. Their names
were cut in the backs of belts. Their girlfriends had frilly
blouses and thick hair. They drank Pabst and eyeballed
Florida. Money moved. Hand to hand to hand. Big blow-
dried boys with pug noses rubbed elbows and watched the
money from the doorway. A uniformed county cop leaned
against the wall. Outside, five skinny Mexican *hombres* in

strapped T-shirts—the clean-up crew?—guys with ban-
danas tied around their heads, tossed knives at the dirt on
the edge of the light. Christ.

Danny talked up to this round-shouldered Abe Lincoln,
a dude tall and too thin in a brown leather trenchcoat—I
thought I was sweating—and tasseled shoes. The guy's eyes
were dry as pennies—and deep. He had the beard. The
nose. Even the mole. His left hand was long and clean and
smooth. His right was gone. He held a martini with this
metal-clamp gizmo engraved with a flowered, tiny vine of
leaves. Florida's smile was stuck. A few huge moths circled
in the light. Abe looked me up and down. Danny pulled
me over. "Here's Cade, Mr. Musk. My luck."

Mr. Musk spoke through his teeth in a high but raspy
voice out of the south somewhere. "Pleased," he said. He
raised his glass, a red plastic sword poking over the edge.
"You ever seen a dog fight, Cade?"

"Not this kind."

"They're never kind," he said. "Just honest."

The music stopped. An overalled, bald guy with thick,
clear-rimmed glasses straddled the fence and grunted into
the ring. He checked a silver watch strung to his bib pocket
with a leather thong. "Fifteen minutes, fellers," he called.

"Happy to meet you, Cade," Musk said as he turned.
"Your sister's one woman I admire. Shame about your old
man."

"I feel for yours, too," I mumbled, but he was gone.

Florida kissed Danny's cheek. She said, "I feel so good
about it." She excused herself through to the fence. I
parked next to her.

A guy back of me said, "I'll take two-fifty."

Across the way a side door behind Musk and Bobby Bull
Shiftlet opened. A broad, bleached blond guy, wrinkled as
a turtle, gold chains a tangle around his neck, stepped in
and tightened up on the silver leash he held. I knew the

guy, but where? The dog, Vice, solid white except for the
pink of its eyes and mouth, came to his knees, rocked from
side to side when it walked, two legs, two legs, two legs.
"More like ice," I said. Solid, wide, it threw its front paws
up over the fence and stood, held, even though the old
blond guy tugged.

"That's for sure," Florida whispered. "It's Vice's daddy
got Musk's hand. Did you know that?"

"Shit," Danny said, near us, hatless, wearing rawhide
gloves. Danny leaned to Quicky—Quicky black striped, yellow the rest, longer—lifted the dog's square head with the
tips of a glove. "C'mon," Danny said. The dog's tongue
dripped from the side of his mouth. The dog leaned against
Danny's good leg.

Florida hugged my arm. "Check Quicky out. What's the
deal?" And the room silenced to a whisper of moths and
dogs and trees.

Danny tucked his gloves under his belt and left Quicky
with L.G. Then he carried a bucket around to Vice's side.
At the same time, Old Blondy turned Vice over to this
younger blondy guy and hauled a bucket over to us. With
L.G. checking every move, his bleached hair clearly a rug,
the ex-wrestler got on his knees and carefully washed
Quicksand, nose to tail. Danny did the same to Vice back
of the other corner with the young blond guy keeping
watch. Florida said, "There's poisons and stuff you can
spray on, even stuff so the other dog won't bite. But look
at Quicky. His last fight went over an hour. Something's
not right. He's gonna cur out here before he's even in."
The wrestler dried Quicky, and the dog, blinking, wobbled
under each pass of the towel.

"Bring 'em in," the man in the middle said. Quicksand,
tail swinging, ropey muscles in his shoulders changing
shape, pulled Danny, but at the other side, Vice reared
against the chain and dragged Old Blondy in, straining to

cross the ring, gurgling, twisting, fixed on Quicky, tail wag-
ging to a blur. Danny wiped his forehead and glanced at
Florida. He licked his mustache. She held up crossed fingers. "Behind your marks, boys." And Quicky did tug now.

Each dog, fired through the eyes, hackled, collar off, an
arm under its head, a hand gripping the back of its neck,
twisted, struggled to cross the ring. Baldy in the overalls
backed to the side. He shouted, "Pit 'em!" and by the time
his shrill voice died, the dogs had collided in the center, in
dust, had thrown their heads, had slashed and snapped,
and now the white one gripped, twisted, bit into the darker
neck of the yellow, Quicky, held and tore and tore the
bucking shoulders. They spun. Danny and Old Blondy circled them, screamed: "At's it, at's it, at's it."

The crowd yelled: "Kill him. Flip him. The throat, goddamn it." Some threw bottles.

Florida said, "God."

Beneath the hollering, the sound was breath, dogs gulp-
ing at the air, and feet, toenails scrabbling at the hard dirt,
the tan dirt bloodied beneath Quicky's open back, beside
the spattered white fence, but still not whining, no quit,
Quicky lunged, twisting, tried to shake loose of the white
dog turning red. The white dog tossed its head, bloody
foam at its teeth, pushed, drove, until Quicky tumbled, legs
wild to the side, fell, rolled, spurted red, his mouth still
crazy. "Okay," the bald man shouted, but the dogs kept on.

"Get him off!" Danny screamed. He pulled at the white
dog's leg. The monogrammed belt crowd, standing, quickly
lit cigarettes, looked away, quieted, and what the hell was
I doing there? I just sat. Itched. I lit a smoke in that wild,
grunted breathing—still without a whine. Florida leaned
on my arm. Shivered. "Christ," a guy said. "Fuck it." His
neck chains busted in one hand, Old Blondy got the white
dog off finally, towed it—the gasping dog shaking spit,
backing out on its hind legs, still pushing for more—Young

Blondy and Shiftlet holding too, tugging at the leash, dragging Vice outside.

Quicky stayed put. He lifted his messy head again, but it fell. Danny held up a red glove. "Cade, hurry! L.G., c'mon!"

Quicksand's heart pumped through my hands. As fast as Danny could go, we ran with the dog—hot, slippery, stiff, feet up—Danny and I at his bleeding neck and shoulders, L.G. behind, wearing Danny's hat. We hefted him into the back of the wagon beside the dog box. I smelled blood, stale already. Danny said, "You drive, L.G." Danny leaned over the backseat, talking to the dog. "You're a tough shit," he said. "Sure you are, no matter what they fed ya, goddamn 'em. Hang tough." I held my knife, I don't know why, open in my hand up front.

As we skyrocketed out of there, Danny said, "Doc Nort," and silhouetted in the barn doorway stood Florida, lighting a cigarette, primping her hair. "Shit," Danny said. "Shit, shit, shit."

13 —— THE BOY WHO WASN'T THERE

Okay. They died. His closed eyes. Hers. Two funerals in two weeks. Other than the dead skin outside their eyes and that low purple room, I don't remember much. I remember sitting still.

I remember sitting with Hilda against a wall on hot asphalt on the school playground back behind our house, sitting in a slope of shade. Hilda didn't know the truth about Skink. It was just the dying then. And Gandy was ashes or dust or whatever the hell they tell you happens. I put my hand on Hilda's head while she sobbed against my knees. I remember a kid I'd never seen before shot baskets out in front of us, the ball bouncing, that silly, hollow sound. Whatever it was we brooded about, whatever it was that made death matter, seemed to be over there somehow, in that kid with that orange, noisy basketball.

Sitting. In front of Hickler's. The guy wasn't a statue. Sure he saw the change. He must have. For one thing, we hardly ever budged, hardly ever talked or played or anything. We made Captain look like Speedy Gonzales. We still stuffed ourselves—six-ounce Cokes, Hostess Snowballs, Necco Wafers—but that's all we did. The four of us.

Most of the time only four of us sat on Hickler's red stoop now. Gerry didn't come out much. Once Matt called us the Four Fathers. Lance laughed, but it didn't stick. Nothing stuck. Nothing lasted. I'm sure everybody thought we were down because round-faced, little, happy-go-lucky Skink died. That wasn't it. We'd discovered something. Anybody could die. We had proof. And nobody could be trusted. Those are the kinds of shit-eating goblins that left us just sitting. But what really had us stunned, I think, was we'd done it to ourselves. Jesus. Kids. Just kids. Nobody to blame. Nobody to cry to.

"You're Carlos, aren't you?" their parents always said now—like they expected more, or less, or something. I wonder how many knew. Jesus Christ.

Just kids.

I think Lance sat still those first few weeks so he wouldn't piss us off. That's as deep as it went.

One night, with the sun gone, with the air warm, bats scissoring the paper-thin blue twilight, sprinklers hissing, the five of us—Gerry there, white and sad—sprawled shirtless in a loose circle on the center island. Mosquitoes let us alone. And we were Indians or Africans, the first men, the first sons of bitches to hunker down together and talk, to find language. Shipwrecked sailors discovering words for it. A night ocean. A spaceship: We wake after eons of sleep. What year is it? What month? What country? What planet? Cars sometimes sizzled past, through that darkness inside everything.

We whispered. Matt told about this caveman a scientist found frozen in a giant blue ice lake in Antarctica. The caveman was still alive. He'd been in hibernation, or suspended animation, or something, Matt said. On a stack of Bibles.

And Gerry says, "Are we goin' to hell for what we did?"

We're ghosts in that weird, dirty light, silent, dirty ghosts. Mosquitoes stab me now. Lance laughs. "You believe that stuff? Pygmy red devils with pointy tails? This big bad barbecue? That's for scaring babies. And even if it's true, Satan and hell and everything, even if, the accident *was* an accident. Skink was dead—good as. We all know that."

Okay.

The weight of snow. Holding the houses in place. Snow. Shovel it. Snow's insides are black. Snowy snow. Kick it to powder. Pack it. Snow. With an empty thud flattening in round white lumps on passing cars' doors. Snow. Sliding cars sideways into more cars. Snow. No place to hide. Against the big blank of. Snow. Your footprints won't be left behind. Snow falls. Snow drifts. The wait.

I don't really remember snow or winter until that year. Galoshes. Hilda's heavy, ragged underwear. Mama, yellow, that awful weight holding *her* down, hardly ever getting out of bed, let alone sitting up. Papa didn't cook. He opened cans and jars and bags. I don't remember meals, just servings. One thing at a time—with a spoon stuck in it. Winter—heavy, flat, long, all its pieces in a press of snow, losing shape.

Sleds and snowmen and igloos and angels . . . Sure I can

go back to earlier memories that are wet and white and cold, a fistful of postcards from somebody else. That year, though, winter was mine. *I* went through it. I outlasted the cold. Barely. January and February—a white fire in my fingers, toes, and ears. My galoshes were too big, my coat was too big, my mittens were too big, and my orange knit cap I knew came from Gandy was too little. Hilda looked like she'd been dressed by a lunatic too. We dressed ourselves. We stood lost in our winter clothes like two adults who'd shrunk.

On the slush- or ice-covered playground, we stayed close to the building—never together. We watched the boys and girls. I even laughed sometimes. Their winter was white and clear: red and yellow quilted snowsuits; and padded gloves; and red rubber boots; and cartoon-character thermoses of hot chocolate and soup; and pocket-size, silver, lighter-fluid-fueled handwarmers. Snow rhymed with rainbow for them. A dream. Walking in a winter wonderland. Hell, a teacher, whose right thumb had two ends, two nails and all, even had us shape little snowmen out of cotton. Can you believe it? Those Disneyland kids made ice slides and snow forts and circles for fox and geese, and they stood in clusters like deer, breath steaming from their smooth, hooded heads.

Once in a while another charity-clothes scarecrow mysteriously appeared beside me, back against the frosty red brick, eyes down, hands deep in deep pockets. This boy would maybe shiver, would always have caked, icy nostrils and lips, would usually be black or Mexican or Indian— probably the only one in the school, like a ghost—and would smell of too much life in that cold, still, dead air. Sometimes the kid beside me had a metal brace on his leg. Most of the time I waited for the bell alone.

At a morning recess around Valentine's, a window-display kid told me I looked like a bum and probably had

runny sores on my butt. I punched him, his green left eye
shocked against my knuckles. When he dropped in the
muck, I was on him, my thumbs like screws at his windpipe,
his voice like wet sneakers. Two guys dragged me off. One
was Lance, Lance snug as a Christmas present in this Es-
kimo parka he had. He winked inside the furry hood and
said, "The kid's smaller'n you," even though the bloody
little son of a bitch on the ground was big as a Labrador.

That winter Lance and I hardly talked. Nothing much
to say. We both knew how things stood. Mutual interest,
it's called, although right from the start none of that shit
was in anybody's interest. When a teacher with tits as big
as children hiding under her red coat hurried over,
grabbed me by the neck, and said, "You devil," Lance took
a deep breath and said, "Ma'am, ma'am, he had to. This
guy"—pointing down, a black glove with white stripes—
"called his sister an ugly name." The bastard didn't deny
it. When she asked, he stayed quiet. That was that.

Usually, though, nobody helped me—or could have anyway. I sat through a lifetime's ration of boring hours in the
principal's office. His waiting room was a thick butter-
scotch-pudding sort of tan and his secretary this gray-
headed, whiny potato—no neck, no chin, just lumps. "Don't
kick the chair legs," she whined. "Pick your hat up off the
floor. You boys that can't behave . . . Real discipline is what
you need." She didn't smell, but right around that bitch
the air was empty, gone. "Dr. Scanty will see you now." She
batted her few ragged eyelashes toward his tan door.

If she was a potato, His Royal Highness Dr. Benedict
W. Scanty was a potato chip, crisp and thin and curved.
He couldn't have stood up straight with a .38 in his back.
"Sit down, my boy," he always started. He swept one arm—
the bruised, purple face on the big watch below his worn
shirt cuff, the long, sharp nails on his long, sharp, hairless
hand—toward a butt-ache, silver bird cage of a chair. His

mouth tight, his eyes dry, and his thumbs locked together, he leaned out at me from his creaking seat behind that desk huge as a goddamn pool table. "So soon, Carlos. So soon." When I didn't answer, mum and numb and cold as hell in my soaking clothes, he said, "What am I to do with you? Your parents show no interest. Are they good to you, Carlos?"

"Yes. They're my parents, aren't they? Why should they do your job?"

That whitened his thumb joints. "Because," he finally said, in a low voice hollow as walls, "we learn to behave at home."

"I behave at home."

"Your sister told me as much."

"Well?"

"Your teachers tell me you're a bright boy, when you apply yourself. They think a lot of you, Carlos. But I'm afraid you have them puzzled. I'm puzzled. Why are you always fighting?" Every time a bell rang, he jumped, but he sat through two now and through a chalky sort of silence, looking at me, waiting.

Why did I fight? Shit, you figure it out. Because I could whip anybody, I guess. Sure, a couple of times some guy's older brother pounded me on the way home. Of the kids in my school, though, there was nobody tougher. They came bigger and stronger. Better fed. But I was fast. I still am. And when I fought I sort of blanked out, slipped into a kind of automatic where moves made themselves, where my fast-as-hell little body couldn't quit—the eye of a goddamn hurricane, that's what I was.

"Can you explain it to me?"

Winter and school. Six of one.

Gerry and Matt went to Saint Paul's, a couple of classrooms—Lance told me once—like torture chambers under the cathedral, with nuns and priests all in black who'd just as soon paddle you as smile. They spoke Latin.

Pep went to Wasatch with me and Lance. Not one of the Disneyland kids, he was still Mormon. The Chosen saw to it he played. He sort of slumped around, always the fox. The geese never ran. Half the time he fell on the ice slide and lay smiling until someone—usually a girl—helped him stand. The name Pep seemed crazy now. His face slept through those games—his colorless, long, soft face. Whenever he saw me, he lifted the corners of his mouth, but he didn't talk. His feet dragged. Even when the weather eased up.

My old man had an Indian-head nickel, another of his screwball treasures. He kept it in his fishing-tackle box in a compartment with his three or four heavy, beaded-silver spinners. "Bank robber give me this," he told me lots of times. "Said it was lucky." After he turned it in his fingers, sometimes he'd let me hold it. An Indian head on one side and damn if it wasn't an Indian head on the other. Shit. I looked at it every which way, tried to bend it, and bite it, and rub it smooth.

You want to believe and certain goddamn things just won't let you.

Most of spring that year, the nickel had a tails after all. No more heavy, mismatched snow clothes. At recess in the candy-store smells of all the goddamn flowers everywhere, I was invisible again. I could play nearer the others. I could stand close to the girls with the clean, ribboned hair and the soft white and yellow dresses and not have them run off. I got pink. The hair on my arms turned white.

As the sun hung around longer and longer after school, furry dogs wandered back to their islands of bones and grass. Hickler put his awning up. Every now and then my old man hunted out a few tennis balls. And the gang?

Alone, I could hardly sit still, for all the birds and their singing, and the green back in the grass. When the guys were around, though, I felt the change, something different, something gone. We sprawled for hours in the open. We'd left pretend in the dust. With each other was the only mirror. Nobody moved much. Nobody said much. In a canyon, in a cavern . . .

"Matt's science project's going to the state contest," Gerry said. "Father Mann says it's the best he's ever had." Matt rubbed the yellow from a dandelion onto his palms.

Pep told about a dream he'd had, of being swallowed by a fish as big as Walker Bank: "Pitch black. So quiet I heard my heart. But it was the fish's heart." Pep's changed body showed now, all puffed out, in the arms, the legs, the tits, the belly, like a damn baby.

Gerry's father kept him crew cut to the quick like a convict. I remember thinking Gerry's eyelids were so dark they would turn black someday. His mom wouldn't let him drink Coke anymore, he said, because he hurt sometimes in the stomach. We listened. Dogs barked, buses hissed open, and sirens squealed.

Lying on his stomach, Lance twisted a silver, ruby-eyed skull ring on the long, dirty middle finger of his left hand. He'd sent for the thing with a coupon from the back of a *Tales of Terror* comic. "Let's all get 'em," he said, but nobody moved in the green grass. He even said he'd help out with the buck and a half they cost. No takers. So he worked it up and down his finger, the smooth, little head with the red eyes that turned his skin green. Sometimes he laughed to himself or groaned and put his shaggy head down. Once or twice, rolling with a quick breath onto his side, he said, "Ya know what I'm gonna do? Make us all rich as Kennedy someday." Funny about Lance—and Lance alone back then—how he saw the future like some limo that had just rounded the corner onto our street, coming to carry us away. He'd stare off over his ring so hard sometimes that we'd all look too. Shit. And that little scar quivering under his eye.

14 ——— CHAPTER AND VERSE

Junior high.

Where Wasatch had been only a street corner away, Bryant was a good half-mile down South Temple. Mornings now, I left my neighborhood like last year's clothes. Kids of every sort followed that sloping, white sidewalk. You took your place in the line and breathed the sweet, gritty exhaust of traffic. Hatted men in big boatmobiles caravanned past, motors healthy, steady—rich fathers, chins high, off to this store, that market, on the dot again. The world turned. You knew you would be missed if you left that frisky, beautiful parade. You were important; nobody was like you; you mattered to everybody. Always alone on that moving trail to your run-down, crowded, piece-of-shit school, you sometimes smoked a desserty, stinking menthol, Mormons or no frigging Mormons. Nobody ever pushed you in that line or passed you.

Lance—taller now, with a freckleless, small face girls seemed to like when it laughed—always moved a clump of others along, held them with a yo-yo, or a comic book, or an imitation of President Kennedy. He'd say, "Hey, Los," whenever we crossed. That was all, no introductions, no mimicking, just, "Hey, Los." His friends, the money kids, the polished, the kids in penny loafers and long-sleeved shirts, the label stitching showing off in back below their collars, with hair so clean it damn near stood on end, without cigarettes, never met my eyes—never. He didn't care. "Hey, Los." You can say a lot of things about Lance Arthur. Ass kisser isn't one of them. He led because they followed.

Pep followed no one. He went nowhere. *Don't miss the Incredible Shrinking Boy. This young man can slip through the cracks in any goddamn group. Now you see him, now you don't.* That was Pep: clean—around the edges; chubby, not fat; not short, not tall; Mormon, but not a goddamn missionary about it; politely dull; and pokey enough to lose himself anywhere. Good old had-the-wind-knocked-out-of-him Pep. If we ran into each other, he patted my shoulder and said, "Hi." His friends, as woodworky as he was, would say, "Hi," like a button had been pressed.

I caught on.

Kids were not the same. They came in different kinds. And they liked it that way. I'd never had a kind before. What do you know? Before, after, and during school, they hung out in alleys and bunched, smoking, across the street back of Boy's Half-Price Market. They shook down any unattended, lonely, little Disney shits—for laughs. No sneakers, no loafers. Zip-up, pointed-toe rib splitters, with taps. Required. Baggy shirts—seasons-old baggy shirts— and washed-out, black jeans, no label on the hip, no belt, cuffs thin as cigarettes. Brylcreem, a curl, a tail, I got the hair right. They were mine, and I knew it. After a few lessons, they knew it, too.

My fists arrived as soon as the next guy's, but faster than thought, to hell with my brain, they found opening after opening, and my feet saw to themselves. Before karate and all that pussy Japanese shit, this was street-savvy, pay-as-you-go, save-your-ass scrapping: creative mutilation—with knives, chains, and brass knuckles. Only a couple of guys fought over anything that mattered a damn—two or three times a girl riled them up. Usually you got into it just to get into it.

Seventh grade. Week one at Bryant. Music. Right. I had to take music and hold my mouth like it had an egg inside, through chorus after chorus of songs for the deaf. Shit. Miss Warbler, or whatever the hell her name was, thought we were supposed to be the Mormon Tabernacle Choir or something the way she worked us those first few days. I strangled my rotten little notes until my throat hurt.

I sat on the back row. Beside me, a short, runny-eyed, blond kid pretended he could sing, too. He screeched like a dying cat, not that I gave a shit. To pass the time, I said, "Just fake it. Think of my ear drums." When I stepped out of the cracked, wire-enforced doors that day after school, alone as usual, there stood the runny-eyed cat with four or five alley toms. He laughed and pointed. He smiled. So did a larger version. I came up just past the shoulder stars on the leather coat of the larger version.

The larger version gestured me over, a cross tattooed on his hand. A missionary. "Com'ere," he said. The pupil in one eye was oblong, like a black tear. "Com'ere," he said. Everything about him was performance—the half-smile, the smooth sweep of the leathered arm. That's what scared me, that I didn't matter at all.

"Hey," I said. I walked up slowly, thinking *brave*, but I left my knuckles in my pockets—just a punching bag. The backups with the kid and his larger version moved away a couple of steps. Three or four girls stopped on the stairs to groan.

"You told my brother to shut up," the big one said.

"He sings like he's sick," I said. "I wanted him to take it easy."

"My brother likes to sing." His blue tattoo: J E S U S
$$\begin{array}{c} \text{A} \\ \text{V} \\ \text{E} \\ \text{S} \end{array}$$

"He could've fooled me."

"Hey, smart mouth, you're gonna apologize. You know that? What's your name?"

"Carlos."

"A spic name." Two guys laughed. "With your hair, you must be a bastard spic."

"With your face, you must be a birth defect." My old man taught me that. The older version's nose started to run. His breathing slowed down. And still my fists were handcuffed in my pockets. I guess that's what kept him off so long—wondering what they held and why the hell I didn't pull them out.

He didn't blink. He licked his lip and spit between my feet. "My brother wants to hear how sorry you are. Don't you, L.G.?"

"Fucking right," L.G. said. I grinned.

"You think that's funny?" Big Brother asked quietly. "Funny will be when you crawl over and kiss L.G.'s pretty little shoes." Others waited on the sidewalk now, silent and still, like I owed them something.

"What's L.G. for?" Two could play the crowd. "Little Grunt?" Some of the girls snickered.

"Kiss 'em, or kiss my ass."

"Lily Guts? If you had a skirt on, he'd be hiding behind it."

Fists up, crusted eyes teary, L.G. stumbled forward.

Big Brother jumped. He caught the side of my face with a right I never saw. The sidewalk weighed a ton; I tried to lift it off my stomach; my cheek pulsed against it like a drum. Big Brother had turned to the audience. His buddies shouted when I sprang—too late. I hit him low in the back, like my old man told me cops did it. Brass knuckles fell from his fist. I saw fast enough what they were for. I unloaded at his chin twice. Jesus God, they damn near broke my hand. They hurt him worse. I stood over him. Nobody moved. L.G. was Long Gone. Big Brother rose slowly onto his elbows. He poked some fingers into his mouth. They came out bloody but empty. He shook his head and winked the crazy eye. "You're a tough little spic," he said.

"I'm not a spic."

"You're tough." Kids were leaving.

"I don't kiss shoes."

"No shit?" Now he got up. He found a crumpled pack of Salems in his coat. He held out a cigarette, his teeth red. "Here. My name's Danny, Mad Dog Danny. I'm not mad no more. Take it."

"Some other time," I said.

"Sure."

Enter Danny Ingus. Try this on, his brother's name, just those initials. God. Danny and I got close, like I said. It took a while. He beat the hell out of me before school Monday. The next Friday I kicked the shit out of him. You get the picture.

Danny showed me what was what. Chapter and verse. I owe him that. What to drink, what to sniff, what to pop. What to want. What I was that would not disappear. He shot out the East High clock one night with his old man's deer rifle. He had this bayonet he said his old man used in World War II to kill Japs. Scratched in the blade was INGUS—VICTORY. He ran that bayonet through this rich kid's baseball mitt at Lindsay Gardens. Then he laughed at the kid and said, "Lookee what happened. That won't catch shit now, but you don't want to catch any shit now, do you?"

Because of Danny, I tried lots of things, but I only threw in on two holdups, both gas stations.

The first one, Space Gas, or Rocket Gas, or who cares, wanted to be knocked over, just four pumps and a white box with blue windows. An old pioneer minus a few teeth watched Johnny Carson on a big sucker of a TV stacked with Pennzoil. We pulled stockings over our heads. The old guy logied at Danny and nearly got his eyes blown out. "All the dough's in the safe in the floor, stupid shits. Should've read the sign out front." Danny shook his head— cool. A little spit and twenty-three cartons of stale cigarettes is what we got out of that hot-shit heist. The smart old fart needed a few more teeth.

The second was with Danny, too, this time a Texaco, whitewall tires racked out front, restrooms around the side, even an air hose hissing between the pumps: the genuine article. A kid was on that night, a big blond kid in a green shirt and a green hat with a red star. Danny held the pistol on him, a shitty little .22, and I was supposed to load a pillowcase with anything I found. The stupid shit, though, caught Danny asleep, I guess, swung a thick, rusted pipe he must've had up his sleeve. Danny hollered, something wrong with his voice. The pipe clattered. When I looked, Danny squeezed his own right wrist. His legs folded. The kid sprang for the pistol on the floor. Sorry, son. Better luck next time. My knee caught the center of his chin, and his hat damn near jumped onto my head. He wasn't out, just groggy. I hightailed it to Danny's old man's DeSoto around the corner, towing Danny like a blind lady, and I drove. Goddamn, I'd like a movie of that drive, the second time I ever sat behind the wheel of one with tires rolling. An automatic, thank God. Shit, I kept hitting the horn by accident when I turned. Danny's arm was busted. I wished I'd kept the hat.

15 ——— THE PEACOCK

The vet said, "I don't know what can be done." With short jerks of his thick, scarred hands, he sewed up Quicksand's back, thirty-eight stitches. The dog, its swollen face splotched with round blue holes, like it had been buckshot, its heavy tongue purple and dry, didn't twitch as the needle slid in, slid out.

Then we stood in the half-lit waiting room, with posters of children holding puppies and kittens, with warnings to vaccinate, that antifreeze can kill, the yellow walls peeling, the linoleum cracked. "I'll get any money it takes," Danny said. "They doped him, Doc. Everybody seen it. This wasn't even half a fight."

The vet set his bifocals on the counter and sipped something from a plastic glass. "I can't test for that. I'll watch him. Call in a few days."

"I'll pay whatever fixing him costs. Don't put him to sleep or nothin' until it's no question."

After the vet's, L.G. bailed at some bowling alley out west. I drove, Danny too shaky and stoned. Even with the windows down, the wagon still stunk of dog, that dog damn near dead.

Two kids kissed under a big tree just up from Danny's. Three in the morning and some TV yammered off in the dark.

"I got nothing to say."

"Just a beer," Danny said. "We wake her up, and you explain like it was. That's all."

"And my money?"

"I'm not through with them, Cade. Haven't I helped you? You know what they done as well as I do. You think you got money troubles? Shit."

We fired cigarettes outside Danny's door, a torn screen door half off a runt stucco job just back of the Capitol. The door wasn't latched. A radio dial shined green in the corner, kid clothes bunched around it. No sound but deep, deep breathing, Rose on her side in a lacy black slip asleep on the couch, Rose hanging tough through thick and thin. Rose—still with Danny. Danny flipped on this red lamp of a horse with a bulb on its head. After tossing his hat through the kitchen door, he sat in the bend of her knees. He stroked her calf and smoked. Once we'd crushed our cigarettes, he shook her. "Rose, hey. Hey, Rose." I could hear the joints in his leg when he stood to turn her, to raise her against the pillow.

She rubbed her eyes, glistening eyes. She looked older only because her mouth hung lower, but she was waking, and when she yawned, the roundness returned to her cheeks. "A smoke," she said. "Light me."

"Hello," I said, as she inhaled.

"Cade," she said. She let go the smoke. "You're still alive." She leaned on her knees, looking at the cigarette, her tits half out of the thin thing she wore. As Danny came from the kitchen with a pint of Old Forester and three Bud tallboys, she said, "You, too."

He dropped beside her. "Sure."

She pushed his hand off her leg. "And why aren't we celebrating?"

"I brought Cade to tell it. The Vice was shit."

"Our dog's dead?"

"It was a fix from minute one. And it ain't over, honey. That's years we're talking. Years to come that won't. I ain't inventing this. Tell her, Cade."

"Danny," I said.

But he held out a hand palm up, and Rose flipped her ash on the floor and said, "Well?"

And I said, "Somebody got to Quicksand. Anybody could have told the dog wasn't right."

She tipped her beer, swallowed. "Get out," she said. "You'll wake Carlie. I got work today."

"The dog's not dead."

Slumped, but at the wheel in the wagon headed downtown, Danny said, "They think they're playing with nothing, Cade, with nobody. Quicky's gonna beat 'em someday. Dollar for goddamn dollar. You watch. And this Castro ain't a babe in the fucking woods. They ain't gonna squeeze me."

"I missed you all night long," Ginny says Saturday over a burrito for lunch at Taco Bell.

"I missed *you*," I say. Flies run across dried Coke on our umbrella table. "Six hours of stud and I break even. With college kids, no less."

Her hair is tied back in a blue bandana. She wears a pink halter top. The tortilla tears and hangs from her lip. She laughs and blushes. "I did a dumb thing. Me and my two girlfriends went to these male dancers. Ladies-only night at this sleaze-ball bar on West Temple. The dancers weren't hunky or anything. They had these leather jock straps and bowties."

"You're kidding."

"I'd never been. The girls were the gross ones, taking off their blouses by the stage, writing down their phone numbers and tucking them in the jocks."

"So then what, dates after or something?"

"Carlos, it was funny. If you knew these girlfriends of mine . . ."

"Jesus, just stop this missing-you bullshit. You had a damn party."

"I missed you the whole entire night."

"What is that, a goddamned hicky on your arm?"

She stretches to me and kisses my cheek. "You jackass," she says. "A kid caught me with the trainer door."

Danny's back in his own buggy on Monday, this candy-apple, beat-to-shit Camaro. His hands are scratched. He smokes quickly, follows me into my bay. Spud's next door pitching a Volkswagen bus to the last hippy. I've got one car waiting. "How's the dog?"

Danny laughs from the shadows. "He's hanging in there," he says. "Christ. Anybody's guess." He drags his leg over now as I wave in this yellow Electra and an old lady driver. "Cade, I got this different deal going. I won't forget you standing with me the other night."

"Forget me. Hey, you seen Florida?"

"Who ain't?" he said.

Tuesday, Danny doesn't even nod. As I walk in, he fires his glass packs out of there.

Wednesday, he surprises me, waiting in the hot dark of my bay, smoking a joint. "Keep an eye open for the fat man," he says.

I take a quick hit. "You're the one needs to keep an eye open." His are swollen and blue. One middle tooth is busted clean off. "Shit, you chasing armored cars?"

"Close," he says. He eats the roach, licks the broken tooth. "Tomorrow I might need a hand with an errand."

"What's wrong with L.G.?"

"What isn't? Your money's coming, Cade. Just do me this favor." A drop of blood rolls from his nose, and another.

"Danny, Freddy, whoever the hell . . . Drop it. Leave me be. I told you I've got business, man. Fucking important business."

"I'm talking business," he says. He spits at the drain. "And *mucho dinero*. This favor goes both ways."

Thursday when I roll in, two black guys with monkey wrenches bang pipes in Danny's bay. "Castro phoned in sick," Spud says, huffing, holding a wrench himself, wet all over. "So I'm realigning rotors," he says. "Gave the boys in these two a couple days leave. Do yours this weekend. You scratch Saturday."

Sure, Danny's gone and I could worry about him, but I don't. The sky's this thin white that fries your eyes, and the heat won't quit. I think about my old man, about Matt and his goddamn cow, about *my* story. The note's in its Baggie in a frozen glob of spaghetti in my fridge. A fire couldn't touch it there.

I sprinkle my sheets with water, the windows wide, and sleep alone.

Friday night I towel off, drag a comb through my soaking hair, and drop the bay door. Spud calls, "See you Monday."

Two blocks up State, Camaro rumbling, Danny catches me at a light. He says, "That errand I was telling you about. I'm counting on you, Cade. How 'bout it?"

And I told Ginny we'd go for ice cream, something chocolate, but Danny is staring straight out, and his cigarette's shaking. "This is money we're talking," he says like his teeth hurt. "I've got your bread. You drive."

And I know better, but I say, "All right." I tell myself I can stop anything stupid, maybe protect Danny. He is my oldest friend. And I should have stopped him once before. I think of telling Ginny, but I don't.

Danny's eyes look better, but he hasn't shaved, and his hat's ripped in back at the brim. He whistles, sharp, short bursts, low in the passenger seat, with his hat tilted down. "A couple of bennies, man?"

"Nah," I say. The wind hisses through the windows, hot and gritty.

He picks at his cheek with one hand, a smoke going in

the other. "Next left," he says. "You'll be glad you signed on. Now right." Between his feet is a blue Dallas Cowboys gym bag.

An alley. South of the post office downtown. A brick and concrete oven of power lines, dumpsters, barred windows, and steel doors with business names stenciled on. The Camaro shivers and growls. And what the fuck do I find myself doing? Idling at the wheel behind Stonehenge, this high-class nightclub with an awning over its back door. Danny says, "Don't fall asleep." He flips his cigarette about fifty feet, unfolds his leg, and gimps inside with the heavy gym bag. Dope, I'm sure. Coke, I'll bet. And there I am in the son of a bitch's car, taking chances for who knows how much cash. Probably none. The bugs are crazy around the alley lights. And, Jesus Christ, I think, what the hell hope do I have with life all the time turning itself inside out?

Danny carefully closes the Stonehenge door, the gym bag gone, gives me the thumbs up, showing teeth like a damn crocodile, and hustles over. "Motor," he says. The tires whine. He falls back in his seat laughing.

"Where's your hat?" I say.

He touches his hair, eyes panicked. "Shit," he says. He pounds the dash. But now he laughs again and jerks back like the noise startles him. "Forget it," he says, "wrecked anyway. It don't matter. I'll get another. A new name."

At the first red light, he tightens up, says nothing, stops breathing damn near, and stares in back of us. "Just drive," he says. "I got all this shit to work out."

I head down State. I'm thinking Tricky Mick's. I'm thinking about cool air and trumpets and this wild woman with eyelashes two feet long who doesn't fluster at any goddamn thing. But my mouth is wrung out now, the heat like another layer of skin. I smoke and it's bitter, and I can't spit.

"Good man," Danny says when I stop at a 7-Eleven. "Two quarts of Schlitz."

And I am coming out with my sixer and his bottles, sliding into the driver's seat, Danny holding out a hand, smiling full-time now, when sirens rise up toward town. This isn't your traffic accident or your kitchen fire. This is business, these machines screaming, rushing together from every side, one long wail just uptown. Danny says, "Sounds like the Fourth."

I circle through Liberty Park and turn on the radio, slowly dial the stations, even though I don't need it, already know I've gone back about fifty giant steps, and my muscles tighten, and I light a cigarette, and Danny says, "God-damn," when the news lady on KSOP says, "The bomb was found minutes before the blast, the Stonehenge nightclub cleared quickly. Still, a man and a woman have been taken to the University Medical Center. Until the debris is cleared, we . . ."

"Cade," Danny says. "They found it because I left it open in the middle of the goddamn kitchen. Couple I can think of should be dead, though. They'll wish they was when I'm finished. This is enough. Hit 'em in the gut one good time. Fuck it. You get what you pay for."

"Roland Musk," the lady goes on, "the owner of Stone-henge, says he knows of no motive for the bombing of his club. Right now, the police are—" I flip it off.

I park up alongside Tracy Aviary. Sprinklers hiss and sputter in the dark beyond the fence. Danny gets out. He leans against the car, the bottle bubbling as he gulps. Out of the night, a peacock trumpets one long jungle-movie wail. The sirens are gone. The only other car's a hundred yards down, by the lake. Cruising teenagers swing their lights past, their radios. In the quiet, wings are moving.

I get out, a cold one in my hand. I step around the engine and stand in front of Danny. He laughs and stretches inside for the other quart. A truck passes with Waylon Jennings on. "You should have told me, Danny."

"I told you money, Carlos. That's it." He pats his wallet.

"This is hard time. I'll take my money."

"Nothin' hard about counting dollar bills," he says. When he lights a cigarette his eyes are yellow coins. "I got something the big boys'll pay for. They don't want to pay. Hell no. But now they'll see I don't roll over."

A cop car wheels by. I see it. Danny doesn't. My skin tightens down. My heart does double time. What if someone saw? Made the car? This is Danny Ingus. And it isn't. Fred L. Castro. Fuck. People don't hold still. They aren't you. They leave you. And do you owe them then?

I smoke to slow my breathing down. "Danny, goddamn it you're dumb. A fucking dumb shit."

"You wait," he says. But he stands away from the car.

"I'll give you my expert opinion. This is deep shit. You're in it. I'd stash my car and lay low."

"Low is where I'm not. Are you that goddamn low?" He sucks the beer. "You scared? That's it. You want money but you ain't got the balls to fight for it."

I've drained one can. I hold another unopened in my right hand. The can is hard and heavy.

"What'd I figure you for? Shit. Get going, Cade. Nobody'll put you there. Go!" he is shouting.

I shiver, the beer cold and hard in my hand. "My money," I say.

"Look," he says, "you won't go, I'll show you something." He drags his leg to the trunk, where he fumbles in his pocket for the keys. "Stand right there," he says, handing me his nearly empty bottle, pointing at the curb. He bends. The trunk springs open. He leans inside, and when he rises, lunges, this goddamn bayonet catches streetlight on its way to my gut and the can in my hand is cold.

16 —— VOICES

No knock. Ginny whispered, "Hey, night owl," and quietly closed the door. She snapped on the lamp Danny left me, her face creased with sleep, her toenails blue. I sat on the windowsill, my feet up, my shoulder and cheek against the warm screen, an empty bottle at my back. She touched my neck. "I got lonesome." She pulled me against her, this thin white nightie sewn with yellow flowers. "It's nearly two. You sick?"

"It's nothin'."

She stepped back, tilted her head. "Okay." She kissed me, tongue and all.

Home alone I woke to the stink of my own breath. I lifted my right hand, moved the fingers to check the swollen, bruised knuckles. Shit. I tried to remember leaving Ginny. A roach crossed the wall. My old man used to catch roaches in this coffee-can trap he made. He'd stand them in the freezer for a while to slow them down, and then he'd melt wax over their feet on bits of tin foil at the kitchen table. They'd live for days stuck like that, twisting their heads, their feelers twitching.

I smoked two cigarettes on the pot. In the window again, I chewed a cardboard chocolate Pop Tart—no toaster— and stared at the city, the cars I wouldn't have to buff that day. Some instant coffee from the tap, plenty of sugar, and I'm ready.

I get the black Spiral from its spot in my closet. I put my pen beside it. I sit and turn the pages, the print too large, too stiff. I will copy this over. I will add what's missing. My hand throbs when it moves. And I throw the goddamn pen against the wall. Mr. Cat pounces across the floor after the spinning silver cap.

The sun slants hard through the window then. I told myself only after dark, but I unlatch the screen at the bottom, check the street, the windows across from me, push so it swings out, reach for the hole where mortar and brick have crumbled away, for the plastic pipe tobacco pouch I bought last night and tucked up there, shaking as I touch it. I slide it out, sweating in the hard sun. I take two fifties from the pouch, just one hundred out of seven, and zip it shut. Only at night after this, I tell myself. As I work it back into its hole, two pigeons cannonball past my head. I look below, and three cars have stopped, drivers leaning from their windows, a couple on the sidewalk, too, holding hands, pointing at me, past me. And Jesus Christ, overhead this hot-air balloon drifts under two small clouds, a black and red balloon lettered UTAH.

I close the screen. I am dripping. I hear the balloon firing its air, a low hiss coming from the sky.

Two big bills in my pocket, my hand sore and obvious, I tried not to walk too quickly, the sidewalk thin as eggshell in the bright sun. They couldn't have found him yet. And my only connection was he picked me up. He wanted me along, I'd say, gave me a hundred bucks for starters. I turned him down, tried to give the money back, he swung, I punched him. Last I knew. Simple. None of my doing.

Now I wondered, Had I wanted to kill him?

My shirt was wet up under the arms, the sun like hot plaster, the sidewalk blank as paper, and I could hear a cop car at my shoulder, the engine breathing. I did not look. I knew who I was, what I could take, what I could give. I needed a car—to be off the sidewalk, out of the sun, to move when my brain said move, to be even. I did not look. The newspaper rack was empty. So what did I need to know anyway?

The clerk at Grand Central said, "You all right?"

"Just ring it up."

A Sony. Classy. In a black case with a strap. This would work. I could hear myself. A new blue notebook.

Had I locked my door? It opened without the key but not a goddamn thing was touched. The closed Spiral lay on the table. Every page there. I lit a cigarette. My screen was latched. Mr. Cat slept on the couch where I'd left him.

I popped a beer, took a long swallow. Then I poured it in the sink. Discipline, goddamn it. To see straight. More instant from the tap. I would talk it—to myself. Why not? I cleared my throat. The cassette turned. My voice swirled the dusty air.

I copied what I said from a tiny earphone.

Sunday morning. A pigeon walked the length of my windowsill, flew when I stood. In groups of scrubbed, frilly children, couples swayed down the sidewalk to cars. A man in a white hat laughed at the funny papers under a tree.

Behind me, behind one thin wall, Ginny lay on top of my sheets, Mr. Cat curled at her chest with a grin on his face.

It would make sense. I hid the cassette and the notebook back over the ceiling. I pushed Mr. Cat to the floor. With her tongue touching my ear, Ginny whispered my name.

And no one knocked. Nothing. Danny's hat must have been shredded.

I bought two Cokes and a paper, but the Stonehenge story was already page 2. The man and the woman—in town for a dental convention—lived. The photo looked like the moon. Police were investigating.

"They think it's organized crime," Ginny said. "I saw it on the news." She lifted her dark glasses in these big orange frames and blinked at the picture. The light changed. The car behind us honked. "They must not love anything is how I figure it. Bombers. We're dead already to those bastards."

She wore this sailor's hat. She folded up the brim. The mountains leaned over us. "You know what I think? Nobody wants to understand anybody. That's the bottom of the list."

"Tell me about it. But right at the top of everybody's? Being understood. Power."

I lit her cigarette and reached under her shorts as she drove. She said, "I know what's at the top of your list," and she laughed, and squirmed, and her cheeks, warm pink, rounded when her lips opened. She turned up Red Butte Canyon, said, "Hang on," which I did, and then she cut down a dirt road and nosed into a shady clump of scrub. The ground was hot and hard and she moaned, moved herself in circles above me, said, "Oh Los, oh, Los, say it. Say you love me."

And I said, "Sure, sure," lifting her, us, sweating, as we both let go.

Canyons. Canyon after canyon after canyon. We went to the zoo, at the mouth of Emigration Canyon, the next one over. Two black metal panthers crouched on pillars at the gate. I looked up the canyon. Why not? Regrets were for dinosaurs. Time did not run backward. Survival was no small thing. Ginny said, "Come on." We started at the children's zoo, The Ark, this huge open-air boat full of sheep, and goats, and ducks. Shit. These high school girls in togas and sandals, with change makers on their rope belts, sold animal food.

We tossed popcorn to white bears from the top of the world. Tigers yawned. The hippo ate like a garbage truck. We ate nachos and snow cones. No dope or booze. No nothin'. We laughed at the gibbons, the chimps, the orangutans. But the gorillas looked sad, too big, too hot. Ginny said, "There's this woman who lived with lions in Africa someplace. They thought one killed her, but it turned out to be murder—this tracker or something."

She held my hand at the stagnant puddle of alligators, three scummy leather logs with snake eyes that would not blink. Flies everywhere. She kissed me by the camels.

Early Monday, I knocked at Ginny's. I couldn't settle down. I owed her. I owed myself. Just a few minutes.

As usual old Mrs. Shiftlet was perched below on the landing in her wicker chair. In a cellophane of dirty light, she rocked there knitting, five days out of seven. Took weekends with family somewhere. "If it's number eight you're looking for," she said very quietly, eyes down, scrawny yellow in her old woman's clothes safety pinned at the seams, "she's out just now—since the sun come up." Her hands fought with those needles in her lap. Her voice jumped when I stepped away. "Pretty one," she said. "Good stock, I reckon. Irish, with a name like that. Good worker, I'll bet. Steady."

"That's her," I said.

"Say," she said. Her needles stopped. "You seen Danny?"

"Last week."

"You do, tell him my boy Bobby's been callin' every five minutes trying to find him."

When her needles clicked back into action I thought for a second of teeth, teeth chattering, cold.

17 —— LIKE LADIES

Fall. Eighth grade. Dry leaves over damp, dark dirt. Jill Arthur tearing her face apart, crying.

I took a splitting, lopsided Bill Russell basketball I found and wandered up the alley to the backboard behind Matt's place. I couldn't hit anything but lay-ups for shit, so I dribbled mostly. A few shots now and then. The backboard was bolted onto a rotten relic of a frame garage. The whole damn thing rumbled and shivered if the ball so much as grazed it. I liked that. I'd wind up and chuck the ball as hard as I could. The walls boomed, paint chips fluttered like moths, and the ball rocketed from hell to breakfast. It was once when the ball bounded clear to the Arthurs' garage that I found her.

Straightening up with it in the dark by rakes and a power mower, I spun around at this sudden noise like slurping through a straw. Nobody. Then the sound again, higher, longer, and I saw her lying all twisted in a ghost-white nightgown on the backseat of her father's Continental, her hands locked onto the silver door handle, her feet stiff, two dirty crescents on their bare, smooth soles. Her chest jumped full through her back and then burst once more into that noise. Finally I whispered, "You okay?"

When she looked up, everything kept on—the heaving, the sound—and her face opened itself, wider and wider. Her eyes. I dropped the ball. It bounced three times, each one a crazier kind of thud. Then silence, without tears, her face the same. The eyes. She swallowed and sort of leaked out, "Get away, you . . . trash."

Hell, I didn't care. Not really. What would I have said? I already understood that damn near everybody only spoke to be heard about ten percent of the time, the rest just reflex and mouth exercise. No, it got me that someone as pretty as I thought she was—her ears perfect for all I noticed them anymore—could be so ugly. One other thing, too, that someone so strong could be so weak. Blood seeped through the tiny cracks in her eyes. I went back to shooting baskets.

The few flies felt like tears on my face, my neck, my arms. Damn. And all the trees looked like ladies.

Jill.

Hilda made her own rules she looked so good. I realized that about her damn near the same minute she discovered it herself. All that kept her outside the dance hall, so to speak, was a clean hair ribbon and change of clothes.

Take my word for it, Hilda had smarts enough for anyone. I'll give you even money I wouldn't be able to read without her nagging me when I was a little pecker. She liked books now the way she liked to daydream before that afternoon when the nosey goddamn universe got a glimpse of how God shaped her. Anytime Papa didn't have her cleaning up or running piddly-ass errands, she parked somewhere, her eyes fiery righteous over everything from Nancy Drew to *Vanity Fair*. She lived books. Her cheek muscles quivered when she read. Lots of cold winter nights, when the furnace flame couldn't have lit a cigarette, she told me entire novels damn near word for word.

Hilda's book savvy brought her the only positive attention she got in elementary school, dried-up spinster teachers sending her from room to room for special reports every week or so. She wasn't about to let her little brother make a fool of himself. We had drills. She sneaked a bunch of flash cards out of her homeroom. She worked me sore-eyed. If I bitched, she sometimes squatted down, tight all through her face, and whispered, "That fat slob that says he's your papa, you wanta grow up to be like him? You might as well let me knock you in the head good right now."

Once Papa caught us. He staggered through the door-way and sneered. Hilda dropped the cards. Our goddamn radio whined way the hell off behind him somewhere. Hilda didn't wait but a second: "I stole all these, Papa, so's Carlie could get his reading down." I backed across the floor toward my bed.

But my old man laughed. "You got smarts, Hildy," he said. He tilted his head and eyeballed the cards. He scratched his neck. Papa left mumbling about "good sense is dollars and cents."

I never knew my old man to actually lift anything, but I always got the feeling he saw stealing as a sort of obligation. "Ownership's one great goddamn game. What's more honest, for God's sake, than sharing what we all fair-and-square was born into?" On one of our trips to the golf course, he said, "Swimmin' pools won't count for shit at any pearly gates. Hell, pearly gates won't count for shit."

After school once, for some damn reason, I whined I was hungry. He said, "You're outa diapers. Hickler's ain't but a stone's throw."

I said, "Okay." I took an old pop bottle I'd found, and while Hickler thought I looked at the candy figuring out what to spend my three-cents deposit money on, I shoved some Hostess Cupcakes inside my hat. Hell, I opened them at home, and my old man made me give him one. He ate the frosting and put the rest on a saucer for Mama.

Anyway, he didn't mind the flash cards. What was to mind? Reading was so far outside his life, it could have been pretend. Hilda drilled me, coached me, worked herself black in the eyes. She believed. And she studied. And she studied. For what? For a little luck maybe. To cover the bets she still had faith were on the table.

Luck appeared for Hilda the June before eighth grade, before her second year at Bryant. *Luck* wore a fluffy yellow dress, for crying out loud, yellow sandals even. *Luck* went by Sissie, the name of Matt Downes's sweet-as-Co'-Cola cousin from Oklahoma here for the summer while her parents traveled overseas. On her wish-boned wrists sparkled a gold charm bracelet and a real watch that chimed. Sissie was smiling at the chimes, her arm lifted like a wing, the velvet of the watchband red as blood, when Hilda and I first saw her.

Away from home, Hilda and I were hardly ever together. But we were rarely far apart all the same. We swam in the same fish bowl, if you know what I mean. Kids were everywhere. Kids were nowhere. Hilda liked the shadows, the deep, dandelion shade under Mrs. Bottoms's maple trees, to read, to think, to plan, to sit with her knees tucked up and her chin on her hands. I'd take the sun any day, shoulders red as bubblegum, blistered sometimes. I sweated till my eyes stung and loved every minute.

I was lying on the sticky grass of the island, roasting, itching, going for heat stroke, when Matt called me to come over. "And," he said, like something routine, "bring your sister."

Hilda said, "Yeah, sure," when I told her. She wore patched cutoffs, uneven like the legs had just rotted away. Supposed to be pink, her T-shirt could have been blue. The blood had drained out of her skin. She marked her book and got up, scratching a head of hair damn near short as mine.

"Honest," I said.

Matt said, "No, this way," from the alley as we stepped onto his porch. I was too hot and thirsty by the time we pushed into his small, redwood-fenced back yard. Each white patio tile held a painted yellow flower.

Sissie sat fluffed out on the edge of a white wicker chair, pressed up at the side of a white garden table where four places were set. Her arm raised, she listened to her watch, like I said.

Matt said, "This is my cousin Sissie from out of town."

Eyes closed, she smiled, rocking her head to the chimes. "Sissie," Matt said louder. "Here's some kids from the street."

We waited by the gate. "I asked Lance and Jill," he whispered with his back to his cousin, "but they had to swim at the country club with somebody. Come on."

Hilda said, "Thanks, Matt," without a blush.

She took three large steps and sat beside Sissie. Wide pearl eyes stared for just a second and then closed again. "That's a cute watch," Hilda said. "So's the dress, but you wouldn't catch me wearing that in this heat."

Eyes open. "I bet I couldn't catch you in a dress," a small kitten of a voice said.

Hilda did the last thing I expected. Stiff as a stick, she stared over the flower bed, and then tears flooded her cheeks. Jesus Christ, Matt went white as everything else out there. I started to think about how I'd probably have to fight him now. Then, sobbing how sorry she was, Sissie knelt next to Hilda. Fate drove a Cadillac that day and said, "Hop in."

Fat, flabby, rouged-up as always, Mrs. Downes grunted open the sliding door and squeezed outside. Matt said, "Mom . . ." Her spreading face said something close to, What the hell happened to my garden? The crying stopped.

Mrs. Downes cleared her throat. "Sissie dear?"

"Is it time yet for lunch, Aunt Helen? We're starved." Sissie got up and brushed off her knees. I winked at her. The corners of her mouth rose to dimples. Aunt Helen blinked at the sky. She rolled her red lips together so they disappeared. She breathed deeply through her nose, fiddled with the pearls on her necklace, and went back inside. Sissie was one hell of a name for a kid like that. She had the nerve of a goddamn saint.

If Sissie decided on something, get out of the way. Sissie

decided on Hilda, don't ask me why—I didn't see all that
much of it. Mostly I saw the symptoms, the little things,
the clues. Hair was number one. All that first week, Hilda
came home with her short, colorless hair fluffed up and
clean, one silver barrette just back from each ear. The second or third night, Papa said, "What're you doin' to your
head?"

"Makin' it cute." Her eyes sort of fluttered at him.

He drew on his cigarette. "I guess you are." Hilda
dodged a jet of blue smoke.

As she quietly moved past the low bed that somehow
captured our mother, Mama hoarsely whispered, "Come
here, Hilda. Let me see what all you done for the boys."

"Boys?"

"It's the way when the juices start flowing." Mama's head,
small as a cantaloupe on the gray pillow, with the skin of
a cantaloupe, too, turned toward Hilda.

"Is that what I'm feeling, Mama?"

"Light inside the ribs. Down there. Warm. Womanness.
I had it once. Maybe not near enough, Hildy. Maybe not.
Maybe that there was the first sign I was goin' to be sickly
and die young." Behind me, the kitchen door slammed.
Papa stood outside.

Hilda leaned over Mama, her hands stroking that cantaloupe, the cantaloupe breathing like it hurt to breathe.

Every damn day from then on, something changed
about Hilda. I'm not really sure what happened, why she
put her books down. Maybe she glimpsed the older girl
blinking through her eyes now in the mirror. Suddenly she
saw herself and looked after what she saw. Maybe Sissie
alone accounted for it, Sissie just possibly the first person
to touch upon *Hilda*, to kneel beside her in anything like
sympathy, if that's what it was. Maybe Sissie's flowery, soft
frills were enough by themselves, Sissie like a goddamn

Mormon fairy tale in the center of Matt's back yard. Jesus Christ, I'm not a goddamn psychiatrist. Something moved her, though, lifted her eyes, her chin, her shoulders, her chest, like she'd been made all over again. And it happened fast.

Hilda and Sissie stayed together until dinner. Papa stood when Sissie came in. He tugged at his nose as he said, "How do, Miss? How do?" I don't remember Hilda ever bringing anyone else inside. Sissie perfumed the place. My old man kept his shirt on and smoked in the alley.

Mama never said two words to Sissie, but she saw her all right. Whenever Sissie passed, Mama's eyes sparked like two matches. Sissie and Hilda would close the door to our room and do who-the-hell-knows what. I tried to peek in, but they squealed and held me out. To see Sissie in my house, you would have thought it was just like any other. Farm-girl polite, but bubbly and pink, what Sissie brought left me wanting to hold her and whisper with her and breathe all of her in.

Usually, though, they kept their distance, off at Matt's or just out strutting around. One practiced step at a time they got to looking more and more alike. Sissie came part way. Every now and then she wore khaki shorts and a crayon-yellow or blush-pink golf shirt. Hilda could have had the witch's ruby slippers. After the hair, glossy, perfect, tapered wings, came earrings. Hilda and Sissie took the bus downtown, and by God, she got her ears pierced. Tiny silver balls flashed when she tossed her bangs into place. Next her fingernails, which she stopped chewing, and her toenails, got coated flaming red. Like I said, Papa never dropped another word about Hilda's changing—but his rheumy eyes cleared plenty. And Mama? Who knows?

I found a razor in a hole in the wall next to Hilda's bed. She said, "A lady looks after her legs." As clean as cafeteria dishes, scrubbed, she tanned up like a million bucks. Except for the clothes—and Sissie left Hilda most of hers when she went back—they could have been sisters.

The Downeses asked Hilda to go with them to Disneyland for two weeks. "Sure," I said. "How about Hawaii? Or the moon?" My old man said to send him a postcard. Dark as chocolate after that trip, swollen somehow, rounded, Hilda ripened. That's the only way to describe her. Sissie too. Like my old man's 3-D picture of Snow White on the window sill, different from every angle.

Whenever those two took a turn up and down the street, faces followed from windows, gardens, cars. Shit, they were a certified event, the beautiful children that guarantee our beautiful-oodleful future. Oo-wonderful-La-darling-La. They rode their hips slowly, slender necks curved just right to lifted chins, eyes thrown always away. They used their legs like talking ponies. "Lovey day for a stroll, yah?" the German professor pruning his roses would say. Their feet would stroke the ground—the air. An ancient lady, deaf as her wicker rocker, would call from her porch, "Hello, girls. How sweet you look. Sweet as apple blooms." People liked to talk to them. They listened, pawing pavement with their toes.

Once while Matt and Pep and Lance and I shared one of Old Man Arthur's cigars down Hickler's alley, hot backs against the cool, crumbly brick, half sick, mouths puckered, Hilda and Sissie paraded by. You'd think they heard music. We stayed quiet in the drifting smoke. We watched them pass like something dangerous. Who the hell should be bringing his slow-motion act the other way but loony-toony Captain. "Hell-ooo, girrrrls," Captain said, holding it so long you wondered where he got the air. They stopped, blinked, brushed the ground. "You've had your babies so soon?" the old man asked. I though we'd die. The girls vanished.

Through the open window over our heads, I heard Hickler say, "They get cuter every time I see 'em," followed by a thud, like his cleaver separating chops.

Lance crushed the cigar butt. It smoldered in the dirt. "What's happened to your sister," he said, and he licked his cracked lip, "is something."

Matt said, "I'll say."

"Aw," I said, "ain't nothin' happened to my sister," in case they were making fun.

18 —— CHANG AND ENG

I am wiping down a lemon-yellow '55 T-Bird, toweling it like a baby, the baby Jesus, because the brunette who drives it is posed by the Coke machine, dabbing at her cleavage with a green scarf, and I can believe in miracles. She lifts a red can, her head, stretches her long, streamlined neck, drinks. Tires whump, short on air, shriek. She throws these big brown eyes right past me. Wouldn't you know it? Two guys in tan sport coats and one uniformed cop are climbing out of an unmarked powder-blue Plymouth nobody but the law would buy. The woman sort of giggles her ass past them, wiggles her tongue, and slides into her bird slowly like she's sliding into bed.

"Call again," I say, but she doesn't smile and the cops don't either. They just sort of sniff their way to Spud's hot little corrugated office. He pries open the glass door to his hut and holds out a paw. "Gentlemen," I hear him say. A short, pigeon-toed gray cop talks, and every now and then they all turn and squint toward me. I'm not scared. No, it's Danny who fucked up. When they wander over—even Spud in that great wounded way he moves—I'm just starting on a Toyota wagon. A lady in curlers, with three kids, is hunched inside writing checks.

"Carlos," Spud says. He and the cops stay in the shade by the vacuums. "When you're finished, these fellows have some questions you might be able to help them with." I take my time.

"Yeah?" I say. I pull my Pirates cap down tighter. The only car waiting starts in. No rush. "What do you need?"

"Castro," Spud says, before the gray one even inhales. "Lookin' for him. These detectives think he might know somethin' about that explosion over to the Stonehenge."

Three cops with masks of bone, these frog-skin X-ray eyes.

I blink. I scratch my neck. I say, "No shit. First I've heard about any explosion."

Spud says, "Friday night."

The gray cop cuts him off. "You two spent some time together, right?"

"We tipped some beers."

"Tricky Mick's?"

"You're mind readers. He could guzzle it."

"Ever say anything make you wonder, think he's a bad boy?"

"Uh uh. He did some time once."

"So did you."

"The State School. Years ago. I was a kid."

"What I said," Spud says. "I would've known."

The gray cop licks his upper lip. "You two went way back. Back when he was Ingus . . . Danny Ingus."

"So?"

"So why the name? Castro. He political or something? He bitch about stuff?"

"Bad luck, same as the rest of us. You asking was he a commie or what? Shit. A dummy's what he was. The name's a joke. He called himself that in junior high for a couple of weeks after the missile shit in Cuba. Smoked cigars. Turned green."

"So give us some ideas."

"Check with his wife."

Spud says, "Castro's his girlfriend's name. What he told me." He laughs. "Jesus. Fred L."

"We asked the wife," the cop says. "His car's back without a print on it. No Castro. Where is he?" His buddies watch my mouth.

"He's not here."

"Where'd he go?"

It was like that, like it always was, like eight ball, but nobody won and nobody smiled and nobody was happy when it was over—because it was never over. I winked at the nun coming through in a church van.

I wasn't worried about cops. I was wet to start with. If they'd had anything on me, they would have paid a weekend visit. The game had rules. I was in it, strong enough, balanced enough, to last, by God, till my story got told, till I got *finished*. Crazy Ingus. If I hadn't been at the wheel, some other sucker would have. And nobody saw. Still, I thought I was through with that shit, for this lifetime anyway.

An old Lust Brothers' mechanic, a retired fire-eater with a white beard to his belt buckle, the guy who sold those Florida chameleons, he told me all about Chang and Eng, the original Siamese twins. These guys, hooked together at the side, like the covers of a book, married two sisters from England. Had separate families, one with ten kids, I think, the other eleven or twelve. So many nights at this house, so many at the other. Jesus. How would it be? Talk about brotherly love. I'll bet they kept the ladies laughing.

"Died a hundred years ago," Old White Beard said, "within two hours of each other." They were connected by an artery or something. When one went—too much nooky?—the other's heart kept pumping blood out, into his dead brother. And there he is, and he can't move, and the pounding in his chest keeps on, keeps on. The blood does not come back. Jesus.

Cade's law. Death loves a vacuum.

The next night, Spud crawls out of his booth again and sways toward me, me dripping over a repo Continental, another goddamn dollar. He looks down, in the eyes, in the mouth, but in the heat he seems kind of empty all the time anyway.

"Carlos," he says. And for a minute he wipes that Lincoln's taillight with a hanky he drags from his hip pocket.

"What can I do ya for?"

"That Castro guy . . . You figure he really planted a fucking bomb?"

"If I was a good judge of character, I wouldn't be spit shining cars at three and a half an hour."

"No. C'mon. I mean, *that* little guy? Cheerful all the time."

"Maybe it made him happy thinking about blowing people to hell and back."

"I'm serious."

"So am I."

Spud shakes his chins loose of his collar and rocks away.

"You'd think he spent his whole life in that booth he was such an innocent son of a bitch. He thought monkeying with odometers on used cars was where it ended, a little friendly catch-me-if-you-can. And I see it, off on the other side of his lot, next to his own green Caddie. "Hey." Spud turns. I point. "You sellin' that antique gas hog over there?"

"It runs. Mechanic checked it out." Spud wobbles above his wide shadow. "I told my nephew I'd try to unload it. You in the market? Two hundred bucks."

"A buck for every thousand miles."

"Not quite. Take it out over break."

So I do. A '65 Dodge Polara 500 with push-button transmission, power windows, a chrome horn ring on the wheel, blue shag carpet over the rust and holes in the floor, and a squirrel tail on the antenna. The front end shimmies a little over sixty. But she hums. The radio gives me George Jones loud and clear. I need a car. Anybody wants to know, it's money I saved with the carnival. What's left'll cover insurance.

Ginny says, "God, it's like Flash Gordon."

We drive up behind the Capitol right on midnight, two blocks from Gandy's now, a wasteland full of lights below, and I think I will just keep driving, not tell her a thing, let her go to sleep, wake her up in Las Vegas, take her to the coast and live on a boat.

Right. The car's twenty years old. Later we'll go. In her car. Or a new car. Amtrak. We'll go. Sure. Me somebody so goddamn hidden away she'll think she lives alone. Right. Who'll pay for the boat?

My alarm clattered. Seven. Jesus, my eyes. Discipline, I thought. I rinsed my mouth with whiskey, ate the usual. Sat at my table. The notebook. Listened. Wrote, dreamed it, sitting there, one cigarette after another—and where the hell was I?

And I walked into bay number three pleased with the sizzle of the spray, the hoarse whirl of those wild, foamy rotors, the look of an Impala inching through, like something being born. I told Doug, the guy ahead of me, to take off five minutes early. Rubbing the planet down, seeing to things, that's what I was doing. The sun was like a woman on my back.

Then these two inflatable muscle men show up, two blond bulldozers in shiny gray suits and white golf shirts. They weren't cops and they didn't pretend to be. They could have been father and son, the old guy just a weathered-up

version of the young one. They could have been albinos
with that hair, but they didn't wear dark glasses and their
eyes were chocolate brown. They looked familiar.

"Carlos. We have a word with you?"

I'm tinkering with a nozzle. Things are slow. They are
walking over from Spud, who watches them like they stole
his magazine or broke his heart. I remember. The old guy's
the ex-wrestler handled the other dog at the fight. "I'm
nothin' but time. What can I do ya for?"

The young one stands just back of the old one's left
shoulder. I'm missing something and I can't put my finger
on it. Dad does the talking in a kind of sleepy southern
drawl. He's got gold chains on his neck, his wrists, his right
pinky. "I'm sorry this idn't a pleasure call, old buddy." He
holds out a hand.

"Noel," I say. "Jesus Christ." Noel Bonus—somewhere
inside a wheat-straw hairpiece and a dozen more years of
hard living.

"Hey," the other says, "long time." And goddamn if it
isn't Noel's younger brother, Stud, mustache gone, hair
bleached.

"You assholes've gone Hollywood. You're not dead."

"Gone serious is it," Noel says. "This ain't pleasure."

"And?" I say. And the world is too goddamn small.

"You palled with a guy name of Castro used to work
here."

"Good enough guy, Castro. But pals we weren't. Shared
a few pitchers a couple times is all."

"And a dog show."

"Strictly an accident."

"More like a tornado." Noel laughed. Stud spread his
nostrils.

"He said I'd be doing a favor if I went. He didn't spell
it out. You know what, at first just now I thought you guys
were cops."

"Do we look like cops?"

"Nah, but they've been nosin' around a lot, about that explosion. I can't see Castro and bombs. Shit he could hardly work a sponge."

"How do we find him?"

"The phone book. I don't know."

A black Mercedes had started through the wash. Noel pulled a hair from his nose. "You'd level with us, right, Carlos? We're friendly, you know that. But see, what we got here is a question of business, big business. You see him, get in touch. We're askin' nice. I owe you one." He handed me a silver card from his breast pocket: STONE-HENGE, with an hourglass and a phone number underneath. "Ask for Anthony. Anthony Nicks is a name I've had for a while now."

"I'll do that."

"You do that."

Noel folded into the back of that damp Mercedes, Stud in the front. A little guy with a neck brace drove, guy with bulgy, watery eyes that followed every move I made. Noel's window hummed down an inch. He said, "Polish the sombitch." Just as they pulled away, I spit and nailed their vanity plate. SHARX it said. I'd send them a dictionary.

Ginny's TV was off for a change. The crickets throbbed. Each hair on her head, each wispy little lash around her eyes shined. On tiptoe, pushing her fixtures right where I wanted them, she licked my ear lobe and breathed, "How's my horny devil?"

"Horny," I said.

"And hungry?" I nodded.

I was glad to sit, watching the smooth seesaw of her ass in front of the stove. Steam set fire to her hair. I said, "You're a miracle to a tired man." I patted her. She rolled it. I liked Ginny. She never made me mad. "I like how your lip puckers out from before you got braces?"

"How do you know I had braces?"

"Because your lip puckers out."

Dinner sizzled. I sipped a short whiskey, chased it with a Bud, and forgot—the Bonus brothers, my barometer reading cops in the air. "Ginny?" She didn't turn. "What the hell's in this for you?"

"We've been over that, Los."

"So I'm a pest. Humor me. You're class. I'm a pest. Why not find some Old Spice rich guy owns horses and plays golf?"

Like that she swiveled all tearful in the steam and said, "Hey, I'm on my own." Her neck burned pink. "I'm okay. Okay? I had braces. So what? Look at me."

"My pleasure."

"Virginia Wenonah Crumpbell from dead, sweet-Jesus Paul, Idaho. Except for TV and can labels, my folks've never seen Chinese food. I cook it. Or a Chinese person. Hardly ever a stranger even. Mom thinks sex is fornication and is between cattle. Sex is something I like. Moo. There. You know it, too. I won't rock this boat. I won't. I never thought it'd float. I like you here. Hear that? You're nice, most of the time. You care if I'm happy. You're different. I don't know, Los. There's something about you an earthquake couldn't budge."

"Atlas," I said. I crushed the beer can.

"Not quite. You sure haul me around with that hay rake of yours, though, I'll say that." I laughed and she smiled, said, "No, what it is, you don't expect anything. You're not going to run away. You don't think you'd do any better. You're not going to want to marry me because you don't think it would make any difference. That's good. I'm too young yet for the farm, too old to be really stupid. I'm flighty is it, up and down."

"Up and down's what I like about you."

"Ha ha. I don't want any Joe who just clomps along like a plow horse. Not yet. Or anybody crazy."

"Count me out."

"Just somebody good, somebody who thinks holding me is special."

"Beats the *Tonight Show*."

Her face tightened and dived back to the burners. A kettle smoked. "I wrecked the noodles." She stamped her bare feet.

19 —— THE WHITE DOOR

There was this morning in high school. I stood on a mountain and squinted at other mountains, white ridge after white ridge. I slapped snow off my pants. The wind froze my cheeks. My fingers would not bend. This time I was alone and I knew it. The last door—closed. White.

The wind blasted the powder on that cliff. Through me blind with white freezing light, breath tight in my chest, my ears burning. I ran that first mile, more—some old slush from sand and salt, mostly ice. I wouldn't hitch. I couldn't. Cars passed and I pulled my hands out of my pits and dove into weightless, blue drifts, knelt behind woodpiles, twice garbage cans. And hurt. I would get back. Find a door. I would not die, not yet. But my fingers, my ears, and Jesus, the wind. The cabin. Small steps would carry me. Small steps but breaths too big, tearing out at my ribs. And I thought, pain, this pain, I deserve it. It is what it should be. Through drifts, against heavy branches of snow, I pushed myself until I had cut into that small canyon, our tracks still fresh, the key where she returned it, under the rock. On her porch I brushed myself off with stiff hands, painful hands. I stood inside until I could stand still. My face tingled. She was not there. My feet would hardly cross the room. But the note she wrote was mine. And I picked it up because the world had forgotten Skink, because I was hiding in this mountain range of snow, and I would not be found. I touched nothing else. I shut the door with the cuffs of my coat. I walked to the road in my prints from earlier. I fell. My hands were gone. I laughed. I ran, the note folded in my pocket.

I slipped, fell half a dozen times, opened a hole in my knee. Counted steps. My feet stopped aching, and I counted, making sure they moved.

Ruth's Diner was a bend away. Heat. But Ruth would read me, know me, hate me, with her long face, with her cigarette ash that could not break, and shit, I made the Jeep up. Nosed into a pull-off the plows had made. Blue. Blue burst of icy light. Ski tracks—four long lines becoming two into a shadowed canyon. Two lines. Disappeared. The driver's door opened, the Jeep's air inside still warm, without wind. A hard pack of Camels on the floor. And keys. By my frozen boot, between the seats, on a key chain with an orange rabbit's foot. Goddamn it. Keys.

I kept the rabbit's foot—left the Jeep in a university parking lot.

And I didn't try to figure it.

I'll leave, I know that. I'm sure. Didn't she leave me? Shit.

There's no funeral for Jill.

Lance doesn't even blink. His picture's in the East High *Leopard* every other day—for debate, or swimming, or even drama, if you can goddamn believe it.

I'm gone. I'm already gone. I do my two or three hours on the midway at Beehive. Most every night I rip something off somewhere—for dope, you name it. I get a couple of chicks drunk and fool around now and then. I do not think, barely feel. I cheat in every class—buy tests, copy papers, read answer sheets in teachers' files. Shit, for algebra I change all my D's to B's in a grade book over lunch hour. My counselor from SIS—the State Industrial Slaveship— says they'll send me back I don't finish school. Danny's learning to use his leg. He's on probation, farmed out to the Shiftlets off somewhere across town.

Mama gives me a carton of cigarettes on graduation morning. Seniors don't have school and it's damn near eleven and too damn warm when I roll out. Mama's got her cheeks rouged. Hilda's gone to work. She's part-time at the U. Mama holds out her gift with both hands. She gave Hilda an alarm clock with gold bells on top. I smoke. She pours coffee. "I'm leaving," I tell her.

"Men's ways," she says. She puts the pot down on the stove, smiling.

"Today," I say. "Just gettin' out. I have to. I'll send you money."

"Course you will," she says, and she steps past me to her room, where flies are dying on the windowsill and the radio makes her sway beside it for just that long, and she lies down, humming to some tune or other with harps and violins.

I thumbed south, through Provo, over Soldier Summit, through Price and Green River into Moab, into heat. When I called Hickler, Hilda would send my mail, and I'd get a draft notice from Uncle Sam, I knew. I'd straighten out, march in Europe somewhere, and learn electronics. For now, hell, I'd get out of the goddamn canyons.

I ripped off a sleeping bag from a church group and camped at Arches with some gray-haired hippies who promised me a ride. They were headed home to Drop City, a commune to the east somewhere, domes made out of car bodies, they said.

They dumped me in a Ho Jo's parking lot in Colorado Springs. I pumped gas, checked radiators, and squeegeed the bugs off windshields at Cowboy Jack's in Manitou Springs. Cowboy Jack'd hose down this two-story, cracked plaster likeness of himself out front, say, "Tourists love that big guy," and kiss his daughter Jeanine on the mouth—period. He had a bad back from bronc riding.

I rented a beat-up, one-room Biltmore trailer that never cooled off. Half the time Jeanine and I were too goddamn buzzed or ripped to get out the door.

The army offered to pay bus fare to Denver for my physical, but Jeanine closed down for the day and took me in the Cowboy Jack tow truck, with longhorns on the hood. I said, "A man's got to serve, I guess." They checked me every which way, tested my brain. AOK, they said. But the shootings. Those goddamn soldiers, who dreamed about blowing half the world to hell, got all bent about my time at the State School. "Morally unfit," this fat ass with tinted glasses muttered and wrote on my form.

"You're one lucky bastard," this black kid told me.

Jeanine said, "They don't need you?"

"Their quota's full up."

The past never went past.

I stuck till payday. Sunday I waited for night, for the heat to lift. I called Jeanine to say good-bye. I owed her that. I drained a few beers on a hammock roped to laundry posts behind my trailer, did a pipe or two. When I closed my eyes, I saw snow.

She showed about five, when every damn blade of grass seemed about as dry as it could get, when every living thing had a shadow about two miles long. She had on this pink shorts suit tight as they come and carried a red nylon back-pack over her shoulder. "Darling," she said.

I said, "Hey, I didn't mean anything by all this. On my word."

The blood left her face. She almost fell off her clear plastic heels. "You ain't got a word. But I got a word for you."

I dragged on my cigarette.

The tow truck pulled in out front, revved smoke into the runty trees. Her old man shouted, "Jeannie! Honey! I told you to stay the hell away from here."

"Go on," I said.

"You'll come back?"

"Cade!" her old man shouted. "You're finished!"

She kissed me. Then she reached up high like she needed something from a shelf, grunted, and brought her hand down smack across my cheek. As she teetered away I lifted a beer.

I stood at the bottom of Pike's Peak in the dark that night. The fifth car stopped, a lumberjack from Oregon in a beat-up station wagon. He'd been to Ohio to visit his brother who'd just come back from Nam. We drove straight through.

20 ——— *THE BRAVE COWBOYS*

I finally see Lance again. Friday night.

With orange lips that must have ripened on a tree, this milkmaid brunette speaks to us on the TV news. "This just in," she says, something like sorrow or Valium mucking up her eyes. Pow. A full-dress photo of the son of a bitch jolts up beside her. Has he died? Not on your life, even though he looks half dead all polished and stiff in a chair between the state's blue flag and Old Glory. "Governor Arthur's oldest daughter, Rachel, was rushed to the Holy Cross emergency room earlier this evening with what doctors say was a ruptured appendix. Listed in satisfactory condition following surgery, Ms. Arthur should remain in the hospital through the weekend. The governor and Mrs. Arthur are at her bedside."

When the screen jumps back to black and white, Kirk Douglas's horse twirls in rain on a dark highway. Long, slippery headlights roar down. He kicks, slaps hard with the reins, but the damned animal won't budge. You don't see it. The horse screams. A semi-load of toilets.

With Mr. Cat cradled in her cleavage, Ginny cried. "Don't laugh," she said. "You have a heart."

"As big as all outdoors." I kissed her knees. I turned off the set. I kissed her knees until her fingers moved through my hair.

Saturday First Security Bank flashed "102." I didn't need a sign. Spud looked like a blood blister in that shed of his. Water beaded on hoods and trunks and disappeared. Soap jet-trailed over anything dark, clouded chrome. And even though it was Saturday, only half-a-dozen air-conditioned crazies came through. I stood there, and I stood there. Twice I soaked my head with the hose. Spud said the shirts stayed on and no shorts. Christ, what he needed were Gila monsters.

There I am half dead in the dark cranny of my bay, wishing I could pant or scream or slit my throat or something, when the powder-blue Plymouth pulls up in back. Three cops climb out—the same three cops—as if they'd just been made, so comfortable and calm and new. Then the guy in the uniform smolders off by the vacuum, while his plainclothes buddies—in shirt sleeves, with steel green ties—stiff-leg it over to Spud. Spud shakes his head once

the little guy's had his say. I itch with sweat now, and
it feels good. Spud calls me over in this high, pinched
voice of his. The gray cop smiles. The other chews gum
like he's trying to kill it. The gray cop introduces himself
this time. "Detective Dolores," he says. Dolores hits the
mark. We don't shake hands. "We found your pal Castro
last night."

"I thought you would."

"Found him sleepin' up Emigration Canyon. In a sink-
hole full of stickers in a field. Curled up under some leaves
and gravel, there was your pal. Stunk. His head was flat
up over his left ear. And cold. Read me?"

I couldn't swallow, but it was the heat, and I nodded.
The uniformed cop had wandered next door, to Spud's
Wonders. He leaned inside an MGB convertible.

The little gray cop poked my shoulder. "You don't remember anybody making noise around Castro, around
Ingus, do ya?"

"You asked me that."

"Once more can't hurt."

"No. Nobody."

"And he didn't drop a word about where he was headed
that night? And you didn't go along?"

"Hey, listen, I knew Danny twenty years. This guy was
my friend. I hope you catch the son of a bitch did it."

When they'd gone, after I'd wiped down my next crazy,
Spud called me over again. His eyes couldn't have been
deeper in his face. "Carlos," he said, "can you fucking believe it?" I laughed. His air conditioner rumbled in the wall.
Spud closed his sliding door slowly. "I don't know about
you," he said.

"One dozen of the yellows," I said. After all it was his
money.

The florist lady had Bandaids on every finger. "They're

the flower that endures," she said. She held one to her
crinkled lips.

I wrote:

Dear, dear Rose,
Fate is in the driver's seat, crazy-ass Fate.
Be strong. Good luck.

All my love—

I nursed a couple of beers at the Astronaut before I went
home. With an Indian guy, I wasted time on this pheasant-
shoot game. You perch next to a control table wired to a
black box with a white button in your hot little hand. Out
in front of you, hanging from the smoky ceiling, this wide,
narrow screen blinks with two cartoony hunters. The other
guy, the Indian, has a box, too. He hits his button and up
jump two birds on the screen, two dots of light that arc
over the hunters' heads. Your hunter is fat and has a
red vest and a red hat. When you punch your button,
your hunter lifts his gun, and blam-blam, you hit or miss.
Then it's reversed: You're sending the beads of light and
the Indian guy's pulling the trigger. But nothing flies.
Or dies.

The Indian doesn't even look when I go. He just sort of
lifts this hand of heavy turquoise and silver and then says,
"Any other hotdog thinks he can shoot dese ringnecks better'n me?"

Stretched out by the TV in a frilly, little blue nightgown,
Ginny blinked was all when I got there, the place stale with
Mary Jane. John Wayne towered over some big broad son
of a bitch of a desert. When I whispered, sliding my arm
up and down her back, John Wayne mouthed marbles the
way he did, and she said, "Shhh."

21 —— *THE ISLAND*

A scorcher again. Screw the heat. I talked into the tiny microphone. Ice cubes cracked like bones in my water.

Out on the landing on a Sunday, a first, Mrs. Shiftlet didn't knit. She held a section of the paper, the rest folded at her feet. Her wicker chair squeaked. She didn't turn. "Hello," I said. The light was whiskey yellow, dim as ever. Her gray, trifocaled head swayed above the comics. And she chuckled. I'm sure that's what I heard.

Then Ginny's wearing this orange bandana of a bikini when she opens her door. She has white goop smeared on her nose and Gillette Foamy or something under her arms held out. "I've had the best idea. Just a sec." She giggles and wiggles that Swiss-movement ass of hers off to the bathroom. I look mean in her mirror. She calls, "To the lake. We're going to the lake, to Antelope Island, my treat."

I shake my head. On her counter sits a brand-new picnic basket—still red-tagged SALE—stuffed with napkins, grapes, and beer. She's singing, "May I have this dance for the rest of my life?" When she comes out, I hug her, one hand on the world's smoothest tit, and kiss her, careful of the sunburn goop. I lower the orange bandana. That's all it takes—so fast Mrs. Shiftlet might have heard something like a bicycle pump if she heard anything, or Ginny's crazy laughter.

Ginny inhaled two fat joints on the highway. I helped. I said, "Look. You'd think the rocks were hollow and the whole damn thing floated out there," when we drove into the narrow causeway smoky with heat and birds.

I'd been to Antelope Island once before—with a blond

named Belinda or Dorinda or something weird, who had
great hips—late the day Hilda got hitched. We met at the
reception. She said I looked ready to hurt somebody. The
causeway was dirt and gravel then. Whatshername called
it "a dream." Crossing slowly, the sun melting red in black
water, pelicans opening into the air like a thousand goddamn bridal bouquets, *was* out of this lost mother of a
world. Then the sun pooled gold, was gone. The lake and
the sky darkened together around two headlights of road,
two silver wings of water. Flying away. Driving on water.
Could we go back? Would we want to? Could anyone from
anything?

Dorinda or Belinda and I zipped our sleeping bags
together on a small mesa in space and slept hearing nothing but a few horny mallards and the French kiss of the
waves.

Ginny and I did not find that untouched, quiet, hidden wonder of an island. And who in hell could drive on
water?

The car shimmied, the road out paved a licorice black
now, soft as skin. I heard a windy river while that rocky
red son of a bitch floated bigger and bigger. I pulled the
salt smell through my nose. And between the blue of water
and the blue of sky, white Styrofoam cups and the dirty
white bodies of used-up pelicans and gulls bobbed against
stones in yellow suds, in a long strip beside us. Bugs
splashed the windshield.

The place was crowded, bodies strung across the white
beach on our right, clustered in the shadows of the few
pavilions. We stopped on a ridge of dry grass. I tried to
forget the people, to remember just the lake without
boundaries, the wild meadow to the left carpeted down to
a broad bay.

A chainlink fence not a hundred yards off cut the

damned island in two, kept this part public and that part private. I pointed past the fence. "See that chocolaty clump clear over by that mountain? Would you believe buffalo? One guy owns all that."

An orange Jeep raced in a white spray back and forth through the green marsh below us. We drove to the north end and parked by the noisy pavilions. We smoked two more in the car, quietly, getting hotter each second, and then we broke for it, burst across the sand to the water, the cold, scummy water, the bottom like peanut butter. Where the water's deep enough, you can stretch out and you don't sink, and who gives a shit, right? But these people as far as you can see are in the water with their heads and their feet and hands above the gray surface, shouting. The sun is lightning. The salt burns your cuts. It's a lot of laughs for about twenty minutes. Besides, the smell makes me sick.

We wade back, not too fucking sure where in God's name we are. The sun dries us, bingo, and the salt is another skin that tightens and itches. We sit on a picnic bench. We laugh but it dies. The saggy, pink mother in the family with us hands a small, sandy boy a slice of apple. The boy bites it and juice runs over his lip. He says, "The rain leaked out," and starts to cry. A fly lands on the apple he has dropped. We stumble through more sand to the car, salt yanking at the hairs on my legs. The picnic basket is still on the backseat. Ginny shakes her head.

"Can you drive?"

"Yes," she says. "Tell me where."

We looked like dead fish. The basket scraped my leg as we climbed the stairs. I said, "Nice afternoon" to Mrs. Shift-let, still bent over a picture of Pete Rose, the same sports page as before. When I bumped her hand, the paper slipped down her legs to the rug. Air groaned from her nose.

Ginny said, "No."

In spite of the dope and the beer, Ginny didn't cry. She just stared, empty eyed, and mumbled a prayer or something. Mrs. Shiftlet's pulse throbbed through one loose string in her neck. She drooled. Her eyes were dry. I told Ginny to call, that someone should stay with the old lady, watch for any change. And Pete Rose, holding his hat high over his head, grinned.

Ginny talked to a young cop on the landing while two white-coated Oriental guys carried Mrs. Shiftlet outside on a stretcher. A couple of our hollow-cheeked fellow boarders coughed into their hands and closed their doors.

"A stroke, they think," Ginny told me. "God, how would it be? Trapped in your own body." Her voice was too high. I sat in her kitchen, smoked.

She stood at the window. "Why'd you hide? You could have talked to the cop."

I said, "I guess that's right. I don't know."

"Just like that she's gone," she said. "My mother doesn't even know where I am. God." She tilted her head back and closed her eyes. After a while she whispered, "I need to be by myself a little. A nap maybe."

The ceiling tiles hadn't budged, and the spaghetti sat tight in the corner of the freezer, but hell yes, I could tell someone had looked my place over. The sweet, phony stink of hair tonic. Draped off the mattress, my top sheet was caught under a bed leg. Sloppy.

Why the scavenger hunt? I wondered. Had Matt called him? Why not turn the screws? A reconnaissance visit. Maybe I should phone some ace reporter, cover my ass, break *my* story. Great timing. Send the cops Xerox copies with Danny still on a slab somewhere. Goddamn Danny. It was *my* story.

Maybe Mr. Cat climbed across my dresser. Maybe. Maybe Ginny rifled through my closet when I wasn't looking. Maybe my last good goddamn brain cells jumped ship. Maybe I'd better wise up.

Bobby Bull Shiftlet opened my door and then knocked, backhanding slowly with woolly knuckles. "Cade," he said. "You got a visitor."

"Okay," I said. I unfolded from the window ledge, wobbled some. "How 'bout a cold one?"

His curly head brushed the door frame. More sweet-pea cologne. A gold chain on his wrist. And his black shirt had a gold golf ball on the breast pocket. Dapper Dan. I couldn't put it together, what the hell he'd want with me.

"Mom," he said. "She's in bad shape." And he lisped a little, his voice too low somehow. "I hear you found her, stayed right by her side."

"For what good it did."

"I'm grateful." He sniffed. "But, Cade . . ." He dropped one of his heavy paws onto my shoulder. "It's Danny's dying done this to her. I been looking after my mother. I figure who done Danny, well . . ."

I pulled away. His arm fell. "How about you run it past some of your buddies fight dogs?"

"They didn't do it."

"They'd tell you?" I popped another can, fired another smoke.

"They'd tell me. They told me they had reason—lots of green reasons—but it wasn't them. You'd tell me, right?" He took a step closer, wiped his nose. Another step, I have my knife. There is a mole like a black beetle just under his chin, a target. "Cade, it's good you got friends in high places." He shakes his head, licks a shine back onto his teeth. "And I owe you one. I'm paying it by not asking any *tough* questions. Understand? When you know something, you'll call me. I'm sure you will." He turned. "And Cade, stay the fuck out of things. You're over your head."

Hot air. All bluff. Bobby Bullshit.

Disguised as red rubber, the sort of bumpy rubber they make those no-skid bathtub mats out of, my back stung. I was cold, goosebumped, shivering.

Ginny sat in her kitchen crying into a wad of paper towels. She said, "He told me his mother loved horses."

I said, "I'll stay here a couple of nights till you feel better."

Mr. Cat bivouacked at her place, too. He looked better than the sun-broiled two of us—and she liked him, even when he shit in her pink bathroom sink.

"The flowers helped," Rose said. "I've been better. Somebody's gonna pay."

"No question," I said. I turned in the phone booth—on a shady corner of the City and County Building grounds—so I could see the police station. All seven stories. A fleet of clean cars. A thousand pressed shirts. Pistols. Badges. People who decided nothing. They followed paths, the paths of others following paths. The flag flew. "We'll figure it. The cops will."

"Anybody can figure it. Mr. Big Dog, he's it. He'll pay."

"When's the funeral?"

"We burned him," she said. "It's over. I'm glad."

I lit a cigarette, watched the match flame and flicker. "The cops let you?"

"They got him all recorded. They don't care. Know what we done? Spread him on the lake this morning."

"I was just out there."

"His old man hired a boat. All these birds swooped around us. Maybe he's the first. L.G. said the salt would keep his ashes the same forever." Then she said, "Thanks, Carlos. Call me some other time."

22 ——— *LAUGHING BACKWARD*

I swear, sometimes when tires squeal or the wind wails and whines, I hear her again, like something trying to scrape away that blue winter blackness.

Nine o'clock maybe—not too late—and I'm crunching down our alley over the crust of old snow. I am in ninth grade—barely. My jaw is broken from a fight weeks back with some nobody kid. It hurts in the cold. On Valentine's, next Tuesday, the wires come off. I am tired. Of secrets. Of fighting with my old man. I have come home early for bed for a change because I overdid it the night before and the night before that. Because I hate sleep but I want it to work. I hate sleep because even with a busted jaw I hate dreams, and when I am awake it's hardly awake anyway: fights, glue, booze—*high*—laughing my ass off, but never laughing enough. And girls. I am restless against my desks, in my bed at night. One girl. I have one, and she is the only warm thing about that night, the thought of her.

My old man dragged me and Hilda out onto the islands one spring way back, when two strays were at it, this ribbed-out, frothing, white mutt with one black eye, and a grizzly whore of a Saint Bernard. Ride 'em, cowboy. My old man said, "Okay. That's how babies is done. It's called fornoccasion and screwing. Men and ladies do it, too." When the dogs finished, panting to beat all, wandering in wobbly circles locked up together ass to ass, he said, "Any questions, you ask me." I never asked him anything. I doubt whether Hilda did. For months I half expected to find people out there on the islands humping each other like that.

When I heard her that night in the drive, I didn't think of *those* dogs. I thought about dogs in traps. Cats, too. I thought about Skink face down in dust, breathing gray, snotty bubbles. I thought about pain. I wondered if the sound came from the radio. The kitchen was dark. And now somehow outside my body, alert as I've ever been, I walked toward it, through those two, yellowed, cold rooms, searching out that sound. My mother stared at the one hot light bulb on the ceiling, a ragged quilt tight at her chin, her eyes dry as Ping-Pong balls, while the terrible whining kept letting itself loose. From my room, I realized, *our* room. Jesus.

The door is open inches, the light out, the sound awful. I turn on the light. The sound. The smell is whiskey. Sweat. Her dress—a new dress, new for a dance probably, paid for from her job as Teen Consultant at a ladies' clothing store—is bunched at her waist. And he is crushing the sound out of her, his ass like a boulder falling, falling again. And his eyes stay shut, even when I shout, "Get off her! Get off!" He is drooling down her face. "Get off!" The eyes shut, his hands like clamps on her wrists above her head, this is not my father. Goddamn it. I am beating his back, but the stranger continues to fall at my sister and pushes me off. I am screaming into my teeth, reaching for something, hunting. In the hole in the wall, I find it. I am calming down. I see what will happen. I smile. I open the razor and lift out the blade. I walk to him, whoever he is. I reach out and lunge, hardly touching his neck. He stops. Still she squeals. The shouting is his. I can't believe the miracle of it all when he stands, the red just barely spreading on his yellow shirt under the line around his throat. He lifts his scarred lip at me, jerks up his pants, and, groaning, stumbles from the room.

Hilda rolls into a ball. The ball gushes into its hands, turning itself inside out in throw-up and a new noise which I don't want to hear. I tug the dress over the roundness of the ball. I hear a door slap shut in a deep distance. I stagger past my mother. She moans. I slug the kitchen wall so hard I crack the plaster, and a picture of two children in leaves— a crummy, framed print from somebody's trash—crashes to the floor, glass everywhere.

Mama said, "Dreams can fool ya. Take you clean away." Once or twice, as I tiptoed past her bed late at night after my old man turned his yellow ass and bolted, I caught her in the middle of one, shadowy, like a corpse trying to wake up. Her eyes fluttered, and her hands slowly waved on their backs from the dirty sheets.

Hilda never made sense to me again.

That cold son of a bitch of a night when it happened, she slept where he left her. The noise. In her throat a needle stuck on the empty last grooves of a record. I tried to be quiet while I cleaned up the stuff she'd heaved, but World War III couldn't have roused her. My mother watched me as I passed, eyes wide and dry.

I locked the door and braced it with a chair. I spread a coat and a braided rug over Hilda. I turned off the light on those two. I shivered and my head hurt.

The space heater flickered. Icicles threw fangs against the windows. I got under my covers in my clothes with the razor in my hand. I believed the bastard would come back or that some cop would come to say he bled to death. I waited.

And I remember thinking that I wasn't strong enough

or even the smallest bit loyal enough to nursemaid two poor cripples—maybe nut cases if that's what they turned out to be—but I sure as hell didn't want them on my conscience, the little I had.

Hilda had left by the time I forced open my eyes the next morning. Sunlight, gray somehow through the windows, tried to warm the room. Mama's pillow lay on the floor beside her empty bed. I stubbed my toe on the goddamn doorway and staggered into the kitchen. Like a sack of light propped in a chair at the table, frosted, white light, Mama, in her linty nightgown and her month-old Christmas bathrobe, a gift from Hilda, sipped a cup of coffee, her lip raised. Faint behind her, the radio preached, Brothers and Sisters, of being born again. Jesus Christ. The framed picture of those kids, minus the glass, hung on its nail. I heard Mama swallow. Her teeth separated black: "Let's pray that evil, awful tramp stays gone."

It took weeks for Mama to get her color back, if she'd ever had it before, for her to stand much longer than a few wobbly minutes to scramble an egg. I guess most of the groceries those days came thanks to Hickler and his church. You got to give Mormons gold stars for patching over plenty of cracks. And I stole a lot those few months to keep our bellies comfortable. To keep busy.

Hilda? Hilda had gone to school that day. See what I mean? I stared at Mama a while, sucked an egg mixed into some old tomato juice through my wires, and left for school myself. As I hobbled over the icy walks, hearing girls laughing, seeing a couple of the Disneyland kids chuck snowballs at some other Disneyland kid and his father in a blue Mercedes, I got real cold. All knotted up like that, I couldn't believe I would make it the next few blocks. I tried to forget. I pretended the bare trees were maps against the sky, maps of rivers and mountain ridges, maps of countries I would explore.

But the birds looked so goddamn pitiful on little stick legs. And dog shit made brown pockets in the snow. I wanted to take out my goddamn wire cutters, open my jaws, and scream. I stopped. I turned. And I punched this red-headed, freckle-faced kid who happened to be behind me. I don't know if I'd ever seen him before. God, he was standing on a piece of ice and you would have thought he wore skates the way his feet shot out from under him. Well, he bumped a kid behind him, who fell, who bumped another kid, who fell, who bumped . . . You get the picture. Just like that these five pedigreed pissants were on the ground. The red-headed jerk didn't say a thing. I was warm then. I took off my hat and showed him my hair. I hit a lot of guys till spring.

Hilda needed to. I mean she looked so cold all the time. She stayed tight: her arms folded almost always, her hands in her pits, and, sitting, her legs crossed so the bones whitened her knees. She got up, nibbled a piece of bread with jelly or a bowl of cornflakes, if there were any, spent at least thirty stony minutes concocting her face and dressing—making herself suddenly older looking, better looking, with sexier clothes—and took her grown-up hips to school. At quarter to four, down the alley she came, dark in the eyes but just as smooth as you like.

She parked in the kitchen in her bathrobe and read. Ragged books from the library. Read and read, like the old days. Before Sissie. Mama sat across from her in a brown sack dress, yellow-rubber, fur-topped boots on her feet, a nail file busy at those colorless things that were her own weak hands, and looked only at the radio—if Hilda hadn't switched it off—or out the window. They never talked, as far as I know, except for basics. Sometimes Mama threw back her head and screamed with laughter until her nose and eyes ran. Hilda read. Do-it-yourself dinner from cans. The heater flickered.

I hung around, too, waiting for the heater to ignite in

its noisy rush of flames. I kept an eye on things. Honest to
God. I mean, Jesus, my sister and my old lady lived like
lepers or something.

After school the last cold months that winter, I hit
Smith's Food King, or Albertson's, or Crystal Palace, or a
lot of smaller places. Shit, show a little confidence and you
disappear. More than once I left with a case of you-name-
it, I mean a whole, sonofabitching box. Now and then
Danny Ingus went along. The guy could have top-billed
state fairs with his moves. He'd look at a bottle of ketchup
in one hand and slip spaghetti sauce, noodles, and Par-
mesan cheese up his sleeve with the other. French bread
on the way out. His fingers had fingers. Sport. Except for
cigarettes and beer, he stole for *me*, because I told him we
were hard up. That's all I said. I left my old man out of it.
Danny didn't care what the problem was anyhow.

A time or two he sat in the kitchen when Mama pressed
him, but ogling Hilda while she fired her eyes on more of
those yellowed books got old in a hurry. After a couple of
cigarettes, we left. "Night, ladies." We shot pool. We shot
dope. The tail end of winter was another Ice Age. A dingy,
goddamn sky, a dingy, goddamn world, week after week
after week. A sonofabitching wax museum.

The second week in March the wind died down and the
sun tried to warm up. Finally. I opened a window, so rotten
the glass fell out. Next day the world went cold again. I
taped cardboard in the hole.

Hilda read. And Friday afternoons, and Saturdays, she
still punched in—was still Teen Consultant—at Bob's
World of Fashion, or Bridal World, or some shit. For "Teen
Consultant" read Cheap Model. Bob's three or four "girls"
liked the work because he got their pictures in the paper.
I didn't think anything fishier went on. I don't. Hilda said,
"Bobby told me I needed cheering up."

For Valentine's, see, Bobby gave her, of all the choices,

this little, yappy, black-as-a-bat toy poodle. It was ugly and had yellow gunk caked around its eyes, but if you whistled once it would sit up, and, twice, roll over. The damn thing could have been a cobra for all I cared the way Hilda giggled and nuzzled its black curly head. I laughed when the dog, Fifi, rolled over. Mama screamed. Fifi screamed, too. We all cracked up.

Fifi never whined or barked or whimpered unless Mama did. Mama did it so Hilda would smile. Fifi licked Hilda's face in bed off and on through the night. Instead of reading after school now, Hilda walked Fifi, to the park, around and around the block. She still kept to herself, but she'd whisper in Fifi's ear all the time, whisper so quiet I could never hear. Lots of afternoons when I got home, they'd be in our room staring at themselves in the mirror, another gift from Bobby. Once while I smoked outside in the alley, waiting for the phony sun to get lost, I heard her ask Fifi, in a smooth, serious voice like she was talking to Sissie or something, if maybe sweet Hildy wasn't getting a little tummy. I damn near choked, but I liked it, I really did.

23 —— BLUE MOON

Wednesday night I pull an orange sheet over Ginny and punch off her TV. The dingy hall light, sleepy and pink, leaks from two glass roses beside the fire extinguisher. A house waiting, four-story kindling in a city on fire, an antique pioneer of a house whose time is nearly gone.

Over the downtown the moon's steamy blue.

The air moves just enough. A great cat howl of a siren rises and dies. Hedge leaves rustle. A few cars race black shadows. I am real, I remind myself, in this sludgy sort of nonlight that seeps from the moon.

I walk. In a bright, second-story window over a copy shop, a woman combs her golden hair and smokes. In the gutter trash, a skunk bristles, its little eyes hot and slick. Holds still. And then munches again its nightcrawler or Juicy Fruit or Big Mac bun. I cross at the corner.

A pile of bones sleeps on the grass beside the dark Center for the Blind. Two bikers roar by. South Temple jitters with traffic. I am the only walker. I like my Pirates hat. I could be anybody. I am going to see her. It is late.

I pass twin, gray, squat apartment buildings, and even through the traffic I hear the mumble, or maybe feel it, of TV's in those walls. Even in this light, beer cans shine. Hub caps shiver and shine. Every goddamn window shines. Turn around and the whole fucking skyline glows, with the moon over it all like a faded Good Housekeeping Seal of Approval. God. I'm two blocks away.

This is his, this and hundreds of other places—Panguitch, Payson, and Provo, Kearns, Coalville, and Copperton—all of it. Throw in mountains and rivers and desert. Throw in a prison, a State Hospital, roads, throw in the works and what he says goes. I want weight rooms at the blind center. Check. Move that scuzzy son of a bitch passed out on the lawn. Right. Tell those bikers to muzzle their hogs. Check. Women. Right. Cars. Check. Parties. Right.

Look at the mansion the state puts him up in. Two hulking, smooth stories of granite, lights sighted just right on the tall pines, the flagpole, the columns, the gate. Cars slow for me as I cut across the street. Crickets trill in the governor's yard. His downstairs windows are bright—someone is awake. The guard has a face like lava and no neck. His badge shines. He leans from his booth by the gate. "May I help you?"

I smile. "Yes, I'd like to see the governor's wife."

He smiles, eyes tight. "I'm afraid the governor and Mrs. Arthur is out for the evening." His voice is soft and clean.

"You can leave a message if you like." He takes a pad from a small shelf beside him. He holds out a state pen. One hand is always free. His walkie-talkie growls.

"Nah, I'm not much with words. Just tell her her brother is back and came by. I heard about their kid on the news. This was a get-well visit. So long."

He taps the pen against the pad when I step backward into shadow.

"Cade."

I was sweeping suds into a puddle around the drain, when they called to me. I thought I'd imagined it what with the steamy, dizzy darkness of my box. Nope, there they stood shimmering in the heat, my favorite law-and-order window display, right down to the green ties and the powder-blue Batmobile. "Like to have a talk," the short one, the gray one, said when I got there.

Spud's eyes were pinholes in his face. Chins dripping. "Civic duty," he said, his tongue thick and careful. "Gave you the afternoon off."

"With pay," Lieutenant Dolores said. The name came back to me. "That's mighty big of him, wouldn't you say?"

I laughed. "What isn't? I'll be right with you boys."

I combed my hair in a little mirror I kept tucked back in one corner of my bay. I leaned into my own shiny squinting face and said, "Those guys are bush league." I swigged the last of a Coke, put on my watch, and switched off the rotors. Alone in his glass case, staring, Spud could have been some new zoo display, an ape-man or a toad.

"Hop in," Dolores said.

Big-city police stations always smell like old socks and new shoes. You walk sandwiched in lights, the bright, buzzing ceiling tubes, their reflections on the speckled, white linoleum floors. The young men are stiff and trim, the old ones stiff and bellied out. The ones who run things look somewhere in between, like Dolores. A blond lady in a tight uniform inked my name in a book and then, with two painted fingers, typed me into a computer. Dolores studied her buttons.

Next I was in a cold room behind a green door. The latch clicked. The walls were tiled with those BB-holed pasteboard squares, like my ceiling, different pattern. "Sound suckers," a guy I knew in Dusty called them. Nobody screams. My hands were flat on the hard white table. Across from me, Dolores held a tape recorder the size of an electric razor like he wanted to give me a shave. In the silence, the tape whispered in its spools. The other detective, the guy who liked to bite the heads off Doublemint, sat on the table, his wing tips dangling, one rubber heel sometimes clunking a hollow metal leg.

"And you got no ideas what happened to Ingus?" Dolores talked out of one side of his slit mouth like the other side was Novocained or resting.

"Cross my heart."

"How about a fellow named Anthony Nicks? Know him?"

I shook my head slowly. I studied my shoes.

"His mama christened him Noel. Noel Bonus."

"So he changed his name?"

"So everybody does it," Dolores said. "So I'm Frank Sinatra. What's the difference, right? You hung out with Bonus."

"Sounds real important."

"Calm down," the gum killer said.

Dolores thumbed his collar a minute, squinted at me, and then stiffened again. "Bonus and Ingus shared a few interests. Ingus is dead, Bonus visits you. Food for thought."

"Bonus asked my thoughts on what happened."

"And?"

"I don't have any. Hey, listen. In all this bullshit, everybody forgets Ingus was a friend of mine, a damn good friend. I'm as interested as anybody in who did it. I'd like to get ahold of 'em."

"What about dog fighting?" the young guy asked. Maybe he'd swallowed his gum. "You were such good friends, you know something about dog fighting, I'll bet."

"Yeah. And life on Mars." And my hands were still, and my heart was a Bulova, and I wasn't even warm. But I believed then someone would talk: Florida? L.G.?

Dolores smiled. Dolores smiled the way Mr. Cat smiled, so that if you moved the smallest goddamn fraction of an inch, you couldn't see it anymore. "Danny Ingus fought dogs. Ingus bet the ranch on one bout—a ranch wasn't built yet. Could make folks mad. Maybe you heard something."

"Nothing."

"Nothing about his champ getting killed a week before *he* did?"

"The whole truth and nothing but the truth." I raised my right hand. The young guy waved it down and stood up—chewing again.

"Listen, Cade," he said. "This whole business stinks, and it's getting worse. You lie to us, we'll find out." Heard that before? It must be the first thing they teach them in cop school. This guy was probably top of his class—Joe Polygraph. "Where were you Friday night? That wasn't one of the times you and Castro grabbed a beer was it?"

"We've been over that."

"Come on, Cade . . . Ingus's last. The night Stonehenge blew."

And I smiled. "How do you know that was his last?"

"Makes sense. We got ways."

"I don't think I saw him that night. Out drinking. Yeah. I guess I went drinking after work. Spud gave me the next day off. The Astronaut. Played this shoot-the-pheasant game. Ask 'em."

"Uh huh," Dolores said. "Sure, they'll remember you. Maybe you went out drinking with Ingus, blew some of the wad he stole."

"What wad?"

"C'mon, Cade. Celebrating the big explosion. Then you nailed him for the money."

"What money?"

The young cop leaned down. His knuckles popped as he flattened his hands. "The wad he ripped off at a vet's office on his way to Stonehenge. Seven hundred and eighty dollars. Quite a night."

Doc Nort, I'd bet. Danny *had* cracked. Would Nort talk? Had he already? "I'd kill my oldest friend for seven hundred and eighty dollars?"

"It's happened."

"Jesus."

They were getting bored now, had been guessing. Their eyes wandered from this silly goddamn piece of work to watches, fingernails, the floor—small stirrings that said the show was over. They were slow to bring the curtain down, though. Cops hate to leave the stage. For the next hour or so, the room got stickier and stickier in the sick spearmint of gum, in the white glue from cheap fluorescent tubes. The lights hummed. When Dolores and I finally stood to leave, our chairs groaned.

The young guy opened the green door a shoulder's worth and stopped. "Where'd you go to high school, Cade?"

"You've got my life story."

"East, wasn't it? Me too. Must've been a couple of years back of ya. You're related to Hilda Cade, Hilda Arthur."

"Her brother."

"Yeah, I barely remember. When she was a senior, she won some beauty contest, didn't she?"

"Miss Utah."

Dolores cleared his throat behind me. "How 'bout that?" he said.

"She got a trip to Atlantic City out of it anyway."

The young guy started to say something, thought better of it, popped his gum, and Open Sesame.

Dolores said, "Later, Cade." He took a side corridor. My high school buddy saw me to the front desk. Just for the hell of it, I winked at the blond with the buttons. She rolled her plastic eyes.

"We'll be in touch," the young guy said.

I turned to leave. Then this dead-as-the-desert voice says, "What have you got this one in for?" The cop who wrote up the Shiftlet deal is standing by a water cooler. A big bubble farts inside the glass. With a frown, he crumples a tiny white cup.

"Questions about a murder," the young guy says. "You know him?"

"I thought . . . Nah. Hell, I've got to watch it. I'm starting to think everybody fits in someplace."

The door is heavy but it opens.

24 —— ANSWERS

I doubt Jill ever did a single damn thing she didn't want to.

She didn't disappear into the background along with everything else those winter weeks I nightwatched at the Cade wax museum. She wouldn't. Sure, I changed plenty when my old man hauled ass. But the goddamn thing of it is this, Jill always sat there separate somehow, and deeper than the crap. No question. Somehow it had to do with that pretty, thin girl crying, thrashing on the wide, dark seat of her old man's car, telling me to get lost. Maybe that afternoon with my sister, too, but I don't know how. And this other time. Those come back first—and strongest. I can't really say why, since later was so much bigger and wilder, clearer, between us.

I hardly come here at all anymore.

When the ball bounces it smashes maple leaves against the black asphalt. The leaves are orange and yellow and brown. Leaves are stuck in the net hanging from the rusted hoop on the shitty plywood backboard. On lay-ups sometimes they come loose and drift down like the dry skin of the basketball. I smell them. The sky is pink. I think about dinner because my old man is still there opening cans, and I can still chew. I shoot and I shoot and I shoot.

She touches my hand and I think it is a dog's nose, and I look down at her shoes, those black, shiny shoes reflecting the two of us against the pink sky. Last year Jill cried in her father's car. Now twelve months later she is back, taller, rounder, her hair longer in a ponytail, but with the Continental behind her, with the basketball not three feet away, a year disappears and I believe she has just come from that wildness. I expect more shit, more bitterness.

"Carlos." Her smile seems very brave.

"What?" I try to pinpoint the times I've seen her since the last time and I can only think of one. I saw her trying on a pair of sandals in the Paris department store. She was alone. A tall, bald man knelt at her feet buckling the straps with hairy, fat fingers. Jill waited. The man worked. I'd never seen her in sandals. I watch us in her shoes.

"I want to ask you something. Do you have to be anywhere?"

"What is it?"

"Come in here."

"Your old man's car?"

"He's in at football. He won't know."

The garage is dark and stinks of bug spray. The door is huge, the light bright, the seat deep and quiet. The door swings, shuts, the air stands still. Perfume thickens my tongue. I expect nothing. A vault. "Will you ever tell anyone if I ask you something?"

"Who'd care?"

"You promise?"

"Sure." I can just make out the shape of her face at the other side of the car.

She takes a deep breath. Then she pushes herself across the seat and puts one of her thin arms behind me. "I trust you."

"I promised." I think she is nuts but I am curious, more than curious. Will she cry again?

Another deep breath. "Am I pretty?" I feel the words on my cheek.

We aren't touching, but she could be hugging me for all the pressure on my chest. I want to push her away, and I don't. "You know you are."

"You think so? Do you?" Her arm rests on my shoulders. I'm hard as a rock and hating myself for it because hell, this is secret and important and sex is still in some ways something you must suffer through.

"Very, very pretty."

"Really?"

"May I go to hell."

"Will you kiss me?"

Jesus Einstein Christ. Here I am with Jill Arthur, who's always been upsetting in some rose-garden sort of way—who stole my sister's clothes—a diamond-in-a-case kind of power, in the back seat of a car Danny Ingus could have

gone to prison just touching, breathing all the damn roses
in the world, her hand on my shoulder. It's all too goddamn
strong. Somehow I am not there.

"Kiss me?"

If I move my mouth just a little, our lips will meet, she's
that close. "No."

Her fingers tighten. Her breathing stops. I like her silhouette. "You won't? Really?" Quietly, she bites off each
word.

"I'll kiss . . . your ear," I say. Our eyes trade information.
I hear my heart. She leans into my arm and breathes.

"Okay." She flattens a palm against my chest, pushing a
little, as if she might change her mind.

I close my eyes, smelling the good smell. Remembering
her soft, pink, flexing mouth, I touch her cheek and turn
her head. The ponytail is like water on my hand. I kiss the
tiny pucker of her right ear and kiss it. I am in it with my
tongue, with care, kissing it. She is crying now, heaving in
my arms. Now she pushes me away and slides across the
seat. My hand is wet with tears. Once the door opens comes
a rush of cool, clean air and light, and she is standing. I
say, "Jill, I promise you're pretty." She leaves.

I slam the door with all my might.

I get my basketball and go. What the hell? Some things
you just have to live with. I wasn't sorry and I'm sure as
hell not now.

When Hilda was in ninth grade, before the nightmare woke
her, she blinked at me—I was in seventh—over some damn
picture book and said, "Carlie, I want to know everything.
Really. Why clouds float, why rainbows are all shaped the
same, why leaves turn orange in the fall."

Sissie redesigned the wheel the summer before Hilda's
eighth grade. After that Hilda had it all her own way at
Bryant, I think. I can only guess. I mean, a hell of a lot of

junior high happens in locker rooms and bathrooms. And I only saw her that last year.

When she walked the halls, the current moved with her. Boys *and* girls turned, lifted their eyes to what she had—whether they liked it or not. Even I felt it. Who knew I was her brother? Who cared? She headlined. I played the stands. I did my thing, painted the town red as the first apple, and she paraded herself, a queen in a garden, no putting out, no putting on.

Shit, she could have done it all, only good Hilda wanted to "know everything." You saw that in her blushing wonder at dances. Sure, I went to two or three—too many—of those goddamn dog shows. Hilda took best of breed every time, believe me, hands down. She had spine, too. Whenever we bumped into each other, there, or in the cafeteria, or in the halls, she always said to whoever tagged along, "I want you to meet my brother." I liked that. Usually. Sometimes I cut into an empty classroom if I saw her carrying too big an audience.

Guys acted like idiots around her, pushing each other, messing up each other's hair. At night she was out of reach. We didn't have a phone. When a kid came calling—and quite a few did—a couple of words from my old man, like, "Go cool your prick somewhere else," sent him on his way. Hilda never complained. She read. I hope she sneaked off now and then. Who knows?

She was young.

She liked to lie in the bathtub under an ocean of bubbles and sing nursery-rhymy kinds of songs. (My father listened with his head resting on his cigarette hand, his scarred, loose mouth open to something like a smile.) She liked to do the stupid things girls do, swing and swing in the park, make dandelion chains, work hard on her tan, and paint and repaint and touch up her nails.

Sister Hildy was young. The real thing. A true-blue dreamer. Those books she read could have been Monkey Wards' catalogues. "People own whole herds of horses," she'd say. "People live on their own islands loaded with tangerine trees. We can be anything we choose. We can." She wanted to be an architect, she said, and design island cities to float on the ocean.

Still, for all that, something old as starlight belonged to her. It must have, the way the kids mooned and stuttered and milled around her. *They*—none of my friends— officially made her their queen at the end of ninth grade, for the graduation dance. I didn't go, but I saw her at home just before done up in some of the extra fancy stuff Sissie left or sent. Mama sighed. My old man shook his head and lowered his eyes again. A cowboy yodeled on the radio.

Without surprise or worry, as though she understood, Hilda took her place at the center of the pack, a sheep in wolf's clothing, or something like that. I don't think she ever had friends after Sissie, just attendants, the pretty, quiet girls who didn't pine to be prettier, happy girls who liked themselves and fairy tales.

Lance didn't stand out from the crowd for Hilda then. Nobody did. Anyway, he was a year younger. In junior high girls could be ruined hanging out with younger guys. And in those days, I think, Hilda and boys cruised different sides of the highway.

Jill missed the entrance ramp. Hilda controlled patterns. Jill Arthur didn't see them. An exception is what Jill god-damn good and well was. The few times I saw her at dances back then, she looked right through me, right through walls. She went: period. She stood around with the kind of girls who wore flannel skirts and glasses. They weren't ugly. They weren't anything. They did well on tests. Someday they would be pink ladies in hospitals and dream over the ads in slippery magazines. Then they'd die, and the hospitals would find volunteers to replace them. Their husbands would buy new wives, wives younger and sexier. Their kids would shoot another nine holes. Shit. Background. Camouflage. Hell, once when they trooped away, Jill just stood there, arms crossed, loafered feet apart, without the faintest idea they'd gone.

She was different. Alone, she walked all the way home in a downpour one time with her umbrella closed. I followed along, splashed after her about a block behind, just to see if she stuck to her guns.

I didn't know this then, but when she was in eighth grade, she rode the bus downtown and had some fat grandma gypsy lady tattoo a spider, as big and hairy as a tarantula, low on her stomach where nobody would see it unless she wanted them to. A spider.

Once, lots later, she told me she wanted to feel everything a person could. She called it "an obligation" to take our cars through all their gears. "Otherwise," she said, "we never change and find out who we are.

"Everyone's perfect," she said. "You know? We should live up to that."

25 —— *THE CROSSING*

*J*uiced again his last autumn home, weaving around the kitchen in his undershirt, my old man drops a can of spaghetti and meatballs in a bloody splash to the door and says, "Mop that up."

"Screw you." I barely get outside.

He shouts through the screen: "You goddamn, sleazy, maggoty little son of a bitch, come back. Come back here.

Get your bastard ass back here, boy. You'll wish to fucking God you was an orphan when I'm through. So help me."

Bottoms's place is silent when I pass, lights on in every room. Then through a slivered hole in her window glass, I hear her whispering, whispering high pitched and thoughtful: "That Tommy's been naughty again. When will the child behave?" Bats chop through the gloom. I remember their ugly, pinched faces in the science books at school.

One reefer. My ears sting with cold. Headlights flare down South Temple. It's dusk, a foggy kind of gray, but I can still see the big bright houses outside the strip of road where I walk backward, shirt collar up, shoulders hunched, thumb out.

I am hoping to God for a ride with a working heater, hoping to get to Danny's before he's gone for the night, and this brand-new, yellow, two-door sports job—no plates, temporary tag—slides over behind me. The horn bleeps, but I'm running already. A girl is driving. Nice legs. "She loves you," the Beatles sing, "and you know you should be glad." The leather is warm.

"Hi." Jill's face. Her pretty, square face, lips slick, barely open. "Where you going?" The soft neck of her white sweater tightens my stomach.

"You stopped," I say. Clever.

She glances in the rearview. I close the door. Her perfume. It's been a month. She flicks off the radio. Her bracelets jingle. "I didn't mind what you did," she says. "Only at first."

Heat. My fingers loosen. When she pulls into traffic, I say, "You steal it?"

"Right." She bites at a fingernail but laughs a little. "From Daddy. For my birthday. From Sweden."

"Some present. How old?"

"Seventeen. You . . . You're what?"

Lights fast flash by—burger joints, gas stations. She holds both hands on the wheel now, eyes straight ahead. "Fifteen," I say.

"You're still at Bryant. That's right." She takes a left through a neighborhood without trees. "You seem older." The mountains darken, a high, rounded wall just ahead. We pass the zoo into Emigration Canyon. "Want to go for a ride?"

"Beats freezing."

We wind past A-frames and rock historical markers, this the Mormon trail. The canyon and the darkness deepen as the mountains rise, and I imagine things, like ghost wagons and ghost pioneers, like Jill's going to ask me to kiss her ear again. "Bug you if I smoke?"

"No. I'd like one, too. I like to sometimes."

I wonder if I've ever ridden in a car with a female driving who wasn't somebody's mother. I light our cigarettes. I crack the window. The chilly air whooshes in. Ruth's Diner dives like a submarine. Then Jill brakes hard, we brace ourselves. Our tires shriek. We damn near smash two mule deer, their eyes burning until Jill taps the horn. In one amazing leap they're gone.

She laughs too quickly, accelerates, and smokes, one long drag, with her fingertips—like a movie star. "You ever think about . . . dying, when, where you'll go?"

"What's the point?" I let out a big breath.

"I know," she says, and the sky's sharp with stars. "But sometimes I can't stop myself. I just picture floating—in this empty grayness like in an ocean, but no currents, no movement, no sound. It's not hot *or* cold. It's not anything. Give me another cigarette."

I listen to the windiness of the tires as they pull us through these huge waves that are mountains, as Jill turns into a narrow, climbing side canyon I recognize. Danny and a bunch of other buzzed-out fools took me there one night. We cut our lights right about where Jill down-shifts now, and drove with the moon. "Devil worshippers," Danny said. A spooky stone house hunkers beyond the stream in pines back of this tall fence with shiny spikes that stretches up the road. Danny sprayed FUCK SATAN in red on the stone gate post. We pitched M-80's over the spikes until a damn siren blasted from these speakers on the trees.

Jill says, "Heard about the satanic cult? These four queer hairdressers own the place. God, they're in their sixties. I've hiked with them. They don't know how the story started. They've been brave." She honks twice. The road is steeper after a sharp bend, the air black.

She swings onto dirt through a tunnel of scrub oak and stops. Off across a rickety, bleached-out bridge, a log cabin, windows shuttered, squats in aspen and sage. "This is ours." She grinds her cigarette in the ashtray. "Daddy knows I'm here. Sometimes it's good to get away. Want to go inside? I *don't* mind. I think we're a lot the same."

Crickets sing with the stream and it's cold and a cave kind of dark with stars close enough to touch. From behind the seat she lifts out a quart bottle of Tab and a Bob Dylan record. I've never heard of Dylan. She laughs. As we cross, the bridge bounces and squeaks. Jill pushes her round ass up to me beside the porch when she bends to lift a rock where they hide their key. She says, "You won't tell anybody it's under there."

The cabin smells dusty but isn't when she lights two kerosene lamps, one on the mantel of the stone fireplace, one on a knotty-pine counter between the wide front room—dining room and the kitchen. This "cabin" could hold my house three or four times, I'm thinking. It holds my heat. Indian rugs Old Westernize the walls, and hanging spears and feathered pipes. I'm crashing a little from the dope, and the elk head on the chimney has teeth. Once Dylan is pounding down with all the tin his voice can muster, Jill goes to the fridge. "Want'ny Tab? There's beer in here."

"Beer."

She brings chips and dip too, and we sit on a deep couch by the hearth sipping and crunching and looking at each other sometimes with glossy, cool eyes. Christ. One minute I'm chilled to the goddamn marrow, hoping anybody'll let me shiver by their heater a second or two, and the next minute I wouldn't change a son-of-a-bitching thing.

I'm on my second beer. The lamp flame's bright. Jill just told me the history of the cabin, that it was built by a polygamist in 1850 or '60 or sometime, that one president of the church owned it for a while, next a senator, that for two or three years a famous doctor from South Africa held it—"a vacation house" he used each May was all, and that her father picked it up from the doctor when her mother was still alive. "Mama died right after I turned seven. I barely remember. Daddy kept the cabin for us, I'm pretty sure, but now he entertains here a lot." Dylan's harmonica screeches to a stop. The record player clicks to mountain silence—water and wind.

Jill lowers her bare feet to the floor. Her bracelets jingle. She shakes her hair. Looks at me. Licks her lips. Sighs. "You know when I asked you that question before? That afternoon? Did you mind?"

"It was okay, I guess."

"I've got . . . I've got another. I do. Only this time, if you don't want to answer when I ask, just don't, walk out. Don't lie. Please don't lie. And promise, promise you won't tell."

I smell her perfume. The collar of her sweater is folded over and soft. I remember her head against mine.

"You don't want to?" I can hear her breathing.

"I don't know. What's with the questions? Why me? 'Cause I'm handy? 'Cause I don't matter?"

She touches her fingers to my cheek. "I'm asking Carlos Cade because I think he sees things pretty straight. That's why. That matters. It does. I'm going in that room over there for a few minutes. When I'm ready to ask it, I'll call you."

I sip from the cold beer, peel at the label.

"Okay."

The cabin is chilly, but I am hot right then, damp around the eyes, itchy in the face. Why do I go? She might be making fun. I step into the room. At first this is a stranger shy behind that small smile, the garden-green eyes. For a moment it *is* a joke because I don't know where Jill went. This girl, naked on the bearskin on the wide double bed, is so much I've never seen before. Jill lies on her side, legs crossed, a Y of the softest-looking goddamn yellow hair you ever saw below this monster blue spider just under her navel. Her breasts, full, nipples stiff and broad and brown, are white as shell, and now the shy smile is gone. She smokes one long drag, taps ashes into an Indian bowl.

"Okay?" she asks.

I swallow. I nod. I nod and say, "Jill . . ."

Smoke slides from her nose. She sits up some. "Carlos, am I . . . sexy?" The crickets go nuts, way the hell out of sync.

For quite a while we listen to those crickets. Finally I say, "God, yes."

"Do you know how many boys have seen me like this?" She blinks to the side like maybe she wants this to end but is scared to move. "My father and my brother and Carlos Cade."

No girl except Hilda had ever seen me. And who had I seen? The ones in magazines, with pubes shaved and tits polished like goldfish bowls. I'd stared for nights through a keyhole in the sealed side door of the Art Barn at models on tall stools or stretched on a quilt. My pants move, and I don't want Jill to know, so I sit on the bed.

"The spider," she says. "A tarantula. I went to this gypsy lady four different times. I wasn't afraid. But I am now."

Her cigarette smolders in the bowl. I lift it to the floor. I look at the log walls, the dark walls hung with tomahawks and guns, the wall over Jill's head holding one of those big cat-house pictures they stick in cowboy movies, a meaty whore on a red couch, waiting—Jill's pose. I laugh. I laugh and put my hand on her side and we both jump. She lowers her head and laughs hard into the fur of that black, god-damn bear. Then we breathe. Then the crickets take over.

Her smile is scared. "Will you?" She turns onto her back. "Put your hand here. I'll show you. Please."

Hell, I'm in ninth grade. I have touched girls before— I know what they have—but always the dark, and panties, and maybe even someone else across the room kept the girl just a girl, and Jill kisses my fingers on the heavy fur of a bear. She lifts my hand. "Yes," she says, "that is the spot."

She twists her hips in slow circles. She reaches for my buckle—and I remember where I am and who. For a long time the crickets stop. Her eyes shut. When they open, she asks, "What's wrong? This enough, Carlos? That's okay." But when she says my name I can't breathe.

"Where's the bathroom?"

I look scrawny in the fancy mirror with those hundred burning bulbs around it. I take off my jeans and hang them on a hook on the door. Christ, my underpants are fifty shades of brown. I lift the band over myself, throbbing now, to get them off. My cock sways blind and mean above the sink. I wash it. I scrub the son of a bitch, softening down, because I want her to like it, if this amounts to anything, better than anyone else's ever. I'm pouring paper cupfuls of warm water over it—me, the knife-eyed fool in the mirror—when she calls: "You okay? We can go."

And she is on the sheets, arms at her sides, feet under covers folded back over dark bear hair, her legs wide. She blinks and draws herself together. I sit, bend to her, touch her. I love her wild eyes. And she is holding me, and I'm as big as life. She opens her cool mouth around me for just a minute and jumps like something dying under my hand and tightens and moans damn near screaming. I slide alongside, my chest so full my ribs will break. And with the warm silk of her belly heaving, I come and come and come, and she catches it with her hand and wipes it over everything.

I have never been so heavy. She can barely talk. She says, "I would have let you. You could have. I've never been . . ."

"I couldn't . . . I couldn't wait."

And my hand is nestled in her hair, and my cock shiny and dead, looks like something the spider killed.

"I turned you on. You can't say . . . I didn't."

We stayed until the sheets were ready in the dryer on the back porch. Showered. Lay across from each other on the couch after, so I saw every angle, got hard again in her hands, and she whispered, "Go slow. I'm used up. Let me. Show me. I want to." Her hair across my stomach. Her lips.

"We are a lot the same," I said. "We are."

26 ——— *CLOSE UP*

I felt nothing.

When Hilda pulled in all by her lonesome in that monster, gray Cadillac and called to me, you should have seen Spud's face—like a pizza, hold the cheese. Old Spud didn't even peep about the twenty or twenty-five minutes I shut down my bay.

I guess I expected her—I'll see your visit and raise you—because when she honked and I turned, and her tinted power window opened, I just winked, nothing else —no surprise. She waved a yellow scarf. I finished a Gremlin.

As I close her heavy, quiet door, I change planets: air conditioning, perfume, leather, and the long fingers of her hand on mine, which I pull away without a word. She is pretty as ever, prettier maybe, and I like that about her, but it's two years since we talked, saw each other, a horseback ride with her kids to Bridger Falls, so anything like who we ever were is in the backseat but probably not even there. "Mama's dead, Loskie." When she speaks, her neck tightens inside a thin necklace with a diamond like a tear. Her eyes shrink. "I thought you should know."

She lights a cigarette—when did she start?—one of those long brown ones. Vents in the dash suck up thin clouds and sigh. "Sunday night," she says, picking something from her lip. "She died in her sleep."

"So now it's official."

"I thought you should know." Her chin sags just a little underneath, like Mama's.

I light a cigarette of my own. The smoke slides to her inside the windshield. "Told the old man? I saw the posters."

"Lance'll get him word. I didn't even know he was alive. Then here he comes born again. And again. And again. Night after night." She stops. Shuts her eyes. "They thought Lazarus was good after what, four days? How about fifteen years." She steadies her eyes. Slowly shakes her head. "You don't do badly yourself."

"I'm walkin' on water, Hildy." I nod toward the wash.

She studies her hands, the long, high-shine nails, shaking, the cigarette, and finally looks at me. "The funeral's at noon tomorrow. The press loves it. I guess you missed the headline this morning, the predictable tripe: Rags to Riches, Poorhouse to Statehouse—garbage. A photo of Papa all tearful. Third grade classes will write and praise me as a tribute to liberty and the church, complete with crayon angels holding flags."

"You're a tribute to something."

She laughs for her own eyes in the side window behind me. "I guess I am." We're quiet. Finally she says, "By the way, your message . . . Rachel's well, thank you. You spooked the guard." She laughs again.

The kid in the next bay is amazing he moves so fast, a super ant, wiping down a Galaxy like he can wipe it away.

"How long've you been back?"

"Not long. Something just over a month, I think."

She lights another cigarette.

She blinks at the bays, the fat man in his glass box. The color has left her face, all except a red circle floating beneath each eye. "Cops told me where I could find you, not that I asked. A Lieutenant Dolorian or something called about you—about Danny." Her voice breaks, but she sits completely still. I remember the sound when Danny fell into the bumper. I remember the shriek of the peacock. "I'm sad about Danny," she says.

"He must've been in something deep—big time."

"A bombing, they said."

"Not Danny." I turn to the street. I hate the silence in this machine, idling, blowing cool air, burning gas. "They warn you about your wicked brother?"

"Just questions. You're in trouble?" She looks me over again.

"No."

"If you are . . . You know, I could give you money to leave . . ."

"I'm not."

"Hey, Mama died. *That's* why I came. I just wanted to talk before some reporter found you, and . . . And, Loskie, I just wanted to ask you to please stay out of it. I'm the First Lady of Utah. Please, no trouble."

"Okay." I push-button the window down to get a little heat on my bones.

"Promise?" she asks in a whisper.

"Sure." I open the door and stand, leaning in toward the dark coolness of the car, my arm burning on the polished roof. "The governor can't throw me in the can for going to the funeral, I guess."

"He wouldn't want to. He never has, not even over that bear." Her mouth widens. "You know, that bear tore the cupboards off the walls."

"What happened to that bear?"

"We ate it."

And then she drove out of Spud's, her black windows rising.

We sat Indian style on Ginny's floor, the thin light from her kitchen frosting her hair, our plastic cups, the ashtray. Just a crack or a creaking now and then, the Samson was quiet as ice. An iceberg—drifting. Matches exploded in her eyes. I pulled my cold fingers through her warm hair, warm smoke. Alive. Alive and changing, Ginny's cheeks, her red mouth. We stared. My eyes ached. And I finished an Old

Crow on the rocks and groaned, I think, or she did, and
she whispered. Whispered, "Gees, are you wound up" as I
lay spread-eagled on the bed. Breathed over the hair on
my chest, my neck, my arms.

I said, "Ginny, do you know how much I . . . Ginny,
I . . ."

Spud gave me the day off for the funeral. "How old was
she?" he asked. I didn't know. What did age have to do
with a goddamn thing?

When Ginny asks why I'm home, I say, "I'll tell you about
it sometime."

It is six o'clock. I'm on my third beer. I do not finish the
pork chop. *Bonanza.* She kisses me during the ads. The
news helicopters in. The cemetery, a hole wide and deep
as the Kennecott pit. She's up like someone yanked her
with a leash. She points. She says, "You."

I hold her arm, trying not to spill my plate, to get her
to sit down again. Jesus, the cameraman must have climbed
a tree, and a small, ash-faced procession is filing out below,
me smack in the middle in tropical technicolor. "Yeah."

"Why didn't you tell me? God." And she drops back on
the couch.

Close-ups: Lance, stern; Hilda, coping; me, Elvis Presley
fifteen years ago, before the fat, in some island movie—
Hawaiian shirt, gray pants, combat boots; my old man
heavy and yellow and packaged in black. He says, "So you're
still kicking?" He wears a tie, if you can believe it. We ride
in the back of a limousine alone with his smell. My knife
is closed in my hand. He is shorter, one lower tooth gone,
the scar on his upper lip like a red zipper, and he stinks.
His hands hang between his legs. He's missing one thumbnail. He moves that hand over his head, across the greasy,
gray-yellow hair.

I say, "Why couldn't you stay the fuck away?"

His head rocks with the turns. He looks to me. "Same reason as you, I guess." He scratches his neck. "She is married to the governor."

"So what?"

"And something you ain't never done." He sits back. His pointed tongue jumps out. "Talked to Jesus. More than once. Go ahead and laugh." I put my knife away. A cop purrs past on a Harley. And my old man shakes out a Pall Mall, lights it, and coughs. Leans over his knees and coughs until his eyes run. His cheeks are wet at the funeral—like somebody real.

The solemn music is broken by the sax in an ad for Carlson's Cadillac and Olds, the lot a pattern of banners and cars. Ginny cuts off the set. "I'm sorry," she says. "Your mother."

"Her head went a long time ago. Rest home–itis."

"Still. And your sister is married to Governor Arthur?"

"Last time I checked."

"You didn't tell me."

In the kitchen for another beer, I look out over the roofs. The moon is a "C" for Cade. "You stupid shit," I whisper against the glass.

Then I tell Ginny I'm ashamed at how little I've made of my life, that owning up to a first lady of a sister isn't easy, that my old man's crazy and I'd rather forget. Twenty minutes and she's crying for my old lady the way probably nobody ever did before.

Not one reporter asked me a damn thing.

And I would find him and see him again. I would hear his crazy ass out in a church and I would follow him. Did he really visit her before she died? She was already dead.

In this hairy, twisted hand with the blue cross tattooed on the webbing between the index finger and the thumb, my pen moved. The cassette. Circle after tiny circle. I could run. I could chuck the whole damn business, but what would running get me? Bigger circles? The voice was mine played back. Moving forward.

Mama said, "Dreams can fool ya. Take you clean away."

27 —— *THE SECRET*

The first little while after my TV debut especially, Ginny doted. "You get comfy," she'd say. She asked would I like another beer every two seconds. And she held back, bashful, super ticklish and giggly all of a sudden. No more dope smoking. "Just trying to cut down," she said. Then one night when I undid her shorts and rolled against her, she smiled all kind of embarrassed and said, "I don't think I like it on the floor anymore." In bed she cooed and whispered, "Please, honey, please stay."

The first red-eyed pigeon of the day paces my windowsill. Mr. Cat sits beside it behind the screen. I lift my machine and my notebooks from the ceiling and I try, but I don't care. I can't even doodle.

Ginny.

She says, "You all right?" The pigeon flies. I did not hear the door. Her hand, cool and smooth as flowers, opens onto my neck.

"The heat," I say. "Has me dopey is all."

"I know what." She dumps her coffee into the sink. "Let's drive to Brighton. Cold in the mountains." And steep, I think, and high.

We pack a bag of beer and sandwiches up the winding, chocolaty trail to Lake Mary, a black mirror of water cupped in gray, slabbed granite between peaks still tipped with snow. "The guy Brighton," Ginny says, "named all the lakes after his wives."

We cross a cliff you want to remember. I hold my breath. Ginny yodels, "I laid a little old lady who . . ." Her voice, faint in all that air, comes back.

She said, "I want to freshen up."

"You're fresh enough," I told her. My shower steamed, but I couldn't get warm.

"Surprise," she said, turning, when I opened her door. In a black, slinky dress cut to leave this perfect V of neck, shoulders, and cleavage, Ginny kissed me with pink lipstick and then stepped away to pose, one hand behind her head. "My prom dress—and it still fits."

"Your parents let you go in that?"

"I made it myself. My mother cried."

"Who'd blame her? Hell, it's a lethal weapon."

"I want to be classy as anybody for a change."

I lit a cigarette. I said, " 'Classy' has a credit card. Besides, nobody's got any class on you."

"You're a bullshitter. I picked out a place. Go put on something real downtown nice. Okay? My treat. I haven't wasted ten cents outside a grocery store since Christmas. Go on. Bullshitter."

The best I could do was this ragged khaki shirt and a watermelon-red tie I picked up in Florida with inside a blond in a bathing suit and fishnet stockings HAND PAINTED IN HAWAII.

"You look like Jack Nicholson or somebody," Ginny said.

A pedigreed place: bar, mirror-tiled; green neon tubes snaking in and out of deep, round, smoky corners; thin people with thin watches and thin, clean laughter, born just for this, a drink in one hand, a carrot stick in the other. Easter-eggy covers from the *New Yorker* hung in chrome

frames like windows. The George Dickel knew all my
strengths. She drank wine, swirled her tongue around her
lips. We chewed each other's ears no matter who gawked.
I said, "You know the secret? The secret is to invent yourself
before someone else does."

How could I leave that night?

A breeze cooled the valley. I walked to work, trying to save
my piece-of-shit collector's car, and everybody smiled. The
day was solid gold, with birds—on State Street, in the gut-
ters, in the shadows, everywhere—whistling louder than
any damn engine noise. And Spud stood up and spread
one of his silicone-giant, magazine centerfolds against his
window. "Hey, Cade," he said. "How ya doin'? Get a load
of this. Geez, I'd like a taste of hers."

Once I'd foamed good old bay number three into action,
though, things changed.

Noel and clone and dumpy driver, still in his neck brace,
Mercedes damp in all the right places, roll smiling from
the rotors. SHARX.

You remember the new Noel, Anthony Nicks. I saved
his ass one time, and here he is—dog handler, ex-
wrestler. A swell guy. Sure. Gray suit, white golf shirt,
bleached plastic hair, chains enough to sink a carrier.
Comes with a spare about eight years younger whose
teeth are whiter. The driver's waiting for a brain from
Ronco and hardly blinks. While I dry with my chamois,
Noel and his reflection, Stud, climb out and pump
themselves up as best they can. Quite a show. "I'll be
damned," Noel says. "Look who's putting the luster on our
chrome."

"If it ain't the governor's ass wipe," Stud says.

"And I thought we were friends," I say.

Noel's jaw might as well be wired shut. His eyes are

bloodshot, loose. He growls between his teeth, "You got it."

"Huh?" I ask, even though I heard. Stud has his dumpster of a back to us now, staring off toward Spud, whose head is down.

"You never called."

I'm on the windshield now. The driver squeezes his eyes shut and looks like maybe he should have "Highly Explosive" stamped on his forehead. "Nothin' to call about."

"Sure," Noel says. "We don't know you have the dog, Cade. Mm mm. It's just that nobody else has him. See? It might not matter what we know. We might start guessing. So listen, good buddy. If you're holdin' him, turn him over. No questions. You'll never fight him. We'd hear. And money? You ask a dime, our senior partner snaps his fingers, your heart self-destructs. Got it?"

The car gleams. I step away and nod. "Got it."

Noel smiles and folds his arms.

"No. I mean, I haven't got it, but I understand. Come on. If I was hiding anything with this shit flying, I'd have to be one of the dumbest assholes on legs. I'm not. I don't know a damn thing about any dog."

"You've got my card."

"Check."

"Vice is back by this time tomorrow, we clear the books. Simple. The governor ain't in your corner, Cade. Word is he wants to go easy on you, but these're his friends' places gettin' detonated. Find the dog, buddy. That's all. Or we will. Try anything after tomorrow, your nuts are moon dust. Anything." Stud turns around and grins, showing off his horse teeth. Noel knows he's been clever and stands there long enough for me to appreciate his greatness. Sorry, Noel. "And, Cade, one other matter has a lot of people interested. The heat's on over this Castro thing. What do you know?"

"Nothing."

"Tell us who done it, some big guys'd be grateful to the
tune of some big bucks."

"So you're still looking in graves?" I say.

Noel tightens his eyes down. "Be glad it ain't yours."

They move like they're laminated, and fold themselves
into the Benz. The birds sing.

I'm not pissed. And I'm not really scared of those small-
timers. But I don't like it about the dog missing. I want
things to calm down. I'm not afraid, because I'm bigger
than they are—than *he* is—with what I know. I go wherever
the hell I please.

Somebody had put my room through another skin search.
The door didn't look jimmied, except for some tiny
scratches by the latch—very professional. But the place was
too tidy, every cupboard shut tight, drawers snug, rugs,
pictures, hangers, sheets straight. No one wanted me
hurt—not yet. Too dangerous. Just a frisking when my
back was turned. The curtains shivered. Mr. Cat broke
through them and thumped to the floor. The ceiling hadn't
been touched. Still, when ghosts walk, you get nervous.
And you get mean.

So I'm strung together with barbed wire. And I drink
icy beer and watch—how's this?—Gregory Peck search for
the likes of Moby Dick in fuzzy black and white. I think *I*
have it bad.

My shirt is off. My bare feet are crossed on a chair between me and the set. Ginny kneels behind me on the couch.
Her hands work the wire out of my shoulders. I wonder
if I'm losing the little sense I had. I'm threatened. Shit,
then my room gets overhauled, I'm sure of it, and an hour
later Milwaukee's lightened my head about twenty pounds,
this sweet woman is rubbing me down, and I'm into a goddamn whaling flick. Almost. I've got to care. I've got to.

But Ginny is so bashful, so gentle and full of sex in her

eyes that I'll feel like I've left her exposed, spread to all the open-mouthed Spud sort of shit in this shitty, twisted world if I drag myself back home. I tell her she can count on me. I smile.

"God," she says. "This is getting old, honey. You fill me up and then empty it all out." She turns in perfect curves under the sheet.

Her door locks automatically. I hate the leaving. The halls are haunted. The house stinks with it.

28 —— *PLACES IN THE DARK*

I'm home—from Cowboy Jack's, Jeanine, Colorado, from a nice try but no cigar. Hickler says, "I may know somebody. How bad you want to work?" Sometimes your own life just kind of hunts you down.

At $1.60 an hour, I sweat over this whining, rattle-trap conveyor belt at the Cornitt Wool warehouse. I tug dried sheep turds out of fleeces Jorge, this grinning Mexican kid, dumps on. Up from me, Curly, a wrinkled, stoop-shouldered giant, "grades" the wool, feels each fleece with his eyes shut then lobs it like a head of dirty hair into the correct cart for baling. Along with the rock-hard clots of shit in the wool, I uncover sticks and burrs and bugs—and dark glasses, a pocketknife, a set of false teeth. Once I open this fleece crusted with mud and find a porcelain doll's pink head. Mama calls it a "headstone." She says, "That's a good joke."

Hilda's off with Lance half her life. He honks. She rushes out. For most of two years, it's just lip service whenever Lance and I cross paths. "How's it going?" he says with his forehead wrinkled, like *he's* looking after things. I'm shaggy as a damn sheep with hair to my shoulders, and Lance is the same, the same as ever. He winks. He talks to Mama in a whisper.

To hell with it. I rent a two-room, cracked-plaster roach trap out on North Temple. This family of painted concrete bears is flaking away around an empty motel swimming pool across the street.

Most days on the belt I stay loaded and then warm nights at the Bonneville Speedway fire up this rusted mother GTO I bought. I am strictly C class, but my engine roars, my wheels smoke and squeal, and plenty of girls polish my pipe. Danny Ingus goes, too, on Sundays sometimes—his one day off. The state turned him loose. He's driving cabs, shacked up with Rose.

Sometimes I want to make something of myself. Sometimes I tell myself I have.

I am. Not dead. Not hiding like these wetbacks. At break their faces hang empty around the dirty rings of their mouths. Not married. No lackey to Lance. *Not* knotted up. Not yet. I am. Something. Legal. Alive.

Hilda saves me a story from the *Tribune:* After all those years pot-bellied with glass eyes, with that slouch, his feet dragging, Pep managed to dive over a grenade in Southeast Asia. The purple heart. Probably tripped.

You think Lance will get the purple heart two college years into the future when his time comes? Right. How about officers' training school and whore-house reconnaissance? With Pep's example to keep him cautious. Lieutenant Arthur. I never thought he'd go. But that son of a bitch had the game mastered. The Arthurs "went to war."

When two guys thrash it out in a back room one lunch, Jorge says, "Man, you'd think we'd learned from Nam who the fucking enemy is."

"Name's Noel," this big bald guy who'd just hired on said, "like the grassy one in Dallas maybe hid a second shooter."

I thought of that whenever I looked at his smooth head with the strip of strawberry hair shaggy around it. Over forty somewhere, raised next to a Kentucky coal shaft, Noel damn straight knew it all.

He said, "I come to town to fetch my brother, 'cept his woman might die, looks like. Had herself a head-on. He ain't budgin'. I can wait."

No problem Noel could heft a four-hundred-pound wool bag. But he only put out about five minutes of every hour and smoked cigarettes in the dark hideaways in the warehouse the rest. "I'm just passing through," he'd say.

He drove a rusted, redone Fritos truck, painted black over the pictures on the sides. It had beds and shelves and drawers built in sprayed purple. His gear shift was an eight ball with a compass in the top. A couple of lunch breaks a week, Noel perched on the bumper, the back doors open, and moved plenty with the Mexes—mostly jewelry, now and then a radio or a rifle—cheap. "Let me tell you, son," Noel said, "a big man needs big plans."

He said, "We wait for the cool. Then we motor south, the desert, and dig. Big dough, Cade. I'm a grave dog, a treasure detector."

"Just buried out there," Noel said, "stuff for the next life. For this life's what I say."

A pebble cracked the windshield. The brother, who called himself Stud—a wiry Noel with this mustache clear down his chin—pushed a wad of gum into the hole. His skinny blond sweetie, Bitsy, with a blue scar beside one eye, did some acid on the bed in the back. I said, "Why's she along?"

"I'm somebody to be reckoned with," her little voice called out behind me. "Ask Mr. Stud if I'm not." We drank malt liquor.

We're doing seventy-five and Noel squirms his gut up against the steering wheel, works his tooled, chained-to-his-belt-loop wallet out, and pushes a crisp fifty into my face. "Take it," he hollers. "Your first day's pay."

We dumped Bitsy in Flagstaff.

High up over this orange-red, worn-away world—the air thin as flash paper—Noel finally cut the engine of the over-heated army-surplus Jeep. "Jesus," I said. We took our time getting out. Little Stranger Gulch fell away to the south. Up from the flat where we stood, a ridge climbed through patches of blue and green, leveled, then climbed still more into the San Francisco peaks. Noel stared at a crinkled sheet of yellow paper. "This has to be it," he said. We'd split the takings five ways, one for the guy in Flagstaff outfitted us, drew our map from some prospector's report, looked after Bitsy, and would move the stuff, and two cuts for Noel, the contractor and the nerve.

Noel hobbled around a black boulder where the slope started. He threw some brush aside. Crouched. "God-damn," he said, "I'm a wonder." He flipped his cigarette into a good-size crack right back of that big rock.

Stud said, "So far it's just a hole."

"There's holes and then there's holes," Noel whispered. "Tomorrow we go underground, Cade."

As the sun smoldered out that night, we pitched a rag-ged, camouflaged tent in a stand of junipers.

"Silted up," Noel said as he crawled inside. "This tunnel coulda been big enough, maybe five, eight feet high."

"Snakes," Stud said. "Remember snakes."

"Just crickets," Noel called out of the darkness, "them blind boogers with no blood. I'm watchin'. C'mon, Cade."

The crickets, milky white, clung to thin black knots of

roots. Roots, Jesus, the air so dry my eyes itched. The cold walls chilled down, sparkled in spots when the carbide from my hardhat bounced across. Hands and knees. Noel grunted, dragging the huge, worn soles of his boots behind. Noel stunk, and I followed.

The tunnel widened at a turn, tilted in these purple stripes. Hunched sideways, we squirmed our way farther in, maybe fifteen feet, and Noel stood, and my light opened into this rock room with an orange powder floor and more crickets and a pile of gray fur and bones. "Cougar gave up the ghost here," Noel said. All that earth domed over me, I pulled out a cigarette. Noel moved through the cavern, poking with his toe in the dust.

"Looks professional, don't it?" Noel said, his pants powdered now, and his arms. The Coleman lantern hissed. He'd blocked out the floor with tent pegs and string—five squares maybe eight by eight apiece. "We take 'em one at a time, Cade, move this dust and see what's what."

Whenever we went in, Stud perched on the cliff edge outside, holding fancy binocs and this beat-up Marlin .30-30 with a brand-new scope. He toked down plenty of weed. I figured he'd drill a few rock squirrels or buzzards. Nope. Stud could concentrate. He kept his eyes locked on the road we'd four-wheeled in on. To stay alert, he said, he now and then did a run of push-ups or sit-ups right there on that lip of rock. Every hour or so he brought us cans of Colt 45 still cool from the nights.

Now we're coughing on the third day in the chalky light of that goddamn hole, still being damn thorough, even though we've found nothing but cougar bones. On our knees, we scrape and scrape, as far as square number four in the back corner. Noel stops for lunch, takes his sweet time crawling in again, says, "I know this other spot on Black Mesa," but we work that next-to-the-last square. I'm sliding my hands through the powder, my eyes shut, and I feel something, a sharp, pointed rock that I wipe on my shirt and pass to Noel. He sits back. "Damn," he says. He stands and slaps my shoulder. "They *was* here! Now she's mine." He lifts the hissing lantern to a short ledge beside number four.

Stud comes in to say dinner, but Noel says, "Not tonight," and scoops and brushes, and grunts and hums—and smells—like a damn bear. He is working at a shallow hole. He's got this little stack of stuff on newspaper off to the side, more arrowheads, seven or eight, these strips of what he says is yucca, chips from busted pots, and now, before Stud ducks out through the tunnel, Noel rolls onto his heels. "Hey," he says, his hand caked and bloody at the nails around a dusty wad of gray. "A sandal." I would not have known. But when I hold it, I understand how it worked, fit a foot, and I hear voices, but I turn and the tunnel is empty and it's Stud and Noel there chuckling as Noel chisels slowly deeper, hits rock, a slab, taps to find the edges, to loosen this lid, and lifts, opens a hole, dark, with something in it, something Noel carefully raises, something shorter than his forearm wrapped in skins. I say, "What we got?"

After a long time with his head bent, Noel twists his dirty eyes on me and grins. "A baby," he whispers, so I hardly hear. He sets the thing out on a wrinkled sheet of newspaper. "Mummified," he says, "mummified," like it's the word he found. "God, the face is somethin'." And it is when he dusts it off, like one big dried leaf shrunk over a skull, eye holes worn in, a nose hole, a tight, tiny slit mouth. "By Christmas, this'll be some Tokyo rice merchant's prize possession."

"That?"

"This, you bet your life," Noel says. "This, Cade, is the jackpot."

"You know what?" Stud whispers. "Bitsy wants kids."

"Well, she can't have this one," Noel says, and he laughs with Stud just staring, shaking his head.

The next night four Indian boys in jean jackets rose up in the wind on a red ledge above our Jeep. Noel winked at me and slowly leaned back. Stud turned a burrito in hot grease, our fire jumping. "Come have a bite," Noel called, but the kids fell away.

"Well," Noel said, "that 'bout knocks this spot on its ass. Got the old moccasin telegraph goin'. Some chief'll call the forest service sure as shit. First thing tomorrow we'll just hop over to another cave I heard about. I might even run the baby to town."

"I can go," I said.

"I know these roads."

"We'll everybody go," Stud said.

"For Christ's sake," Noel said. "There's trust for you. All right, we'll all stay. We move the operation and stash the goods till we're finished. Stuff's been out here this long."

I said, "We're talking what for the baby?"

"About the same as a rich live one you sell it back. One hell of a lot safer, though. How's thirty-five g's?"

"Enough for smart guys to stop on."

"Or to stay on," Stud said. "What's another couple of days, Cade?"

The sun set like a car in flames. Out of all that dirt and rock, coyotes wailed.

We tossed slugs of tequila and poked our fire. Clouds rolled in to hide the stars. "Kid," Noel said to me through the orange light. "You touch the baby, I'll bust your neck."

29 ——— FALLING

"Look what nature brung." Noel jerked back the tent flap.

Snow! A moving wall of wide flakes. The steady sigh was snow. No wind. The tent sagged. "It'll stop," Stud said.

"When, Mr. Weatherman?" Noel asked him. "An hour? How about a week? And tell me this, how soon are the Indians gonna drop in? Or how about some damn rescue patrol? We hustle now we got a shot at gettin' out."

With one lousy sweatshirt apiece was all, with just one windbreaker, which Noel pulled on no questions, we packed up. Last thing, Noel crawled back into the ground, into the black hole in that crazy smoke of snow, and fetched the baby. He wrapped it in burlap while we held a sleeping bag over him. Then he laid it down easy in a Styrofoam cooler. My pink hands ached. How long had it been buried?

We fishtailed, straightened, and dived. Gravity took us. "Like landing on a aircraft carrier in fog," Noel said. The tiny wipers scraped the glass.

"You did that?" I asked. Stud grinned back at me with the rifle between his legs. Noel popped a beer.

We shimmied down this skinny ridge and how Noel followed it who the hell knows? He pumped the brake and pumped it, slush all through his fringe of hair. "I busted my knee sledding one time," he said. The wipers squealed. We slid, wobbled, fell. Fell and kept falling until the bottom, where we twisted sideways and the engine roared out this huge cloud of blue smoke and died.

"No problemo," Noel said. The motor caught. But these thick-cleated, son-of-a-bitching tires just churned deeper in the mud. Twice we laid down mesquite, rocks, cardboard, the works, and pushed the damn Jeep out—just to have it sink, tilt, stall again. "Well, goddamn," Noel said.

Up to his ass in orange clay, his hair and eyebrows white,

Stud said, "I'm gonna fly over this place sometime and laugh. I am."

Still behind the wheel, Noel chugged the last of the tequila. "Fuckin' blizzard." He threw the bottle and it disappeared. He swiped a match at a wet book of matches, a cigarette shaking in his mouth. "Fire," he said. He dropped the matches. His chin bled into a red bead where it must have hit the wheel on the trip down. His red hands wrapped the wheel. "Christmas," he said, but his eyes were closed.

Stud stood on the passenger seat. "So okay," he said, and lifted the rifle. "Okay. We get a ranger." Three huge booms swallowed by the snow.

"A ranger?" I asked.

"Indians," he said.

"Right. Just who we want." And I knelt on the backseat and yanked our stuff out: beer, tuna, chocolate, toothpicks, tortillas, spaghetti, sausage, Sterno, shovels, tent, sleeping bags, flares. Chains. At the bottom in an oily cardboard box. Atlas Chains. But it was too goddamn late. My hands. My legs burned. My toes. The snow would not slow down. "The tent," I said.

My fingers, numb, fumbled with the poles. Stud and I stomped the stakes into mush and mud. The tent turned white. "Jesus," I said. "Look at him."

We dragged Noel from the Jeep, his face edged with snow, frost inside his nose. We pushed him through the flaps. We could not untie his boots. He drooled onto his cheek and groaned. "Christmas," he mumbled again once we'd wrapped him in a sleeping bag.

Stud got the rifle. I slid the cooler with the baby up beside Noel's head. My ears hurt. I zipped the flaps. To hell with food. Matches crumbled. My lighter caught. Fire—a Sterno flame, small and blue.

Stud smoked a number on his side in his bag.

I ached with wet cold curled in mine. I dried cigarettes over the blue flame, Camel filters, with a desert on the crumpled pack.

"You stupid goddamn, no-balled, chickenshit bastards," Noel said. His breath steamed, stunk. His chin had swelled, bruised. Gunk beside his eyes. Christ. He stuck his head outside, pulled it in, kicked back at Stud. "Assholes," he said. He kneed me.

"Watch it," I said. "You were damn near froze. No way to make it in that snow."

"The snow's over."

"Yeah, *all* over," Stud said.

Noel closed his eyes. Then he stretched flat so he could work this bottle of pills out of his pocket. He swallowed plenty. Stud fired a jay.

I pushed my face into the frozen air. The sky moved, purple, slid low over white stands of rock big as banks. "We got chains," I said.

Noel shook his head. "We got toothpicks, too." He wrapped his bag around his shoulders. "How far'd we get?"

"Down anyway." Stud said.

"Listen." Noel held a finger to his lips, cocked his head. "Nothing, I guess."

I said, "We could take the baby back in case somebody shows."

"You got snowshoes? Hey, nobody's comin' in this."

I said, "The slush underneath is freezing down."

"Get some sun tomorrow," Stud said. "Melt her."

"Into mud up to your mouth," Noel said.

"Here's what we do," I said.

Stud said, "I wouldn't put it past Bitsy to show up on a snowmobile."

"Here's what we do when she doesn't," I said. "We sit

tight till dawn, the very first light. Everything out there
ought to be about as frozen as it'll get, the best chance we
got for the chains."

Noel stumbled with the baby to the Jeep heaped with snow
in this crystal blue windless world. The moon was ice. We
waded in circles, hunting up our gear.

"Lunch at Wendy's," Noel said, his breath thick and
white. "You watch. Three big bowls of chili."

Stud swept the seats. Noel kicked trenches by the tires,
then stooped to mount the chains. "Goddamn redskins!"
he shouted. "Nails in every one." Stud fast swung the rifle
over all that empty snow.

For a long time we stood there in the blue light, getting
colder. I wondered how many ways it could end. "The
Injuns show again," Noel said, "we maybe trade."

"I'll tell ya," Stud said, "I wouldn't put it past Bitsy to
ride out here on a damn snowmobile."

Who did show up on snowmobiles somewhere around
noon, everything going to slush, were four rangers in green
snowsuits and silver shades, with pistols out as they roared
in a slow circle around us. Stud ate his last two joints.
"We got a call," a bearded ranger said once we'd crawled
from the tent blinking. "Looks like everybody's lucky
we did."

"Just a simple thing like snow," Noel said.

The grayest of the rangers, his pistol by his red ear,
opened the cooler. "Jesus," he said. "A mummy baby. Look
at that face."

"We just found it," I said.

The old ranger said, "So'd we. Lean up against that
Jeep."

Noel phoned his partner. Noel who? I heard him shout
clear in my cell. Stud said, "Well, Jesus, where is she?"

This fat guy who'd puked all over himself in the next cell said, "She's in Texas."

Ice was silver on the window mesh.

The rangers said we'd violated the Archaeological Resource Protection Act. "You're federal prisoners," the sheriff said.

The receptionist at Beehive accepted the charges. "Have Lance Arthur phone," I said. "Understand?" Old Man Arthur holed up most of the winter in Palm Springs, but I didn't want to risk getting him with a call to their house. The lady read the number back. "Tonight," I said. "This is serious." And I will never ask for another thing from them, I told myself. Ever.

The guard said, "Your arraignment's in the morning." He said, "Goddamn Mexicans," about the guys shouting in Spanish from the last cell on the other side. They'd laughed at us as they stumbled past.

Noel said, "Shut the fuck up down there." They hooted.

Stud said, "Sheriff's got to get us a lawyer."

"What's the worst?" I asked.

"Five big ones," Noel said.

"The worst," the fat guy said, "is getting hidden away so can't a goddamn soul remember where you went."

The light bulbs burned all night in their own cages.

The new guard had a black eye.

Noel said, "What about breakfast?"

"Takin' Mr. Cade here down the hall," he said.

"It wasn't easy," Lance said, the connection noisy.

The sheriff sipped from a mug at a desk in the corner—watched me. The dispatcher filed her nails. I said, "Oh."

"This embarrassed my father, Cade. He wants to leave all this."

"We just found the thing."

"That's what we told them. I know you, though, Carlos. Remember?"

"Like hell."

"Listen, when you hit town again, there's work at Bee-hive. Try to keep your nose clean. Make an effort."

"How about my friends?"

Noel said, "Jesus, man, how the hell'd you do that?" Dirty and starved, but laughing, we stepped into the sun out front of the jail.

"This genie in a lamp," I said.

"Well don't rub him the wrong way."

His partner's pawn shop closed, nobody answering the phone, Noel said, "The bastard." His truck hadn't budged from the alley, though. The side door screeched open when we weren't thirty feet away, and skinny Bitsy, in this shiny red jumpsuit, came loping out carrying a half-eaten donut, white powder around her mouth. "Hi!" She kissed Stud on the lips.

He pushed her off. "Where you been?"

"What do you mean, where have I been? Why right here where you left me. Aren't you glad?"

"Goddamn it," I said. "Let's go."

30 —— THE CATCH

Too much beer, grass, and a lot of lazy up and down, I stumble in around midnight. First, I smell cigar, faint, bit-ter. I close the door in silence with the rubber sole of my shoe and ease out my knife, let it warm in my hand. I crouch in the dark, slow my heart, my breathing, then inch around even though I don't for a second believe any fool'd be dumb enough to wait. Harassment is all this goddamn is. This isn't the dog boys. They visit the Suds. Why? Why not grill me at home? Because it's Shiftlet's? Because they're scared of accidents?'

And this? This visit? This is psychological warfare, smoke, a reminder, a nudge, nothing more. He thinks I'm crazy, has come to believe it, I'd bet my life. If it wasn't for what I've got on him, he would have straitjacketed me off to the state hospital a long time ago. He filed my mother. And how about my old man? Harmless. Born again too many times to remember, only to be used. I got the ranch instead. Now, he thinks he has me. He thinks, If I can just push that son of a bitch a tiny bit, the next step or two, he'll fall into the hole he's found.

I circle through the gray light, ready, take my word for it, to remedy some mother's mistake if anybody moves. This shit is going to stop, I think. The smell sweetens. A sappy, sticky kind of barber stink that I sure as hell would never pay for. Mr. Cat rubs my ankles. He would be hiding someone's there. He mews. I pat his side. Listen. I turn on the light. Mr. Cat's ear is scratched—a hairline of red from base to tip. "Tell me about it," I say. He mews. On the arm of the couch is a black spot in the green thread, a burn, stogie size. No ashes anywhere.

Everyone's perfect, Jill said. Right. The perfect past. The perfect present. The perfect blow to the perfect skull. A perfect hole in the perfect ground.

And at the dog fight, Florida had smelled sweet like this, but honest, sweet so I wanted to push my nose through her hair. She had squeezed my arm. And standing alone in the light from the wide hole in the barn as we bounced out of there, she had controlled everything, the air, the moon, the heat cooling from the blood on my hands.

I'm glad I do not have a phone, because I would call Lance and tell him he has reason to be scared.

I drink whiskey for a while. And sleep.

Ginny wanted us to camp in the mountains near a trout stream, with a fire in a circle of rocks and stars, never mind mosquitoes and ticks. "I love to fish," she said.

"Yeah, with my fly."

She'd get up at dawn " 'cause that's when they feed, dumb ass," and then fry her catch with potatoes and drink coffee with the grounds.

"But we don't even have sleeping bags. Let's just try an afternoon. Tomorrow. Somewhere close."

"I do know a place the state stocks. This guy I work with took me there one night."

"When?"

"Last year. Skinny dipping."

"Have a good time?"

"He was married."

"So?"

"So it felt funny."

We drove her bug to East Canyon Reservoir. You snake up a mountain forever, until sometimes you see hawks, eagles maybe, floating their long, smooth circles below. I sipped a beer, trying like a son of a bitch to come back from that other canyon, to snap the trance of all the morning's goddamn words and to forget the married skinny dipper when I did. "Any dope?"

"Didn't bring a thing," she said. This rainbow-striped bikini cupped her chest. In dark glasses, she looked a little like Tuesday Weld. Those thighs in those shorts. She wouldn't let my hand between her legs until we dropped over the mountains to the sage flats, magpies, a stream blue as the sky. She drank 7-Up and smoked Carltons and smoothed loose hair off her ears under the brim of a goofy fishing hat. She hummed. She smiled. Even a stinking, goddamn herd of muddy sheep blocking the road didn't get to her. She honked her way through and laughed.

Loaded down, eyes open for rattlesnakes, each of us

saying, "Shit, shit, shit," we hustled over orange dirt almost too damn hot for bare feet, and through scratchy blue sage, to the cool mud of the shore. The lake held an icy slice of sky, until some loud-mouthed ski boat chopped it all to hell. At the bank the water rocked scummy and thick with butts and cups and shit like that. Ginny opened two folding chairs.

We ate first, mayonnaisey turkey sandwiches, pickles, and chips. I emptied some beers. "Good it was dark for your swim," I said.

"You're right." She smiled. We rigged our poles, her poles. I'd fished plenty on the ranch, but Ginny added swivel, sinkers, and spooner as easy as buttoning her blouse. She waited, tapping her watch.

And cast—swiveled at her waist, a crease of smooth skin opening, her arm a quick clear circle—and laughed. On the transistor on her chair, Casey Casem took us down that week's top forty. Ginny hauled in two pan-size rainbows, nodded each time. She held them like friends and clubbed them with the butt end of a Swiss army knife. She slipped them into the Igloo and then splashed her hands in the lake to get off the slime. "They'll cook up real nice," she said.

I'd had four bites but no takers. Ca-sey Ca-sem introed number nine when—bam!—my rod nose dived and my line scribbled like crazy over the water. "Keep your pole up, up," Ginny said at my shoulder. "Let *it* play the bastard. You reel. Smooth." The fish broke, out about thirty feet, and splashed flat like a goddamn speedboat. "Shit," she said. "Monstro. Remember Monstro?"

My arms felt it now, the pull, the rush toward the darkest waters. I turned the reel and turned it. The fish *was* coming, goddamn it.

"He swallowed Gepetto. Pinocchio's father."

"You're shitting me."

"Pull up, pull up."

The son of a bitch burst out again, trying to shake loose of that ten-cent piece of metal that suckered him into the big finale.

He's strong, this goddamn fish, without arms or legs or anything, this storybook giant of a trout. It's all I can do to reel and reel some more. I am soaked. Ginny, laughing, "Oo, he's a beaut," wades up to her knees and scoops this piece of thrashing silver out of scum. The bastard flips in the net, which she holds with both hands, and won't quit. I take him, surprised at the weight. "Four pounds easy," she says, sliding her arms around me from behind.

He knows it is over and is still. When I bring the heavy stick I have found down on his sharp silver head, his eyes don't change.

She sits on my lap. I sip beer across her chest. She kisses my ear. "Loskie," she says. "You're a good dude, Loskie. You are. You like to have fun. You like the right things and all. I'm going to tell you something that could tick you off." She's crying.

"About the married guy?"

"Jesus, Carlos, that was nothing."

I hold her away. Her face is tense but not sad. Scared is more like it. Hot. "Come on."

"I'm pregnant," she says. "I'm pregnant with your kid and I'm going to keep it."

The sun dragged our shadows deeper into the brush. Mostly we stood, now and then sucking at cigarettes, the radio off. A few boats rumbled by. Here and there a trout threw itself out of the black water. The fish we caught arched inside a wave.

"You're pregnant?" I said. "Isn't this the twentieth century? Twelve-year-olds get the pill with Tootsie Rolls. Ginny. Even I know about diaphragms, and IUD's, and foam. Goddamn it, why the hell did you go and get pregnant?"

"It takes two to tango, Smart Ass."

"I figured you saw to business."

"Business. I should carry a card—Professional Screw."

"You know what I meant."

Steady, controlling everything else, she cried, her tears splashing tiny craters in the dirt. "Listen, you stupid asshole, I'm the one who's pregnant. I'm going to have a kid. Period. You can go screw yourself for all I care. Buddy, this is no shotgun wedding. I left those way behind in dear old Paul. I just thought . . . I just hoped you'd feel something is all. Hey, I told you before, I'm glad you never got hot to marry me."

"I do feel something." I felt Ginny's eyes. "Okay. What I feel is, you're strong. You are. You're going to make it fine, that's what I feel."

"Is that a promise? How about a guarantee?"

"Ginny, you should . . . get an abortion. Nothing to it."

"No." Now she sat, started another cigarette with the last. She flipped the stub into the black water. It sizzled. "I won't. And for your information, asshole, it's not like getting your ears pierced."

"That right?"

"That's right." Her lips tightened white. Her toes curled. "I ever kill another baby, I'll kill myself."

A baby. I touched her flat stomach. She wiped her face, the hat lopsided on her head.

"Whose was it *then*?"

"None of your business."

After a long time staring at her hands, she said, "A welldriller's boy. Drove all over Idaho. Came to my farm and on he went. I was fifteen and four months. I told my parents, my LDS parents, Jesus. My mother wanted the boy arrested. She ranted about the devil, about the serpent in the garden. My dad didn't work four days. They told me to let the church take care of things. The church runs this kind of adoption agency. Bad girls go live with good Mormon families and have their babies. The families keep the kids, the girls go home, and God's kept His hands clean.

"I said no. I had a razor blade hidden in a tree in the woods—I was ready—and they said go to my bishop and talk it over. I didn't want to talk—with anyone. 'Well,' Dad said. 'We'll see.' Saturday morning he left in his truck in a swirl of dust like I couldn't remember. By lunch he was back. By dinner I'd been to Idaho Falls, and by bed I was empty, my parents pressed up against me praying, hoarse. Someone'll saw down that tree someday and find a razor smack in the middle."

The sun. Long shadows. The water deepened. "So keep the kid," I said. She stood. I still sat. "It's up to you."

"Let's go," she said, pink as the sky.

"What did you want me to feel?"

"Forget it."

"What?"

"Well, maybe a little like I do."

"Which is?"

"I don't know."

"Which is?"

"Which is glad it's yours." Her lighter flashed. "Like maybe it won't be all bad. Loskie, maybe you'd like a kid. Did you ever give that a thought? Huh?"

And the light, her mouth, a warbler, the sting of mosquitoes. I laughed. I shivered, close to goose bumps, maybe tears.

She kissed my cheek, a quiet, soft kiss.

She said, "You're a shit eater."

I laughed louder. I laughed and pulled her over. "I'd give every lake your name."

She whispered, "I love you, asshole." Clouds bandaged the sky.

I said, "No you don't."

"Suit yourself."

We sat beside each other at a fire on the shore till nearly eleven. No dope. No sex. Just fire and stars. And guess what? We forgot that monster trout, left it out there in the dark.

I'm not scared to be happy. So I am happy, happy that she wants *my* kid, happy that she thinks I deserve it, that she thinks enough of this world to bring another asshole into it. But I'm ready, too. Always.

What's the catch?

Hell, we've only gotten it on about six weeks. Maybe she's not p.g. Maybe it's not mine. Maybe it's got no heart— no younameit. Maybe it's triplets, or quintuplets, or Siamese twins. Maybe it'll look like my old man. Maybe she'll lose it the day after we get hitched, if, *if,* that ever happens. Maybe she'll die pushing it out. Maybe it will grow up to be as rotten a son of a bitch as I am. Ha ha. Fat chance. And by then they'll need another one anyway.

In bed the next night—okay, I slept *there* mostly now— Charles Bronson killing faster than commercials, Ginny only smoked one cigarette. She wouldn't touch dope anymore, she said. She whispered, "This life of ours is going to work out. You watch."

31 —— *IN A CANYON, IN A CAVERN*

Her Volvo snarling like a guard dog, Jill dropped me off in the cold. She said, "Don't forget." The hot eyes that were her taillights snaked around the island and up her drive. Her exhaust slowly disappeared. I wondered if maybe I wouldn't sneak away with Jill all through high school and then marry her and work for her father or something. I thought that, light-headed with the frosty air, everything blue.

My old man whispered, in his toothless, wet way, "Whose pants you been in?" as I slipped by.

"My own."

He chuckled. Bedsprings creaked. Mama moaned.

As I lay there not giving a shit if I slept, I thought about how I'd been buck naked with a girl twice as pretty, for sure, as any my old man had ever set eyes on.

We didn't talk for two weeks. You can bet I caught her Volvo zipping all over hell. I couldn't turn around. And half the time I closed my eyes I saw her spider, ink and skin. But shit, I couldn't call her. And I wasn't fool enough to hang around her garage or anything.

Whenever I wandered through the neighborhood those chilly fall days and nights, I took my time—rerolling a cuff, looking over a car, watching little kids on the islands, where I'd been—hoping she'd drive by, maybe stop. Otherwise I stuck to the script I'd followed for a couple of years now: saw logs through school; afterward blast off on dope or glue; roar up and down State in some older kid's rusted-out shit can; stop for a Coke and a footlong if I'd managed to lay my hands on any change in gym class or the cafeteria; and go home with my head somewhere over the rainbow.

In here somewhere, Kennedy got shot. I liked his accent. I hated his kids. The principal sobbed over the intercom. They gave us the afternoon off.

The only thing about school that woke me up at all was some *High Noon* sort of warfare between the betas and the greasers: The betas had JFK's fluffed-up hair, stuck silver in their loafers. The greasers, hair heavy in oil, carried rat-tail combs in the back pockets of their tight pants. Nothing very complicated—the old story: them what has and them what hasn't. I played along. Sport.

I fought a big kid with the soft, know-it-all face of a teacher or a cop, because Danny bragged that no sissy, ass-kissing beta could beat Cade. This kid was the best they had. Fowels, or Bowels, or something. On weekends the coach trained him for Golden Gloves. His dad was an FBI agent. Everybody knew days before. Greaser girls brushed against me in the halls. Beta girls frowned, knotted tighter in their packs.

So Wednesday, at the head of this dead-end alley, bundled up like a bunch of goddamn snowmobilers, a crowd gathered clear from Farr's Ice Cream to the corner of Seventh East. I shivered in the center, a circle of breath and cracked cement, bouncing on my toes, blowing into my fists. Cassius Clay in Russia. Bowels pushed in wearing a Texas A & M sweatshirt and creased Levi's. He didn't look mad. He didn't look scared. He didn't matter. I hit him, and he hit me like I hadn't been hit before, right on the point of my chin, so that I slipped on an ice patch onto my left arm. It hurt like hell.

Then Bowels stood there, open hands halfway down, grinning like a queer. Pain or no pain, I kicked him in the nuts, laid a right across his forehead, and, when he was on the pavement—the crowd crazy—kicked him in that big soft teacher's face until blood ran out of his flat, twisted nose. Somebody dragged me off. Bowels didn't move. Ha ha. Buddies held my coat around me and elbowed through the crowd. Nobody patted me or said anything.

In his dad's DeSoto across from Farr's, Danny passed me a joint. He said, "Goddamn, you showed them what was what." But he looked at me funny, glanced off to other things, chewed his lip, and maybe I had overdone it in the fight. Bowels homered one punch was all. My jaw remembered. My left arm burned.

Quiet, small piece by piece the crowd was breaking up. Bowels finally rose to his knees, a couple of school officers holding him. You couldn't read his sweatshirt for the blood. Breath drifted away. And she drove by, slowly, Jill in her soft curls. Behind her there's this kid I don't even know kneeling and busted, probably still goddamn sure that difference meant something. For just a flash, Skink blinked back from my reflection in the window then—Skink!—his wide, glad face frosted on a mound of dust red as dead leaves.

"Catch you later," I told Danny. "Maybe tonight." My chin throbbed.

The sharp, cold air straightened my brain a little. Still, I wobbled toward home on stilts, stilts stuck in my shoes, toes spattered with blood. My gut hurt. Jesus, one punch and every goddamn muscle in my head cinched up around my skull. My arm.

A block, maybe two.

She honked. Orange leaves. I almost fell on some damn dentist's lawn. Her door jumped open. "I'd hate to be him," she said.

I backed into the seat, trying not to jar my arm. She squirmed past and locked my door. Her loose soft sweater. Her green skirt bunched above her thighs, her long leather boots. We pulled away.

"You all right?"

She turned on the radio, a crazy burst of "Surf City." Somebody honked three long times. "Eat shit," she said to the rearview, her eyes shining just then, the real joy of it all spreading through her lips.

I switched off the noise. I talked through my teeth: "Light me a smoke, will ya?" The cigarette didn't taste. The heater helped everything except my arm and my jaw. She touched my neck.

"You hurt bad?"

"A little." I took a drag and held it for the full goddamn effect.

Along dead slopes gashed with bloody, muddy ruts, we circled the university. She braked hard once for a red-footed, bounding Siamese cat. Something speared me in the head just below my ear. Whatever I did then, she was slow starting and a long damn time just squeezing my hands and staring at my face. After that I smoked and tried to hold my bones together.

Jill bought a box of Kentucky Fried Chicken on Foothill Drive. The smells: stuffing, fresh rolls, butter.

"Girl next to me in algebra," she said. "The suffering sister. How's that for coincidence? She moaned her baby brother was going to have a big, bad fight. With the devil. All teary-eyed she called you names and just *hated* all the attention she got. I'd seen the brother. I knew . . . I knew you'd be . . . tired. God, Carlos, you . . ."

Darkness almost hid the scrub oak, the boulders, the stream. I wanted all that—every sound, every stick. With just her fingertips, she led me across the bridge.

I swear I smelled our last time there. She made me lie on the couch by the fireplace. She brought me aspirin. "Take these." I touched her ear. Her hair. She massaged my arm. And her eyes rolled over me, over, and over, while I drank her old man's beer. "Eat some chicken?" she asked. She lightly kissed my chin. "Maybe later."

The logs she lit popped. Cracked. Finally my arm began to forget. With her boots on the floor and her stockinged feet tucked under her, she smiled when I reached inside her skirt. She moved my hand gently, fingers soft and smooth, nails tracing up my arm. "Not tonight," she said. "We don't need that tonight. Wait."

She took a book—*Listen to the Worm* or some damn thing—out of a dark case in the corner. She lifted my head into her lap. "Shut your eyes," she said. "I'll read to you."

But after two weepy, lost-love poems, her voice too loud, too strong, I said, "Spare me."

"Sorry," she said. And honest to God, she slid out, stepped to the fireplace, and dropped the damn book in. I couldn't laugh. She said, laughing, "I keep forgetting this isn't a TV show." She pulled her sweater over her head. She undid her bra, slipped it off, and sat beside me. "Just hold me gently. Okay? Lie back down." I wanted . . . "Just hold me."

The fire hissed. My good arm tightened across her smooth stomach, beneath her breasts, her face. The fire. Glowed.

And then, her sweater on, she rocked me slowly, held me, kissed my forehead. "Come on now, Champ. Come on." A new fire, pine logs split and rough and yellow, was already set. My empty bottles were gone. "Your face looks bad."

She sang quietly in the car in the canyon. We were hidden in stars. I ached, but I tried not to care. "You know what, Carlos? Some day you might hate me for all this. You just might." Her breathing went deep and she didn't sing again.

32 —— *AMATEUR HOUR*

Spud whistled me over the minute I showed up. He slid his door open, waving a newspaper. Sweat beaded the folds in his face.

"Spud?"

He let out a long sigh, inhaled. "Hey, so you and the Bat were buddies, huh?"

"The Bat?"

"I knew I'd seen the guy before. Two or three times he came through, wasn't it?" The paper trembled under my nose, behind one wide, dirty thumbnail. "I used to watch him on TV—but always in his outfit. He was mean."

Like a barbell on the front page—the headline, FORMER WRESTLER SLASHED, with a dark photo at each end. Probably a police shot, one picture showed Noel after the desert, back before he became Anthony, before the chains, the coat, the shirt, the tinsel hairpiece; his face empty of anything but patience, a mean load of patience; the face I remembered. The other was an eleven-year-old publicity pic of pro wrestler The Bat, a.k.a. Anthony Nicks, in this stoned-out crouch, as broad in the gut as my old man, in black boots and tights, and a black mask with white rings around two real, ugly, bulgy eyes and a pudgy mouth.

"What'd he want with you, Cade?"

"To wrestle," I said. He didn't smile. "Hey, see, he's a guy I used to know."

Behind the paper, I checked the street for serious traffic, trying to figure if all this meant a damn thing to me yet. I said, "He worked over at Stonehenge. I cook pretty good. They were lookin' for good cooks."

"And?" And God was Spud red. Mobile Stroke Lab One.

"It was only for two weeks. In the kitchen till midnight or one, then cleanup. No thanks. Got a girlfriend." Now he started to relax that punch bowl he stared out of. "Beats magazines."

I expected Spud to laugh at that, and he did, just the right amount if I was being friendly, but then he stopped real sudden just in case I wasn't, and got stern, if that's what all those new wrinkles were about, in case I'd forgotten who was boss. He blotted his forehead with a rag. "Nothing the police might be curious over?"

"I told you."

"Do me a favor, will ya? When you're on the job, keep the visitors down."

I held onto the paper.

And I was being sucked into some black place where my past always seemed to go, dragged in, everybody pushing.

I thought goddamn hard about not going home that night. About skipping town. But I had the note. I had the truth. I had Ginny. Ginny, Ginny, Ginny.

I bought her a six-pack of Welch's grape drink, which was where she was at those days, and a bag of Cheetos. She modeled the green bikini she wore—all of her. "This isn't going to fit too long. Better get my money's worth."

"Me, too."

"I'll lie out on weekends till I get fat."

"Good."

I spread the paper on her kitchen table and popped a beer. A spider dropped from the ceiling, hung there, shinnied back up. Somebody burned rubber, a high scream below. "Guy at school's uncle." I tapped the Bat on the chest.

"Jesus, Carlos. Everybody's dying."

"You got it."

"He looks like . . . like something a kid made up."

She sulked into the living room and flopped on the couch with a handful of paperbacks—name books for babies. I read Noel's obit again:

Noel's old man trained horses. Probably doped them, too. Probably trained dogs. No mention of a mother. Stud's real name was Yule. No kidding. Noel did a stint in Korea, then some time for forgery and armed robbery. Nothing about caves. No Indians. He "reformed," according to the paper, quoting his brother, "thanks to a helping hand from the present governor." Lance had taken him on, Stud said, as a bodyguard. Shit.

Lance got Noel started in the ring. The ring played out five years ago, but Noel, now Anthony Nicks, became manager of a club, Stonehenge—recently investigated for possible liquor and gambling violations. Stonehenge's owner, one Roland Musk, said Mr. Nicks was a "hard-working, effective manager," and called his killing "an act of savagery." Behind Stonehenge between eleven and twelve on Monday night, Mr. Nicks's throat was opened, as was his abdomen. DOA, University of Utah Medical Center.

The story saved its one real tidbit for last. Musk bought Stonehenge from Beehive Corporation. Good old Beehive had done right well by Old Man Arthur. Lance got controlling interest. Beehive sold Stonehenge in '80. How about that? The year Lance became governor. Manager Anthony Nicks kept his position under new ownership. Do tell. The Bat Fan Club had scheduled a memorial picnic the next afternoon at Liberty Park.

I flipped to the TV listings. I lit a smoke, pulled it deep. And what I saw then was an ad for Melody Lord all that week at the Westerner. Damn. Moon's heartthrob.

The Melody Lord show. Loud. Hot spotlights. Purple lips, cowgirl hat, blond hair, earrings like flashbulbs, pants somewhere between pantyhose and body paint. On a scale of ten, she got a six, down from nine because of all the "sweet-darlin' " talking she did between verses. Same old voice, but she could use it now. She knew how to moan through a slow number, along with her pedal steel, and Ginny and I swayed with our arms around each other in the yellow light on the crowded floor. "She just kissed some

cowboy right on the lips," Ginny whispered. "His woman
doesn't look too happy."

"He does." The grinning cowboy dragged his pouty girlfriend away. A lot of big cowboys sidled in close to Melody
Lord, but not the one I hoped to see. Between sets I parked
Ginny in a corner with a ginger ale. "She knew a pal of
mine."

"Glad you liked it," Melody Lord said. Sequined eye
shadow. She held her cigarette with her painted thumb and
forefinger, like a joint.

"I was wondering . . ." I said.

"Come on," her piano player said, a skinny guy in a Levi
jacket. "Give the lady a breather."

"Virgil Moon. You used to go with him. Still together?"

"Who?"

"With the truck," the piano player said.

"Oh yeah," Melody said. "He rolled his truck."

"Dead?"

"You kidding? You a cop?"

"I worked on a ranch with Moon. He ever tell you about
a bear?"

She smiled, tossed her head, primped her hair. "Yeah.
What's your name?"

"Carlos."

"There's a lot of passion in that name. Well, Carlos, it's
like this. The bastard's on top from what I hear. Married
some tail worth three and a half million bucks. Runs a
record company. Cut an album in the stores any day now.
He never did love me." She shook her head. Her pale blue
hat hung on the microphone. "He loved a couple of my
songs. And you know what? I never did love him." Her
chest had white tassels on it.

"Tell it, sister," the piano player said.

Ginny said, "What'd you expect?"

"I don't know. I thought he might still be with her."

"I'd say she's too hung up on herself to feel it for anybody right now."

We danced hard.

"You know," I said, during a slow one. The beer signs and the stage spread the only light. "She told me my pal has his own record coming out."

"And you believe her?"

"Sure, why not?" I lifted my head. "And I hope it sells a million copies."

33 —— CONVERSION

Spud wasn't in his box. Like the Oquirrh mountains had moved. When I had the rotors up and my first car rolling through, a lanky kid tan as chocolate, with this mangy pelt on his chin and a pony tail, poked me on the shoulder. "You're Cade?" His T-shirt said, DAIRY QUEEN.

"I am? No, you're Cade."

"C'mon. Name's Aaron. I'm Uncle Willard's, Spud's, nephew. Ulcer's giving him fits again. Called me to watch the lot. Said you could handle the bird bath. Aunt Dorothy's tryin' to get him to the doctor. Needs a tow truck. Want a M and M?" He held out the pack. "Mint." I shook my head. "Anything I can do, holler."

"Check."

Aaron wore camouflage cutoffs. He opened the box and leafed through skin books same as Spud. Goddamn it, though, if he didn't sell a red Celica GT to this square-shouldered Navy guy the first hour. Aaron saluted as the sale squealed away. "Sold one!" he shouted. "Just like that. You see me? Wrote a check. A check for sixty-nine, ninety-nine, ninety-five. I knocked off the tax. Bank says fineroo." He stood next to me, waving the check, laughing while he talked. "He wanted something sporty. Sporty! Goddamn." He bounced back to the booth and the magazines.

Ginny cooked the last of her trout. If you think you've had fish, think again. Crisp, buttery mothers—with almonds. And we talked baby names. I almost said my mother's name, Editha, but I didn't. I said, "George Washington Cade."

She said, "How about Abraham or Liberty?" Funny. Then fifteen minutes before Clint Eastwood and *Dirty Harry,* drinking Hi-C cherry in this sea-blue nighty with her nipples showing through, Ginny said, "Loskie, how come you never got married?"

"How do you know I didn't?"

"Did you?"

"Not in this life."

"And?"

"And who the hell knows why? How about you?"

She lighted her first cigarette of the night, shook the match, and laughed—too quickly. "Maybe all that Idaho stuff made me nervous, you know, about losing something . . ."

"But you'd already lost it. Just kidding."

"Control, I guess I'm talking about. Come on, though, Mr. Kidder. What's it for you? You must have had a chance."

"The chance? Some chance, promising someone and some storybook God you'll never be different, never change."

"God doesn't have to be in it. Judges can do it without a word on God."

"So, what's the point? Who the hell's the ceremony for?"

"For the two people getting married, asshole, who aren't

afraid of change. Maybe you've just never felt enough for anyone?"

I stretched and switched on the set. "Ginny," I said, while the ads lied, "marriage is for people who know what they're doing."

"And who's that, smart ass? Really. Who's that?"

I squeezed that soft little hot spot of hers. She squirmed. She said, "Screw you. Watch the movie."

Mr. Cat slapped flies from the screen, stripped off their wings with twists of his head, and smiled as they buzzed in dusty circles on their sides. I stopped talking. I turned off the cassette.

Four months and I'd be thirty-four. Older than Christ. Just where my hair used to puff out so goddamn right on each side of my head, two gray patches were spreading. Drainage ditches next to my eyes. Teeth stained. White hairs on top of my nose. My paunch folded over my bronco buckle when I sat down. My back popped. My pecker dripped. Fast going to sleep and slow getting up. Sure, I tried. Fifty push-ups when I thought of it. But my kid coming into the depot left me thinking too damned often how soon I might be going out. And maybe I'd hop the real thing and vamoose, as a birthday present—to both of us.

But then I caught myself. I crushed my cigarette and turned on the tape recorder. "I am not my old man," I said, "and never will be."

"Uncle Willard's still under the weather." Aaron wore a T-shirt air-brushed with a he-man's physique. Hell, for a second I thought he didn't have a shirt on at all. "And with *his* gut, that's a shit load of weather to be under." He laughed, his eyes white, until he realized I didn't. "I'm just here keeping everybody honest." Stenciled across his back was EMPEROR'S NEW CLOTHES.

I hadn't been there an hour, when the hairy bastard leaned into my bay, whispering, "Hey, Cade. There's this blond chick wants to see you. She was scoping this Lincoln town car. She spots you and her jaw drops. Kind of acquaintance every dude needs. She slipped me ten bills to let you off a while. No problemo. She says it won't take long. I'll bet it wouldn't."

I'm no fool. I wondered about it, but she leaned, her arms folded behind her back, against a yellow Porsche at the curb. The kid ran the next bay flipped me the bird, wagged his tongue. Welcome to Wonderland.

Florida lifted her dark glasses and left them on her hair. Her hair blew in smooth curls around her cheeks and neck. She wore a hippie blouse open way down her cleavage, green shorts, and little silver shoes, her toenails painted to match her eyes. Her lips were red wax. "Hi, Carlos."

"Small world."

"I couldn't believe it was you. I thought sure you'd've come see me."

"You've crossed my mind."

"You've crossed mine," she said. She reached around my head and pulled me close. "Let's go somewhere."

Ginny did not smell like that, didn't know half of what those fingers sliding circles in the wetness on my shoulders knew. "Well? A half hour, Carlos. We'll talk. You drive."

A dirt pull-off in Memory Grove. She told me Danny had said I could be trusted. She missed Danny. Her chest rose under her hand. She twisted a Kleenex in her lap. She smelled like spring. She put a hand on mine. Rings, round flowers of rock, on every finger. The cool air up my pants. The engine idled. I squeezed her hand. She smiled. "I'm scared," she said. "Real scared, Carlos." She lowered her hair, her head, onto my shoulder. "What happened to Danny? And that dog got taken. Now Tony Nicks."

"Hey," I whispered. "It's okay." But her hand had moved between my legs. Her lips against my chin.

"Tell me what's going on."

I cut the engine, pulled the key, opened the door. The stream sounded like tinfoil unfolding.

From the car, she said, "I'm a woman needs help sometimes, Carlos. Come on. You don't need to hide on me."

"And you just stumbled over me at work, right?"

"I won't lie," she said. "I don't. I knew you were there. Cops told me when they asked about Danny. I thought I'd spook you if I just showed up for you. But that's what I did." She took a pill box from the glove compartment. She tossed two into her mouth and gulped. "We'll take a night out sometime. You'll tell me why I shouldn't be scared. I'll give you all I got. Carlos, I got it all." She touched her chest, that tan V of rising skin. A pickup rattled down the road behind us, two teenagers, a boy and a girl, with a malamute in back, with Elvis on full-blast. "Heartbreak Hotel." I tossed my smoke into the water.

"Florida, I don't know anything more than you." The sun broke like glass in the trees. "But if you want to talk, stop by when I get off some night. At ten."

"I'm working."

"An off-night. No hurry. Hey, my time's about up."

When she smiled, her long teeth were too far apart and yellow. And she tried to kiss me when she dropped me back, but I couldn't.

"I bet I got it figured," Aaron said. "Her husband's at a medical convention right now, probably talking about

money, about his investments with some young squeeze
from the bar."

The next morning I felt loyal to the entire son-of-a-bitching
world. But my coffee had barely dissolved when three times
a heavy fist pounded my door so hard the key clattered
out inside. "Hold your horses," I yelled. Already I stood
on a chair in my closet, sliding my tapes and notebooks
back over the ceiling tiles. "Take it easy."

Bobby Bull Shiftlet carried an attaché case, one hundred
percent alligator—dead. He kept the other of his pile-
driver hands in his coat pocket. Thick, icy glasses. "Carlos,"
he said, with his whispery lisp. He lifted the corners of his
mouth in this long, steeped-in-deodorant pause. After staring over my head at my rooms, he cleared his throat and
said, "Mom's recovering better than they'd hoped. She'll
have her own room. She likes the pies. A survivor."

"I'm glad."

"She asked for Danny once. Doctor said don't hide things
from her. I told her the truth. What I know of it. You never
called."

"Nothing to say."

"That happens." His gold chain slipped up his hairy wrist
when he tucked his glasses in his breast pocket. "Right now
everybody's quiet. Especially the wrestler. He's real quiet.
You wouldn't know anything about that." I shook my head.
He tilted his and glanced over my shoulder again. "Since
I do owe ya, I'll take your word. Your word *is* good, Cade.
I'm sure it is. I dropped by about something else. Mind if
I come in?"

Mr. Cat leaped from the counter and raced for the bedroom. Bobby Bull set the attaché between his legs, tugged
up on the creases in his pants, and sank onto the couch.
"Mom loved this building, *loves* this building. I was born in
number seven. Did you know that? Lucky seven."

"I thought she told me five," I said. I parked backward on my work chair.

"My dad's repair shop was in five—till he died. God-damn building. Hell, I could have given her a house on Walker Lane, a dozen houses. This place was her obligation, she said. Always swore she'd die anywheres else. Might as well have. Yup." Now he looked at me, patted his curly head. "Times change. I love my mother, don't get me wrong."

I put some more water on to boil, leaned against the fridge, and blew smoke at the floor.

"Cade, it's like this: With Mom gone and this part of town getting so damn neat and clean all of a sudden, the savvy business decision is to turn this place into condos. You've probably thought of that. The smart old people with money are staying in town, planting themselves in their own apartments to have as few headaches as possible."

"The rich old people."

"There you go. Hell, you can see what the sense of it is. World's a dangerous place. Money's holding us up right now. You got to keep money strong. You got a month," Bobby said. "Plenty of time. I'm payin' you back by bringing this message personal."

A month. Months mattered. Used to be days. Hours. Shit, I'd had minutes matter more than whole years. Seconds. Getting old.

"Cade." Shiftlet stood and threw a left jab at the window so he could check his watch. "You seem smart. You got nerve."

"What I got is a shitty job, no apartment, and half the town after me with questions."

He twisted a pinky ring, a ruby-studded horseshoe. "We've *got* questions. And the job's your choice. Your connections'd get you work. Also, the thing is, I need a good boy right now, Cade. Worth a couple hundred. Might even

find you another nice place. You and your girlfriend." For
a second I thought Florida, that somehow that was *his* game.
But he said, "She took it real nice. She said she'd be grateful
if I could turn up something."

"We'll turn up something. And hey, money isn't way up
on my list. I can manage."

"Is that right? Easy money? I just need somebody to
check in from here every couple of days." His attaché had
combination locks. "I don't want any bleeding-heart shit
hitting the fan when another building converts."

"This town loves conversion."

"You know what I'm saying, from rental to private. Ran-
kles some people. Could be a few of Mom's prize tenants'll
drag their heels, make noise."

"These geezers don't even make water they're so damn
quiet."

He opened his glasses, covered his tiny eyes, adjusted
his shirt cuffs. "A few phone calls is all it is."

"They'll *go*. You don't need spies. Wherever the hell
people always go."

"A month, Cade. You're making some hefty mistakes."
I flashed across his lenses when he turned.

For twenty minutes or so I leaned on the edge of my
table, talking to Mr. Cat about the chances people never
really had, about my chances, about his odds of a yard
someday thick with spinach-green grass crawling with mice.
I smoked Pall Malls and my coffee tasted like salt.

I laughed, because most of the time only a laugh will do,
and went into the hall. Nobody plotted on the landing. Big
surprise. Did they know? Eighteen separate doors. Someone flushed. A rush of water in the walls. Maybe the news
had moved one of those sorry, broken, tottering relics to
shit this morning's Product 19 into the rusty pool given
each boarder to perch above, ass bare.

Ginny fiddled with the elastic of her turquoise shorts.

Was it her toilet, her call to arms? Her TV flickered without sound. Wile E. Coyote shot by Roadrunner over a cliff. He didn't fall. He looked at me, his red eyes bulged, his mouth opened, and then, in three tiny puffs of smoke, he dropped. The sound would be a bomb falling. Ginny turned it off. "How 'bout some black stuff?"

"Sure," I said. "Got a cigarette?"

"By that little poodle on the table. Thought you were cutting down."

"Or I'd light two or three right now. Shiftlet drop in?"

The cups steamed. She crossed her legs. "About redoing the place? Yeah."

"He didn't tell you to amscray."

"Gave me a month. That's enough. Four weeks. This ain't the Hilton."

"So we'll move to the Hilton." I touched her cheek.

"I can stay with these two friends of mine in Sugar House if I have to. Moving goes on the bottom of my worry list."

"We'll find a place."

Now she heaved enough breath to tease my hair, and slumped farther on the couch. Her eyes fluttered. "You know I like you, asshole. I've told you. This baby can have purple eyes and purple hair and purple problems up the wazoo for all I care. I'm keeping it. I'm keeping *your* kid. I told you you don't have to marry me. You don't. But listen, you stupid shit, you stupid, stupid shit, if we move in together, I'm gonna be your wife, your dumpy, little pregnant wife. That's the only way I can do it. It is. I'm scared, but I need to be tough, and I won't be tough if I depend on you and you can leave, and . . ." She reached her cup onto the table. "We're together," she said, eyes wild. "Or we're not."

"You're my lady, Ginny." I curled her damp hair around her ear. She lifted her head. "I've only really wanted one

other person before. You're good. You're good and real—
and, Jesus, what a swimmer in the dark." Her mouth shivered. I laughed. "But you don't know squat about Carlos
Cade."

"Marry me."

"I'm bad medicine. Poison."

"Marry me. Just do it. Just marry me. Have some balls
and marry me."

"Shh. Hey, calm down."

"That's all I need," she said.

So I lied. I put my arm around her shoulder, wrapped
my fingers through hers without rings. She lifted her pearl
blue eyes, too pretty for the likes of me. I had business,
that's all I had. And she'd be fine.

And after we drove all over town checking out places to
rent, me getting loaded, Ginny chest-deep in the classifieds,
nothing turning up without orange shag carpet or decals
on the fridge, she separated eggs and baked me an angel-
food cake. She whistled, something slow from a musical.

We held each other. Beneath us someone coughed up
through the ceiling, mumbled, and dropped something
heavy, an iron or a kettle, or maybe just dropped. We quit
for a second or two, listened to the tick of Ginny's watch.
Then she moaned and lifted her back. My back snapped
straight and I'm sure I groaned, too, as we pulled.

34 —— ALMOST DEAD

The fight with Bowels will not go away.

My jaw has a knife in it, heavy and hot, that moves
whenever I do and even when I don't.

When I think I'll start to shout, I get out of bed. I zip
my coat but I'm frozen before I'm even up the alley.

Snow starts to swirl in big, twirling soap flakes that dissolve on my coat at first but then gather there. I can see ahead a house or two. The streetlights in the snow are burning fuses. A doctor could stop this.

Doctors. I have seen very few. Hilda broke her arm once. Who fixed it? Twice a year my old man dragged me to the county health building. With him picking at a mole on his cheek, we rode the bus to a red brick box. They looked in my ears and rubbed my arms with cold alcohol before they stuck me. That was where the son of a bitch got the pills for my mother, too. Fat ladies at the desks said, "Hello, Lester." Once, before he could reach, a lady handed me those shiny brown bottles crammed full of hard white pills.

White pills melting.

The laundromat, empty, is hot and steams into the dark. *Reader's Digest*. Candy bars. Bleach. I have got a pocket full of change, so I put my coat and socks in a dryer. The floor is warm. I turn on a TV chained to the wall, for fifteen minutes of some woman telling about tomorrow's weather.

When the snowy cop comes through the door, he lifts off his hat and hits it twice against his leg. "What's the trouble, son?"

I want to say my clothes got wet and I ducked in here to dry them. I can't talk. He bends down. I groan, "I'm okay," but it sounds like groaning.

"Better have that face checked out."

"No."

I point to the dryer. He gets my things, a good guy who stinks of cigars. He helps me with my socks, my coat. When we are outside, losing the warmth, another cop steps away from the window, blinks white eyelashes, and says, "Well?"

"Looks to have a busted jaw."

"Probably slipped on the ice," the other cop says.

"Yeah."

I slide into the back of their very warm car.

My old man trudged in wearing a beat-to-shit gray overcoat and a red plastic rain hat. He hobbled like his knees hurt, followed by a tall man in a shiny, blue suit, squinting through heavy glasses.

"So he's your boy?" the tall man asked.

"Sorry wasn't me did it." My old man stood there in that overcoat and the hat. A little spit bubbled on his lips.

"We're waiting for the swelling to go down," the tall man said. He patted my leg, then left.

Left my old man breathing hard. "When you're fixed to come home, call Hickler.

"What you starin' at, boy?" he all of a sudden said to J.J. Flyte, the black kid in the next bed. J.J.'d run into his sister's ex-boyfriend in a bar.

J.J. grinned, *his* mouth already wired.

Mama never came—no surprise. What did surprise me, though, Hilda, always smiling, stopped by afternoons. She'd slip out of her dark sort of pea coat, and even the old polygamist in the corner opened his bloodshot eyes for that sometimes. When she sashayed closer, skirt sliding over knee-socked long legs, I loved my sister and hoped she'd be a movie star.

Hilda brought me a lime green, stuffed dinosaur with snaggly white teeth. "He looks just like you with your chin all bruised out like that. My dinosaur man." She wedged it over my headboard. "You know, it's time you stopped being . . . being so hard on yourself."

"Yeah," I mumbled, "I shouldn't have slugged me."

"Just try. Even Danny Ingus says this stuff's gone too far. He came by to see about you. They suspended the other kid in the fight. You're smart, Carlos."

Later, after Hilda left, J.J. Flyte said, "Danny Ingus? A friend of yours? I know Danny. He gets around." J.J. went to South High. "Man, me and him got loaded at this canyon party the other weekend. He's still in ninth grade?"

"Held back or something. Wild guy."

"Tell me. He had some drunk chick in the back of his car showing off this tattoo."

"Tattoo?"

"Right up on her thigh between her legs. This Cupid. Shit. He even had a gun."

The night before *I* would be wired shut, Lance peeked in, stepped in shy as a cat. He carried a big envelope with both hands—the skull ring long gone. This is the first time I remember Lance and Hilda together. Hilda stopped whatever she said and stood. Lance, in beta boots, tan cords, and a yellow parka, stared. Swallowed. Hilda said, "Carlie doesn't talk too well."

"Oh." Lance glanced at the envelope. "Hilda . . . Hilda, do you think I could see Carlos a minute on my own?" Those freckles, his cowlick, the same lift to his mouth, everything—I saw him on the limekiln made from stone. "Just for a second?

"I heard the guy who hammered you couldn't see till yesterday he got so puffed up," Lance started, his hands turning the envelope and turning it. "You're tough." He winked. The young politician. "But, Carlos, I'll tell you, I think this beta, greaser stuff is nuts. Fighting over nothing."

On TV, Lucy, in some Mexican outfit, with a big mustache, and Ethel too, shook their heads at Fred and Ricky reaching through the bars of this little adobe jail in a desert.

Now Lance blushed. He whispered, "She told me to bring you this."

Her blue handwriting. Why didn't she come? He said, "Okay," lifted an open hand. "So long." He squeezed by Hilda at the door.

The envelope smelled like cigarettes and soap. An angel in a blue gown folded just out from the silver card, an angel in fiery light, an angel with Jill's face smiling, where she had glued it. JOY TO THE WORLD was stamped inside. A smooth, blue scrawl at the bottom said, "Your present has a spider on it. The black widow. Get better. How could you? More than love, Jill," over x's, a whole row.

My mouth is too small. The nurse pulls the tubes up my throat, out of my nose, and I can breathe. I tingle. With another hose, she siphons my sinuses—Shuhhhh. My eyes water. I am alive.

J.J. blinks from a parade float that is a bed, and this white-white parade float of a nurse holds out a marshmallow and swabs around my nose. My head is packed with fat, warm water balloons.

That afternoon, dressed, standing alone next to my bed, J.J. spreads his silver smile. "Dinosaur Man," he says, not too loud. "You're all right. I always got deals goin'. You need anything, you got my number. Rattle my door sometime."

Hilda said, "I'll bet my dinosaur's ready to leave."

"Like a comet."

"Guess what. Jill Arthur's driving you. In her brand-new car." The mountains rose right there, white outside my window. "Lance must have asked her or something. She stopped me in the hall today and offered."

"I thought you two . . ." I said. "You know."

Hilda's face tightened. "I . . . I don't even dislike her anymore. She's spoiled and everything, but . . . what it is is I feel sorry for her. I do. How she's always sort of . . . separate. Know what I mean? Not loneliness exactly, but sad, sad clear through."

"I guess. Hey, I might stay that first night at Danny's or somewhere. There's no point in hurrying home."

"Suit yourself."

"They won't even know I'm out of here, for all they'd care anyway. What the hell's the matter with them?"

Hilda brushed the bangs from her eyes. "They're . . . They're all right. They're just jealous, I think. Jealous of everybody."

I nearly slept in Jill's heated car, the blue sky blinking past. In the slush of the turn toward the canyon, I said, "I'm glad."

"What? Oh, Carlos, you silly." I put my hand on the cool skin of her leg beneath her plaid skirt. "Hold on there, stranger. Let me drive."

I smoked. "Thanks for coming," I said. "Gutsy."

"Just nuts."

The plows had cleared right up to the last, drifted leg to her cabin, logs chinked with snow. She tightened her arm inside mine. Smoke swirled from the stone chimney, around a white moon already out, a cold eye over the crusted trail, the frozen bridge. When she closed the door, I leaned toward her, but she pressed me away from the warmth, the fire, toward the bear's yellow teeth, the covers folded open. "Take off your clothes. You don't look too frisky."

"Frisky enough."

The spider. When Jill stepped through the door without a stitch, she said, "I don't want to hurt you."

"You couldn't," I said. "Not now."

35 —— *THE NORTH POLE*

Ho ho.

My old man's last Christmas home, five weeks or so before he took off, was damn near merry, thanks to Hilda.
Like I said, she came into her own her first year of high
school, with something definite about her laugh and her
green eyes that kept her apart and a little more important
than anybody I ever saw with her. Now girls' fleshy mothers
were all the time picking her up or dropping her off. Her
job played a big part in it, I'd bet, a place where she was
loved for the striking young woman she suddenly loved
becoming, where no one pretended beauty could be more
than skin deep. In spite of my old man, boys elbowed each
other all over her life, I'm sure, even though I only saw a
couple tagging after her. But Hilda possessed herself then,
every pore—no mirror, mirror stuff. She carried her bones
like royalty. Or deer.

Over vacation she worked hard and had lots of new
clothes to show for it. No matter what the weather, mothers
still pulled in and out. My first weekend back, Hilda went
skiing with some Italian family. They strapped orange-
crate slats to their Saint Bernard's feet, she said, and skied
it down the mountain. Jesus.

Her life spilled over into the house. Christmas with it.
She bought a sack of candy canes and one of sticky mint
Christmas trees that I sucked between my cheek and my
wires for days. She taped shiny paper reindeer and Santas
in the windows. Mama said, "Pretty."

Papa said, "If Christmas ain't a crock . . . Like worship-
pin' comic books."

Hilda laughed, shaking her head, her curls. The Mormon Tabernacle Choir sang "Jingle Bells" on the radio on
the stove.

Hilda almost always brought home some new treat and waited to take off her fuzzy coat until Papa had tasted it—a cheese ball, a pecan log, peanut brittle. Then Mama got a bite, straining the scrawny strings of her neck. "God, that's good," Papa would say. He would kiss his finger and touch Hilda's forehead.

Mama would just say, "That's enough, no more. Thank you. Yes, yes."

All those sweets damn near drove me bonkers, wired up the way I was. But Hilda smelled like sugared berries and cream, or lilacs, and when I was there I glanced at the door as often as anybody, hoping she'd burst in.

Sure I went out those nights into that winter frozen clear through, even though my old man wanted me in by nine o'clock sharp, no shit, or busted jaw or no busted jaw the antenna would sing carols on my precious ass. I bowled sometimes. Bowled! Those crazy Ingus brothers coat hangered into a Mercedes outside a ladies' club on South Temple and hot-handed a doctor's bag tucked up under the dash. With the dough they made on the jet fuel in that bag, we could have bowled three lines a night for fifty years. In the chips. Danny bought a diver's watch. He wore a leather coat with silver studs and a hat to match. It goes without saying he was fired out of his mind all day and that the money wouldn't hold out till the first of the year.

Okay, I got plenty loaded too. What the hell? Five-to-nine or so, I'd traipse back to the rot of the Cade family shack. Shrink. Pull a chair up to the kitchen table. Usually the old man had soup steaming in a dented kettle on the stove—"dinner." I slurped through those goddamn wires while he sucked on Pall Malls and spit tobacco flecks at his shoes. The radio shut up only in the dark, and now it buzzed its scratchy Christmas tunes over and over. Sometimes Mama called out something crazy from a dream.

Three nights before Christmas, some chickenshit chicken broth scalded the living Jesus out of my tongue. I rifled the bowl into the refrigerator and leaped up, pushing my chair over. I tore Santas and snowmen and reindeer and popcorn strings off the front door. The old man thumped me so hard alongside my head I dropped onto my knees. He'd drunk enough to miss my jaw. "Get your butt to bed, you son of a fucking bitch. Git." The door jumped open as I got to my feet. Hilda—in an icy white powder.

She looked us both in the eyes. She cried. "It's Christmas," she said. "It's Christmas, for God's sake." She hurried through our parents' room and slammed into ours.

In that rusty squeak of hers, my mother said, "Father's a big man, ain't he. Beats on kids is what he does."

I cleaned up. The old man slurped instant coffee and smoked until *Public Pulse* with some damn Paiute chief for a guest. The chief said his people had lived in the desert for centuries.

"That's living?" my old man asked, his eyes crinkled up.

Hilda knew words. That Christmas vacation my turn came.

I lit out early the morning after the old man knocked me down, before the papers, before the plows scraped darkness back onto the streets. My hands ached in the cold of my shitty pockets. I passed Hickler's, head down, feet dragging, and a quiet voice said, "What you running away from?" As if he didn't know, Pep, his *Tribune* bag creasing his shoulder, stood grinning stringy clouds beside a snowman. His eyes, with frosty rims, funneled into his shallow face. Blinked.

"Just running," I said. "From Christmas."

He laughed. He clapped mismatched mittens.

I walked. Downtown. I needed buildings to get warm in, where I could wait—and wait and wait. My jaw wanted to shatter. My toes splintered into my feet. Jesus.

Warm ghosts of car exhaust haunted each intersection. I passed no one. My short footsteps hated the smooth sidewalks. Cold kept me moving. When the sun finally bloomed around my frozen shadow, God how bright the snow was then, white, white, white.

The Hotel Utah lobby. All I could think of. What a nervy little shit. Patched jeans, a too-small, oil-stained, phony sheepskin coat, a broken mouth. I told the old fart who wandered in every ten minutes or so that I had orders to meet my dad there, a repairman. "What's he coming to work on?" One hand tightened on my sleeve, dead eyes fastened on my awkward lousy mouth.

"Screwy hookup on your angel outside."

"Oh," he said.

Their Christmas tree damn near touched the two-story lobby ceiling. I catnapped in a deep, warm chair and looked at the million sparkly trinkets dangling from the limbs.

At quarter to nine, I shook myself out and zipped my coat. A hand squeezed my shoulder. The old fart dead-eyed my mouth again, only this time he smiled—a gold tooth, flecks of food. "Take it," he said. He pushed his other hand at me. Five bucks.

"Merry Christmas," I said. "Really."

With a passel of blind women beside the *Trib* Christmas tree, a nun looked me square in the eyes and said, "Peace on earth." When I finally made the library just before ten, I was warm and up: warm with hot eggnog from Walgreen's fountain, up with five cups of java—pass the sugar. I paced the place, the Children's Corner to the record collection. Pardon me. The radiators, hung with green and red tinsel, creaked and hissed, and the dusty, musty, trusty air smelled like Gandy.

With over three hours till two, I checked out the manger

scene, chipped plaster figures splotched with paint; ink drawings of one-armed John Wesley Powell; a cloudy glass case of pink, petrified dinosaur eggs, hard-boiled, by God. And not far behind the desk and the dumpy, puckered duo of petrified librarians stood a long, black table of books with honest-to-God, beat-to-hell cowboy boots for book-ends. Above it on the wall, a lariat looped wide around fat, branding-iron letters: ZANE GREY—WESTERNS OF THE PURPLE PAGE—whatever that meant. In a tight, warm cor-ner with a radiator on the second floor, my damp coat wadded behind my head, I started in on *Riders of the Purple Sage.*

Lassiter. Black leather, lightning. The awful ache some-where deep in my teeth got lost in that desert, in Lassiter's fury, his cold courage and purpose, in Jane Withersteen's helpless, beautiful heat. A woman of words. Wild horses of words.

And *the* Word. Bishop Tull. I knew Mormons, and Tull fit just fine with what I knew—full of GOD, feeling zilch, human as a rattlesnake. Sure, Hickler damn near redeemed the whole lot. Damn near. All those Christ-eyed kids, though, with White Stag parkas, and thermoses of hot soup, and collies that fogged up car windows in parking lots, in their guarded, postured groups at quiet lunch tables, not a gold-plated word for anyone who didn't stink with Dial or Dentyne. Age 'em. Fatten 'em. The sheepdog sheep of the purple sage. Just ask Lance.

For two and a half hours I lived those words as fast as I could and faced down the meanness in life with Las-siter: That Arabian son of a bitch of a shop teacher who straight-armed me into the storage closet and said he'd plug my thumb into a dangling, goddamn light socket if I ever wrecked anything else. He called me "godless." Lassiter had his number, for damn sure. Pow! And the fat, hairless slob with the jobs passing out phone books, who asked what ward I belonged to and said, "Give somebody else a break," when I told him I didn't. Lassiter hardly even bothered over shitheads like that. He knew what mattered—right from two-bit righteousness—and so did I. I ran my finger under each line. I rode with Jane at my back.

By two o'clock I'd walked the place again. I'd pissed twice in twenty-five minutes. My jaw ate through my face. With her mittened arms held out like wings, Jill ticked her heels like clocks through the silence, trailing a long, tasseled, green scarf. "There's my dinosaur. Come on." She led me into the stacks. Under her knit cap, her soft, sweet hair, her blushing face, her mouth round and open. We kissed between a map case and a dusty shelf of poetry.

She hugged me with her hands moving, and I undid her bra, squeezed her chest, sucked her neck until my knees would not stay locked. She said, "Oh, God," and fell away, sat, laughing, her legs straight as the chair's, in blood-red boots. She looked again and laughed, eyes shut, chin up, and I looked too. If my pecker wasn't pole vaulting right out of my pants, I'm Joseph Smith.

And that was that. Silence. Snow. Icy trees. I caught my breath and sat across from her at that wide pine table. Between us our initials filled the ragged heart I'd carved two days before. This was not enough. The cabin was enough. We'd been back twice.

Her blouse rose high. She smiled as she fastened herself. Her stomach was damp. "Lance is right. You're trouble."

"Lance?"

"He asked me why someone like you."

"Like what?"

"A loser. He says you'll ruin me."

"He's smart."

She laughed against my hand then kissed it. "All he really knows is the card at the hospital and that sometimes I meet you here. He just plays he-man, shakes his fist, and says he'll tell Daddy if I don't stop. He won't."

"He might."

"You're right," she said, "he might. Who cares?"

"Daddy?"

"He wouldn't believe it."

"You'd lie?"

"On a stack of Bibles, I like you so much." She flicked the tips of my fingers with her tongue. "But you don't really like me, not really. I'm just different, huh? That's all."

"That's enough."

"Promise?"

I grinned. I yanked the back of my hand across my teeth. Then I held her fingers, blood gathering at the cut below my knuckles. "I promise." I pressed my hand, palm up, onto the heart.

She saw me to a chocolate shake and left me on a shoveled corner two blocks from home. Her father was throwing a party at the cabin that night. Jill had to eat at her aunt's. "I'll miss you. I wish I didn't have to go to that club garbage tomorrow. Daddy needs me on Christmas Eve, though. He does. I'll see you on Christmas. Dream about me all over you. I'll dream it, too." Her Volvo's tail wobbled in the slush. I waved.

Lassiter rides again.

Visit number two to the Arthur stronghold. The cold burned my nose. My breath hissed into silver balloons and sank onto the swept, iceless concrete of their porch. I shivered in the empty light. A red banner ribbon across the holly wreath on the door said NOEL. I rang the bells again.

She'd driven out not five minutes earlier. The Volvo slipped on the slope of the drive and lost itself in snow. After a couple of shitty, restless hours at the laundromat— *my* laundromat—and a sticky little donut shop that smelled like rotten milk, I'd staked out my street. Once she was gone, I stomped a tingle back into my feet and worked my way down a slick sidewalk to that porch, to those three clear chimes inside. My mouth hurt.

The pen light of the peephole darkened, flashed back. A lock snapped, the latch popped, the door sighed wide with heat. Lance, light flaring behind him, looked like a goddamn religious painting. Try Christ in the tomb. In a tweedy suit and a blue tie, each hair in its place, this was the Lance of the glossy posters in the school halls, the Lance of the goddamnedest, most dignified smile you ever saw, the Lance that ran for Bryant president and lost, but would only lose once more in his life. Say cheese! "Carlos." The opening narrowed around his shoulders. "How's the chinny, chin, chin?"

"Broken. Your old man here?" I was losing the frostiness, the pain. I was losing.

"Listen, Carlos, I've got a . . ."

"Your old man here?"

"No, my . . ."

I pushed past him onto the deep, green carpet of the hall. I could smell roast beef. Without taking off my gloves, I undid my coat and waited for my face to relax. "I like being with your sister," I said.

The smile grew. Even though he was taller, he backed over to the piano. "I know that. I don't blame you."

"You told her to stop, that you'd tattletale to your old man."

The smile and a quick nod.

"Why?"

Now he met my eyes, became serious, tightened all over. I'd seen that before. "You know why. You're a bitchin' guy. I like you. Honest. But you and Jilly are different kinds of kids. God, I don't have to spell that out on the blackboard. She needs a real boyfriend. She needs . . . Shit, I mean at least some guy her own age."

"She could get a *real boy*friend if she wanted." Right then I knew I stank, my dirty clothes, my filthy goddamn hair.

"You've got her wasting . . . time is all."

"No I don't. And, hey, what I want you to know is I *like* being with her."

"You said that."

"You tell your old man about us I'll tell her about Skink. In a minute."

"That's history, Carlos. And maybe she knows already."

"Who you trying to kid?"

"Carlos," Lance said, with a return to the smile, stepping over, patting my shoulder. "I trust you with my sister. I always did."

"Don't forget."

His body wanted fins he looked so slippery. "Listen, I've got to . . ."

"Good night, Lance. Merry Christmas."

36 —— THE LUCKY LADY

I'd left the window up on the Polara, so the vinyl burned. The wheel. Fifty minutes late, I hung corners like Richard Petty on speed, just missing two nuns on either side of this pregnant girl.

The orange bay doors were down. Padlocked. Taped on each was a curled sheet of blue paper. A half-dozen more covered Spud's booth. Under a wiper on every heap in the

lot next door, another blue paper. Quiet. No flies. No trash.
Nothing. A holiday? Closed by the state? That's what I
expected, that Spud had been into more than heavy breathing in a glass box, that the clever son of a bitch had seen
to darker dealings all along that caught up with him.

Midnight's what caught up with him.

In a border of wavy ivy, or worms or something, each
blue sheet read:

WILLARD FIRTH CHOMPY
OCTOBER 31, 1931—JUNE 27, 1983
HIS BUSINESSES ARE TEMPORARILY CLOSED
HE WILL BE MISSED

I thought back on Spud, sweating over those sex-posed,
flesh-perfect honeys he'd never meet, see move, touch,
Spud in his box, his new one, his heavy skin, his swollen
eyes.

And death? Death shut those eyes. Turned him off.
That's all. People died. A smudged photo and some ink by
the want ads.

I told as much to the dandruff-coated, do-right of a
chaplain they had pray over the shaved heads of heathen
delinquents at reform school. I said, "You know, if you
weren't always rubbing our damn noses in fairy tales, maybe
we'd relax."

I cupped my hands around my eyes and looked into
Spud's booth: a green chair, a stack of magazines, a cash
register, a telephone, two unopened rolls of Tums, a
framed picture of an Airstream trailer, a Peanuts strip with
Charlie Brown missing the football, and on the shelf above
the window a small silver trophy I couldn't read, with a
race car on top.

———

The Mission Cafe was cool, the beer warm, the chili somewhere in between. I drank to Spud. Then I counted the bills in my wallet for the third time: sixteen bucks. Add to that the $422 stash in the wall, and I still didn't have much for a guy whose job had two fat feet in the grave. "Pass the *Tribune*, will ya?"

An old dawdler two stools down, glazed like a donut, hunched over a cup of coffee and a wet cigarette butt, slowly pushed the paper. "Any change?" he asked. "Just a couple of bits?"

"Change is where we're at, Padre." I folded the second section to the obits. The old guy dragged deep, hacked for a while, licked his lips, and dragged again.

CHOMPY, Willard Firth.

I could have guessed that pumpkin head was born on Halloween. Grew up (and out) in Idaho. (Where else would Spud be from? Next door to Ginny's parents, probably.) Fought in Korea. No shit? Survived by his wife, Dorothy J. (Lucky to survive.) And I'd missed the funeral. They could have been lowering his hot tub of a coffin right then. I lifted my beer a last time. "Go for it."

"What?" The old guy cocked his head. "Just a couple of bits?"

The Indians in the gloom back by the pool table started to laugh, to howl, to pound the butts of their cues on the linoleum.

My tiny waitress had a sticky looking blue hair net. She said, "You sure I can't get you anything else?"

I brought Ginny a shiny black rock I found in the parking lot. She gave me a long, wet kiss.

Who could tell? Dorothy J. might make me manager. Sure.

In the morning, the trees looked nervous in the rain. The sky had black wings, diving from the mountains. Talked out, written out, I closed the notebook. Mr. Cat studied drops skidding down the glass.

Thunder. Jesus, nobody would be at Spud's, nobody half sensible anyway, which ruled out Spud's relatives from what I'd seen.

I bought a five-pack of piss-cheap White Owls at Skagg's and a pint of Old Crow at the state store: birds of a feather. Ginny was off in the rain somewhere teaching kids how to turn their wipers on. If I had seen my father, I would have killed him.

I light a cigar in a phone booth across from the Salt Palace. Two to an umbrella, young women tiptoe past on spiked heels. A tall guy in a yellow rain suit jogs by with a Doberman. Businessmen. "Dr. Downes is in surgery until two."

For an hour I play asteroids and drain a pitcher at the Dead Goat. I tell a waitress she has nice legs. She says, "Big deal." The last time I saw Matt he was home from college in the east, with a ponytail and this chick with no bra and hair under her arms. They threw a Frisbee on the island.

The rain has stopped, and it comes back to me that when I called that time before, nightcrawlers squirmed in puddles all down the sidewalk. And Matt made up machines to keep the dead alive.

He is not surprised. He says, "I appreciate your feelings about this, Carlos. I'm very busy."

I squeeze the phone. I say, "All you do is sign. I have it all written down. I wrote up what happened to Skink. All straight. We give it to the paper."

"There's Hilda."

"People should know. Hilda is strong. It's not like he'll go to jail or anything. It's just the truth, so people will see."

"Let it die, Cade. You'll hurt yourself. We were children."

"It matters. You sign. I'll see to the rest." And what will I see to? What *is* the rest? The cigar sours in my stomach.

"I told him, Carlos. I told him you called."

"I've got lots more."

"Not with me. I'll level with you. I feel sorry for you, Carlos. I wish I could help. I can't."

"I help myself."

A bus roars by with wide fins of white water.

Drinking fattens my room, heats it. The cassette spins. The sun falls behind the rain. Lightning throws itself at mountains. My hunger has forgotten food, but when I see Ginny gliding to the front door with two less-graceful girls, each holding a sopping newspaper over her hair, I shout, "What's for dinner, beautiful?" unhook the screen, and lean out as far as I can. I could fly.

Except for a difference in width, Ginny's friends came from the same mold. Middle-aged, I thought. Their faces starting to pinch around the openings, they wore their hair short, swept onto their foreheads. Each tried for sexy cowgirl in her outfit, which was okay by me: shirts fastened low, tight yellow and blue riding pants, monogrammed belts, eagle-toed cowgirl boots. I hadn't smoked so much dope since my Fourth of July on the ranch. The icing was two snorts apiece of nose candy.

Ginny held her own—dancing to an Elton John record by herself most of the night—even though she didn't smoke much and left the powder alone. Once Emma and Ginny danced a slow one, while Paula shrieked, "God help me, " by the lamp.

Ginny said Emma and Paula worked in the shoe department at Sears just up from South High, where she taught driving. I couldn't figure out why that would make their fingers blue, but they were, and cold, and I winced each time one of them squeezed my cheeks and kissed my forehead. What a pair. I wondered if Ginny brought all sorts of wild strangers to her place early in the evening while I worked. She said, "Don't be dumb. Hey, what are *you* doing here?"

"Dancing. Getting stoned out my ever-loving gourd."

"Come on."

I tightened my hands on the angel globes of her ass. "You know what?"

"Tell me."

"Really. I'm not Carl Sagan or Isaac Asimov or one of those guys."

"Had *me* fooled."

"I mean, at the university. I haven't . . ."

"What?"

"I'm just not doing so hot."

"Hey, hold me there. Yeah. You're doing fine."

Paula shrieked, "Dinner's ready."

We sat at Ginny's shiny little, rickety-legged aluminum table and tried to swallow pizza burned on the top and frozen on the bottom. Emma said, "I could eat a horse. I'm so friggin' hungry I could eat a horse."

Paula is the last thing I remember, lifting her glass. "To the baby."

I woke up in somebody else's tomb on Ginny's floor, the sun in my face. Paula and Emma were gone. Ginny, her nightgown up around her neck, yawned on the couch, purple lipstick on her cheek. She hugged me when I kissed her.

"Girls," Aaron said.

He wore a red beret this time, soaked through the top

like a bruised apple. The mercury must have topped a hundred. The mirror lenses of his dark glasses twisted me and glared. Empty beads of sweat slid across his pink, bony chest. He'd been dancing around out there in his camouflage pants and sandals since seven, he said. A goddamn freak.

"Got a cigarette?"

He worked a crooked Benson and Hedges Menthol 100 from the pack he kept tucked at his waist. "Cade," he said, snapping his Zippo shut. "You're lucky. We're only keeping one bay open for now. And you're the afternoon man. My uncle would keep *you*. Shit, I feel for them other guys. But business is. Sorry to boost 'em from the bird bath. *You* got two weeks. Mornings you can hunt up something else."

"Girls?"

"Got to." He swung his cigarette around the lot, past three painters—compressor chugging—spraying a bubble-gum pink over the stained outside walls of the car wash, past the guy hammering yellow siding around Spud's booth. A sign painter stretched on a ladder, adding the finishing touches to LUCKY LADY RECONDITIONED CARS and GO GO CAR WASH.

"See, Cade, we'll have a chick in the booth from now on. Idea is she'll feel lucky you buy a set of wheels off her."

"And a bunch of girls with Miss Universe stats are gonna rub down Datsuns in this Death Valley heat? Sure. They'll look real good, work real hard."

"The chicks'll be in swimsuits. Bikinis for now, someday maybe topless. We'll keep a sort of shower spraying all the time. They can hop through whenever they please. Shit, Cade, you know women. A chance to pull decent bucks showing off their bods and soak up a righteous tan besides. Man, I'm gonna have the Dallas Cowgirls in here."

"Dead from heat exhaustion."

He bounced off toward the sign painter.

"How about winter?" I asked.

"Overhead heaters," he hollered. "Chicks'll wear pink snowmobile suits."

"Sounds horny," I said. He flipped his curly ponytail over his shoulder.

The black guy ahead of me in the one open bay finished up a Jeep. He nodded and said, "You the other *lucky* one?"

"Yeah, two weeks lucky."

"Spud'd love this. Crazy. Man, why'd he do it?"

"Probably in his will."

"No, I mean off himself."

"He just kicked is all."

"In his car at midnight, according to Aaron, tapped into a nice long exhaust hose."

Like cardboard over the downtown, the full moon looked fake.

I gulped beer at the Astronaut. A fight on the TV ended in a TKO. Two Indians blasted pheasants. A fellow redhead down the bar winked—at some other guy.

Four or five blocks of gold-plated, pawn-shop waste, a long, empty train of windows between the post office and the stock exchange, and I stood just up from a flashing dome of lights—Stonehenge—dead-ending a noisy street. One night I might step through that loud, canopied door, to find Stud, if he was there, to get out from under everything.

Maybe I'd say, Yeah, I've got Vice. What's he worth to you? Too iffy. All backbone, no brain.

Maybe I'd say, Did you see Noel's neck? Imagine that in *your* collar. Remember who your playmates are. I may be the only person you can trust.

The doorway steamed. Blue smoke. Strobes. A red

convertible unloaded low-cut fancy blonds too thin for Florida.

The moon slipped farther away. This long-legged teenager in a wrinkled miniskirt, with a sparkly gold star on her cheek, stopped me on my first block back north. I smiled at her halter top, her hips. She might have been seventeen. "Twenty bucks is a good time," she said. She touched my chest. Her little girl's face floated there, the star, her eyes. She licked her teeth.

"You got a smoke," I said, "I'll buy it for a buck."

"Get lost." She backed into her doorway. Then she tittered. "Wait." Her purse, sparkly as her star, thin as a glove, jangled when she reached inside. I half expected a pistol. "Here," she said, a tooth missing from her grin. "I found this. Just your speed." She held out this cheap, silver heart, scratched, blank. "Where's the buck?"

And the next morning, the damn heart on my table, I caught every skirt on the street, the tick-tock of hips, the practiced glide of high heels. I chugged an Instant Breakfast and tried to think of other things.

37 —— SALT

"**M**erry Christmas, Dinosaur Man." Hilda shook me. The box springs groaned. Stale light melted through the doorway to our room. From the wires, my lips were a stiff kind of raw in the morning. Hilda hugged me. "It snowed again in the night," she said. "It's beautiful. Christmas. You'll see." She shifted her feet in fluffy pink slippers, modeled a quilted, yellow robe.

"One of 'em's just gonna get sore."

"We'll try not to let 'em. Okay?" She winked, but then she blinked, and her mouth tightened. "It's Christmas. I want it to be Christmas." She pulled a blanket around my shoulders.

Mama and Papa, like people waiting for a train that might not come, looked up from the table. A choir had the radio shaking on the stove. Wrapped in a robe like Hilda's, Mama trembled. Papa wore a new blue-flannel shirt. A white tag dangled from the sleeve. He puffed on a cigarette. Their coffee steamed.

Behind me Hilda said, "For you." Shiny green paper, a crisp red bow—her nails red around it. I backed away from those two aging, sorry children who were my parents, away from this sister of mine who should have been born somewhere else, someone else, in some other goddamn time. "Please," she said. And beside my mother's bed, crumpled wrapping, a card, Santa creased beneath a shoe, the smooth loops of Hilda's writing, "Merry merry Christmas."

"Hilda," I said, "I wish . . ."

My old man lit another. My mother squeaked through her eyes somehow. I took the package and tore it. I shook my head at the gunfighter in black on that boxed set of books. He smiled.

"Susie Sowett, this girl I know who's part-time at the library, spied on you. She said to get you these."

"God," I said. "You don't give up."

As she hugged me, she said softly, "I can't."

With a candy-cane striped apron over her robe, Hilda cooked breakfast, bacon and scrambled eggs for them, Cream of Wheat with real cream and maple syrup for me. They put away two helpings. The radio caroled on. My mother tottered back to bed, a strip of bacon in each hand. My old man said, "Yup."

They turned the thermostat down that day, or maybe other times the heat held over from the dryers. I kept my hat on. My shoes sounded frozen on the yellow concrete floor.

I wasted my eyes: soap operas on every channel but one where sport has-beens tried to pump up the Blue-Gray Game with dope on the players, a bunch of boring, all-American baby talk.

When Jill honked, I felt like I should shout so long to somebody, I'd spent so much time there lately. And Jesus, before I pushed outside, the announcer said, I'd swear, "What a catch for the big senior out of Arkansas, Carlos Cade."

We decided against a movie, which Jill said would only "keep us from ourselves." Her old man still held the cabin. "You know," she said, believe it or not, "it might be neat to go to some church somewhere. Stained-glass windows, us praying and singing carols with a choir full of strangers. I want Christmas to mean something. You know?" Then she laughed, shook her head.

We drove north, away, the heater saving my feet, Jill rubbing the knots out of my neck, Janis Joplin choking on snow, howling across that blue ocean of sky with something like pain, the highway wet and narrow and black, the mountains chiseled from ice.

"You talked to Lance," she said.

"Yeah. What'd he say?"

"That he won't tell Papa. That I'm a big girl. And he says he guesses you're okay."

"What'd you say?"

"Thank you."

Jill kissed my neck. "We're out here," she said. "Almost gone."

We followed soft, shadowy tracks over the unplowed road through Syracuse, snow fresh enough for traction. Christmas lights wrapped a tall row of pines. We made it to the lake. The snow-covered causeway—unpaved back

then, a thin, miles-long dike smooth as dough—curved out
through the blackness of that lake which never froze, out
to Antelope Island, a floating castle carved from soap, from
foam, from salt. We stopped at the gate—CLOSED FOR THE
SEASON. She cut the engine. In the snowy wind, the gate
clanged at its lock, like a bell. No tracks from here. Black
water, the white land.

Jill kissed my cheek. She lifted a small gift in silver paper
from under her seat. "Open it." It smelled like my old man.
One of her old man's cigar boxes. A woman in a blindfold
on the green label. Smoke, all right. In a fat Baggie. "The
girl I got it from says it's the best around, Mexicali something. You like marijuana?"

"Sure. You shouldn't be buying grass, though. Big, big
trouble for a lot less than this."

"Just once. She won't tell. I've never smoked it."

"Guaranteed to jingle bells. Got a pipe or papers?"

"Only a syringe." We laughed at that, at the snow, the
lake, the sky. She fished in her purse.

I touched her arm. "Here," I said. She beamed at the
tiny package, tore the purple, velvety paper.

I'd lifted the locket the week before from Shoe Fly An-
tiques. Danny kept the old lady busy over some Nazi crap.
Nothing to it, really.

"Little roses," Jill said, "even birds. It's pretty." She
kissed it.

When she squeezed the sides, the silver case sprang
open. Our initials took all but forty cents of the Hotel Utah
money. The jeweler charged extra for the swirls.

"Put it on," I said.

She got stoned. And we managed in that tight bucket
seat, with just my zipper down and her skirt up. That was
Christmas.

The Great Salt Lake.

On New Year's Eve Jill and I will ride a train to Park City
and back and smoke dope with the conductor. In four
weeks my old man will split. In five weeks I will get my
wires cut. Now I am buying cologne—can you believe
that?—looking for something in a classy kind of barbershop
bottle that doesn't cost too much. Christmas was three days
ago. This is the last time I see Gerry:

His sister's tits balloon wider than her arms and sag,
perfect, clear to her waist. Power, even though she has zits,
and black hairs curl out of a mole on her chin.

She is behind him, looking, head tilted, while he stands
in one of those three-angle mirrors in ZCMI. He wears a
black suit, a Christmas present, I think. He is trading something in.

I lift my eyes from a display case, and I see her from
the side, like this great cushioned doll. Gerry doesn't move,
stares. From those mirrors two heavy faces that are his, that
are gray and swollen at the eyes, that are scooped out at
the cheeks and cored empty at the mouth, gawk back at
this stiff boy whose sister's mighty breasts, for all their glory,
cannot soften his fall.

Thanks to Danny Ingus, with plenty of help from Old
Man Arthur, I am in reform (ha ha) school that summer
when Gerry does it. Sure, I've wondered, but everything
seems right, as right as things that final always are, can't
help but be. Lance told me, though, told it like he was glad
no one got to me first.

September—still hot—and the sprinklers hissed, and I
lay spread-eagled on the next island, loving the sun and
hating it, missing Jill. Eating Red Hots with a couple of
butterflies and half a dozen bumblebees.

Lance's shadow covered my eyes. "You're back. How was
it?"

"Fuck you."

"I'm serious." Lance posed, in a yellow shirt with a red stallion on the pocket, madras shorts, and white tennis shoes. I never saw him in cutoffs again.

"They work your butt and spike the mashed potatoes with saltpeter to keep you from jackin' off."

He smiled, his dimples like wounds. "I'm just asking."

"I'm just telling."

I wanted to get to him. I wanted him to know how much was his fault. But he studied the neighborhood slowly, like Captain. Maybe he didn't see a damn thing, not even the Volvo.

Now he sat Indian style. Picked at some clover. "Carlos," he said. "Gerry killed himself." Just like that.

I pushed onto my knees. At Gerry's house the grass was too high, too brown, the windows white with blinds, the place so goddamn vacant I imagined for just a second that Gerry killed his whole family. "Two weeks ago. His father found him. In their basement. Ant poison, a bottle of it. Wouldn't even've felt it. Quick, my dad says." He snapped his fingers. "Then there was a bunch of Catholic crap about suicides can't be buried or something. But they did it."

Lance swallowed and tossed his hair into place. He whistled as he walked back home. I finished the Red Hots.

I figured Gerry left a note—and I didn't give a shit. I thought about his sister, though, and wondered what she'd lost. She probably felt guilty.

38——— *BETWEEN A ROCK AND A DARK PLACE*

Where I Told Her

1) Away.

   Even with Ginny's windows open, with her fan winding up the air, the Samson would not let go of the day's heat. Beer didn't work. We drove out in the Polara at eleven, the parks jammed, radios yelling.

2) On a boulder on the south slope of Ensign Peak, crickets full throttle. Below, like machine spiders, cars wove lights through the city. We held our knees. The moon turned everything around us to yellow powder. I tasted it. Our Schlitz cans glowed. We tossed our shirts across the rock.

Why I Told Her

1) When I rubbed her back, my hand made a suction noise on her wet skin.

2) Moonlight.

3) I couldn't remember what anything meant or whether I cared.

4) I was not afraid.

5) First thing when I got home, she said she had a house for us. "Two-fifty a month," she said, "including utilities. At least a couple of acres, with apple trees, and a garden, and creek bed right on the edge of the yard. Emma and Paula found it in *The Advertiser*. I mean, Bountiful's only; what, ten minutes from town max? There's this incredible view of the lake. Let's just do it, Loskie. I'm not scared, and I'm the one that should be. Let's just get married and try."

6) She whispered, "Really, cross my heart, I do, I love you."

What I Told Her
1) "I would miss you. I know that."
2) "Something important, though. You haven't the faintest idea who the hell I am. I've never been to college. I've robbed people plenty, and I like it. When I have to, I'm mean. I did time in the State School. I'm not worth a shit. I don't deserve you. I don't deserve much in the way of anything.
"And I want you to listen now. I'm getting down what I've done, what I know—making this record of it. That's what I do every day. Plenty's been buried. In that model house you've got picked out, some paid gorilla might just enjoy finding you alone while I'm gone."
3) That my job was at a car wash. That I was canned.
4) "Because you're beautiful—really—and our kid needs his old man to be a human being, if I had to choose between getting the past out, down— getting even—and you, I'd pick getting even. I would, no matter what I feel with you—or because of it, or something."

What Ginny Did When I Told Her
1) Cried into long sobs, then breathed deep through her nose, out through her mouth, eyes shut.
2) Stared just over the city.
3) Slowly smoked three or four cigarettes and finished her one beer, while I rubbed her back, the dampness gone from her skin.
4) Looked at me, chewed her lip.
5) Smiled.

What Ginny Said After I Told Her

1) "You know all you told me is crap. You know that. What you are, Loskie . . . what you have been all along—every doggone minute I've known you—is scared to death you might have to really give up some of yourself to somebody else. You talk tough, but you're so weak you think a little softness might just get you killed. Sure, the whole world's after you. Right."

2) "I've known all along you were some kind of liar. I have. College was a lousy story. Hey, I even called up and asked if you registered. And you know what? I used to park down Ninth South and watch you at Spud's. I did."

3) "Why are you all of a sudden all wrought up over me? If I'd be in danger in Bountiful, for God's sake, shit, I'm in danger now." And she shouted up the slope into moonlight, "Go ahead, kill me. Get it over with."

4) "I like having you around me, that's all."

5) "Nobody's what the hell they say. It's a sideshow. Don't you see? The Greatest Show on Earth, Ladies and Gentlemen. Get it? Ladies and gentlemen." She slipped from the rest of her clothes. Spread her arms, yellow, smooth.

Why I Told Her

1) Because I dreamed of Skink's face, Danny's. Mama's, her skin beginning to crack and flake like bark. Of finding one other, mouth and nose worn away, opening its disappointed eyes.

2) Because Ginny, standing, glistened there alive above a city of half a million sleeping, dreamless, worn-out sonsofbitches.

What I Told Myself

1) You love her and you like her and you want her and that feels good, but love is moonlit, goddamn witchcraft.

2) You are afraid after all, you dirty, fucking, yellow-bellied coward. Get rid of it. Live. If you want a kid, then, by God, have a kid. If you want Ginny, then, by God, take Ginny. To hell with them. To hell with him. Make getting even EVEN, goddamn it.

What I Didn't Tell Her

That Florida said, "I keep my word, don't I?" I had four cars to go. "Ready when you are." She batted her eyelashes and puckered a smile, one ringed hand on one round hip. Moths swarmed the floodlight edging her in gold—white, heavy halter top, hot pants, black net stockings, high heels. "I'll be in front. Whenever."

I changed my shirt.

Her treat, we ordered top sirloin at Little America and three drinks. She folded her legs beside the table. The busboys damn near popped their bow ties. I already knew we would get a room, that I had lost. Her smell filled the place. And that line of freckles across her nose, of all the damn things, kept her young in spite of the orange powder, open.

"Can't a girl just need company?" she asked. Her hand slipped over mine. "Why not?"

" 'Cause you've *got* company—all you could want."

"All that would want me," she said. "Not see me or know me." She leaned over the table so her tits pressed my hand. "I told you before, I'm scared. Honest."

"There must be some guy."

"Was, always was just some guy. This last's out to Point-of-the-Mountain. Fifteen years for pushing. I didn't know. A crazy guy. We're better with him gone."

"Kids?"

"Good kids. Livin' with my Mom in Kaysville till I get things calm. Amos, my boy—I ought to carry pictures—calls me Sugar Candy."

"Must be tough."

"You come meet 'em. You could stay the night. I'm one man at a time. I'm true."

"How come me?"

She spoke in puffs of smoke. "I don't know. You hold back. You see how fucked it all is. No games. It's the games I'm scared of." And men had grabbed her, stuffed money in her G-string, taken every bit they could. "Stay with me a while. You'll be the only guy."

"Tonight."

"So what's the matter with tonight? That's how you find tomorrow night. Hey, your job's up. I've got money."

"How do you know my job's up?"

"I just know."

And I wanted that wanted woman all over me. But she wasn't even there. With Florida, motel rooms were bedtime stories for kids. This time I kissed her, though, right there. And her mouth was hot and tired and too wide. She touched her tongue to my lips. She said, "Danny and Tony, and I can't sleep sometimes. What happened to the dog? Who took him and how come?" Her hands were tight on mine.

I stood, ground out a smoke. The busboys looked away.

I said, "I don't know anything. Thanks, though, honey. Really. You're the stuff centerfolds are made of. My God. But I've got my own nightmares and I'll never know what the hell you want from me."

As I walked from the dining room inhaling myself in that clean air, she called, "You *don't* know anything, not half of it."

And I didn't.

39 —— VISITORS

Slow. Hot.

Three very dirty cars—period—in an hour and a half. Two big pretty boys pulled in once but then backed out—hoping for the foxy go-goes, I guess. Why would any driver pick that raunchy wash, one lousy bay, especially with the goddamn pink sign? Workmen sawed and pounded and sucked down Gatorade. Three or four times Aaron—his hair in braids now, so that he looked like Raggedy Ann with a beard, a raggedy beard at that—tried to make small talk: "Ever seen anything like it? Cade, I had this vision. A little imagination and a lot of nerve, that's the good old U-S of A. Me, right here, with an idea, man, that's where it's at."

I was sweating to death, rocking on the old aluminum kitchen chair by the rotor box, counting flies, when Ginny's training car swung in. A boy in dark glasses drove, and I didn't recognize her at first. When she climbed out and waved, I blushed, I think—for her. Four teenagers watched us through the suds. "Can't you talk now you dropped out of college?" She lifted her eyebrows.

The low, blue Buick shrank me on its bumper, fried me on its grill. I smiled at the decal on the front door. She did teach driving. "You work for the state?"

"Highway patrol sponsors it. Sure. I work for your brother-in-law, big man."

A girl in the backseat leaned and kissed the cheek of the boy driving. The grill beaded with tiny clouds. I reached for myself through the finish.

Ginny said, "I took it. I took the place. Do you hear?" Hot metal. "We can move in day after tomorrow, if you want. Saturday, Los."

"I have to work."

The kids cranked down their windows. Their faces crowded out. "I'm about done," I said. She kicked me, grunted, drove her foot hard into my ass. My forehead hit the windshield. A black girl laughed like a damn hyena.

And when I slid down, Ginny raised her fists. "If you're so tough," she said.

"Yeah, sure. Beat up a helpless man."

"With pleasure."

"Hey, we'll move on Sunday."

"Lady, is he causing you any trouble?" Aaron pushed between us, stroked his mustache. "I'm the manager, and if . . ."

"Trouble?" After a silence of giggling kids, Ginny stepped over, pulled me down, and kissed me, long, slow, all she had.

A girl said, "God." Ginny grinned. Her eyes watered. She swooped into the car on a wing of red skirt and slammed the door.

And once they were gone, flies all over his head, Aaron growled, "She needs a good screw."

"Yup."

"Broads," he said, and yanked a crumpled pack of smokes from his jeans.

Labeled in big, marking-pen letters—KITCHEN, BED-ROOM, BATHROOM—a line of liquor boxes, as straight

and regular as train cars, ran from Ginny's front door to
the TV. I smelled grass. "That you, Loskie?" Her hair tied
in a red bandana, wearing just a tight, transparent bra and
green panties with yellow hearts, she stretched deep into
the cupboards. "Hi. What do you think?"

"You have a nice ass."

"I'm almost finished."

I rubbed her stomach, a smooth lift below her belly button. I kissed her damp neck.

She said, "I rented the littlest U-Haul."

"Let's drink a lot tonight, a hell of a lot—to us. You can
this once."

"You're not mad I came by?"

"You turned on the guy with the pigtails. You turn me
on."

"Yeah?"

"Scout's honor."

"You know what I'm excited about?" She arched into
another cabinet. "Seeing Mr. Cat outdoors climbing trees
and hunting birds, acting like an animal. Isn't that silly?
But I really am."

I called Shiftlet—at his office in the Musk Enterprise Building—a half hour before work on Friday from a booth back
of the toys in Grand Central. Bobby Bull said he'd send
our damage deposits. Sure. And our new address? Right.
Uh huh. And I was just born. I said I'd pick up the money
next week sometime. "Good," he said, "I'd like to see you."
No wonder his mother got old.

Then just when I hung up, L.G. said, "Hey, Cade." Red
eyes. Hair gunked with dandruff and fuzz. "Long time."
He leaned by the phone, blocking me in the hall to the
fountain and the bathrooms. Two boys ran between us.
L.G. smelled liike something buried. His boots were

scraped and curled, his jeans shiny with grime, and his shirt torn in the pit.

He knows, I thought. My knife was there, and I considered it, stepped to the fountain, drank. He popped a fat pink bubble. He wobbled. He said, "I followed you. We need to go over some stuff." And his eyes were down.

And I lit up, breathed, tossed the match into the fountain. "Okay."

"Cade, what the hell's goin' on with this goddamn dog?"

"You tell me. Cops and half the world've asked about it."

"Somebody ripped off Vice," he said. "I know that." He chewed. "Right before what happened to Danny." A man in a Yankees hat excused himself past us with a baby in his arms.

"Big-timers think you know something, that it?"

"Think I owe 'em money. Shit, Danny was in to his eyeballs."

I stepped over then and whispered, "And you killed Nicks, didn't you?"

His two big mitts jolted me back. All the life left his face but the blood red in his eyes. "What's with you, Cade? We're in the same corner."

"And you," I hissed now, hissed because I needed to know. "I'll bet you're the asshole doped Quicksand."

"I wouldn't!" he said, so loud a silver-haired clerk steamed around the corner and said, "Please."

"I wouldn't," he said, fists balled up, quieter. "That's one thing I'm needin' to talk over." He checked the aisle in front of us, the doors behind. "Doc Nort still has Quicky, Cade, wants to sell him back, says it's money he's owed 'cause Danny rolled him over. Hell, I don't know what to do."

Jesus. "Quicky's gone," I said. "Forget him."

He grabbed me under the arms, lifted, held me. "I've been tryin' to forget." I smiled.

A kid came out of the toys and said, "You two shouldn't roughhouse."

"Yeah," I said. He let me down. "And the cops catch you with the dog, what do you say? You'll never fight him."

"He ain't the same anyway."

"*You* could sell him."

"Sure. Nort wants three grand."

"He'd take less. You rent Quicksand out for stud."

"For stud," he mumbled. He scratched behind his neck. He slumped down right there, squatted over those lousy boots, that huge, stinking, stupid bastard, and unwrapped another piece of Bazooka. "To cover what they say I owe. Yeah."

"Yeah," I said. This was a man with absolutely nothing left.

"You're smart," he said. "Danny always told me." He looked up, sniffed. "Who done Danny?"

"I don't know."

For a long time he sat. Then his eyes changed, sharpened, and he stood. "I'll remember you give me advice today, Carlos."

Three cassettes and my notebooks. They'll ride with me in a garbage bag in the cab of the truck. In a Styrofoam cooler by my door, the note is still frozen, the last thing I'll load. And I like my window, the heat, the light.

The truck is where I parked it at the curb. Ginny is on the ramp, carrying two boxes, singing. Now an old man I've never seen hobbles on with a box. Here comes another old guy. Goddamn. She draws us all to her.

40 —— THE RED WHEEL

Just last week my old man split. I watched over the wax museum. My mother changed poses a couple of times a day at the kitchen table. Every so often Hilda changed books.

Valentine's.

The receptionist and nurse, plump and gray, wore red hearts on the stiff fronts of their white uniforms. I waited alone in this small, windowless room of ocean paintings, plastic chairs, and ragged magazines. I smelled something sour, like vinegar. I had the idea I'd die when the doctor put me under that morning to take off the wires.

A red-headed, freckled priest came back from the examining rooms. "It's the fire in our hearts," he said to me.

The nurse said, "Good-bye, Father."

I thumbed through an *Outdoor Life* with bow hunters stalking a bull moose on the cover. In the last seven days, I'd beaten up five guys who'd done nothing, with faces wide and empty as snowmen. Not one touched me. None of their friends rushed forward to make me stop. Not one. My teeth were wired shut, goddamn it, like a goddamn stuffed animal's, and nobody came at me. Shit. I *would* die.

The nurse moved her paper heart closer. "Carlos," she said. "Everything's fine. Calm down. This is the doctor's, Carlos. He took the wires off. Close your eyes. It's all right."

My tongue touched my dry lips.

The doctor never came. I did not see him that visit. This same nurse was the one had needled me with Valium and told me to count backward. Now some part of me wondered who really opened my mouth again, and why I wasn't dead.

That afternoon I walked the anesthetic off downtown. The sun melted ice into shadows on the sidewalks.

My stiff jaw did not want to open. But I ate a cheese-burger and fries. No one seemed to notice. I talked to myself—to feel the words escape. I sang on Main Street, State Street, Broadway. By four o'clock, beat to shit, I was slumped in a deep chair in our corner of the library, my Valentine to Jill inside my shirt, goose bumps everywhere.

I couldn't read Zane Grey's too-goddamn-tidy books. His world turned as easy as a top. His people didn't change, didn't move. They got clearer, to themselves and to the reader, that's all. Smaller. They straightened their masks and that was that. I doodled a big heart with an arrow through it on the last page of *Code of the West*. When Jill whispered, "Hi," I was chewing on a library pencil, feeling the muscles itchy in my cheeks, trying to climb loose of myself through the black branches outside the icy window.

I pressed my teeth together and they squeaked, stayed in place. I shivered and swallowed more of her father's bour-bon. The fire roasted the backs of my legs. I faced a gold-framed portrait of a thin woman with black hair, with a wide smile. She wore riding clothes, a velvet coat, and knee-high boots. Beneath her Jill lay on their blue couch. "She's pretty as you," I said. "Your coloring's different is all." Ice cracked in my glass.

"She *was* pretty. She . . ." Her quick laugh brought more tears. She lit a cigarette. I wanted to go home, or some-where—someplace where life didn't take so much so long.

"Maybe your father'll come back," she said. All I'd told her was that he left, that my mother and sister were like strangers or dead people.

"No way."

"He didn't say why or where or anything?"

"Nope."

She tipped the last of her third glass of wine. She said, "I had just turned seven. Two weeks before, she gave me

a party I won't ever forget. With a pony. And then . . .
Then she took us to see our great aunt who rented a cabin
every summer in Brighton. Except for the fight with
Lance . . . He caught a toad on the trail, real excited and
proud. She made him let it go. He got that look he gets.
Except for that the day didn't need anything. Except for
that . . . She patted my head inside this big roof of trees.
Then we stepped into the sky it seemed like. I remember
her fingers in my hair. I remember smelling pines and
feeling her hand and she was everything, that huge bowl
of mountains, the blue, the smell—touching me. I loved
every single bit of her. He lunged at her, pushed.
And . . . When she went over, I wanted . . . I saw this red
hawk swoop out of the trees, and I thought . . . For a second
I thought Mommy was flying. I wanted to fly. Until the
scream. Lance . . . You know what he is . . . Do you? Then
he . . . he pinned me in the dirt above the cliff and said,
'She won't come back. Not now.' "

Hugging her knees, Jill sobbed under the picture of the
smiling woman who tumbled from a mountain and died.
More shivering. She whispered through her hair: "I never
talked . . . before to anyone . . . Never. Never ever."

"We shouldn't be here," I said.

I sat down next to her because of the yellow, jagged,
jumping light, and the cold, and the fire snapping its fingers
at my back. My teeth ached.

From the frosted chandelier down her upstairs hall, light
melted into her room, turned blue against her walls, and
should have been romantic. Like a water-smooth stone, Jill's
curved back inside those pool-blue sheets. I could not see
her face. A clock on the dresser sounded like someone
coming with a cane. Where were we?

Clean where it counted, I folded my clothes on the floor

and slid in beside her. Her skin. I kissed her shoulder.
"Happy Valentine's," I said. I'd said it before. I'd written,
"Your mine, Spider Woman (the only one)" inside a pink
goddamn Cupid card from Walgreen's. Hers said, "Love
is life." Her pillow smelled like the hospital. Now we lay in
her blue room in her empty house.

Through the narrow doorway beside us, against a tall,
tiled wall, a cold white toilet crouched by a sink like a pris-
oner. Her own bathroom. Her own television, her own
stereo, her own minirefrigerator, her own phone. Whenever we met to hold each other, to forget or remember or
whatever the hell we did, she came from this. Someone
wanted her to need this not me. I'd had nothing all my
goddamn life because nobody gave a shit. She'd had everything, for the same reason. Then all around those useless
things, I saw her: white-faced, old-timey dolls; stuffed
birds, perched, an owl, a hawk; clay jungle animals parad-
ing on a shelf; and witchy, blue bottles, bottles and more
bottles, empty bottles.

Two posters hung in the blue, one of a man in a suit,
tie, and derby hat, his round head a red apple. Why an
apple? I wondered. Why not a grenade? Why not an egg?
How about a dinosaur egg? I thought it was funny, and
funny didn't matter then. A pale, naked woman lay on a
striped couch in the other. She looked at us, her plump
face pretty but cold above a body of bone, a beautiful, big-
breasted body of bone. She looked at us, saw Lance living
in this house.

I listened—for the stairs warning of someone home, for
hinges, for dogs barking, for sirens, for ghosts, for the end
of the world. Just the clock with its cane. Just my heart.
Lance had a party, her father the cabin. When she'd told
me last week that they would be gone—before my old man
vamoosed—the excitement had itched behind my eyes, in-

side my chest. Valentine's Day. Our Valentine's. My teeth ached, and I hated my father, and now I had this other thing to hate.

The springs squeaked when she rolled to me, spread her chest on mine. Her wet lips. Her tongue. Her leg wrapped me. She moved against my thigh, where I felt through her hair now, her dampness, my hand, and something in me liked it, liked it fine, but not enough—and I was his son, I smelled like him. And Jill. Stop, I should stop. I said, "Jill . . ."

Her lips lifting from mine, she breathed, "Please, Carlos. Save me."

Her hips, and her hand. She slid across me like water . . . her wet mouth. "Jill." I reached. Touched her head below, the two of us a circle then, her mouth. Her taste. Everything. She rose. Rolled. Opened herself. Wailed my name, that I was doing it, saving her.

Afterward, slick and hot and salty as the lake, she said, "All the rest happened, but not to us. Remember that. I'm going to remember. Not to us. We're the only thing that's happened to us."

And I said, "The time with Hilda, when she ran home . . ."

"Oh, Carlos." Jill's hand moved up and down my side. "It was . . . I was mean. We were playing dress up . . . in the attic, my, my mother's gowns. I took Hilda's things. I was awful. I know I was. This is now, Carlos. This is us."

I gripped her hand. Okay, I thought, she *was* mean. Mad at her life, she got mean that once. Look what I'd done in my time.

I left her sleeping, moving her soft eyelids. Now she *was* beautiful. She was so goddamn beautiful.

Valentine's Day, 1964.

The breeze that Valentine's night, warm with Jill and bourbon, swirled newspapers across the island like ghosts through leaves. I *opened* my mouth ear to ear and tasted every last star, the lemon of the moon. I sat on the island and smoked three, four cigarettes. My piss steamed and smelled—sweet. I went home. I could not think.

Hilda shifted in her bed. It squealed. I lifted a corner of the curtain and in the sudden, soft gauze of moonlight saw this scrawny dog beside Hilda's head. Fifi's arrival. Hilda opened her eyes, smiled. "Isn't she pretty?"

"Go to sleep."

The dog yapped first thing in the morning. The dog had done plenty on the floor in the night. My teeth throbbed.

The world had changed.

White and deep, on windowsills, cars, even telephone wires. Snow. Flakes still fell, feathers of sky, a great, white, wild swan with wings big as mountains. I stood at the head of my alley up to my knees in powder. I had not heard myself laugh for eight weeks.

But by afternoon, after school, the streets splashed an oily slush. The library windows were spattered and streaked. I wouldn't read, not today. I went to Hilda's friend, the librarian's helper, who saw me as some damn Horatio Alger or something. "Just a moment, please," she said. A voice for Story Hour. She swished her petticoats into a back room. She returned with a small box and smiled. She patted her red hair, but her steady blue eyes bothered me. "This way." Her chest brushed past. Her perfume through the stacks. As she threaded the microfilm onto the reader, she stood on tiptoes, her legs tight and nice, her skirt above her knees. "Just turn the wheel like this. Try it." The pink flesh in the corners of her blue eyes could have been gum. Our shoulders touched. Her freckles thickened until she wasn't pretty. "Where's your friend?"

"Friend?"

She cleared her throat and whispered more softly, "Hey, I've seen you."

"And?"

"And I . . . I just thought, well . . ." She twisted a thick orange curl. "If she's ever, you know, I . . ."

I held her arm. "You're all right," I said. "Really. But I'm . . . I'm pretty serious with her. We'll see. I won't say nothin' to Hilda. You don't either, huh?"

"Sure." Her ears were red. What did she want? Her heels tapping off through those roads of books reminded me of the clock the night before, which reminded me of Danny shooting out East High School's clock, which reminded me of my old man nursing his wounds who the hell knew where—or dead.

I turned the wheel. A stream. A ribbon of news. *The* news reel. Unwound. Page after page, day after day, one entire year, 1955. Shrunk to this, a strip of . . . a roll of . . . the sound of . . . smoky plastic. Flickered through winter, spring. Ads shed their clothes. The Easter Bunny came and went. I wanted summer. I knew that. Business, politics, plans, promises. Most of it boring. The city grew. A small quake Richtered across the valley. Half a dozen polygamists got rounded up.

July.

> *July 1*—"Don Jesse Neal Nervously Faces Firing Squad Death as Pleas Fail."
> A cop killer had one day to go.
> Temperatures were below normal.
> Neal claimed innocence.
> A half-gallon of ice cream cost 75 cents.
> *July 2*—Kennecott Copper struck.
> Neal paid the "full penalty."

Ninety-four had died so far that year on Utah high-
ways.

"Neal's Execution Draws Large Crowd."

July 4—"Holiday Traffic Claims 243 in US."

"Bear Raids Tent, Carries Off Baby."

July 5—Yes. A washed-out black and white of that
thin woman, here in a dark floor-length dress, a
white flower above her heart: "Attorney's Wife
Dies in Mountain Fall." It was a picture of Jill
grown up, grown older.

Rachel Children Arthur, 34. Rachel Children, eldest
daughter of a Lutheran minister, came from Boston to Salt
Lake City the bride of attorney H. Malcolm Arthur, recently of Harvard Law School. Arthur's firm now repre-
sented Kennecott Copper, Silver King Mines, and Geneva
Steel. Mr. Arthur had just opened the very successful Beehive Amusement Park. As Symphony Guild President,
Rachel Arthur raised over $50,000. She chaired the March
of Dimes campaign. Her neck broke in the fall. Her body
would be flown back east. Mayor Harkness's wife said, "This
loss is inestimable." Such emotion, Mrs. Mayor.

A spokesman for the Mormon Church said, "The president offers his respects. This energetic woman will be
missed." About a Gentile, no less.

I flashed on my old man, his neck ripped open like it was,
dodging into darkness, and I wished to God I'd pushed him
off a cliff. You bet I did. He wouldn't have made the news.

July 6—"Rioting Convicts Grab Control of Washington's State Prison."

July 10 (thick letters)—"ARTHUR SUES OVER WIFE'S
DEATH." In the photo, two white, dotted lines,
one across, one down, joined in a V on a moun-

tain. Old Arthur blamed the forest service. They should have reinforced that stretch of trail for holiday traffic. She wouldn't have fallen. He thanked God his children were spared. On the day of the unfortunate mishap, Mr. Arthur was fishing in the high Uintas. Just four weeks earlier, he and Rachel Children Arthur legally separated. But he loved his wife. Their situation did not make her death less tragic.

Just more understandable, that's all. Christ.

July 11 (a box at the bottom of the page)—"Arthur Withdraws Suit." Experts walked the trail and told him no go, his wife stumbled. I looked at her dotted lines again: the accident, where Jill's mother breathed one final time then dropped right through her bones.

41 —— RED ROCK

I drove the U-Haul. Ginny followed in her bug.

We lugged our shit through a breezy heat into our new hacienda, the Eagles wailing about desperadoes from the eight track in her car. When the album ended, we stood quiet for a long time on the baked and rocky dirt of our yard, our sweaty arms around each other. "Like my own private postcard," Ginny said. After we dropped the truck and brought the Polara out, we forgot ourselves like that again, on our sides on the red, van-size boulder just north of the house, a giant Jonathan beside our "orchard," two prehistoric apple trees.

Here we were on a ragged ledge above North Canyon, halfway to Mars, the highest house but one toward Cave Peak. Our gully out back probably only ran steady two months a year, a trickle down to the west, to the lake, that huge mirage of hammered silver and red, rugged islands like petrified apples that smashed when they fell. The wind blew sweet. Dry. Clear.

Her skin gleamed. Her smooth eyes stayed closed. I tried not to give a damn about any binocs in the house around to the side above. Ginny even took off her panties.

Before we jumped from the rock, each of us pink, damp, she said, "You're right about one thing, Loskie. There's plenty to be scared of. I'll grant you that."

On an old, lopsided barbecue she pulled out of somewhere, Ginny burned a few hot dogs. She called it a house warming. When darkness finally happened, we unknotted on our mattress on the back room floor then went outside stripped to the bone. The moon torched the tops right off the mountains when it rose. Wrapped in an itchy blanket that smelled of cedar, we leaned against one of our trees and fell asleep. Around four-thirty I carried her to bed.

I inhaled sage first thing. And dry grass the brown of bread crusts. Our slopes climbed clear to the sun. My back was a little sore, but not like a kidney punch or anything. I had not heard Ginny leave for work. I rested my head on my folded arms on the windowsill.

Two big magpies twisted their spiked heads this way and that, perched in the heavy, dusty scrub oak bunched around the shed. When Mr. Cat slunk across the drive's yellow gravel, closer, closer, his shadow black-panthered beside him, the magpies barked, and he ran, his fur frizzed, his ears flat. I laughed. Before he reached the house, he did a flip then flipped again.

I could have turned a few somersaults over the sun-baked goddamn perfection of the place myself, everything but the house. The bathtub was red from rusty water, like the slab under the water heater in the basement. In half a million places, the sky-blue kitchen linoleum was worn through to the rotten wood beneath. The walls peeled in milky green flakes big as chestnut leaves. The oven window had a bullet hole in it. The fridge rumbled like a Greyhound. And half the dirty windows were cracked and ready to fall out. They trembled in the wind.

The wind always blew up there. With wings wide as overpasses, big birds rode that wind all day, drifted circles over the sun-cracked, rain-stained, collapsing adobe house, the sandstone path to our door, the two mammoth pines in the front yard that shaded me in the window. Mr. Cat sauntered to a tuft of yellow grass at the knotted base of one of the pines, turned his ass, tail high, and shivered clear to his sharp little toes, laying his claim to everything.

I only heard one car that first morning. Amazing. I fired up some water for coffee on the lousy stove and leaned on the sink to look again at the mountains. A Jeep whirred down a ridge to the east and then growled past on the tiny paved trail that wanted to be the road we lived on. In the green canyon just south, a dog hacked its ever-loving head off. I wanted a dog—to chase deer, guard Ginny, and howl at the moon. Another moon like last night's and I'd be howling.

I'd stashed my garbage bag, with my notebooks and tapes, in the crawl space up behind the water heater. Somebody'd need X-ray eyes to find it. I didn't tell Ginny.

Up there where the moon burned acetylene and red-tailed hawks sharpened their knives against the sky, nothing but courage would do. Justice. And when had I shown courage, taken charge of anything? Assholes had taken charge of me as long as I could remember. Lance. Lance had always controlled *his* own life—and everybody else's. Not me. I let myself get mean. You name it, I bent. Skink. Danny. Dogs. Yet here I was with chances left to stand up for real. One more chance. To make up for plenty.

I remembered only three things I had ever *decided* to do:
lure a bear into Lance's ranch house, come back to make
Lance pay, and go to my mother's funeral. Lance would
pay. I would make a difference.

And my old man would pay, would leave or worse, would
one way or another stop his lying revival scam. I saw them
as they were. And who else did? I leaned over the entire
Salt Lake Valley with power—courage. My voice. The tape
turning. Finally.

They made me. Because I let them.

The rock of spaghetti thumped the counter. I put Jill's
frozen note inside my shirt. Here with Ginny, the icebox
wouldn't do. On the way to the car wash, I stopped at
Walker Bank and rented a safety-deposit box.

For eighteen years, I'd carried it, hidden it, seen to it
myself. Everything led to this. A bank vault of small, secret
drawers, and one with my number on it.

Our house stayed dark when I cut the headlights. An owl
carried in on the wind, three shorts and a long; who, who,
who, whoooo. Mr. Cat leaped into the window, like a damn
ghost, and I jumped. A pistol in my hand, Mr. Cat's gone.
He sat as calm as a lamp. So nobody stayed behind, if
anybody'd been there in the first place. "Ginny!"

The drip pots for the storm the night before were put
away. Mr. Cat said, "Meow, meow, meow."

"Shut up," I hissed. "I'll feed you to the rattlesnakes."

The place looked damn near like I'd left it, dishes in the
sink, an Orange Crush on the table, our new baby-blue
phone—Ginny insisted on one "for emergencies"—in its
cradle. But the TV . . . The TV was gone.

"Ginny!" I called again, out back. "Ginny! You up
there?"

Her tiny voice whispered "Yes," from the slope.

Ginny, smiling, on the boulder on a blanket, said, "What's wrong?"

And I said, "I thought somebody . . . The TV. What the hell happened?"

"Oh. Don't be mad. I put it in the shed. So I won't watch anymore. Yeah."

I told her I would quit my job. She would not be alone at night again. She said, "Bull. This place is safe as the Temple grounds." She said I should be thinking hard about another job, not dumping that one with a week and a half to go. What the hell *was* I going to do next, she wanted to know. "Maybe your sister hears about jobs—in state parks, or museums. You could ask."

I pulled Ginny tight against me. I said, "It's a long story, believe me. But I'd rather rot. And I won't rot. There're ways."

Then here came the moon again, melting a little bit of everything.

Aaron talked the future to the two guys overhauling the bays, took an hour coffee break, and looked in on me. He wore wash 'n' wear suits with his braids and sandals now. And he brushed his teeth. I noticed, since he smiled so damn much.

"Yesterday," he told me, "I was empty, man, clean out of ideas. Remember that, Cade." He adjusted his tie, a green one with pheasants, the knot wide as his neck. I stared back at myself in his shades. "Now this"—the lot where each car had a fish bowl–size plastic heart balanced on its hood (and chained to its bumper); his grass shack, tropical booth; and the bays, puckering with plaster and paint. "Tell me about it sometime, man, what's wrong with the world. Then check this out, and think about the outrageous potential of imagination, Cade. That's what it's about." He gave me a cigarette, lit it with a fancy butane. "Got to run," he said. But he dragged his sandals away slowly.

Great, baggy purple clouds settle around the mountains
like a tent. The valley steams. Ropes of mist. Then the rain
comes—heavy, slow, silver.

Aaron clutches a red umbrella, and he's running. "Your
lucky day, Cade. I'm closing up. S'posed to do this all night."

At first I think, Yeah, some fucking luck. I stop by the
Mission Cafe and eat a hot dog with a bowl of chili while
two Indians shoot pool. I buy a cigar. I ache through my
shoulders.

And it hits me how married I am. I want to call Ginny.
Take her dancing. Buy her a ring like Florida's with the
last of Danny's money—all of it. And I wonder what happened to my mother's ring. The old man probably sold it,
what do you bet? My old man.

At the second Safeway, I find a poster—a new one. All
this week, "Bear Testament" with Ministers of the Gospel
Tiny Markem and Bernice. "Banish the demons of Obesity,
Greed, Lust, and Debauchery! Jesus heals!" I tear it down.
This is what I will do on my *lucky day*.

The parking lot is full. I run half a block through the
hard rain. Lightning yellows the air, booms as I squeeze
into the long, narrow church where a woman far away
bends at an organ and sings, "I am a pilgrim and a stranger
passing through this troubled land." When she's through,
those in the back with me work their way forward to empty
spots on the padded pews. I sit by a woman in rollers. Her
hands clutch her knees through her thick skirt. Her breath
whistles. A voice calls, "Jesus!"

"Hallelujah!" everyone answers.

"I said, Jesus."

Louder now: "Hallelujah!"

He must be Tiny Markem. What you would expect. A
small face, mostly mouth, hair sprayed in place, a plaid suit.

What I didn't expect was his voice—an eerie kind of whisper, even with the microphone damn near down his throat. "Jesus has but one door. You must knock. I said, You must knock!"

"Jesus! Praise Him! Praise Jesus!"

"To get in, you must knock. You must knock for the Lord!" Tiny Markem dropped a loud fist on his flimsy pulpit. Thunder cracked outside. "Knock for the Lord."

"Yes, yes."

"Knock and the door will open. Knock in the dead of night and the door will open."

And a door did open. A yellow door at the back of the stage. And through it stepped my old man, in a white shirt and a wide green tie. He kept his head down.

"He knocked, ladies and gentlemen. Brother Cade knocked and the door opened wide. You know his story. A drunk. A drifter. One of God's lost children. He came home. Step up here, Lester Cade."

"Praise Him! Praise the Lord!"

"Step up here and speak of Jesus."

My old man took the microphone. He raised his face, his eyes big. He spoke slowly. "There is a Satan. I've walked in Satan's shoes. Who hadn't? Huh? Who hadn't tipped a bottle with 'im? Huh? Lied for 'im? Lusted with a lust from hell?"

A man rose, a thin man, tall. He rolled his head and jabbered. Just plain jabbered. The woman next to me said, "Mr. Holt."

My old man said, "Listen to God. He is with us." A baby whined. A woman screamed. The rain sprayed the tinted windows. Mr. Holt waved his long hands above his head and jabbered.

"Only Jesus," my old man said, "can bring you home. Go home. Knock. Hey, Jesus *will* let you in."

And spit bubbled in Mr. Holt's mouth as his loud, tangled words came out.

"He is calling you!" my old man hollered. He reached one arm over his head, waving us in. "Calling His children."

"Yes!" Tiny Markem shouted. He stomped the stage. "Yes!"

"Yes!" a fat, fat woman called. "I hear the Lord." She shook in her tight dress with eyes all over it. Small, horn-rimmed glases were deep in her shiny face, the lenses like chips of ice. Mr. Holt still yammered, hitting himself in the chest. The woman said, "He that hath an ear let him hear what the Spirit saith."

Tiny Markem stomped again. "We hear it!"

The fat lady rocked slowly from side to side. "Behold, I have set before thee an open door, and no man can shut it."

"No one!"

"And listen!" the fat woman almost sang. "Listen! I have heard the voice of many angels round about the throne, and the beasts, and the elders. And the number of them was ten thousand times ten thousand."

Mr. Holt stiffened with a jolt and fell, banging the pew. The group gasped. "Glory!" Tiny Markem screamed. Two men lifted Mr. Holt, sat him up.

My old man said, "Come home." And Bernice jumped in with the organ. The heat. Good God. The lady next to me moaned.

"Come home," Tiny said. He paced the front of the stage. "If you feel the spirit, come home. Come forward and say, 'I have come home.' Come forward." People filled the small aisles. They stood before the stage, and Tiny Markem leaned to them, pressed his thumbs to their eyes, and they shrieked and squealed and dropped back into the arms of those waiting, until they blinked and smiled and staggered to their seats. The organ—so loud—and lightning burst through the windows. My old man loosened his tie, raised and lowered his arms, shouting, "Praise Him, praise His name." He sweated so his face shined and his shirt darkened and clung as he moved.

The air was empty, sucked out. I wanted a smoke, but I stepped into the crowd, slowly moving up front, closer, closer, men shouting, children crying, women calling, "I'm coming. I'm coming."

I yanked my old man's pant leg. He said, "Jesus, Jesus." He opened his eyes, big eyes, dark eyes, smiled, and said, "So!"

And I said, "Save yourself." He couldn't hear. He stooped down, and I took his tie in my right hand, and I said, "Save yourself. You're going to stop all this." He smelled like gasoline. The small scar under his nose tightened. He rolled his head and laughed. "Stop," I said. "Stop. You've done enough damage. I'll make you stop." He dropped back, sat, laughed.

Tiny Markem shouted, "Praise God!"

I pushed my way out into the air, the rain pounding down. The trees were black balloons. Cars sliced across wet streets.

Cutlip, Crow, Cross, Cox, Cain, Cade. Norval H., Danine S., and Lyle T. I smoked with a burning cup of coffee at the wall phone in the Sears snack bar. I ran my finger down a list of people I'd never heard of with my last name. No Cade, Lester. Water ran down my face and spattered the page.

42 —— BREATH YOU COULD SEE

Thursday nights those cold months, Jill's old man, Malcolm the Great himself, played cards downtown at the Alta Club.

At five to six, give or take maybe ten seconds, his Lincoln swung its big beams out the drive. By six Lance had hot-footed it into richer neighborhoods to the north, where crew-cut boys shot eight ball in basements, ran through their old men's tough-sounding words, smoked a stolen filter cigarette now and then maybe, the windows open, maybe rolled their eyes over a *Playboy* centerfold unwadded out of some kid's wallet, and believed the whole, half-assed shebang amounted to growing up. I put that much together just on his brags.

By seven, whatever the weather, Mrs. Jove, the black housekeeper, stood at the bus stop on South Temple, a string-handled paper sack in each hand, the peacock feather waving on her red hat. I watched between two spruces next to the Downeses'. I said, "Bye, Jove," to myself and laughed.

Jill waited in her dark garage, mittened, hatted, wrapped in a long blue scarf. If we had any grass we smoked it there, huddled on tires that leaned against the frozen walls.

Before going inside sometimes, we wandered the smaller, dimmer streets, our arms around each other, talking about nothing in particular, stopping over strange sounds, staring at the silhouettes down long tunnels of chalky blue television light behind windows thin as cellophane—like seeing real human beings inside those stale sugar Easter eggs with the view holes in the ends. Maybe somebody watched us, too.

Dope wouldn't have been dope, though, if it hadn't made me crazy plenty of times so that I couldn't slow down or stop laughing. I hung from trees, flapped angels in the snow, slid on icy sidewalks, rifled snowballs, pulled her skirt up, took my pants down, and sang, yodeled like a goddamn idiot. Neither of us pretended to be happy the way happy is supposed to be—ever. But on our way always to her back door and her bed, we forgot ourselves a lot, which I guess is what everything's about. Sure Jill laughed, even clapped, her face open to anything, like a cat's, a wildcat's. Her eyes pounced on leaves, icicles, shadows, strangers.

One of the first warm nights in March, not five minutes from home at the corner of Second and "T" Street, a red and white DeSoto shot up, sprayed the walk with silver. The foggy window came down. A girl with heavy mascara streaked beneath her eyes said, "Fucking cold. Hop in the back. Don't sit on my coat."

Danny turned at the wheel. "Hey," he said.

Jill said, "Hey."

"My friend Jill," I said. "Danny Ingus." Neither girl smiled.

"The old man blinked," Danny said, "so I borrowed his wheels. Get in. You're freezing my ass."

I smelled glue. The girl had a dirty rag up tight against her face. She gave us the once-over with those barbed, puffy eyes. As Danny fishtailed back into motion, he said, "You picked a good night to climb aboard, man. Got any bread?" A pile of greasy *Argosy*s shifted under my feet on the floor. Jill pulled her knit cap over her ears.

"Nada."

"How 'bout your girlfriend? She don't look like no orphan."

"Damn near," I said. "Forget it. No bucks."

"Any smokes?"

Jill gave him her last cigarette. The girl held a big Zippo with both hands. The flame sputtered.

"I'll need a couple more now in a hurry. You'll see why." The car wobbled through turns, Danny low in the seat, one hand on the wheel. "Just to get my head straight. Hey," he said. He laughed up another puff and pulled over. "Listen, I'm shaky like a cripple tonight. Look at my hands. Too much animal food, man, popcorn and Crackerjack."

"Sounds familiar. Shitty idea to drive all over hell, then. Swing around and drop us. Let your girl give you the cure." I put my arm around Jill. "We'll walk from the tennis courts back there. No sweat."

Danny's chin sharpened over the seat when he smiled. "Let's go," the girl said.

"What I'm askin'," Danny said, "is will you grab me some smokes? All I'm askin'. I can't see a store right now."

Jill stared like somebody watching me fight. I nodded, and she tightened her fingers on my leg. "Okay. But then we go home. Deal?" The girl hung on him as we shimmied to life again. "Albertson's. The one on Seventh East."

I worried they'd be gone, hauling Jill all over hell. Nope. The DeSoto hummed exhaust in its own messy corner of the parking lot. Danny grinned, Jill said something to the girl. Like ghosts inside those windows gray with breath. The radio pounded now. I slipped the carton of Marlboros from under my coat. When Danny'd finally torn out another smoke and pulled two or three big drags down, he said, "Much obliged. I'm a crazy fucker."

"Home."

"No no no no," he said. He gunned the engine. The tires squealed. I thought about cops. Jill, tired eyed, pale, smoked too. "You gotta see this."

This followed a long drive along the boulevard, the car choked with cigarettes. *This* became us, headlights killed, outside one of those no-money-down, split-level jobs behind the Capitol. Gandy's garage was two streets over. The city spread below us like oil. A car shined in the driveway, a new car, the sticker still in back. The house slept, without lights. "Let's go," the girl said.

"In a minute." He rolled down the window and flipped a hot butt into the darkness. Smoke streamed away. He turned to me and held up his arms. "Look at me now. The old hands came home." He reached across the girl, opened the glove compartment, and brought out the .22 pistol he'd fooled with before.

"Come on. Stash that thing," I said.

"In a minute. The dude lives there manages the Big Boy where my old lady works—worked. She told my old man he grabbed her in a back room and she hit him, so she got canned. Goddamn. My old man got plastered, that's what he did about it. My old lady split." He steadied the pistol on his left arm.

"Danny, you stupid shit."

The gun exploded. The girl screamed. Jill didn't move. The glass burst from the big picture window. Danny squeezed off another for the window by the door and a final thunder for the window with the sudden light behind a tree.

I heard dogs. A guy in a white bathrobe stepped onto a porch two doors up, and Danny laid down rubber damn near to the corner. He ran stop sign after stop sign until the Capitol intersection, where three cars waited to turn. When he finally slowed down, I took Jill's arm. When he stopped, the pistol sticking over the wheel, tight in his steady hand, I threw open the door and dragged Jill after me. The girl said, "Let's go." And she was laughing as the DeSoto's whining wheels jet-trailed onto the narrow road above Memory Grove in City Creek Canyon.

Jill and I were into heavy kissing on the Capitol steps, between two icy, stone lions, when we heard the sirens.

For only the second time since Hilda got her, Fifi crapped all over the kitchen, just let go. If my old man had been there, Fifi would have been more like French toast than French poodle after that, but the old man's ship pulled out who knew how long ago now—a month, a year? I knew it would sink. He was something I didn't have words for, didn't want words for, so I forgot him as best I could.

The place stunk. Mama leaned against the stove, her sunken cheeks white crescents under her bleached-out eyes. Too empty to bother with, her mouth hung open. "Bad dog, Fifi," Hilda said. "Bad dog." A tiny knot of fur growled and shook a washrag in the bathroom. Hilda duck walked cleaning up. Then she sprayed perfume across the floor. Mama coughed.

I said, "Give my lungs a break."

Mama rattled at the stove again, over liver sizzling in onions and a pot of stewed tomatoes. Hilda'd bought the liver. I'd lifted the rest, and the cherry pie for dessert. I smoked to cut the smell, tapping my toes, thinking about the shots the night before. Jesus, the knocking was so light I believed I made it up, until Hilda opened the door and Fifi bolted out, yapping at the stranger who was Jill, Jill in a blue, ankle-length down coat and a red knit cap. Jill picked Fifi up and patted the fluffy head. She said, "Who's this?"

"Here," Hilda said, taking her dog and stepping back. "Come in, if that's what you want. It's cold."

Jill looked at me, eyes calm, clear. "Want me to?"

Mama shouldered Hilda out of the way. "Them's manners for ya," she said. "Come on. Pull up to supper with us."

"I can't," Jill said, but she moved in far enough for the door to close and tugged off her hat. "At least I won't eat. I already have."

"You're the Arthur girl, aren't you?" Mama squinted. "I remember you . . . you playing with my Hildy summertimes."

"Jill Arthur," Hilda said. "You heard Mama, Jill. Take off that coat. Sit down."

"Hold on," I said. I lighted another smoke. I held the pack out for Jill. "Maybe we'll go for a walk."

"She came to see *you*?" Mama clicked her tongue, smiling. "I didn't know. All the more reason." Mama's hand trembled on the radio until she found violins. For a moment her head moved to the music.

Hilda ate quickly. Jill smoked. To violins. Jill said, "Going to the game?"

Hilda checked her watch, Hilda so dark glancing down then up at Jill, blond, colorless except her mouth, red, and her eyes. "I've got a date with Leo Montrob afterward. Makes me feel like a munchkin. Coach says he'll be all-state."

"The giant curly guy?"

"You know him?"

"Just who he is. My old . . . My father knows his father. We ate with them at the club one time."

"Oh." Hilda covered her mouth with one of the green-checked rags we called napkins. "Excuse me," she said. "I have to get ready."

I stood too, to get Jill out of there; away from the perfume, the comb print in the floor, the dark round tips of Mama's fallen tits poking out of her new robe, showing through her ratty nightgown. Nothing doing. A gray shock of Mama's hair puffed at her forehead like a soap pad. It wobbled as she said, "We lived here since before you was born."

Jill touched the burning stub of her cigarette to the new one in her mouth. I sat back down.

"You was a beautiful little thing, always frilly, always in the cleanest, softest, brightest dresses." Mama slowly reached over and squeezed Jill's hand. "A lot like me when I was a girl. An awful lot. You was always a picture, a lady, spittin' image of your mother, bless her soul."

"You remember her?"

"Like yesterday. I run into her two or three times down to Hickler's. Her voice was like Loretta Young, that movie star from here. You know Loretta Young?"

"Yes."

"Just like that."

"Jill, let's go."

But my mother rose, collecting dishes, and Jill took them from her. Jill passed me her cigarette. "We're not in any hurry. Are we?" A spider crossed one of the peeling cupboard doors.

A car horn hollered up the alley. Hilda kissed Mama's cheek and said "Bye-bye" in a burst of fresh, frozen air.

"Bye-bye," Mama finally said. Fifi yipped.

Mama changed the radio: accordions, polkas. Jill fumbled in steam at the sink, sloshed her pants.

"No kind of work for a little lady," Mama whispered. She sat by me at the splintered table, turning a cardboard egg carton into "a pencil holder." She muttered, punching holes in the bottom, drawing tear-shaped petals around the outside with a red felt-tip pen, wheezing through her nose. "No kind of work for a lady."

Jill twisted her hands on a spaghetti-bloodied dishtowel, then ran her fingers through her hair. She smiled. I said, "Let's motor."

"Okay?" she asked Mama.

"What's okay?" Mama drew a red star on her hand, then another. "I've lost my looks is what I've done. What's been done to me." The pen trembled a long line around her wrist. "What's been done to me, God knows. I'm okay okay. Don't go getting any fool notions otherwise. Hear?"

"C'mon," I said. Fifi yelped and ran from the room.

Jill kept both hands on the wheel. We moved slowly over hollow tracks through new snow. I passed her the last of an old pint I had. "No thanks." Finally, after five or six empty blocks, she talked again: "Did you see the paper?"

"Yeah. Pretty nifty."

The thick headline on the inside section: COUPLE WOUNDED, GIRL DIES IN FIERY CRASH. Idiot damn Danny tumbled into City Creek Canyon and blew sky high. The girl had a Spanish name, Dulcinea Rodriguez, called Dolly. In her yearbook picture, with the story, she smiled. Daniel Cody Ingus, 15, was in "serious" condition with a broken neck, a smashed leg. He might be charged with attempted murder and manslaughter, and some shithead DA said he would see Danny tried as an adult. "These punks with records two miles long have reached the end of the line."

The halfwits in the house had just turned in when the glass exploded. Ike Wilson Foshnet ran to the living room right on time to catch a bullet in the thigh through the window by the door. His groaning got his wife out of the sack. She flipped on the bedroom light, and blamo, shoulder shot. Danny was one lucky son of a bitch, first to go two for three, second not to kill anybody. Not that he didn't want to. Shit. I'd read it over and over in the library that afternoon, stared at Dolly, with her milky newsprint eyes. Then I lost myself in this western called *Beyond the Desert,* about a cowboy named Ross McEwen. Hightailing it for murder, he got caught because he stopped to nurse a poor-as-dirt Mexican family dying in the middle of nowhere.

I didn't think Jill and I had a damn thing to worry over. I told her that. She laughed, beating the steering wheel with her mittens, until she cried and pulled off. The Volvo slid and bumped the curb. With a deep, empty sigh, she lifted herself to me. She shivered, kissed my neck, my cheek.

She said, "You know what, Carlos?" Steam surged into our darkness from an apartment's dryer vent. "Sometimes, I believe nothing's dead." I kissed her hand. "Every little thing in the whole demanding world's mine, isn't it? Is me, isn't it? You know, scientists can prove all kinds of ways that rocks are dead." I laughed. "But I can prove to my-self in a trillion ways that nothing is. The something that lives in me, that lives through me, can't just disappear, is . . . is in everything—like a gong."

"You rang?" No smile. Her hands shook. I kissed her hair.

In the arc light on the corner, a man in a yellow snow-mobile suit shoveled slush. The windows had crystaled.

She lit two cigarettes. "My father was up when I got in. He patted me—like a dog or something. He said he knows how young people are. 'I don't want you getting mixed up with the wrong element, though. You have the makings of a fine young woman.' God. Every now and then he thinks he knows me . . . and owns me and . . ."

"He's your old man. We were late. He cares is all."

"I'm glad you fucking care so much," she said. She reached for the key. "And then Lance this morning, he tells me I'm 'playing with fire.' Listen. The paper was folded right to it on the table."

"Forget the spooky stuff. Drive."

43 —— WAYS TO DISAPPEAR

I set down my pen and touched a match to a cigarette. The son of a bitch must have moved just then because I caught him about a hundred yards up crouched on the rubble of the slope: khaki pants and shirt, binoculars. I stashed my stuff in the basement.

My visitor hightailed it over a lip of brown rock as I climbed. He did not look familiar. No rifle. No nothing. Why did he run? I slowed up to get my breath. A hairy damn tarantula backed into a hole and closed a lid of dirt and rock that fit so well it disappeared.

Same with my peeper. The footprints were there okay, pigeon-toed, with deep heel holes—cowboy boots— pointed at my place. I lost them on a patch of shale, which I circled, but no luck. I found a rusted-out doll buggy in some bushes, a snail fossil. Not much else. Could have been some nature lover just wandered over that way. Sure, there in the middle of Yellowstone. Could be whoever paid the call wouldn't be leaving so easily the next visit.

I'd just pitched the fossil out over a side canyon when a powder-blue Imperial broke from the bluer knots of scrub oak another good toss farther below. Christ. Houdini. He'd had a car with him underground. The car made dust, a red funnel.

The phone rang. The phone would not stop ringing, like it knew I stood on the porch staring at the lake, that I would take my time, to hell with everyone.

"This is Lance," the voice said. Something clicked on the line. "How are you, Cade?"

I took two deep breaths, to remember all I needed to know right then, all of it. "I'm sure you get reports. So why are you calling me?"

"To make life simpler," he said. "I want to help you."

"My old man's scared, is that it? I know you heard from Matt."

"I spoke to Matt. Friends call when they're worried. I'm worried about you, Cade. I'm worried *for* you."

Two dragonflies zigzagged over the yard. A bumblebee crawled across a fist-shaped rock. After two years, we talked, and who the hell did he think he was?

The click again. A lighter? Maybe Utah's governor smoked Kools in his private office. "Maybe you'd like a hand getting started somewhere else? Not charity. A loan. If you want it, I've got a nice nest egg for you and your girlfriend."

"I've got something for you," I said.

"Carlos, I am not afraid of your story. I was twelve."

"She left a note," I said.

"What? Who left a note?"

"You know who. She wrote it that morning. I've got it, and by the way, she gets it straight about your mother."

"It's a fake."

"You know it's not. And it's in a nice safe spot. Anything happens to me, others know how to get it."

After a moment of what I imagined as one or two puffs beneath an eagle or a flag, he said very slowly, "So sell it to me. My sister was . . . very disturbed."

"Tell me about disturbed. Tracking me down is disturbed. Spying on me is disturbed. Pampering my old man is disturbed. You don't know what he did, do you? My old man . . ." And the words weren't there, even if I had wanted them. "My old man, he ran out. The note . . . The note's mine till I decide I don't want it anymore. When that time comes, you'll hear."

I hung up. The sink dripped in the kitchen. The refrigerator kicked on. I could feel my lousy Timex ticking on my arm.

The ragged gray sky must be what kept the yokels away through a good chunk of rush hour. Once Aaron and the workmen packed it off for the night, I smoked and swung at flies. On top of Carpet World across the street rose a technicolor, big-as-a-bus Coke sign: THE REAL THING. A just-minted, strawberry blond burst from blue water, her teeth marble, her smile red licorice, her painted fingers fastened around a black bottle—reaching to me. I lit another smoke. I heard Ginny say my name. She wasn't there.

"A word or two, Cade." Lieutenant Dolores and Boy Wonder, arms heavy in sharp short sleeves. "Come over here a minute."

I flipped the match just shy of them. "Pretty please?"

Dolores laughed. He scratched his square, gray head. "I'd be testy, too, Cade, if this was where I turned a living. Give up the act and come over here. Pretty please." Boy Wonder tightened his lips and shook his head. Their green ties looked bulletproof, heavy as anchors.

They stopped by the vacuum. Dolores stepped up onto the concrete base to jack his squint to my level. Boy Wonder leaned on the pink garbage barrel. He nodded to the uniformed cop at parade rest beside their naked powder-blue Plymouth. I wondered if I could have made a mistake about the morning's visitor driving an Imperial—no way. I had an eye. And I had a secret. A secret they wanted. They looked me up and down.

Dolores's breath stunk. "Dead people love you, Cade. How come?"

I laughed. I said, "I live to talk to you guys, but I can't leave right now. I'm the only one on."

"This'll do fine," Dolores said. "See, you seem to be tied into a whole hell of a lot of my business. Whippet, tell Mr. Cade what I mean."

Whippet stared at me, without blinking, as he pulled a brown notebook from his back pocket. Its pages were ragged and gray. Five'll get you ten he never went to school with Hilda. All that Miss Utah shit probably came out of that dirty little book. "Simple," Whippet said. "After some action at a dog pit, your old pal, Ingus, is sore. He's in hock big-time. We hear a dog gets swiped. Stonehenge blows. Then Ingus, or Castro, drops his guard for good, which you don't know anything about, Cade."

"So?"

"So," Whippet said, his eyes in the book, "I won't mention Spud. Oh, he did himself, sure, but there you were again." They didn't miss a trick. And I didn't show a thing. "Turn around and Anthony Nicks gets slashed. Where did he work? Stonehenge, and we're back to square one. This baby's in your neighborhood."

I spit against the wall.

Whippet licked his lips. "Everybody comes to Cade. Everybody believes in you, Cade."

"We believe in you, Cade," Dolores said. "Honest to God. We believe you know what's going down. Somebody's trying to sell a dog now, we hear. Cade, we'll find this dog and bust these fights wide open. We're gonna catch the killers, count on it. For now, you let us know where the dog is, we'll smile on you any warrants come around."

"My pals."

"You never know," Dolores said. "You don't help us, somebody else could help you."

"World's a funny place," Whippet said.

"Ha ha."

Dolores lowered his voice. "You want to tell us anything?"

"Nothing to tell."

"You didn't go after Nicks, did you? Getting back for what happened to your old buddy Ingus?"

"Are you kidding?"

"Keep your hands clean. Call anytime. We will." Dolores lifted his arm, damn near saluted, and stepped down. "We find out you've been sitting on anything, you can kiss your sweet little life in the mountains good-bye. Hear?"

In that frozen tear of white water, the woman on the billboard forced a grin.

If anybody crossed my slope the next morning, I was blind. The only person I saw was that rummy, bug-eyed son of a bitch holding the microphone, watching me, like a ghost on the clean glass of the window, the stupid goddamn idiot who'd gone to Danny Ingus again in the first place.

————

"So what is it?" Rose asked, her voice sloppy. "If I'm so important, drop by sometime. You did send me those flowers. I've got a heart, you know, same as you."

"I've been busy," I said.

"Tell me about it."

I scratched my initials in the black paint of the phone. A freckled woman carrying a violin case waited to call. She stepped closer, shifted her weight to her other foot, and muttered something right outside the booth. I nodded, held up my knife. She backed off some. A gas station. Over my head, SHELL in gold letters. Flies. Heat. Sweat. I would not use our phone. And I would not visit Rose. But who knew about Rose's phone?

"You still there, Cade?"

"Rose, I just want to get a couple of things straight. The cops keep coming by and they've made me curious. A dog got lifted."

"Okay. That's out of my league."

"Come on. An important animal, what I hear."

"How important?"

"Thousands. But you can't help me?"

"Cade, I can't help myself."

"And L.G.? You know he's thinking of getting Quicky back?"

"No he ain't."

"Ask him."

"As far as I care, every damn dog is dead, Cade. They say dogs look like their owners? All their owners is dead. Come see me one of these days. I got a little life left. Forget this other shit. Leave it alone."

Beside Ginny's head, a rusty voice drawled along with a pedal steel on the radio. She lay on her back in a pair of white shorts, her perfect chest spread over her. She lifted her legs and let them down slowly, counting, "One, two, three, four, five." On "five" they touched the floor.

I worked on beer number two in our easy chair. "I been thinking," I said. "I might move out, somewhere close by maybe, just till the baby's born."

"No," she said, "three, four . . ."

"Ginny, honey, this ain't Paul, Idaho. Somebody important's worried about me. I know a few things. Worried can get scared. Scared can get mean."

She pushed up onto her elbows. "How long have we been seeing each other?"

"Ginny."

"How long?"

"Something like eight weeks. But that . . ."

"Two months," she said. "And in two months, what's happened?" I tapped a cigarette on top of my can. She sat up. "Huh?"

"Plenty," I said, "that you don't need to know about."

"What that's so scary all of a sudden?"

"Somebody went through my rooms. Then yesterday some fruitcake prowled around the rocks up there with binoculars. He bolted like a jackrabbit when I went to check him out."

"Why didn't he shoot you if you know so much?"

"Shooting's too complicated. Just keeping tabs for now." The windows were shiny black above her head. "I've got something. It's hidden. It might save us."

"I don't need saving. What I need is you to relax. Okay? *Okay?* Hey, everything's on the upswing." She raised her legs. "We're going to make it. One, two, three . . ."

"Ginny. Ginny, I'm different than I used to be."

"What a surprise. Hey." She flipped off the radio. "If I saw you charging up the hill, I'd beat it, too. Guy was probably counting field mice or something." She pulled away. "What's going to get us, Carlos Cade, is money. Where are you going to work? You got any idea what it costs to have a baby? This summer session of mine only goes till Pioneer Day. Hey, who eats in August, right? I'll have four weeks with next-to-nothing coming in. So we'd better get on the stick and stop worrying before we have something to worry about. You could do lots of stuff, something with . . . with, I don't know . . . Carlos, it's nothing with the police, is it?"

"No."

No wind, no clouds, nothing but stars. I drank three more beers in the perfect air outside. Then she couldn't get enough of me.

Outside my window the next morning, a range of mountains, from tan, to red, to blue, to black way the hell in the distance. Nothing bothered the sunlight. The shadows stayed put.

44 —— *WINTER LET GO*

Hilda left for work early Saturday morning. Fifi slept in the bathroom. Mama made the beds.

After sitting a few minutes, letting her breathing calm down, Mama swept up. She dragged her slippered feet sideways after the broom, like a cripple. Black hair matted her bony, white legs. Dark stains already bruised her new flowered robe. I smoked at the table and drank extra-sweet instant Hills Brothers, waiting till the stores opened so I could pick up a few odds and ends. Then I'd hit the library and glance through the paper. I watched my mother like a circus act.

"It's up to us now," she said, her face damp, yellow, "now

that the beast run out on kith and kin. Good riddance, by God. Good riddance, I say. Last night we had a guest in this house. Oh, Carlos, she's a chippy. She is. If we keep the place right, she'll come see us all again. She will, won't she?"

"I doubt it," I said. But Mama called that one. From then on she acted like Jill was her doing.

"I knew you was comin'," Mama said that night, smiling up from a red bowl of pork 'n' beans. "Sit down there next to your boyfriend."

Hilda licked her spoon. "I'm finished. Honest. I've got to run. Sit here." Jill set a sack by the door, slipped off the long coat, and tossed her hair around her head.

"I brought something I hope *you'll* like, Mrs. Cade." Jill opened the sack and took out two hiking boots—scuffed at the toes and heels. She set them on the floor beside her. The ankles leaned away from each other. "They might fit," Jill whispered. "They were my mother's."

"Nice okay," Mama said. "Nice. But them shoes don't suit me."

"Nothing to look at, I know. Good walking shoes, though, I'll bet. In bad weather. That's why I brought them."

Mama squinted, her elbows on her knees. "What walking I do's indoor walking. I'm sick so's the cold could do me in."

"Baloney," Hilda said. She looked and smelled and moved like half a million bucks when she sashayed back into the kitchen. "You'd think you were chained here. Mama, this is your *house,* not the Tower of London. If *he* did it, if *he's* the one told you the world would eat you up you step through the door, he's gone—gone, Mama. If the world wanted to chew you to ribbons, it would have by now, and maybe it has. You've got to go out sometime, Mama. What can you lose?"

Calm, Mama turned. "I don't know nobody. Anybody sees me'll laugh like crazy. I'm not young. I'm a sick woman." Her chin rose and fell with two deep breaths.

"You okay?" Jill touched Mama's arm.

"And just what if he come back and I wudn't here?" Mama's head tilted like a puppet's. Her wet eyes could have been painted on as she looked at Hilda. "What if?"

I said, "He's not coming back. And, you know, what they're saying's true. Somehow I never figured you *could* go out. You can. You better. I don't like my mother just a fucking sack of bones in the dark."

"Curb your tongue," Mama said. Her tears speckled the concrete floor.

The *Tribune* had put Danny under the crease on the second section: Odds were he'd be tried as a juvenile. Found guilty as an adult, he could get thirty years. And on top of the girl dying, Danny lost his left leg to the knee. I wanted to tell Jill. I wanted to tell Mama. I imagined bullets breaking every stinking window in the house.

The night Jill brought Mama the boots was one of those clear as tears and cold as stone. Still, you wouldn't trade being alive those nights for anything—drugs, money, or promises.

We left Jill's cabin close to twelve. "Sex," she whispered on the porch, made her believe her life could be "good. *Good* sex, that is." I said the same, except I said with her. Almost always when she came, she knotted both hands down there and damn near pulled herself apart. I wondered how much had to do with me. But God loved us steaming that way, stepping across an untouched crust of snow, the air slapping every cell to life, the stars like needles.

Jill drove slowly, sleepy eyed, an unlighted cigarette between her fingers. "I wish it wasn't so early. But I know he'd say something if I got in late, more of that shitty, almighty stuff fathers are made of."

I circled through the Downeses' alley after she kissed me. On the island a snowman winked two bottle-cap eyes. My mother's gray head rested on the kitchen table, like something dead. A straight razor lay open next to her left ear, an uncorked fifth of Old Yellowstone, a third gone, beside her right. She snored. I couldn't see any blood. Her arms hung heavy at her sides.

I am in ninth grade and strong but not big. When I lift her there is no strain. I am a farm boy carrying a scarecrow to a field. She snores against my chest. I take off her filthy slippers and tuck her legs beneath the covers, her feet wrapped in dry onion skin. Her face caves in around her mouth. White shows between her eyelids.

In the morning water dripped from the eaves, the sky the ocean color on postcards.

"I heard some birds today," Mama said. "I changed my mind." She was dressed. I sat beside her and finished buttoning my shirt. Fifi scratched to get in. Mama looked small in outdoor clothes, in the bulky blue sweater and the long brown skirt, and I remembered her weight, the hollowness of her bones. The steel-wool thickness of her hair was combed, organized around a part. She nibbled her toast. When I looked down, I knew what I would find. They were the boots of a dead woman, all right, heavy and dark and scuffed, but on her ankles narrow as pool cues, Mama's fire-engine red socks belonged to the living.

"After coffee," I said. "And a couple of smokes."

That Sunday morning that year, winter let go. Dogs raced through the slush on the island, tearing up great dirty gobs, until their legs were sopping brown. Sparrows

yammered on the tree limbs. Families walked in long strides
to church. Mama held tight to my arm, the boots scraping
along the wet sidewalk. Something sounded loose in Mama's chest, but her breaths stayed even, her chin up, and
her squinty eyes busy just under her purple knit cap. Closed
for the day, Hickler's held no one inside its blue glass to
judge or pity us. But then I heard footsteps and I turned.

"I saw you," Jill said, pushing a mittened hand through
Mama's arm. "You're out. That's excellent."

"Mm," Mama said. "You don't forget."

Jill smiled across at me while Mama watched her noisy
feet, watched them and clicked her tongue. Jill's smile did
not reach her eyes. She said. "How do those fit?"

"Like they was mine," Mama said. "Some things you
don't forget."

I checked the windows along the way and saw no one.
When we reached the corner at last, Mama was trembling.
She looked at the street sign with those shuttered-up, yellow
eyeballs of hers, and moaned from the bottom of her
throat. When her knees gave, Jill caught her, startled as
much, I could tell, by the lightness of Mama as by the
sinking spell. Mama never lost consciousness or anything
like that. Hell, she talked the whole way home, pulling her
head up from my shoulder and saying, "Glory, glory,
glory," or, "I'll like to go somewhere now."

"Sure," Jill said. She patted Mama's veined hand.

I held Mama while Jill undid her coat and unlaced the
boots. Before the covers were tight beneath her neck, Mama
slept. Jill said her pulse seemed strong. And Mama looked
better already, alive again, with flesh instead of yellow wax.
Jill and I shared a rumpled pack of Pall Malls at the kitchen
table and whispered:

"What are you doing over here in the daytime? Your
old man'll scream."

"He's not home. He went to the hunt breakfast at Log Haven. Lance's watching football."

"They'll find out."

"I'm tired of being . . . of being a damn secret."

I lifted her fingers and kissed them.

I forgot Hilda. She finally dragged herself into the kitchen and let that sorry excuse for an animal back out. Jill and I worked on our right hands, pricking the webbing between our thumbs and forefingers with inky pins. Jill drew blood without a sound, without squirming once. My homemade tattoo, the cross, that's when I did it, but most of it got done to me. Jill had one, too—hers more like an eagle or an angel.

It took a lot to startle Hilda. She squeaked in a breath and spread a hand on her chest in the neck of her bathrobe.

"Want one?" I said. Hilda tried to laugh.

Jill put the pins and the ballpoint insides back in her purse. "We took her for a walk."

"Fifi?" Hilda sat beside us.

"Your mother."

And Hilda's eyes fluttered, fast, turned on me, then finally Jill. "Please," she said, "don't . . . Don't treat her like a joke."

"You know we wouldn't," Jill said. They stared at each other.

Hilda smiled quickly. "I'd better get going."

Mama woke long enough to mix together a dinner of Kraft macaroni and cheese—that was all. But when I got up the next morning she sat over coffee and toast in the kitchen again, already dressed. "Perty day."

"Mama, we've got school. I don't think you should go out alone—for now. Remember yesterday."

"Bluebird weather."

"Wait till we get home."

"I won't leave the drive. I'm a doer when I get the notion."

I skipped the library that afternoon. The valley was brown and bare inside a white wall of mountains.

"Well," Mama said, after I closed the door and shooed Fifi to the bedroom. "I feel like folk from the Bible, the way I come back and all." She looked like someone from the Bible, skin centuries old, fingernails petrified and rough. But her lips had color, and her eyes shined. "Went to Hickler's, I did. Bought me a candy bar. Sat there on the counter and ate it." She laughed, something I'd never heard. And I saw at least four missing teeth. She snorted. "Old Hickler, you'd think he seen a ghost."

"He did."

"I could cry," she said. But she didn't. "I feel like I just been dug up. Some things you don't forget, I can tell ya. No sir. Roamin' the world is something ain't nobody can forget."

The stores downtown stayed open late on Mondays— Hilda worked. Jill came just after dinner. She wore a red bandana around her head. She kissed Mama's cheek. Mama beamed. She yawned, but she didn't seem tired, the way she talked and talked to Jill, while I made cups of instant coffee and chain smoked. What she said she slurred half the time, and most of it made as much sense as baby prattle. But Jill listened. Now and then she asked a question. And Mama worked hard to come clear to somebody at last.

She told about hunting elk with an uncle on Mount Timpanogos. She shot a big cow, she said, and God didn't like her for it. My old man only got mentioned once: "I married Skipper in the spring because new leaves was on everything." And on it went till Hilda got home.

Jill and I drove up behind the University Hospital and did it about as fast as three or four buttons and a zipper.

As I left her garage, a sliver of moon hooked in the soft flesh of that warm sky, she said, "What's going to happen to her?"

"Who knows?" I said. "She made it this far."

"I sent flowers," she said, "without a name, don't worry—to the people Danny shot, that girl's parents, too. Carlos . . . Carlos, sometimes I think we just ought to run away."

Jill let out a deep breath.

Jill showed up again Tuesday night. I'd swiped a Sara Lee pound cake that afternoon. Mama ate two big pieces and talked some more, but—with Hilda in and out—never got rolling like before.

Wednesday Jill didn't come. I stayed home expecting her, leading Mama to expect her, and both of us got a little testy around eight when Jill wasn't there. "I'm going to bed," Mama said finally, pushing herself up. "Don't bother me now. Don't you bother me." I smoked two or three joints and kicked around town a couple of hours till I thought I could sleep.

Thursday night I watched old Arthur's Continental rock down the drive for his outing at the Alta Club. I circled to their back door. I damn near shit when Old Man Arthur himself, big as a goddamn statue, opened the gate. He said, "Get in here."

45 —— INDEPENDENCE DAY

Forty-five minutes late, eating wadded-up stale bread and smoking with one hand, steering and wiping at sweat with the other, I damn near dumped the Polara in North Canyon. Missed a mail truck. Two cats. She overheated, sure, but I held her at sixty. A job for the lowliest of the low and I rushed to it. Why?

All I had to do was stop. Right? Hide. Take Ginny away to some freshly minted piece of real estate in a desert somewhere. Get a job sacking groceries, pumping gas, anything. We have our kid. She goes back to work, teaching driving, selling cars, maybe, modeling for some local ad rag, whatever. The kid crawls, walks, talks, and then rides a red Huffy dirtbike two manicured blocks to a school named for JFK, Martin Luther King, or some desert flower, and after school pedals half a mile to the golf course where he caddies for retired realtors down fairways spitting with rainbirds. At night we watch cable TV in our air-conditioned mobile home, shows about families with kids who ride red Huffy dirtbikes. And we sleep like the embalmed. We sleep. And we do not matter, even to ourselves.

Or grease sizzles. A circle of pink neon buzzes around the clock. Flies never wait long. The two waitresses don't have uniforms, but they wear the same outfits day after day, getups that let you know they're female or once were, tight, naked, lonely clothes. Sometimes brainy high school or college kids hang out in a booth eating hamburgers and fries on wax paper. A trucker. A salesman. Old guys. Or guys that look old, smell it—stained cups, dirty fingernails, torn sport coats, missing buttons, busted shoelaces—who tremble, hands like gloves on bones, their cheeks so sunken they almost touch.

Ginny stops at my booth, fist jabbed against her hip. And I want something. I look back at my cup, the fly walking across my knuckles stained with smoke. "I haven't got all day," she says.

"Sorry I'm late," I said.

Aaron, in swamp-green slacks dripping at the cuffs around his bare feet, his knobby feet frisky on the steaming,

cracked asphalt, rubbed down a blue Granada. His pigtails
looked like pigs' tails.

"Shut up, Cade." He threw the chamois, but missed and
splattered the driver's window, where a silver-haired nervous lady tried not to notice. "Man, if I had anybody else,
you'd be amscray, Jack. My tough luck. Listen up good,
though. You're late again, it's bye-bye. A week or so's shut-
down till we switch over won't kill nobody. Comprende?"

My old man stood alone at the open back door of the
kitchen, blowing smoke past moths through the screen.
Bernice looked up, eyeshadow rising, and said, "Sorry, this
is closed off to the public." She peeled an orange.

Behind me a woman hollered. "Yes, Jesus, yes."

"That's my boy," my old man said.

Bernice said, "Oh, why didn't you say so?" Her bracelet
jangled with tiny hearts. Her stiff, blue dress spread wide
around her at the table. "Some cranapple juice?" She
pointed to a green thermos with a spigot.

"I just need a few minutes with him," I said. I smiled
like I brought the best news a person could bring. My old
man sucked his lip. When he lifted his chin to run a finger
around his collar, I saw the line, pink, circling his throat.
His tie tack was a dog, a hunting dog, a pointer.

"This is my boy, Carlos. He's grown up real well."

"I'll say," she said. "I'm Bernice Markem. Your father
gives his soul to others, one hundred percent. He's a bless-
ing to us. I'm sure you're proud." She ate a section of the
orange, pressed her lips to a paper napkin, and smiled,
teeth too long, blue around the tops. She filed her nails.
"What's your line?"

"The straight one," I said.

"Amen, brother," she said. Voices shouted beyond the
closed, shuttered doors.

My old man said, "Out here, son."

An arc light blazed over the parking lot, rusty cars, dusty cars, two relic school buses painted THE CITY OF GOD on their sides. Bugs swarmed the light. Crickets blew police whistles in the trees. He said, "I ain't scared. What I been through, I ain't scared." He lit another. We stopped by a Thunderbird.

"That's good," I said. " 'Cause you're leaving town." I grabbed his cool, smooth tie, yanked him close, and he didn't reach my forehead, had shrunk. His belly touched mine.

"I can stay. I'm bothering nobody. Helpin', in fact."

"Helpin' people swallow bullshit, wallow in bullshit, worship bullshit." I shook him. His voice sputtered. He dropped his cigarette. "You've hurt more than you could ever help."

"You're my son."

"You're a little late with that shit."

Blue in the light, with closed eyes, he could have been dead, except for the sounds in his mouth, the drops sliding from his forehead to his chin. "Don't. Don't." Our shoes made noise on the gravel. The organ started up. Like movie music.

I said, "I'd like to open you with my knife, but then you'd win, see, 'cause you'd have turned me to shit like you. I'll give you a choice. I'll be civilized. Go or I'll kill you. Not angry, not hot, cool-headed I'll do it because you have it coming. I thought I killed you once. I liked thinking that. But I want you to *go*. That's what I want."

"Okay," he whispered. I'd backed him against a bus. Inside the bus a baby cried out. A woman stared down from the bus window just over us. "You know I know plenty."

"So do I." I pushed him. His head banged, bounced. I let go of the tie. He smoothed it. I said, "I have your schedule. One week. Next week, I'll come looking."

" 'Cause I'm pregnant, I guess," Ginny said after I'd been home just long enough to chug two slugs of snake oil. So around eleven we motored back to town and squeezed into a booth at Snelgrove's Ice Cream. With her painted toes tucked under her, Ginny wolfed three double-dip butter pecans. I chewed malt balls.

Afterward she said, "Let's walk a little."

"If you can."

She punched my arm. "The doctor said I should—as much as possible."

"The doctor?"

"Yeah, the doctor. God, Carlos."

"So you saw a doctor. What'd he say?"

"She."

"Jesus. Okay. What'd she say? Never mind, I know, that you should walk as much as possible."

"You *were* listening."

"Always," I said, laughing. She put her arm through mine.

She slowed at store windows. We passed Hotel Utah, the stiff-backed statue of Brigham Young—who had been hiding, who had picked this place—and Temple Square, the golden angel Moroni trumpeting from a black roof.

Whooshing blue water. The water gleamed in the narrow, spotlighted fountain stretching half a block behind the Church Office Building. Ginny turned and saw my arc of pee splashing into foam. Her eyes got wide. She looked around. Then she grinned. I said, "Piss on it, just piss on it all."

Musk enterprises held its own on a high-powered, three-piece corner by the Stock Exchange, half a block from Stonehenge. It even rated a cigarette and candy counter in the lobby. The floor tiles were six sided, dollar size. Hard and white as teeth. I winked at the redhead behind the cigar case. For the sake of our hair, I thought she'd smile. No sale. "You got business here?" she asked.

"What business you got in mind?" She hooked one thumb on her skirt waist, lifted her eyebrows, and exhaled through the lipsticked, pretty ring of her mouth. "Why don't you give me a cigar?" I said. "Yeah, that one. I'm here to see Bobby Shiftlet. You wouldn't know where his office is?"

Now she smiles. She shakes her head as if to say, So that's your game. She says, "Wouldn't I?"

Carpet you could eat, thick, chocolate carpet. Four tall oak doors, with frosted glass and black nameplates, open onto this wide third-floor hall. Fancy gold frames window the walls, dark portraits of flabby old-time tycoon types. The elevator sighs. A couple of sickly guys in white suits and buckskin shoes slide out of the office labeled ROLLY MUSK, PRES. They carry papers that they read as they walk. The other doors are tagged MISTY MUSK, V.P. and R.W.T. SHIFTLET, BUS. MANAGER. I fire my stogie, huff a few clouds, and open the president's door.

I am here because this is not a game for children, because I go wherever the hell I please, wherever it makes good sense to go.

The walnut, windowless waiting room is crowded with dogs: toy ones, china ones, metal ones, stuffed ones—five hundred tails, a thousand eyes. Behind her wide, dark desk, beneath a blond rat's nest hairdo spotlighted from the ceiling, a small woman flashing phony eyelashes lifts her chest, her full soft sweater unbuttoned. A silent walnut box on her left sucks up my smoke. "Yes?" she says, with a southern drawl straight out of lousy television. "Do you have an appointment?"

"With Bobby Shiftlet," I say.

"Oh," she says. She wiggles. I breathe her perfume in this goddamn tomb of an office without even the sedative of Muzak. Her hands fidget in her lap under the desk. I expect the door behind her to open. I expect to see, maybe even talk to, Abe Lincoln with the metal hand.

She titters. "You passed Mr. Shiftlet's office on your way from the elevator."

I chew on my cigar.

Two workers move a piano in the hall. A cop leaves the elevator, crosses to Musk's. An older man carrying a silver case leaves Shiftlet's office.

Shiftlet's secretary was deeper, in the eyes, in the cleavage, in the accent, a foreign one, and in sizing me up. Her blue eyes knew my pant length and my cigar brand before my smoke disappeared into the red box on her desk. She would have been something except for the pitted scars on her face.

"Vut is yuh naem?" She repeated my story and the amount into her intercom, and did he want to speak with me? R.W.T. himself pushed through the door behind her as she scrawled in purple ink across a fat business checkbook.

The boxer's ears, the rifle-barrel nose—but he'd bleached his curly hair, that was it. An ascot in his open shirt. "I'm glad you remembered," he said, a wad of pink gum in the front of his mouth. "I pay what I owe. But we all do. I worried I'd scared you off," he added in his soft lisp, almost a hiss, "with my little proposition about the condos."

"No such luck."

"A joke. Good you didn't misunderstand."

"Not for a second. How's your mother?"

"Never happier, I don't think. Hey, she painted this picture of a cantaloupe the other day. *I* would've known it was a cantaloupe. She's great." He swallowed. "Cade, how about if you park your cigar out here and come in? Won't take long. Need to talk."

A green parrot perched on a football trophy on his desk. "Howdy, pardner," the parrot said.

"Sit down," Shiftlet said, and I did, in a deep blue chair by a glass coffee table. "It's funny how often I hear your name." He leaned on a filing cabinet. The parrot hopped to the windowsill.

Shiftlet played with the gold chain on his hairy wrist. "You found a place, a good view I been told."

"So you've been pokin' around," I said. "Get to it."

"Get to nothing. You need a job I'll bet to hold onto that good lookin' tail of yours and that house on the hill." His gum snapped. Cologne. "That idn't any kind of threat, Cade. We just like to be wise to what's going on and play the smart cards."

"We?"

"Me and my partners. We'd like to do you a favor."

"Like?"

"Like you run a few errands a year and you get thirty or so grand, plus a Christmas ham."

"Make it a turkey, I'll think it over."

"Come on, funny man." He moved behind his desk and dropped into the chrome chair. He rolled it back and forth. "We're talkin' a damn good job. No real strings. We'll help you and you help us." A cuckoo sprang out of a clock in the corner without a sound. The parrot said, "Cuckoo, cuckoo."

When the door opened and Musk stepped in, the parrot said, "Howdy, pardner." Musk lowered himself slowly onto the corner of the desk. Shiftlet quit rolling and straightened up. "I was going to pay you a visit," Musk said in that smooth Dixie drawl. "Happy you dropped by." He wore a string tie with a silver dollar at the throat. The tips were

rifle shells. His phony hand opened and closed. And goddamn, the nose, the mole—every damn detail—like a crazy
dream from . . . from what? Coins? Calendars? Henry
Fonda? The highway—a copper bust over a cutout west of
Cheyenne? His boots shined.

Shiftlet's face tightened. "I just told Cade we want to
make things easier for him."

"Cade," Musk said. His good hand opened, rose beside
him. "You're a smart fellow. Everybody says that. Your
sister told me. 'Too smart,' she said. And I say it doesn't
pay to be too smart."

I shook out a smoke. Musk said, "Consider all the ad-
vantages. I need some information, Cade. You need some
help."

"Which adds up how?"

"You saw my dog. Vice got lifted. You know that. Cops
know that. Ingus got killed."

Shiftlet said, "I know who done that." He rolled back to
the window.

"He thinks your friend Nicks did your friend Danny.
Something spontaneous. What do you think?" Except for
his arm and his mouth, Musk didn't move.

My smoke clouded things. "Possible," I said. "So who
did Nicks?"

"You?" Musk smiled.

Shiftlet turned. The parrot cocked its head.

" 'Fraid not," I said. "Risk my neck for what?"

"For the dog, to squeeze a few big bills. I got a note, a
funny note, offering to sell my dog back." Musk's dry eyes.
He stood and set his hand on my shoulder. "Who's peddling
Vice? If it's you, Cade—and I don't think it is—I'll forget
it. A mistake. I just want to know. Cops think I did Ingus.
The dog might change that." The hand was cold. The
woman on his silver dollar had no eyes.

"I heard there's a dog for sale," I said.

"Wrong dog," he said. "We checked. That dog's a mess."
Musk backed to the door.

Shiftlet said, "Arizona."

Musk said, "We could send you and your woman to
Arizona. Miami."

"I been."

Musk pulled his good hand through his beard. "Call me,
Cade, you change your mind. Oh yeah, one thing more.
The governor's too busy for any of your shit. Bring it to
me."

In the lobby I'm torching what's left of my stogie, when
the cigarette-counter looker says, "Hey." She's balanced just
right. She speaks low, to the cash register. "Guy back there
wants to see you."

Stud stands in shadow back past the stairwell, near a
half-open door marked ELECTRICAL PANEL. He nods. He
needs another bleach job, half his hair is brown. He needs
a shave. "Yeah," I say. He starts through the door. I say,
"I'll stay out here."

I expected him sometime. Rage. A brother's rage. His
shirt is wrinkled, smells. No gun. Tired eyes. "They tell
you it was me thumped Danny? They did, they're fucked."
He runs a hand around his neck. He's had a few.

"It wasn't me got Noel, either," I say. "They tell *you* that?"

"I don't give a shit who did Noel. He'd done me a time
or three. They might have said you. And I might have said,
so what? It wasn't me and Danny, though, Cade." He licks
his teeth. His eyes jump, settle, jump again.

"Where they got you now?"

"Oh shit, I haul pinballers, video games. They won't give
me Stonehenge 'cause of something Tony—Noel—said or
something. Hell. I'm not as wild anymore, Cade."

The cigar is getting short and hot. "So you want to earn
some real dough?"

"How real?"

"Real enough. I'll let you know."

A janitor, this guy with bloodhound eyes and a beer gut, pushes a broom toward us. His boots echo.

"I'm still with Bitsy, Cade. Remember? Got a kid. I stick." He gives me Bitsy's last name. Says to call. The money's right, he's on. He says, "You can't float me a few bucks now, can ya? I got stung on this trunk of stuff s'posed to've come from some damn Mexican pyramid. Stupid. Like that deal we had. Shit, Cade, we almost died together."

I leave Stud there with his head down. I wink at the cigarette girl and step onto the hot street. This is what is left of me, I think, a scrap, a goddamn scrap I barely recognize. I flip the cigar butt into the back of a Jaguar. I roll a number in an alley and get loaded alone under a drainpipe. I had a *friend* named Moon—my last friend.

I thought of Moon, and late to work or not, I found him. No kidding. With a white hat, in a shirt with red horses over the pockets. Ostrich-skin boots. On cardboard. I drove to Broadway Records and damned if he wasn't standing in the window, a bigger-than-life–size cutout. I parked and just pressed up against the glass in the white-hot sun, staring. He held his first album—called *Naked Melody,* a joke not too many listeners would get. I bought one. On the front there was this old-timey painting of cowboys roping a bear. Ha!

The guy was a real talent, and I didn't even know. He wrote eight of the twelve songs, if you can believe cover notes, including the best one, "Mud-Eyed Cowboy":

Here's lookin' at you,
I thought you knew
That the range was gettin' smaller,
That the coyote wouldn't holler for long,
He's gone now, too.

Ginny said he was too much like Hank Williams, Jr. But she liked one called "Do You Dance to the Radio?" and we danced, our windows pitch black, and I didn't give a damn. Then with a couple of beers on our boulder, the stars leaking light in from outside somewhere, I said, "I bet he owns one of those mansions in Nashville. Can you imagine?" I pulled her close.

Out of the blue, she said, "Do you ever think about your mother?"

"How could I help it?" I finished my beer. I took a few good hits off a cigarette. For some damn reason, I wanted to tell Ginny about the straight razor and the whiskey, about how I carried Mama to bed. Instead, though, all I could think of, I reached into my pocket and pulled out that crummy metal heart I'd been carrying. I said, "She gave me this the last time I saw her. Her joints were killing her, she could hardly think, and she gave me this."

And that was the right thing, I guess, because Ginny lay back and watched the sky and said almost too quiet to hear, "Can I keep it?"

"That's why I got it out."

Sometimes I press my ear against Ginny's rising stomach and tell her what the baby says, stuff like, "I'm holding your heart hostage. Let me out now or you'll never feel it again." She giggles. I say, "Tell that bald-headed cave mouse to stay the hell out of here." I kiss her there.

Ginny says I'm making it up, that I won't see anything for at least a month or two, that the doctor she went to said if she dresses right nobody will be able to tell till she's five or six months along. I can tell now, honest to God, like a branch about to bud. And I am careful of her there, holding my weight over her with my arms.

46 ——— THE LIVING AND THE DEAD

"**W**here's Jill?" I asked Old Man Arthur. I stayed put in
the cold alley beneath a golden dagger of a moon.

"With her aunt, but that's no business of yours. Get in
here." He held the gate: a big, dog-faced, harmless-looking
old man. I'd seen him once before, the day Skink got his
four years earlier. He'd seemed dangerous, his dark mustache, his mouth, his growl. Now the mustache puffed gray
above his heavy chin, as gray as the wiry tufts over his ears.
Because he stooped, his height seemed like a weakness.

"What for?" I said.

In a deep, tired voice, he said, "Because shooting up
decent people's houses is against the law." He knew.

I said, "Okay."

I stepped inside, trying to act as though I'd never been
that way. Finally he pushed past me in the kitchen and led
me to his den, the den of the heavy desk, the stuffed ducks,
and the dead smell of trapped smoke. He took off his blue
suit coat and dropped it over the back of his desk chair
before sitting down with a tight, nervous wink of his left
eye. "Take a seat," he said. He lit the wet stub of a fat cigar
and blew three rings, one inside the other.

I crossed my legs and uncrossed them and wished to
hell I hadn't. I wanted a cigarette, but I didn't want to get
him too steamed up—for Jill's sake. Why had Jill told him?
How did he make her?

He looked down at his hand, which he tensed into a
broad, useless fist, and then at me again. "So you're Carlos
Cade?" His eyes were so shallow they could have been fake.

"I came to see Jill."

"You've been seeing a lot of Jill, haven't you, Cade?"

I stared at the fading black-and-white photographs lined
up between the bookshelves, photos of Arthur, with a fat

head of hair, in golf clothes; bending over a fan of dead ducks in dead grass, his hunting hat cocked over a good ear; in shorts, at fighting weight, next to two big slick fish balanced upside down on a dock on their long needle noses, and, beside them, holding a fishing pole like a whip, the woman who fell from a mountain, the pretty woman with bones so smooth they must have whistled through the wind.

"I'm talking to you, Cade." Suddenly he rose and ground the cigar into a silver ashtray. His eyes deepened. "What you are isn't your fault. What I am isn't my fault. I don't have to like punks like you, Cade, and I don't." His voice detonated each word, a skill for juries of TV-fried housewives, I figured. He probably made a B+ lawyer. I didn't know a hell of a lot about attorneys then. I thought they just told people off, more or less. His fist boomed off the desk and rattled the ashtray. "But all that's beside the point. We are who we are and where we are and something will be done. You will stop seeing my daughter."

"You talked to her about me?"

"She told me to go to hell."

"So, go to hell." Now I stiffened, ready to take the fist lifting a flame beneath another cigar, if he decided to throw it at me. Before long his puffing slowed, and, running his hand over his head, he sat back down.

"Cade," he said calmly, the cigar steady in the corner of his mouth. He folded his hands. "Cade, this is absurd. I'm not interested in talking you into anything. I didn't expect a headstrong fellow like you to tuck tail and run. I'm telling you to leave her alone."

"And if I don't?"

"I go to the police with additional information regarding a shooting behind the Capitol the other night."

"Where'd you get it?"

"That's my business. I've got it."

"From her?"

He straightened and spread his hands. "You already know what Jill told me, *all* she told me. I learned of the shooting from a private investigator, a damn good one."

"Who followed us? Jesus Christ." Now I pulled out a smoke and lighted it with a pistol-shaped lighter from the desk, and lucky that's all it was. People spying on their own kids. He waited. "Mr. Arthur," I said, trying to be as smooth and cold as he was. "If you tell on me, you'll be telling on her."

"That's right, but I don't think you'll make me do it. There's no percentage for you. Stay away and that's the end of it."

"If you go talking about us in the car the other night," I said, "I'll go talking about a boy name of Skink who was killed by somebody else you know."

"Who'd believe that?" He smiled and tapped the cigar.

"Maybe nobody. Maybe Pep would have something to say, though. Maybe Matt or Gerry. You remember Gerry? He's seemed awful sad ever since."

"You'd be getting yourself in one hell of a big mess," he said. "You know that. You're no fool, Cade."

Now I stood. I was mad. I leaned over him. I said, "Stay out of my fucking life. You hear me? Or I won't forget, Mr. God Almighty. Never. You'll remember, too. And if you spill on me now, I'm gonna say plenty about that precious boy of yours who killed his own mother."

Bingo. I had him. I thought. The color sank from his face. I heard his teeth on the cigar. "That's a lie," he said, but hissed might be a better word for how it sounded.

"Right," I said. I turned to go.

"You're not going to say anything to anybody." I'd heard that in enough movies to think there'd be a gun when I looked back. Nothing, just the cigar smoldering between his white, white fingers. "You wouldn't," he said. "For Jill's sake. If you ever spread any of those lies"—and "lies" was very weak—"it would break her heart. Stay away or it's trouble for you. Hear?"

I left by the front door. I didn't see any light in the upstairs hall. I closed the door quietly.

Friday: The blue sky was man-made. The birds flew like ash, slowly, through air the temperature of skin. Women stood bloodless at bus stops. Men rode by in cars, without control. Kids walked to school because school happened to be on the way to wherever they found themselves going. Their clothes were ironed on.

What did I need school for? I wasn't on my way anywhere, which right then mattered. I was the only one alive, the only real person in creation. Jesus Christ. I cut up "S" Street, then turned on Third Avenue toward the foothills, the mountains.

Their slopes were streaked with mud. Red water sluiced down the creek bed in Dry Canyon. I broke through leafless tangles of scrub oak at the canyon mouth and walked, dark water foaming by the trail. Magpies lifted themselves from one steep wall to the other on thick, navy-blue wings. Then squirrels exploded on all sides through last year's leaves. I hurried, the path stamped with the heart-shaped tracks of deer. I took long, charging steps because that shadow in the bottom of the canyon would chill me if I let it, because I wanted to see the kiln again, to look down that black, ragged funnel hole. Not too much farther and I would reach the band of sun sliding downward, yellowing and warming dirt and rock and weed. Jill would know what all this meant.

I thought I dreamed it, the tinny clang of a bell when I turned that last twist in the trail, when I looked at the crumbling box of brick wedged into the hillside. But it clanged again. I had expected something, sure, in this place, a sign, a miracle. And just as I walked forward, the sun hitting my back for the first time, a sheep stuck its head out of the arched fire hole in the bottom, a very white sheep that moment in the fresh light, with very brown teeth that chewed at nothing, like it wanted to talk. The dented bell around its neck rang when it walked, then trotted, then burst in a butt-thrusting run up the muddy slope. When the ringing stopped, the sheep was still, right above the kiln, far enough up so I could not make out its eyes. What would happen to me? What mattered?

I laughed until laughter echoed out of the kiln, rang through the canyon. My knees took the turns, and I dove, and jumped, and flew from boulders, and splashed down and down and down.

I would not have given up on Jill for anything just then, and I would have found a way to see her that night, or the next, or whenever Big Daddy dropped his guard. I never reckoned to be with her so soon.

From the bottom of Dry Canyon, I shortcut behind the U Hospital. I bounced, my legs were so goddamn strong. I whistled right up beside a long, low, gray building, a dingy, windowless barracks of a place surrounded by sheet metal and sagging chainlink hung with signs: DANGER— RADIATION. Suddenly dogs screamed inside, deep inside. I yelled, "Give it up, you fucking lunatics." I ran.

I swung down across campus, between dark castle pines toward the University Pharmacy, where a newborn could rip off cigarettes. I'd smoke a couple and head for school. Good sense. My shoes were soaked. The spring thaw of '64. A warm, blue Friday late in March.

I almost missed it. Her Volvo, nosed in outside the Varsity Bookstore, creaked and popped under its hood. The owl-faced clock on the sign said 12:10. I kept my eyes off the street until I stood inside the dry cleaners next door. One glance picked out the detective, a broad guy in a fishing hat he probably thought looked college. He sat sideways in the front of a tan Valiant, eyes stuck to the bookstore. Not a flicker for me. I ducked out the alley way and slipped in through the delivery entrance of the Varsity. A trap? But how the hell could they know I'd show up?

"Carlos!" Jill hugged me and then kissed me on the mouth right there in front of a couple of the most astonished goddamn bookaholics I ever saw.

Nothing. The detective had vanished, if he was a detective, and now I squeezed her, and whispered, "Come on."

She held out a twenty for a stack of Zane Greys, and a saleswoman with heavy glasses and waxy beads asked for more. Christ. Jill's eyes—dry and red as cherry bombs. Hurt eyes, tired eyes, stoned eyes. Very stoned eyes.

"For you," she said.

No one watched us.

"The cabin," she said at the first stop sign. "Fuck school. Just fuck school. Light me a cigarette." The tires squealed. After two deep hits on a Marlboro, her eyes calmed down enough to look at me. "Where've you been?"

"I'm glad I found you."

"I prayed you'd find me. All through my worthless chemistry class, I prayed to whatever it is that holds us all up to get you to me."

"It worked."

In Emigration Canyon, threading more bloody, spongy mountains, she let go with a crowd of tears, braked onto the shoulder, killed the engine, and said, "He told me they'd pick you up today."

"They?"

"I don't know."

"Hey, hey, hey." I pulled her to me, pulled her warm, soft, shaking head to my chest. "Nobody's got me yet."

"They will," she said. "I know it. You told him."

"Told him?"

She squirmed away. She pressed her hands to her eyes. "About Lance. You told him. You said you wouldn't, not anybody."

I lit a cigarette, drew a face with three eyes in the window fog. I said it quietly. "I didn't think . . . I thought I'd win."

She wiped her eyes. She licked her lips and shook her hair. "Let's go. Let's go away. Please, let's go away." She fired up the car, jumped it back over the rim of the road, and shifted like she wanted to snap the stick.

"Slow down," I said.

"We're going," she said.

"Okay."

Fifty miles later, at least forty shy of Evanston, where we planned to settle into some old hotel with a fourposter bed and color TV, somewhere just east of Wanship, drinking our first beers of the trip, a siren opened its mouth and howled, and we weren't speeding. "God," she said. "I won't stop."

"Stop," I said. "Maybe your license plate fell off or something." I didn't believe that, but I didn't believe we had a choice.

Two highway patrolmen dressed like white hunters circled wide to the front of us. Their pistols knew right where my forehead was. "Shit," Jill said. "Just shit." She threw open her door. A big Kenworth let go with its air horn and jerked to the inside lane. "What is this?" she yelled at the cops.

"You're okay?" the shortest one said. "Come on over. It's all right. We've got him covered."

"I don't want him covered," she said, and ran at them. When he could, Shorty grabbed her at the waist and pulled her up the road.

The big one, with ears like radar dishes and feet like anchors, said, "Step out and away from the vehicle. Keep your hands high, where I can see them. All right, son. Turn slowly to the top of the car. Spread your arms. Good. Now don't move, not a muscle." When he reached me, he threw an arm into my neck and my head banged the Volvo. Jill screamed.

The highway cops eyeballed her car but didn't check it. They didn't touch her purse. Jill drove herself back to the city—in my dust.

I got red-carpet treatment. They lit cigarettes for me, drove damn near ninety. Whenever somebody got in the way, on went the trusty siren. They didn't talk to me or to each other, and I thought about that goddamn sheep, and a shed full of crazy hound dogs screaming out their last drugged-up days.

47 —— BLUE-TAIL FLY

One of the shocked bookworms in the Varsity, a guy whose neck looked too weak to hold up the heavy glasses on his nose—*he* was the detective, a p.i. named Diamond, I swear, Max Diamond.

Diamond swaggered around me a few minutes in the station that night. I said Diamond could leave. I knew damn well if I made it tough for them they'd make it tough for me—and extra tough for Jill. "Sure I rode along," I said. "But I didn't touch any pistol." I had it figured. I'd get some sort of trial. Jill might go through hell trying to cover for me, or her old man might lock her away somewhere until I got locked away.

This wrinkled-up chief of detectives with wire-rim bifocals said, "We know all about Ingus, Cade, but we'd like to hear it again."

Old Man Arthur played the odds all the way. I thought about Arthur plenty. Two kids, no wife, and more money and power than the average success story could stay clean with for long. And one of his children couldn't feel for anyone. Old Man Arthur loved his kids. At least the son of a bitch loved.

My trial was more like a trip to the principal's: Juvenile Court, with a walleyed judge who couldn't talk. He kept calling me "Cave." His steam-ironed face had never smiled, and if those cold, loose eyes had ever looked on anything pretty, or horny, or surprising, they fooled me. "Found delinquent, Mr. Carlos Cave is hereby sentenced to a term of one year in the Utah State Industrial School at Ogden," he muttered to himself. "With proper behavior, however, he will be eligible for outcasing in six months."

When the goon with the toy gun steered me back through the court's airless waiting room, Hilda stood. She brushed a curl off her forehead. Some tall guy with her stayed seated. "Hey," I said. I wanted to smile, but my escort yanked my arm. "Tell Mama not to wait up. Take good care of her." I winked.

Dusty. The Dust Trail. SIS. The Industrial Stool. Indestructible School. The Farm. The Barns. Mini Prison. Green Form School. Camp Lashits. Fuck U.

They—the lifeless, ageless, sexless, passionless, compassionless, bloodless, shapeless sonsofbitches with the goddamn shiny black name badges over their empty hearts, who thought we were their "job"—called the game "Correction." All of us, kids from eight to twenty-one, teenagers mostly—girls penned in two great convent "cottages," boys in six smaller ones—were *in*correct.

Of the three hundred or so kids in Dusty, not one mistake. Hell, they just looked like kids. Okay, a lot weren't white. Come to think of it, every third face wasn't. But hey, justice is blind, right? Just us.

An orphan? State's got nowhere else. Drop him off. All

the good little Indians down around Blanding won't behave? Send them, too. Start those children who can't be
children down the old Dust Trail.

Correction (boys): Shave their dirty heads. Give them tests,
test after test after test on green paper. Tell them how
smart they are—really. Stick them on wings beyond frosted,
wire-reinforced glass doors with two Black Badgers and
kids in the same ballpark agewise if possible. Give them
stretched-out white T-shirts that say TODAY IS THE FIRST
DAY in blue letters on the front and OF THE REST OF YOUR
LIFE on the back. March them around "campus" to class:
English, math, biology, health, music, gym. Education will
correct them. Slip them two bucks a week when they get
good grades. The chalk-dusty trail to a high school D-
ploma. Training will correct them: auto mechanics, wood-
working. Will keep Dusty tidy: in barbershops, laundry
rooms. And fed—the kitchens.

If they won't behave? If they fight, lie, steal, or run? If
they will not learn, will not be trained? If they will not
smile, speak, wash behind their dirty ears? The segregation
units. The seg rooms. The Buckets. In the dark basement
beneath each boys' cottage are two steel-plated rooms, part
of every introductory tour. Even the ceilings. Plates bolted
in place. Battleship gray. Cold. A lidless toilet in the corner.
A face-size "mirror"' of polished steel like ice on the wall.
A canvas cot. The Buckets magnify sound. Shit hitting
water in the middle of the night. The whimpering. The
shouts. The closing of the steel-plated door with the window no bigger than a pack of smokes. Everybody hears.
Everybody sees the pale bucketeers marched manacled to
meals. Everybody learns to stay busy.

Before all else, keep the incorrect young bastards busy.
Keep them busy, goddamn it. Think of the bee. Think of
the honey. Think of the hive.

Chaplain, come in here, please. Wave your pudgy-wudgy fingers over this pack of heathen creatures, and pray for their correction. Amen.

Brothers and sisters, take this pack of rowdy Gentiles (even those forever marked by Cain) to your seminary Friday afternoons. Give them warm cookies. They'll listen. Of course Christ came to America. Soft chocolate chips. He broke bread with Indians. White Indians. White bread.

To forget, to forget that I was to be forgotten, I pretended I owned the joint lots of the time, that the kids were my guests or servants or family, that I decided the meals we fixed on those goddamn unbreakable, cream-colored, scuffed-up plates. *I* chose the whiny music they piped in over the brown boxes in each room. I *wanted* to get up at six-thirty. I *liked* working in the laundry, breathing those hot, heavy clouds around the noisy damn dryers, hands raw with soap and bleach.

Shit, I wouldn't have had any other roommate: Warren Forbes. When they picked *him* up they missed his mind. He tied his shoes like a blind guy wiring a bomb. His eyes weren't hooked in to anything, just followed his nose. And his mouth just kind of flopped along. If he had a brain, it was pea-sized, prehistoric, hairpin.

Three loudmouth, long-term assholes jumped me in the doorway to our room my fourth night aboard. That afternoon I'd told the smallest, this crazy Groucho Marx—looking guy, to screw himself when he said I should be saving whatever I could—candy, money, matches, pills. His fifth year. If I gave a shit about myself I'd contribute every week. I hugged the floor pretty hard after his lucky first punch, and without a sound Warren swooped off the top bunk. Groucho folded in the hall as shapeless as laundry. His pals growled kind of, and I swear Warren threw two uppercuts at once. Then I finished one and Warren hammered the other again. Hell, we both looked so fresh our wing supervisors believed us that those three had it out all by themselves.

Pretending came easier then, since *I did* damn near own the cottage. Except for his fists, Warren was as helpless as a whale.

When I *could* forget, the place had its points: a furnace and canyon breezes, three meals, TV, and a two-room library with wire-meshed windows wide on the Wasatch Mountains. Whenever I could I squeezed myself up against one of the rickety library desks and read—Zane Grey and Jack London—or watched the spring light turn green. Often enough we got to walk out in it.

Afternoons in good weather, mornings, too, sometimes, the Badgers marched us out over the north road to the school's hundred-acre farm and orchards. A dairy, too, but only old-time kids worked the dairy, thin kids with straight backs and glasses. We'd jerk weeds and dig this and chop that. This one fat boy named Crawford sang sometimes:

> *The hornet gets in eyes and nose,*
> *The skeeter bites you through your clothes.*
> *The gallinipper flies up high,*
> *But wiser yet, the blue-tail fly.*

Nobody seemed to mind the singing. It passed the time. And it covered up a lot of the talk.

One morning a fog took longer than usual burning off the farm. Crawford's fat voice tumbled out of these big clouds coiled all around us. An older kid with a pink birthmark on his cheek and no eyebrows whispered, "We're running. Come on." When we passed Crawford, he winked: "Devil take the blue-tail fly." Two fidgety Navajos smoked Kools up against the canyon by a NO TRESPASSING sign.

Highway cops nosed our hot Impala into a ditch just

west of Richfield close to sunset. We'd been doing damn near ninety and almost rolled, but with a gut full of peyote buttons it seemed safe enough. We laughed into their goddamn service revolvers.

The Indians told me later they got beaten by Badgers that day. I got the Buckets—two weeks. Jesus. But old birthmark got shipped out to a federal joint in Englewood, California. He'd run four times before. Never again. Over a hundred kids had hoofed it so far that year. Time to crack down. Hell, the hear-no-evil, see-no-evil superintendent made speeches in the cafeteria. Ogden's mayor came to talk. 1964. Last year a runaway'd shot and killed an Ogden cop. One out of every three who ran stole something, they said. Ogden residents were arming themselves. The tradition of an open campus was in jeopardy. Fence the criminals in, local bigwigs said. Learn from Dallas. Lee Harvey Buzzword.

Another load to Englewood.

Remember the bee. They pushed us even harder. My caseworker, an ex-firemen with a handlebar mustache, told me, "Your IQ's way up there, Cade. Use it. Bolting's the only mark you got. We can forgive. Mend your ways, we'll forget. This is Christmas next to the California hole."

Foward, harch! I'd stay put. I studied. Two piddly bucks a week. I got tired. But even with all the shit they must have pumped us full of, I still slept plenty restless over Jill.

I got a note every day, never much more than half a dozen sentences. She seemed to know they read our mail. She wrote things like "Pretend you hand's a spider and turn it loose" and "I keep dreaming about your home runs, Slugger"—tough stuff way the hell over the head of any self-respecting Badger. Sometimes, though, big chunks were blacked out with magic marker. Her notes always ended pretty much the same: "I'm sorry it's you instead of me. You're special, Carlos Cade. You're smart, Carlos

Cade. You're my Carlos Cade. I visit your mother. I go where we went. I'm with you." No mention of Big Daddy or Brother.

The week's work, the training, ended at noon on Saturday. Our red-brick pig barns took deep, stale, restless breaths then. After lunch, any visitors were bunched in the cramped cafeteria in the Administration Building. Pop and snack machines chugged against one wall. Tight groups of chairs squealed black grooves in the tan linoleum, in and out from wobbly tables.

My first week, nobody showed. "Sorry, Cade," one of my supervisors mumbled. I fingered through a few chapters in the silent library. The second week, he said, "You're in luck. Your mother and sister."

When I got there Jill jumped up and goddamn, my stomach tried to float away. A hug, a kiss. The smell. Over her shoulder, through the soft lengths of her hair, I saw Warren and a big, broad, featureless man in a green plaid suit and a fudge-colored tie sitting together at one side of a table. Neither spoke. They drank Pepsi and stared into the paper cups. "I love you," I said.

Mama could have been at home the way she watched her hands. "Hello," she said, her eyes glancing shyly up then quickly down. "This must be like college, I'd say. Do you think?"

"I don't know. Maybe," I said. I patted her small hands. "Where's Hilda? They told me Hilda's here."

"They like it just family," Jill whispered. "And . . . And Hilda's gone."

"Gone?" Mama asked, tilting her head. "That's right. Now I remember. On a trip. Yes, Hilda's went to see a friend. Isn't that right?"

Jill nodded. "Matt's cousin. Sissie something. In Arkansas. She flew . . ."

"She flew to Arkansas?"

"I guess Hilda called her or something and Sissie said to come on."

At the next table, a little boy with a pirate patch over his left eye stretched a long, pink string of bubble gum from his mouth and slowly chewed it in. "What about Mama?"

"Me?" Mama said. She held the word out.

"What about you?"

"I'm much better. Much, much better. Really."

"I talked to Mr. Hickler," Jill said. She kissed my cheek. "And *I* look in too." White-shirted, white-faced Black Badgers watched from the doorways. I pushed my hand under her skirt onto the buttery smoothness of her thigh. I remembered Hilda screaming. And I remembered her talking about her tummy to her dog.

"What about Fifi?"

"Hilda took her."

I laughed at that. Warren and the man in the fudge-colored tie stared right over my head.

48 ——— BLACK AND WHITE

We hiked to our ridge, did a few numbers, and ran all the way down. Saturday. Now we showered in the cold hose in the shadow of the shed. "Hey," Ginny said, water breaking over her. "I just remembered." Glistening like that, she looked brand-new. "Only for tonight, I'm going to bring out the TV. This girl I'm teaching told me Channel Twenty's doing an Elvis festival. You're doubles, I mean it—except for the hair. And your nose." The water gushed between us and ran in long dark fingers down the drive. "Just for tonight."

The evening shrank through a red, inky sunset. Dinner

disappeared. Our fan pushed the heat around. An engine growled off on the mountain, idiots four-wheeling. And Elvis, baby-faced in black and white, strummed a guitar and sang a slow one in prison.

When the knocking came, Mr. Cat sprang from the refrigerator drawer he slept in. "You expecting anybody?"

"Uh uh." Ginny lifted her eyebrows.

"Then go out back," I said, talking low. "No, no. Into the basement. Be quiet. Hurry. I'll call you."

"You're kidding," she said, but she stood. She said, "All this big-bad-woof stuff's gotta stop."

"Move it."

"You're nuttier than I am."

I killed the TV. I counted to ten, trying to hear over the soft whistle of the fan—then twenty. Two more knocks. I flipped on the porch light. Dead. Burned out. Shit. You can bet I had my knife ready. "Yes?" I worked to slow my breathing down.

"It's just me," Rose said. "Me and the scorpions. Relax." She moved closer through the black air. Her face shaded, her matted hair held in place with a beaded band, she stood—halter top, short skirt, flip-flops—by the steps, in the washed-out yellow from the window. Parked backward in the drive behind her, Danny's old man's power wagon showed off its desert scenes and creaked.

"Cade, here's how it is." And I itched and tried to see inside the darkest shadows, to hear the smallest sounds. Mouthwash. Her words stunk with mouthwash. She lifted a bottle, rinsed, spit. "You're the only place we could think of."

"For what?"

"For holdin' on. I held on to Danny. You don't think so, but I did. I found me others a time or two. I admit it. But I waited. I tried." A plane carried a blinking light through stars, until the mountains. She whispered now, hoarse, gasping almost. "I worked my end of the street, he worked his. We got by—and they killed him."

My arms tightened. I hadn't figured this. I wondered was it the end. "How'd you find me here? How come?"

"You won't like it. I don't like it." Stuffed up, she breathed through her mouth. I cupped a match and lit a smoke. Headlights swept the canyon far below and stopped. The small motor and the lights died. "Musk and his muscles come after us."

"Us?"

"Me and L.G. Musk wanted his precious Vice, and we didn't say nothin', and the fucker . . . We didn't say one thing. They hauled us to L.G.'s lookin'. When L.G. said he knew where they could get Quicky if they'd just lay off, Musk blew his cool and . . . shit."

"And what else is new?" L.G. said. With his right arm in a fresh cast, in a flowered sling knotted around his neck, he dragged his feet from the side of the house. "All they know is countin' coin and kickin' ass." He passed through the window light, face swollen, crooked, L.G., fat, a roll at his middle behind the sling. "What's new is Musk backed off."

"Bobby Bull's the one stepped in," Rose said. "He's still shook up over his mom. She had this thing for Danny. Then Bobby sneaks by today to say he's sorry about his pals. He swears they didn't do Danny. Christ, some pals. He said we could do ourselves a favor, we talk to you, get you to sign on to some offer. *He* knew you were up here."

"I told 'em no. Now *you're* running their errands."

Rose said, "Cade, you're outside all this with us." L.G. grunted. "Why we come. To help ourselves. Honest to God, Cade, take a hard look at my face."

L.G. said, "Cade, the guy done Danny got his. They'll learn. I'll learn 'em. Musk had these guys bust my arm, and what'd I say? I say, 'Please break my left.' Ha, so they busted my right. I'm left-handed. Bastards."

"*Look* at my face!" Rose said.

"Are you alone?"

"That's what we are," L.G. said. "Your girlfriend here? Shiftlet says you got a woman."

"She's around. My business is my business. When you knocked I sent her out. I'm not achin' for her to know a lot."

"There ain't a lot to know." Rose faked her little girl laugh. She swigged from the bottle again. I shook her out a smoke. L.G. took it. I shook out another. Rose's lips puckered in the flame. "You shout anybody comes, L.G.," she said. "I'm gonna show him, explain it." And when she backed inside, holding the cigarette and the green bottle, when I got a glimpse of her black eyes and her busted front teeth as she turned to the light, I could feel the future closing down. She sat by my table with her legs apart, leaning forward, her chest swinging out. Lightning patterned her headband. I shut off the whirring fan. "Thanks," she said. "I got enough noise."

"Looks that way."

"They wanted him. I didn't say nothin'."

The back door squealed, banged. I fumbled for my knife, and Ginny rushed in. She looked from Rose to me, the blade, her mouth open. Silent. Till the door opened again and here stumbled L.G. "I wasn't chasin' her. I seen her by the shed." As L.G. talked, his nose flat, purple, one eye swollen into the whole damn socket, Ginny went white.

I held her. She sobbed until she couldn't breathe. When her shoulders finally settled down, she lifted her head. I said, "They don't mean anything. I know 'em. I told you to stay in the basement."

"I heard," Ginny whispered, "could hear these noises.

Chains and talking, and I thought maybe you . . ." I kissed her ear.

Blood trickled from Rose's mouth. She licked at it, wiped it with her hand, and then stared at the red streaked across her knuckles. "Jesus," she said. A red line crossed her cheek.

I put a hand on Rose's shoulder. "Ginny, Rose."

Rose lifted the bottle from the floor. She said, "My last name's still Ingus, I guess. Is that how it works?"

"When it works. This goon nearly caught you's L.G., Rose's brother-in-law."

L.G. said, "I wasn't expecting nobody."

"Go outside," Rose said.

L.G. got a beer from the fridge and left a stench like old meat.

"We go way back," I said.

Rose blinked. "Back to the stone age. Hey." Rose tugged her mouth into a smile. "I got two fat numbers. Forgot 'em. That's what I could use. You want to? I could honest to Jesus God use it." She reached into her halter top and lifted out a joint the size of a chili pepper. "How about it?"

"How about the dog in the shed?" Ginny asked.

The smoke curled into Rose's hair, the air that I couldn't goddamn breathe through. "What dog in the shed?"

Ginny said, "There's this . . . this monster dog chained up right by that old washer."

"You know *what* dog," Rose finally said, "the white dog. What I wanted to explain. Just let me do this." She sucked the joint through long dirty fingers. "And I'll take a beer. Then I'll tell it. *The* dog." Rose hunched her shoulders, her boobs swaying, and toked again. "Ouch," she said, and pushed her tongue up over her teeth, the smoke spilling out. She held the beer in her mouth with her eyes shut before she swallowed.

I said, "You brought him?" She nodded. So I had Vice now. I slid out my knife again.

Rose ate the roach.

"What dog?" Ginny asked.

"A mean one," I said. "Used to be man's best friends. Now we customize 'em. Any kind of mean you want. Any kind of dumb."

So loud Rose's eyes broke open, Ginny squealed, "Where's Mr. Cat?" I pointed at him sitting in a laundry basket.

"Everything okay?" L.G. asked through the screened window to the side.

"Peaches," Rose said.

L.G. pushed through bushes and clomped in again, a nifty little pistol tucked in his pants. "Get a move on." He took the rest of a sixer from the fridge and grunted back out.

"All right," Rose said. "And this ain't no story, either. You want her to hear?"

"Screw you," Ginny said. She lifted Mr. Cat, held him. "I'm a big girl."

"I'm not," Rose said. "I ain't learned a goddamn thing." She pulled a smaller number from the dark canyon of her top, a twist of red paper. "Light me." She didn't pass this one. She toked and toked and toked and ate the roach, and something changed, her eyes, her mouth, and especially her risen, rounded cheeks. "What I come for . . ."

"The dog?" I said, to keep the brain behind those wild eyes on track. Ginny sat back down, but, goddamn it, this was not hers.

"What I come for is to give *you* the dog. The dog is the devil, Cade. I swear. All he knows is kill. Brain's gone. But, Cade, here's the other part: This one could be the best fighter ever. Danny said that. Sure Danny pinned big dreams on Quicky, but he knew. I seen this dog two times myself—Christ. And they say he gets faster."

Ginny's eyes were fixed on Rose.

"So, get it out," I said. "What's the game? Why the hell bring him here?"

" 'Cause I'm holdin' on. They tried to beat Danny down. You know what he done to their fancy club. They ain't gonna lick me." She inhaled deep.

"What club?" Ginny asked very softly.

"The night after Quicky got doped," Rose said, smiling and shaking her head, "the very next night, Danny sneaked onto Musk's big goddamn estate in Cottonwood and got the dog. Christ, you should have seen Danny's face. He was worried the dog would bark, but this dog never barks. The Vice ate the steak with the pills and fell over in his cage like he died. Danny snipped the chain link and hauled him through the woods. Danny was all scratched up. And the dog looks like nothin', but Danny lays him in the trunk like maybe he's this treasure or something. We locked him in the coal room under the garage."

"We?"

"Me and Danny."

"L.G.?"

Rose whispered. "Danny said leave him out. He gets turned around sometimes. He's careless with his mouth. This was big. Danny knew this was big."

Rose started another beer. Ginny said, "Give me the matches." Her cigarette trembled.

Rose squeezed the white can. "The bastards missed him when they tore our place apart the first time. Shit, they ruined everything. They stood my girl in the corner of her room and ripped her dolls to shreds. What for? To find their dog? It was the Batman, that Nicks, who done it, most of it. That's what got Danny. That's why he went

crazy." Now tears bunched in Rose's swollen eyes. "I wonder—if they'd found the dog, would they still've done
Danny? I wonder that. I wonder what it can mean when a
dog means more than a man. Huh?" She didn't seem to
know. "A man is worth the same as a man. The Batman,
he found out. Didn't he? He sure as shit did find out. He
did."

"Hey," I said. "Hey, hey. I don't want to know. It can't
do anybody anything."

"And Musk is gonna find out sometime, somehow. Goddamn him."

"You got the dog here now is what we're here for. Did
you send Musk a note?"

"Everybody's after me for money. That's all it was
about."

L.G. climbed into the doorway, a silhouette with a beer
and a pistol. "I was workin' on that stud idea you had,
Cade. But shit, the whole damn world's chickenshit. Doc
Nort put Quicky under—got cold feet. This pup here,
though, is big money. First I knew she had him was yesterday after they left. Honest to God. Christ, we're just
leaving the hospital, and Rose says, 'I'm gonna shoot Vice,'
and, groggy as I am from all this pain shit, I say, 'You've
got him? Well, let's not be too damn quick.' And I was
thinking about you, Cade, your advice, and how they seem
to lay off you. We got nerve to burn, man, but what we
need is help." He moved the pistol to his bad hand and
rested the good one on Rose's shoulder.

"What you need," I said, and I saw it all now, "is somebody to get you off the hook you're hanging from." Rose
shrugged at L.G.'s hand.

"Go outside," I said to Ginny, stepping away. "You don't
want to hear this." She crossed her arms, chewed her lip.
I got louder. "I mean it. Take the cat. Just get out till I
call. Anything happens out there, scream, scream your

lungs out. Go on." My mouth was dry. Rose and L.G. watched my mouth.

"Five minutes is all," Ginny said. "I'm not kidding."

L.G. lifts a beer with his healthy, dirty hand, so the pistol still pokes from the sling. Rose smokes, cries a tear or two with those bruised eyes, leaves the mouthwash alone. For a long time it is like that, nobody saying anything—and I am light-headed in this light. "I get it now. You two have your own program. Right?"

Rose licks her lips and tries to smile. L.G. shakes his head and laughs. His goddamn Hitler hair is so greasy it soaks up light and doesn't move. He puts his hand on Rose's shoulder again, and she closes her eyes, opens them slowly. She says, "So what's wrong with a little romance, Cade? You take it where you get it like the rest of us."

I say, "You're the ones. Shit. You set Danny up, poisoned his goddamn dog. You tried to set me up. Now here you are back to try again."

L.G. moves the pistol to the healthy hand. Rose says, "Nothing with guns." L.G. keeps the barrel toward the floor. She says, "Carlos, you don't believe that."

"I been blind," I say, "blind as shit." And I push L.G. on the chest.

He says, "Hey," and he backs into a wall where Ginny has hung an old fishing creel with two sunflowers in it. He does not lift the pistol very far when I swing. He falls hard at the wall, the pistol to the floor. His eyes are shut. He holds his chin. Something bubbles in his nose. He says, "Is this because we brung the dog? We'll take him."

Rose pushes between us and says, "Christ, where we gonna be like this?"

I say, "Look the hell where we are. You set him up." I lock my eyes on L.G. Rose presses against me, to move me back. "Didn't you? Some big money, I'll bet, and a chance to fuck Danny over."

"Christ, I got a busted arm," L.G. says. He shifts his jaw, pushes to his feet. "You're nuts."

"Like hell I am, lover boy."

Rose says, "Okay, Cade. Okay, everybody cool off. Use your head, Carlos."

"It's all I got." I hold the pistol.

"Why would we?" she says. "Really? Goddamn it." Now L.G. reaches around her waist. "Money? Danny was in hock to his eyeballs over this fight. He'd won he might have left me, left me with a few bucks. My kid might have a father. Why would I set him up?"

I see myself in the dark window holding the gun. I see that I don't know what the hell anything means, that I am out of control. I sight on L.G.'s forehead. "You then," I say, "on your own."

"Shoot me, Cade," L.G. says, showing his teeth. "You think I'd screw my brother, you think that, shoot me."

Rose has her hands on my chest and her breath is too goddamn sweet. "Don't kill nobody," she says. "We didn't know they'd kill nobody. It wasn't us. Don't think that."

"So somebody sneaked up to Quicky that night while we weren't looking? Who else could have?"

"We been over it," Rose says. She lets out a big breath. "I know who I'd put my money on. If the stripper's the one who done it, I figure he asked for it."

For a long time I stand at the screen door, watching June bugs pound the wire. I empty the pistol and tuck it in my pants.

"Cade," L.G. says all gravelly. "Nobody else got near that dog, I swear."

"Bobby Bull Shiftlet came over to talk, I remember. Others, too."

"Hey." L.G. holds Rose again. "For all we know, you done it. That's why everybody leaves you alone." I stare at him, but I don't move. He laughs. Rose sputters up a laugh.

"A joke, Cade. Shit, man. You did it you wouldn't be knockin' me around."

"Whoever doped Quicky," Rose says, "Musk did it. He's the one. Danny tried to get even, the crazy bastard, steals Vice the goddamn next day and takes us all to hell."

I meet her ugly eyes, and she doesn't look away. "And L.G. planning to bring Quicky back from the dead, and you're off trying to peddle Vice. Both fucking working solo until Musk scares you so bad you find your love again."

"Vice was my secret for everybody's good," Rose says. "L.G. told me about Quicky. I thought he'd cracked. Hey, *they* killed Danny, I don't care what Shiftlet says. Remember that."

L.G. says, "Yeah."

Rose says, "You're all we got."

"And this isn't a plant, huh?"

"No," Rose says. She crosses her heart. "I swear."

"You keep him," Ginny says. The screen bangs. She steps slowly over to them. "I'm back now. I live here. I want you gone. Take it away, hide him." Her arms are goose flesh. "Get the dog out of here."

"We *ain't* got the nerve," Rose says. "No more. That's the truth of it. Hell, we hardly got our heads on."

"Kill him," I say.

"You kill him," Rose says.

Ginny says, "No."

Rose says, "You can. Slit his worthless throat you want to."

"But," L.G. says, "I don't know. Maybe we should keep it. Maybe we need it. Goddamn it, they bother us again, we tell 'em, we say, okay, we have the dog, and you fuck off or the dog dies. But maybe you don't need insurance, Cade. Hell, what is it you got?"

Ginny stands between us. "We don't need anything from you."

I say, "Cops have a bombing and two murders on their hands and you want me to hold this goddamn dog that's hooked into everything? Kill it." I open my knife. "We'll bury him on the lone prayer-ree."

L.G. pulls Rose closer. "All right, Cade, you got a brain. Insurance might be dumb. So we peddle him. We're talking thirty g's. That's a lot to watch bleed in the sand."

"And who's gonna pay?" I asked him. Ginny's lips were pale.

"Hey," he says, "there's breeders in Texas and Florida would come pick him up."

"And tell Musk."

"Maybe you can figure it out," Rose says. She spread her feet and stood. She put her hand on my shoulder, a small warm hand. "I could use the bucks," she says. "We got nobody else. You ain't a double-crosser. They owe me it. You can't say they don't owe me it. We stuck by Danny, Cade."

"You sell," L.G. says, "we split three ways. Ten grand apiece."

"I trust you," Rose says.

"Don't," I say.

Ginny says, "Take him."

"You decide he needs his neck opened, go ahead," Rose says. "You got the dog."

"They'll look here."

"They haven't yet. You decide, Cade."

And a peeper had binocs on the mountain.

"We better beat it," L.G. says. "This is pretty big shit. How 'bout my gun?"

"Shit," I say. I want to say, Take the dog, but there is too much to figure.

"Call me," Rose says. She sways over and hugs Ginny. "Things happen." Ginny doesn't move. Now Rose, of all the goddamn things, holds me. "We put a bag of food out

there. He's kind of slow right now on account of a couple
of downers. You decide. You're straight."

"If they come," L.G. says, "tell 'em . . . Shit, I don't know,
but not a word on us, huh? Don't tell 'em nothin'."

The faint growl of the power wagon still on the mountain, Ginny lay with our cat on the couch. Elvis did his
dance on the TV with the sound turned down. I stashed the
pistol in the basement. I had almost forgotten the lies,
the shit. I stood on the porch and smoked, trying to find
the sense, the goddamn calm, to go out back.

49 —— SALT AND ICE

I knelt beside Ginny, our hands together on Mr. Cat, her
fingers curled, claws.

"You *should* be scared," I told her. "Me, too. I tried to
tell you that night on Ensign Peak. You should be pissed.
I'm a stupid shit. I knew better than this."

"God, Carlos. People come to my house and talk about
bombings and killings. This isn't us, is it?"

"It's nobody. It's anybody. You saw Rose's teeth."

"Let's go. Right now. What have *you* done? I know you.
I *know* you."

"Hey, shhh. Take it easy. I went to a dog fight, my first,
with my old friend Danny, the guy Rose was hitched to."

"The one who died?"

"Who got killed after he stole the dog out back. That's
where we're at. Ginny, go. We can't just sit here. Jesus. I'll
meet you when it's over."

She shivered. "Okay," she said. "Okay, Carlos. For the
baby." She slumped against me and looked out to where
the dog was. "Kill it," she said. Her lips were white. "I'll
help you. I will. Let's. Rose said go ahead."

I ran my finger along the inside of her leg. "That sounds smart. I think so."

"Right now."

"But maybe somebody should pay," I said. "Huh?"

"And when will it stop? Carlos, Danny Whoeverhewas *did* take the dog. Didn't he *pay*? I'll tell you what. *You* want a kid, *you* have to pay. You have to give up something." Tears streaked her face.

"I love you, Ginny. But . . . thirty g's."

"Deep love, huh? Real deep."

"I'll kill it," I said. She closed her eyes. I lit two smokes and put one in her hand. I got up. "Come on. I'll do it." I threw down a few fingers of Old Crow. "Let's take a look at this hell hound."

"I don't want to," she said. "I've seen it."

Half the moon was dark. No breeze. Heat. Quiet. I carried a bucket of water. I would give it a drink. Had I ever been in greater danger? Maybe the dog was a plant, one of the K-9 corps, ha ha. Shit, maybe Rose and L.G. were a setup. Maybe Lance and Musk drew up this deal together. Maybe from the start, Ingus becoming Castro on down, this had been one fancy trap—for *me*. Maybe. Shit. Even Ginny. She *did* work for the state. I laughed. I laughed and caught myself. I listened. Nothing.

I turned to Ginny behind me in the open shed door, stars like sparks in her wild hair. I said, "These are our lives. We'll take care of 'em."

Our flashlight, hers, one of those like movie ushers use, with a long, red cylinder on the end, centered a tight, round ball of white light in a faint skirt of red. Eyes glowing with the beam, the night edged with red, this white dog sat on the side of his ass, his front legs splayed apart, thick, big-jointed legs. Every inch of him was pit bull, muscle on muscle. But his white head drooped out from his round shoulders. He panted. Spit pooled under his tongue, crawled with flies. His small eyes were deep and wet. I thought he wagged his tail.

Ginny leaned on the washer. She said, "He doesn't blink."

"Vice," I said. "Hey, Vice." His eyes burned with the beam. I held the light away, so that he sat in its red edge. "Good dog." His thick neck was choke-collared, chained to the center post with big-linked shit that could have stopped a buffalo. "Anybody ever been nice to you?" I asked him, holding out my hand, still maybe four feet away. "I'll be nice. Sure I will."

"Be careful," Ginny said. "Rose was scared of him."

"Hey, pup," I said. I put the bucket of water between the dog and me. "Have a drink, buddy." I stretched and shoved the bucket across the dirt with the side of my boot. His tongue slapped the water, slapped and slapped. His sides heaved. His stomach whined and gurgled. " 'At a boy."

"Don't kill him," Ginny whispered. "Give him back." She wrapped an arm around me. "Why not?"

"To fight some more? To kill other dogs? Maybe to get us trapped."

"Just drop if off. Leave it somewhere."

"You don't just turn these dogs loose," I said. "This dog's not a dog." I had thought of driving Vice to the church where my old man did his act, sending Vice down the aisle to be saved. Or letting the dog out in the alley back of Stonehenge. Anywhere. Musk's house, like a goddamn bear. The ZC mall. "Even if I wanted to, I couldn't give it back, Ginny. These guys have tempers." I kissed her hair.

"We'll keep him, keep him muzzled," she said. The dog lifted its head. Now it blinked. Still panting, it stood, its side caked with something, shit or dirt. Its tail moved slowly, back and forth.

"It won't work," I said. "You were right the first time. The dog should go tonight, for you, for us."

"We can't."

"I think it really will end here. Then we'll try not to worry, just get the hell away. I've got something going, something important. I'll have money."

"I'm not leaving till you do. I'd be too scared." She stepped around and touched my face. "Hear me?" The dog sprang. The chain screeched, Ginny screamed, fell hard at my chest. I aimed the beam. On its flexing back legs, its front legs pawing the red ring of light, its teeth folded open, the dog fought the chain. Its nails had laid down lines behind her knees. I dropped the flashlight, grabbed a two-by-four from the corner and swung, the red crazy in the dog's eyes. Ginny shouted, "No!" But the dog hardly moved. Its head turned. Its tongue bled.

I dropped the board. "Hey, goddamn it, Ginny . . . I'm sorry, sorry you're here." The dog opened and closed its bleeding mouth, and then lowered its head and drank again, slurped.

From the door, breathing hard away from the goddam stale air, Ginny said, "How?"

"How?"

"On the farm, Daddy had this gun with this rod inside."

"I've got a gun now. Too much noise."

Ginny said, "I shot an eagle once. Did I tell you that? I was twelve or thirteen. My cousin Lonnie had a twenty-two and this bald eagle was on a fence post. One of his eyes was gone. Lonnie cut off his legs."

"An eagle has more brain," I said. I lit a smoke to get rid of the stink, to hold off the flies. This shudder started in my legs and rolled right up through me. "You go on. I won't be long."

Sweat soaked my shirt. This had no place in my plans.

I leaned on the washer and tried to think it through again. Had I overlooked anything? I kept the light locked on the dog, Vice. Ice or soap. Salt. I tasted salt. Just a goddamn dog. How to kill him. To remove him. He blinked. I could not walk him anywhere. Too jumpy, drugged. Pour him a nice bowl of antifreeze out of the bottle in the corner? Right. Lap this up, boy. And if he did? Convulsions. Probably puke his guts out. Shit.

"It ain't your fault," I said as I pulled down with all my might on the handle of the rusted ax, as the weight left it. And something goddamn thundered the wall of the shed. My swing damn near threw me down. The ax head had flown off. I had the flashlight propped on the washer. My shadow covered the dog standing there, its tail going like crazy.

I found a wedge of wood and drove it in the top with a rock, to hold the ax head. I fixed on his nose, his cracked, tan nose. His blank eyes. I wanted to say, It ain't my fault, but nothing came out but this grunt as I swung.

I went inside for a garbage bag. Ginny sat pale on the couch. I said, "I don't think he felt it."

She said, "Hurry."

The blunt side of the ax hadn't left a mark. With his head between his legs next to the bucket of water, Vice could have been alive. He didn't blink. He didn't bleed.

I carried him on my shoulders around the mountain. The dusty moonlight was enough to see the ruts. Things rustled in the brush. Small rocks clattered. His stomach gurgled. And what I still heard was that sound he made when it hit him, like a person, like someone taking a punch. I whistled. I wondered if I should chop off an ear or his tail and sent it to Musk. No. I dropped a good-size slope of rocks over him.

And it was over.

———

I opened a sheet over Ginny asleep on her stomach on the couch. Her eyes moved inside her lids. I checked the locks. Our fan pulled the air off the mountains . . . the leafy smell of buried things. In the dark, spread-eagled alone on the bed, I was the buried thing. I put my hand on my chest and felt nothing. The only sound was the whirring fan. I smoked to use my lungs, to work my body. Tiny Markem said my old man "returned from the dead." Like hell. He'd never been alive. And Jill said everything was alive.

I woke up on my side and I could see Ginny holding the phone, staring into the bright white light of the window, wearing only blue panties. She said, "I won't do it the rest of my life, Daddy." The curve of her hips, the lift of her tits. She shook her hair. "I just wanted to hear how things are, that's all."

I remembered that I had just killed the dog. I couldn't think of a goddamn reason why I shouldn't have. I shut my eyes.

When she lay beside me, hot, I said, "We'll leave."

She said, "Now."

I kissed her ear, her neck, her cheek. We *would* leave. I said, "It's safer with the dog gone."

"Carlos, don't ever talk about that. Just don't."

I said, "You called your folks."

"It was nuts."

We lay in the morning sun, just lay there, as white and still as that goddamn dog.

50 —— SIS

April.

Fat green flies come from nowhere to thump the glass, to buzz and thump and die in an angry whir on the windowsill. Warren picks their wings off, and their legs, and still the dying flies—like boogers with eyes—twitch and tremble and spin.

I am a generous dictator in the cottage. Whatever I have—smokes, glue, dope—I hand out pretty evenly. Sometimes I fight—to keep my hold. Sometimes Warren helps, but I have the feeling that one of these days he might not be able to stop his fists.

Jill visits every Saturday: twice with purple flowers in her hair, each time perfumed to stop my heart. We walk the grounds now, Badgers in windows, under trees. We walk. Between the silver lake and purple mountains. The birds are back. They sing. Visitors fill the gravel paths ahead and behind us. The sun glows on Jill's cheek. Her lips move. Tell how it will be when I'm out, play by play, until I hurt. I tell it back again. Jill says her father lets her come because she said she'd kill herself. She says she would. Jill says my mother is fine. My mother stays home.

May.

Ditto. Except for J.J. Flyte just in for burglary. By the second week, he controls his cottage. We meet like Civil War generals in the cafeteria every now and then, face each other across initialed tables, and know the joke's on our troops, who fight for us, steal for us, lie for us, do time in the Buckets for us.

A Ute kid hangs herself from the backboard in the gym.

And through the dirty, wired windows, across greening fields of alfalfa, I dream myself standing in the sun on a flatbed car on a passing, westbound train, the wind like water.

June.

School should be out. My blood says so. Campus is too small, too dry, too little of the wide, wide world. Now kids *really* fight, kicking, tearing at ears, gouging eyes, squeezing throats. Two Mexicans stab each other so well the staff RN cries and they go to the hospital and don't come back. We rip ourselves apart until nothing helps. My right eye is swollen and yellow when Jill comes the second Saturday in June. Her face is peeling. New freckles powder her nose, and I know then that I am too old, that something I want is gone.

"Happy birthday," she says. A quick kiss. Too hot to go out, too jumpy to like being in, we sit across from each other, the small, red present between us. For just a flash, it seems what Jill and I have is there, separate, in shiny foil paper tied with a green bow, something we both would give our measly souls to open but can't, not now, not until Christmas or Valentine's or Easter or Thanksgiving, some goddamn holiday that will never arrive. "Open it," she says. We talk, we smile, we laugh, but there is really nothing to open.

I squeeze her chilly hands. "My birthday's in October."

"Shh," she whispers, her face down. "You're not going to be here in October, stupid. Happy birthday," she says louder, leaning across the table, kissing me on the cheek. I don't kiss back, because she is my sister not my girlfriend, because the Badgers watch us like we might overthrow the world.

I can see where the tape has been torn loose and resealed, and I wonder what the hell Jill could want me to have that the powers would let slide by. The paper crackles. A picture. In a green frame. A color photo of Mama. But

the woman is tan, too straight through the neck. In a rainbow skirt, her hair frizzy clean under an orange, propel-
lered beanie, this woman's from some screwed-up nursery
rhyme. Behind her, stuffed, colored animals—bears, rac-
coons, dogs—are frightened in the eyes. "My mother?" I
ask Jill.

"She looks good. Huh? I just took it Thursday. Had to
beg this photo place to do it so fast."

"Where is she?"

"The park. Beehive." Jill sits back, softly clears her
throat, and says, looking at our hands. "Working. 'Working,' I said. Don't you believe me?"

"No." My chest tightens.

"Mostly she just hunts for stuff in Lost and Found and
helps kids find their parents. A couple of times she's been
on the midway, though, when they needed somebody in a
rush. That's the Water Riot. She handed out the water
pistols, a quarter a shot. They have to fill up these tubes
to win anything. She liked it. Really."

"I'll bet." I study the picture. "How did you swing it?"

"I told him he owes you something," she says with a
sharp nod. "He does. A lot more, too. And he hopes this'll
stop me from seeing her so much."

"You know what?"

"What?"

"You're the only other person in the whole rotten world
who really is a person."

"You're right," she says. "How'd you guess?" We laugh.

Jill glances at the Badgers and the dark, muttering families. "When you're all alone," she whispers, "take out the
picture and look on the back. Okay?"

Fresh from the laundry, the T-shirts and jeans smell like
watermelon or candied apples. I sit in their ragged shadows, the closet door closed, the photo of my mother on the
midway in my lap. Step right up. See the woman with skin

as thin as tissue paper. But her skin has something to it, and I cannot even smile, the wonder is still so great. Outside the hollow door, Warren is not exactly snoring, but his breathing could call a moose. After the check at midnight, I slip from bed.

My fingers are bloodless in the dim light. The bulb buzzes into the hangers. I slide the velvety back from the frame, lift out cardboard, two layers of wax paper. And my body is jolted, shaken by the shot, not because it is of Jill without clothes, but because her legs are spread to the lens, spread on soft grass in a wash of bronze sunshine, her face spread around a smile with light-frosted eyes shut—and more because I would murder whoever took it.

For a week I am tight, angry, hair tempered. When she tells me Saturday she snapped it herself—her camera has a timer—I am suddenly heavy and aching and tired, and for four days I lie in the infirmary with a fever.

On the back, five ten-spots were masking taped in place. If I'd torn her photo getting the bills off, the Badgers would have thought World War III what with the shouting I'd have done.

I ran out of things to want in there, fifty bucks went so far. I wanted out, but I decided not to buy that, not with two months to go.

July.

Warren has a friend. Honest to God. A kid named Steam, if you can believe that. George Steam. Warren calls him Georgie. Georgie likes to tilt back his head and say, "Haw, haw," no matter what the hell Warren says. So Warren blabs his birth on up. And Georgie likes Warren for entertaining him. He talks back. These two big hogs, with as much sense between them as a Dixie cup, yack, yack, yack like Mormon girls whenever they get the chance, one of the damndest things I'll ever hear. And Georgie is every bit the fighter Warren is. The three of us give lessons now and then.

Georgie shot a kid, smashed the kid's leg up pretty bad. Now, shootings are a dime a dozen in Dusty. But Georgie, he talks about shooting pistols like J.J. talks about weed. "Jee-zuz," Georgie says, "you should have seen the blood. Jee-zuz, he screamed and threw himself around. Fuck"— a word he drops like a rock or a barbell. "If he hadn't jumped like 'at, I'd a splattered his head. I'd a killed him like I wanted. Square in the face. That's the truth, Warren. Haw haw. He didn't believe I would."

One day Georgie's eyes lit up. "Hey, Cade. You're over to Bryant, aren't ya?"

"I was. We'll see if they ask me back."

"You want a good gun, there's a kid over there can get 'em."

"Yeah?"

"Cheap. Smart guy. Ingus. Or English. Or . . . Fuck."

To know what you don't know is the bottom line. To remember to remember the secret lives whipping us into stride. To remember never to forget you can know nobody. You matter to no one, really, because no one knows you. Protect yourself. Danny Ingus nearly took you down.

I couldn't sleep. In the closet, I sat with Jill's picture till I wore myself out.

Out. Out was what you wanted.

Whenever you looked in the mirror—cheap mirrors that showed you too thin or too fat or too long or too short— you saw it, backwards or not: TODAY IS THE FIRST DAY. And always you wanted to believe you were near the last day, when they'd give you back *your* clothes, your wallet, your lighter, pants with belts, and you could grow your hair. And in the lines, line after line after line, you read OF THE REST OF YOUR LIFE on *every* back. The rest of your life—

behind faceless anybodies in long, cattle-chute halls that led past barred windows to locked doors. Somebody always got wherever it was, whatever it was, first. Someone always would.

His note came in a gray envelope with gold edging, his name in gold script in the upper corner, "H. M. Arthur"— like a candy-bar wrapper. "Dear Mr. Cade," read type needle sharp.

> This is not an apology. You had a choice, and, as I said, we cannot help who we are. You are experienced enough to understand that. I cannot, however, fool myself into believing reform school of any demonstrable value. You are where you are temporarily, and, I am certain, unchanged. You have been punished for an infringement of the law. I believe, however, that punishment must be accompanied by certain positive incentives if people are to be genuinely assisted.
>
> My daughter assures me that, despite your background, you are a young man of potential. Lance tells me you can be depended upon. I am willing to gamble. Your mother, as you know, is now in my employ. I make the same offer to you. To facilitate your release, you are invited to train and work as a mechanic at Beehive Amusement, Inc. as your time permits.
>
> You may make your reply to my daughter.
>
> > Sincerely,

My caseworker said, "You're a lucky young man."
Jill said, "I think it's for real. I think he's sorry."
I laughed until the cafeteria froze. Jill reddened. Badgers glared. Her hands slipped off the table. Finally I whispered, "No wonder you believe in me."
"I do," she said quietly. "You know I do."
"I think about you every minute."

"Carlos, he says he's sending me to some girls' school in the east. At the end of next month. Carlos?"

I wondered if she'd threatened to die over that, too. Or did she trade?

August.

A month long as the calendar. My last month. I knew the Dust Trail inside and out, down to its least lousy smell and each mangy rat that nosed through the rubbish bins. If I pushed my cheek against my window at night sometimes, I could see the girls undressing in orange boxes of light across campus, like a trick my eyes played. I burned Jill's picture. Saturdays were years apart. Sure I got a kiss off some girl in a back room now and then or during one of SIS's dead dances, but when I saw Jill again, Jill quickly standing beside a cafeteria table, hurrying to me, her smile like a small, white bird or something, I sometimes wondered if I made her up, if I'd lost it completely. I mean, could real be soft and happy and perfumed and beautiful as that? We always kissed. Except that once.

She stood, but she stayed put, smiling with her lips together, her hair combed over her ears. Hilda said, "I thought you'd be out by now. I did, Carlie. Honest. Or I would have written, you know, or something." Jill sat down.

I straddled a chair across from them. I said, "God, you didn't waste any time growing up."

She said, "Oh this," nodding and smoothing the clothes around her chest. "This suit. Sissie's mama gave it to me."

"The suit and, hell," I said, "everything."

Jill said, "You look great. I told you."

"I'm glad," Hilda said. "I want to. A girl should want to." Her hair wanted to, curled like that. Her tan wanted to, and her lips and her nails and, most of all, her eyes. Her eyes wanted to look good, not alert or warm or anything, just good. As good as gold. The pretty girl before had been warm-ups for this young lady, who fan-danced thick eyelashes, her voice smooth as canyon wind: "Mama wants to. She does. I can't get over it." She leaned then to Jill and kissed her cheek. "Thank you. Really." My old man had pinned her, and I wondered. What did I know? I read her face every which way—but came up empty.

"Two weeks," Jill said. "Two more weeks in here is all."

Hilda said, "I thought you'd be out by now."

"They're waiting for school to start. They know what a shit load of good it did me."

"What grade?"

Badger eyes zeroed in when I squirmed, fighting down a laugh. "They're not holding me back, because I passed some test and because the damn librarian out here swore I'd read her shelves end to end. She lied to convert me, I think."

"Welcome to the fold," Jill said.

"We'll only be one grade apart," Hilda said. "Isn't that funny?" Funny. Jill told me once she didn't blame Hilda for taking off. Jill did not know the half of it—just that the old man lit out, that's all. What did Hilda know?

"The principal got some stupid sermon out of mothballs for the occasion," she said. "He called me 'child.' And he patted my shoulder." Hilda's face showed itself here. Her voice too. " 'Child,' he said—patapatpat. 'Nearly *five* months ago you *stopped* attending, and only *now* do you ap*pear* with an explanation, *asking* to be ex*cused*. Would it be *fair* to those more responsible, those *students* who take this *school* more seriously, to over*look* your negligence?" On "negligence" Hilda crossed her eyes. Jill squeezed her hand. They laughed. Then Hilda's face closed down again. "I asked him," she said, "what 'fair' has to do with anything."

"And?"

And Hilda was too busy filling out her suit to answer.

51 —— HEART

The shadows have started down the mountains. *Sixty Minutes* kicks in with its goddamn ticking. "How about something else?" I ask.

"How about football?" she says. "Stock car races?"

Mike Wallace talks about a murder.

"Two weeks," I say. "You're through driving. We pack, and it's off to the promised land. You pick the place."

"It's not just the place."

I catch up by the boulder. "Ginny." Her face hangs. No tears. The side I see is dark away from the sun. The rock's heat is like something she sends. "Mexico." I put my arm around her shoulders, but she shrugs it off. The lake hooks right to the sky. "You saved me," I say.

"We'll decide," she says. "It's us who will decide how *we* live, nobody just barging in. We starve first. We beg before we give up."

"It's over," I say.

"No more," she says.

I say, "A week Tuesday's it for me at work." I touch her ear, her perfect ear. "Call somebody, Emma or whatshername. That night we'll cook out and celebrate."

"Carlos," she says. "I think this is a test or something— I do, this dog stuff, I don't know—to make us who we need to be next."

I pull her skirt up to her waist.

"No," she says. She stands. "Some place wild, Loskie. With fish."

She leaves the rock. The door bangs below.

She does not look when I come in. Gloved hands reach into some bloody somebody on TV, and Ginny stares from the couch, holding Mr. Cat, her hair swirling in the blast of the fan.

"Dr. Clark's other vital organs are what failed him," the TV says, "kidneys, lungs, finally his brain. His plastic and aluminum Jarvik-7 heart . . ." Ginny strokes Mr. Cat. I lean above her from behind. The fan whirs.

Barney Clark sits propped in bed, wearing glasses, tubes in his nose, gauze packed at his throat, his smiling wife bent close, speaking. Battery Man. He died—was shut down— four months ago today, two days before that kid stepped up to me with that lizard, two days before the first of April when I knew I would come back. This year? Jesus. "The autopsy found the air-driven heart perfect after beating nearly thirteen million times in one hundred and twelve days." White-coated doctors walk onto a stage in the same hospital where I had been wired shut, met J.J. Flyte, waited for Jill. And third from the last in the back as they take their poses grins Matt, Dr. Matthew Downes. Matt! Matt and his cronies nod while Jarvik and this clown DeVries take questions.

"Ginny, Ginny, I have a lot to say."

She says, "I want to listen," but she means the TV. I grab a Baggie of Mary Jane and my shoulders ache, and I smoke three j's back on our rock in the dark.

Ginny brushed her hair against the quick rise of hills and mountains and sky, legs crossed on the windowsill. "It's after seven-thirty. I should go. We've been over this." She tied her hair with a purple ribbon. "First thing when we get somewhere, to start it off we get married, Carlos. We have to mean it, too." Her earrings had horses on them. She walked like a horse, muscles rounding her legs. At her car, she said, "Call the landlord." She didn't wave.

I told the landlord I had been transferred. He said drop off the keys. I waited to make the other call.

I sat with my tape recorder. My story. Speaking so it almost wasn't words at all. Ginny *would* know. Understand.

Ginny would stick. And maybe the hard part for everyone
was the time between the family you got and the one you
would choose.

I dialed.

"In meetings the rest of the morning," the woman who
answered said.

"Have him call his brother-in-law."

I smoked. Magpies hollered their dry sound down the
canyon. Grasshoppers crackled when they flew. I doodled,
a chair, a stick man in the chair, smoke swirling from his
head. The kettle whistled. I stirred up another coffee. No
radio. No TV. I started a list:

1) Money.
2) Musk.
3) Old Man.

I shut the windows to hold the cool from the night, but
already I was slick under my arms, around my eyes. I
opened the windows so I could hear the phone. I took my
cigarettes outside. Mr. Cat rolled in the dirt next to me on
the hill. I picked small blue flowers for Ginny. The lake
was not there, just sky. Blue. Space. Outer space. Night
forever, really, this blue, this heat, a cheap trick.

I took my time getting it because I knew he would ring
until I answered. I put the flowers in my coffee cup. I read
my list. I lit another, inhaled, and shit, I'd forgotten my
tape recorder. As I lifted the phone I heard a click, his
machine, and he was the governor. I could see an edge of
the green Capitol dome around the slant of the mountains.
I said, "Hello."

"Hello, Cade. All's well, I hope."

"I'm ready," I said. "I have Jill's note. I have my whole
goddamn life story. I'm ready to leave."

"I'm happy for you," he said. "I understand you've had it tough the last little while."

"I've had tougher."

"How much are we talking?"

Jesus. I had written "Money," and I hadn't thought of an amount. A house. A year out of work. A ring. A kid. A Harley. Stud. This huge goddamn hornet cleaned its wings on the lip of my coffee cup. Shit, maybe the click wasn't Lance's phone at all, but cops. Maybe the whole thing was wired by someone else. "I'll call you in half an hour," I said. "Be there. And no one else listens in."

A phone booth in Hotel Utah without one goddamn thing scratched in the shiny paint. Air conditioning. My list folded open on my knee. No hornet. My head on straight this time. I could not feel my heart. Silence. Busy. The phone would not ring through. Lance stalling. He couldn't figure me. I scraped "The End" into the phone's black box. An old man looked in. I palmed my knife.

Off through the hotel's glass doors, flags and red, white, and blue banners hung from lines strung over Main. Two weeks till the parade, the twenty-fourth, Pioneer Day, the day the Mormons had pushed into the valley—the day we would start fresh. The desk clerk's dress had red polka dots and a clown collar. She handed an envelope to a fat man in a fancy-ass blue sweatsuit and white loafers. Still busy. I scratched "1983 BC"—for Barney Clark—into the paint.

The woman put me through. No clicking on the line now.

"One hundred grand," I said.

"Well," he said, "that sounds manageable," too quickly, and I should have asked for more. "For the note, the original. No note, no deal."

I said, "You get the note."

"That who else knows about?"

"Nobody. But a couple people know where to look, anything happens to me."

"Nothing will," he said. And through the walls I could feel, hear, the hotel elevators rising. "I want . . . I also want this life story or whatever else it is you've got."

I flattened the list, and my voice was steady, and I put my knife back in my pocket. "Tell Musk and his goons to stay away. Tell him his dog is dead."

"*You* stole it?"

"Ingus lifted it, stashed it with somebody who gave it to me. I killed it."

"Musk would have paid."

"Right, a hell of a guy. You knew I'd be at the dog fight, didn't you?"

"Carlos . . ."

"You'll pay. And nothing happens to L.G. and Rose."

"Who?"

"Ingus's brother and his wife. He was my friend. He has a kid. Musk heavy-hands me, anybody bothers them, the note goes out."

The silence came back. "Sloppy can get dangerous," he said. I could never forget how smart the son of a bitch was. Not for a second. "Don't be sloppy."

"Don't you. This is business. You planning to be at the ranch over the twenty-fourth?"

"Yes. Is that where you're thinking? We're coming back Sunday night. I'm in the parade."

I thought I was in control. I *was*, no matter who got photographed with Shriners driving him in the goddamn parade. "Have them stay, Hilda, the kids."

"They're set to ride in the car with me. Then Beehive's got fireworks that night."

"Send them to Beehive alone. You can go later. This won't take long."

"I can do that."

"You and I will meet . . . in your office after dark for a few minutes. You get what I've got. I sign papers if you want. I get what's coming."

I would be in the governor's mansion. He would be sitting and I would look down at him, and he would sure as hell know how much he owed me, just how goddamn much. "I'll feel safe there. Be alone."

"Well . . ."

"Be alone."

"Security is cut back to one guy. I'll send him on an errand. *You* be alone."

"I'm bringing a friend," I said. And I hadn't called Stud, and what if he couldn't? For the money I'd be talking, he would. For all of it, he would. And the later I told him, the better. "Just in case. He won't know anything. He sees I'm fine, he leaves. Nine-thirty. The whole valley's busy with sparklers and cherry bombs."

"All right. I think so." The slow breathing again. "I'll work out the fine points—what door, the watchman."

"Get the money together." And asking for more could have been too much pressure. Ginny was in this. "I'll open an account. I'll call you with a number. They say you can transfer it in. That Friday at two be by your phone."

"We leave for the ranch Friday. How about Thursday?"

"Let's say Wednesday—two o'clock." My rules, goddamn it. "That'll save Thursday for business."

"Business? Cade, I don't get these goods on Monday, I'll track you down."

"Hey, I have other business. I'll call. Be ready. The money moves in the pipeline." I would get it right. "You don't even need to cross the street."

"Originals of everything."

I shook out a smoke, put it back. I stood. The walls of

the booth were cold. "One other thing," I said. "The old man, he splits, too—all by his lonesome."

Lance cleared his throat. "What can he do? Forget him."

"Find a way," I said.

"Hold on," he said.

"Lance," I said, "hey!" but the line had jumped to Muzak. Frozen full of light, the icy lobby chandelier swayed above clean, overdressed men and women with name tags.

The music ended. "Carlie," she said, a voice in a long tunnel. "Carlie, leave Papa alone. Lance says you . . . you want Papa gone." This faraway voice barely reached my ear, it was so tired.

"You know why. He has no right."

"I have rights," she said. "Leave it alone. Leave the past inside somewhere. This way . . . This way he's harmless. I don't know why you called or why you all of a sudden care. I don't."

"You're my sister, that's why, my sister, for Christ's sake."

"I'm a lot of things. You, too, I'll bet."

"I want to see you, Hilda. We'll talk. I would have tried to get you. I'm leaving soon."

"We *should* talk."

When Lance came back on, I said, "The old man, he's my affair. Fuck it. Two Wednesday, I call."

In the center of the lobby, a bearded guy took photos of a long-legged knockout in a fur. She wore white gloves lightly wrapped in a thin gold leash hooked to a blond Afghan hound at her feet. The bearded guy said, "No, no, no. More passion."

The desk lady in the polka dots held a silver balloon shaped like a dinosaur.

In the dark air rushing over us from the fan, Ginny said, "I told them, Carlos. This is my last session. And, Carlos,

I sold the V-dub. This student driver who's saved all summer, he's giving me eight hundred dollars. That last Friday
I give him the keys. Kiss me. Just kiss for a minute."

Above her perfume, I smelled the dog, dirt, boulders,
mountains.

52 —— *THE SOUND OF MOUNTAINS SHRINKING*

Those last two weeks hung on like winter, like flu.

J.J. Flyte told the guys trailing after him to sit somewhere
else. One gulp of orange juice and he ate pancakes oily
with syrup, spattered with butter too yellow to be butter,
that melted like Styrofoam breaking down. Swear and
smile. Hurt and smile. Bust bones and smile. Eat and smile.
Ssss-mile. J.J. said, "Nine days."

"Yeah," I said, "but they keep their hooks in."

The smile, locked in place. "What they got you on for
outcasing?"

"A business guy in my neighborhood fronted me a
handyman job at Beehive."

"Experience running Ferris wheels. All right. How to
keep the merry-go-round running round. Man. I'll be emp-
tying trucks after school. I mean a dude needs to get his
back used to boxes, right? Yeah. This way I get the mini-
mum cage, I mean wage, and a Get-Out-of-Jail-Free card.
They get yours truly live and in person. Fair is fair, right?
Right on." The rest of the cakes and J.J. pushed his tray
over to a pug-nosed kid just leaving.

"Too bad you can't take your staff."

He laughed. "A man can always find help. How'd you
like to be on my team outside?"

"Right."

"Hey, I ain't about to roll over and play dead for these fuckers." He lowered his voice. "I got some jobs figured. Easy jobs. Candy store jobs. Gingerbread houses, man. The golden eggs. What I don't know? Tell me. Man, I know whole neighborhoods' floor plans. Even here in Ogden. No shit. I know watchdogs' names. Who's got alarms? All in my treasure chest." He tapped his forehead. "And a team— I got a smart team all ready. This is a superliner, man. I'm your ticket."

"I don't think so."

Warren and Georgie played crazy eights in our room after dinner that night. Thirty minutes before lights out, they put the deck away and stomped the shit out of me. No bones broken, but Jesus.

A Friday so perfect—no clouds, no heat, the air brand-new—I was scared to walk into it, to cross the empty parking lot to her car. A day, I told myself. A day can be like this. You *can* have it. She took my hand despite the goddamn Badgers propping the doors like gargoyles. "Hey, make a decent life for yourself, huh?" this monster supe named Mule said.

The peroxide queen behind the desk said, "Have a good day."

I said, "Don't work too hard." Shit.

School started Monday. My school. Jill was supposed to leave for Connecticut on Sunday. "A joke," she said.

Far out to the right of the highway, the gleaming lake pressed against the sky. "I can't wait," I said, and I pushed my hand up under her hair and watched her drive, wondering if I had changed.

We lay on a blanket on the slope behind her cabin—at each other better than before, and, in between, smoking, drinking, drying in the sun. Until dark. In the dark Jill said, "I'm not. Don't worry. He knows I'm not. All this is part of the game he plays to feel good about himself as a father. I'll promise not to smoke any more or something and he'll give in."

"Don't go."

"Shh."

I snapped on the light beside the bed. "I want to look some more."

A quick kiss—her tongue tip—and she rolled toward me, onto her side, bikinied in white, white skin, the black spider trembling as she breathed, my name tattooed beside it. I kissed her stomach, the fur of the bear silky around us, the sound of the stream and the crickets a rush of air. CARLOS. Written in skin.

"Because you were the first," she'd said.

"You might be sorry someday."

"No."

In her garage at one-thirty that night, I hugged her one last time. We would meet at the park swings Saturday afternoon at two. And I woke Hilda and the old lady, who could have been strangers, in what could have been a different house.

The thing is, Jill didn't show Saturday. I waited an extra hour, the city knotted in those mountains. I knew.

"You can go," she said, "then drive it back." She wore a pink hat trailing a green peacock feather. She winced when she blinked her red eyes. Her clothes—the skirt, the blouse, the shoes—did not belong any more than the hat, like some costume she chose for just this stupid scene in a play about herself. Cartoon clothes, wrinkled and crooked.

My mother said, "Come in, sweetie. Have some French toast." Hilda dabbed her mouth with a paper napkin.

Jill trimmed each word: "Thank you. I can't. I've got to

go. Now. Really. My aunt's in the car. Carlos, please. They said you could."

I threw a brush through my hair.

"We'll miss you," my mother called.

Jill's slow feet, her shiny shoes, wobbled through the gravel. Lips tight, she said, "He won't stop. For my own good, he says. Maybe we *are* just kids, Carlos. Maybe I *am* bad. I won't see you, not for a long, long time. Send me pictures. Write to me. I will. All the time." She lifted her hat, there her brown hair chopped short, ragged. "For you," she said. "I won't look good for anybody else." I kissed her cheek, her ear.

Her Volvo—angled badly at the curb. In a yellow dress, a plump woman with a tight, gray helmet of hair and dark glasses with sequined horns stood stiffly while I scrunched in back. "My aunt's going with me to Connecticut. Aunt Stella." Aunt Stella had a mustache. "Papa said you keep my car."

"What?" I couldn't hear. Aunt Stella smelled like toothpaste. Aunt Stella never looked at me.

Jill drove the speed limit, but Aunt Stella said, "Hurry now, dear, hurry," every damn block.

Jill held my hand between the seats.

Two days out of SIS and where was I? I didn't really know just then. Those coming up the long, cool airport hallways laughed or cried. No one looked at me. Those going down, went down and down and down. I expected the Dusty motto on their backs. Jill's fingers moved through mine.

Time to board. Doors opened. Aunt Stella locked onto Jill's arm even as we hugged. I kissed Jill's neck. In my ear away from Aunt Stella, her mouth a flame, she said, "I loved you." She squeezed the keys into my hand.

The window shivered with the airplane's roar. For one

long second on the takeoff, the airplane, balanced on its
tail, its silly front wheel already off the ground, would not
rise, could not fly. Goddamn, I thought. Good goddamn.
But the rear wheels cleared the runway. The jet rose. The
sky was tin—dented, torn, when the plane broke through.

I unlocked the yellow Volvo. Her car? Jesus. What was the
hitch? I didn't want it. I didn't want anything to make up
for what I had lost. Shit, I didn't even have a license. She'd
shown me a few times, let me drive. And Danny'd given
me a couple of lessons. But a car didn't matter—would not
matter.

Hot seat, air hotter, I rolled the windows down and
breathed—still smelling her. I managed to get the damn
thing home. Goddamn it.

High school. That's about it. Whatever I could get my mitts
on: reefer, acid, pills. I steered clear of horse. Too damn
smart for that shit, I told myself. For a while. I didn't want
to die, just live somewhere else, as someone else.

I did hate the goddamn car at first, I did, all the time
just waiting empty outside, a reminder, a sign, a coffin. I'd
give it back. "You can't buy me," I'd tell Old Man Arthur.
"Spoil Lance with two cars."

Lance got his license that summer—and a forest green
MG-B to use it on early that fall. Shit. An air freshener
shaped like a pine tree dangled from his rearview—in a
convertible no less.

"Drive it up your ass," I'd tell her old man. And plenty
more.

Then her first letter came, eight thick pages, mostly sexy
stuff, but enough about the girls' school where she'd been
jailed to damn near make me hitch to Connecticut. She'd
been so long in writing because Aunt Stella stayed and
stayed and wouldn't allow it. "I'm glad you've got my car,"

she wrote. "Sleep in it sometime. OK? Race it up the canyon and pretend I'm with you."

"You could give it back," Mama said that night. She sawed at her pork chop.

I was wired so my eyeballs burned. "That's not what I meant. I don't mean sell it either. Just use it or something. God, it's only gonna rust and . . . I'll take trips, cruise around sometimes."

Hilda said, "If they want him to," with one ear cocked for whatever boy would show up the second she cleared our table—our new round oak table.

"Damn right, Hildy. Why not? Hey, let's us take drivers' training. I'll give you half time with the Volvo you finish— and make sure I get through, too."

That next week a fancy horn I hadn't heard before trumpeted up the alley for Hilda before school. The first time. Maybe I knew when I saw them. Maybe I'd been waiting. Laughing, Lance pushed open the door to that damn toy car of his, and Hilda, like a dancer, just flowed in.

In the back of the drivers' trainer that afternoon, me so stoned I'd blast off for the sun when my turn came, I whispered to Hilda, "Not Lance. Huh? Anybody else. Please."

She froze me with those perfect, madeup eyes. Then, her red nails touching her red mouth, she muttered, "Jill made you happy enough, I noticed. And she had . . . problems. Well, she did. And look—without the Arthurs, where would we be?"

I skipped dinner. I walked to the library. Walked hard. From the lobby, next to all these crazy, bloodied-up Halloween displays—Bram Stoker, Poe, and Lovecraft stuff, pumpkins, witches, and ghosts—I called J.J. Flyte. I told him anytime, if he still needed somebody. Just to drop by my house, and I gave him directions.

The letter I wrote Jill afterward in our corner upstairs

couldn't say anything she hadn't heard before. I went through four cigarettes. Then they threw me out.

53 —— DOUBLE OR NOTHING

"**D**ouble or nothing."

"You got it." I shaded my eyes, watching the can. A lizard parked right next to it.

Stud shifted on the rock, leveled the pistol on his knee, and squeezed off another round. The barrel jumped, the canyon boomed, but can number two still stood. "See, you aim low. Make it part of your hand. Tighten your pointer . . ."

"But you missed. You owe me four bucks."

"Where's the lizard?" He winked and lifted the bottle in the bag. He wore these beat-up brown wing-tip shoes, no socks.

"Shit. Lizard just ran off."

"Hey, this short-nosed baby you got ain't made for target practice. We'll sit closer."

"Let's stand closer. I won't be sittin' down."

"How 'bout me? What's the gig? Not just shootin' lessons."

"An errand," I said. "I'll tell ya."

Stud tucked the pistol in his pants. He lifted his cowboy hat and wiped his forehead. We hiked above Vice's rockslide, through stickers, grasshoppers bouncing off our legs. He drew, not ten feet from the can—and missed. "I got to split real soon," he said. "Where the hell'd you get this cap gun anyhow?" He took off his T-shirt and hunched up in the shade of an overhang.

He threw out instructions—"lower, higher, let her kick"—and worked on the bottle. It got to where the explosion didn't surprise me. The can jumped off its rock half a dozen times. Each hit, Stud whistled. He said, "Musk's dead by now." My cheeks hurt from squinting.

"Nobody's dead," I said. "It's not Musk. Nobody dies." He shrugged. "This is an errand. That's it. An hour's work maybe, the night of the twenty-fifth. Pioneer Day. The twenty-fourth's a Sunday, so they moved it."

"There's the rodeo, man. Bitsy's got us tickets. She's kind of a mess."

"Two hours max. Listen, hell, you can meet Bitsy there. This is real money."

"That's the kind I like." He looked at his dirty nails. He nodded.

"Three thousand locked in an account for you the Friday before. A check for another seven the day after our errand."

He whistled again. "Ten, huh?"

"You know what Noel would do. Business came first. Easy money."

"Noel's in a box because he was dumb. Don't talk to me about Noel. Don't talk to me about Ingus. I'm smart. As long as I'm alive, I'm smarter than those assholes."

"Tell you what. Five before, five the day after. An errand is all. We'll meet at the Walker Bank Building, the three o'clock closing that Friday. You can see for yourself it's in."

He stood and heaved a rock down into the scrub oak. A ground squirrel raced out and over a rise. "It's Arthur, ain't it?"

"What makes you think so?"

"A few rumors. Musk wanted you at the dog fight. I know that. This *is* Arthur."

"It's nobody. I'm dropping something off. I check things out first, lead the way. You bring up the goods. You leave. Cake. I'll tell you the details an hour or so before. You won't be going in blind." He wiped his face with his shirt.

I shot. The can clattered. "And I'm tellin' you, nobody dies. Your piece of it's cake."

"So why the big bucks?"

"Because. I want to keep you honest. You got a pistol?"

Stud nodded. Spit.

"Bring it."

"But leave the bullets in the drawer this is so easy, right?" He laughed. "Okay." He drank, pulled his wrist across his mouth, and passed the bottle to me.

The woman at the bank had said no problem, just have them sign these cards. Back at the house, Stud squeezed the pen like maybe you had to to get the ink out. He held his tongue between his teeth: "Yule Bonus."

"Yule?"

He tipped the bottle. He stared out the window. "My old man named us after Christmas," he said. "He did a lot of crazy-ass things."

His beat-to-hell black pickup bounced out of the drive. He called from the road. "Hey, Cade. I won't let you down." He honked and rolled away.

The last car in the line of three honked. Aaron, soaked again, held his watch up to me, and shouted. "Fifteen minutes late. Goddamn it, Cade! If I had anybody else, anybody. I count on you and what do I get?"

I left the headlights on a second or two longer to try to read her. She kept her head tilted back against the porch railing, her arms around her knees against her chest. I heard him when I cut the engine—Moon. "Ginny," I said. "Hi."

Through the lighted screen, Moon sang, "Out on the Salt Lake Desert, the water runs away."

Ginny said, "Hi." She did not move. Her eyes stayed closed.

Moon sang, "Your canteen's dry, but you can't die, you're lost on the old Salt Flats."

I said, "How 'bout I shut that off?"

I could feel the crickets in the quiet. The dark hid the mountains. I opened a beer across from Ginny on the steps. "Four more days in the wash," I said.

"Give me a cigarette." She lowered her head. I loved her mouth in the matchlight. She said, "I went and saw Mrs. Shiftlet." The cigarette glowed. "She remembered me. She's thin so her joints stick out. I took her perfume. She'll never get better. God, think about that. Never."

"She's old."

"She dies, and everybody dies, and no one else feels a thing."

"We're going."

"I put an ad in the paper for the yard sale Sunday." She leaned back again, pulled on her cigarette, and then flipped it in a trail of sparks down the walk.

"Her son came," she whispered. "Kind of nuts around his mother."

"Kind of nuts period."

Now she laughed. "That's what he said about you." We listened to crickets. I lit another smoke for her. "They said you went with Danny Ingus when he shot up a house once. You got away. He lost his leg."

"I wrote it down for you," I said. "It wasn't like that. Ingus had a crazy streak."

"He blew up that club, the one Rose said?"

"The cops think so."

"And he died. You said you'd tell me."

"He tried to get even for doping his dog. He stole the white dog. That pissed the owner off and he leaned on Danny. Danny got mad. Simple."

"And the owner killed him, the owner of Stonehenge? How do you know all this?"

I walked into the yard. "Ginny, do you see how rotten this shit is? That's why we're going."

"Where's the money coming from?"

"Why the third degree? My brother-in-law, he owes me, Ginny. I swear."

"The governor?"

"That's right."

"Mrs. Shiftlet said stress is the worst thing for a pregnant lady."

"You told her?"

"She knew. In the middle of something else, she just said it."

"Did Bobby Shiftlet hear?"

"I don't know. I don't care. Loskie, I've made up my mind. You can be the Werewolf and I won't care, not as long as you're nice."

"This is almost over," I said. I kissed her cheek. Kissed her. "You should know . . . There's a hell of a lot to understand. Shit." Ginny cried like someone lost forever. Stumbled out into the moonlight.

Our slope to the moon. Our arms around each other, the sky rising right from our skin, we dragged our feet slowly higher. We didn't say one word. To the top of the mountain where we stood and turned. All the way down.

But when we got back, some kind of bird whimpered almost, jumped from the porch, and scissored through that nervous light into the canyons. Ginny said, "Where did that come from?"

Then on our couch, her blouse undone, she sat up. She said, "Mr. Cat. He's not here, Carlos." She hurried out. She shouted his name. Spoke it, her skin swimming in the moonlight. I called, too. We hunted the yard, the shed, the scrub oak, the road.

———————

Saturday, in the night, she cried again, spread-eagled in the current of the fan. "I know animals aren't people. I'm not flaky. It's just losing. That's what it is. Losing. Getting what you don't want."

I said, "Hey. Hey." But that's what I thought, too, and I listened for trouble, danger, strangers, damn near till dawn.

Just before eight she left. I heard the bug, remembered it was Sunday, tasted something like warm, rotten wine, and thought, *She finally gave up.* Right smack in the middle of my body, just under my ribs and my heart, a sharp pain started, a burning. Walking, taking deep breaths, helped some. Had she gone? How could anyone leave a place so empty?

I found her things, our things, in neat rows on the lawn, on board-and-brick shelves she'd thrown up from scrap out back: coats and shirts and socks and jeans; silly knick-knacks—ashtrays, records, earrings; two hair dryers and two old radios. A lamp stood by the tree. She'd set a saucer of milk and a bowl of catfood on the top step of the porch.

When she got back, her long fingernails were gone, chewed away. "They'll be here," she said. "Get ready. I put up signs."

"Didn't we just unload this stuff?"

Old ladies and twitchy old guys in leisure suits came first. They asked if we'd take less for everything they touched. They bought all the plates and silverware. Families came. Thin girls in halter tops with babies on their hips. Ginny sold one the pink ceramic poodle the well-driller's boy in Idaho had given her. She said, "Wait," and then, "Hell no, I don't want it," when the girl tried to give it back. One of our neighbors from above climbed past in his Jeep without slowing.

Then Ginny lay in her two-piece on her stomach among the things no one took, and the Jeep rattled back, stopping at our drive. A hairless, shirtless muscle boy in gym shorts got out. Ginny lifted her head, fastened her top. "I saw your signs," he said.

I said, "Take a look around."

"No," he said, "the cat."

Ginny said, "I taped on notes." She stood quickly.

And he reached into the Jeep and lifted out a dirty Mr. Cat. "This the deserter? He crashed in our Kayak last night. Friendly booger." Ginny hugged Mr. Cat. She kissed the kid, held his neck.

Mr. Cat licked his saucer of milk, cracked the tiny stars in his bowl. "I thought that bird had just carried him off in the dark," Ginny said, grinning but still shaking. "For what we did."

54 ——— *CANYON REACHES*

On Beehive Amusement Company letterhead, the note said only, "Report to work on Monday in the Maintenance Shop, room 5. Mr. Bolten will be your supervisor." Folded in the note was the title to the car, an insurance form, and a check for two hundred dollars. In the blank on the check next to MEMO, he had written, "Transfer fee, taxes, etc." I tucked the papers back in the envelope and sat down at the kitchen table. I felt too old to live much longer.

The house smelled—like pie, perfume, pines—like the blossoms bursting at the necks of green wine bottles in each room, flowers Mama got from the greenhouse at "The Park." And paint. Clean, baby-blue, yellow, and pink, the bright walls were almost too happy, too new for the few faded pictures stuck on them: my old man smiling crookedly in a pickup truck, Gandy as a beanpole of a young woman tanned damn near black, and Hilda and me standing by a fire hydrant somewhere sometime. Paint from "The Park." Labor from Matt Downes and his younger brother Frank, if you can believe it. Jill sent them over, Hilda said, and told Mama it would be deducted from her pay. Who knows? Matt would be famous, Hilda said, already working so hard to save for college and being a genius and everything. I folded the envelope and stuffed it in my pocket. My old man stared at Hilda from the wall.

We sat on real wood furniture. Thanks to Hickler. One day he showed up with a truckload of stuff he said some family tossed out. Would Mama like it? I can imagine Mama in the doorway unable to talk, just stepping aside. And those men from Hickler's ward, those broad, hairless men in sleeveless white shirts shadowed by the garments underneath, moving like convicts, empty-faced, disciplined, carrying the ratty shit of most of Mama's years out into the sun and then hauling the dusted, heavy, luxurious overflow of somebody else's life into her three impatient rooms.

I had stolen nothing since Dusty, and still we ate well every night. Meat. Plates full. Mama pleased. Hilda, always counting bites, always counting. Fifi, trained now, perched on her hind legs waiting for scraps.

I could not remember my hands on Jill's waist. Only a cutout of her eyes—and hair. A cutout.

The setting sun jutted orange through new curtains. Another Friday night. I tried not to recognize the horn. Why didn't he come to the door? "Bye," Hilda called. Everything pretended to be real: her prancing up the drive, the smell of lamb and potatoes in my house, birds chirping their lungs out.

Before long maybe I'd be idling up some cute little horny girl's alley, honking that Volvo's horn, waiting for her lipstick and her giggles and her thighs. Her spider? Fat chance.

I smoked. I picked my gums with my fork.

Mama shined the low red-brown boots she called her "Girl Scout shoes." Every work night after dinner Mama rubbed dark polish into the gummy leather. Then she buffed and buffed. The radio whined with Beatle songs on violins. Mama said, "I'm glad they seen fit to finally let you go."

"Likewise."

"The devil was here," she whispered over her red hands. "Night foreclosed the day. Foreclosed it. God done me like Job. And . . . And I give up on God. Satan's gone now. Gone gone. Remember that. God come back, right *here*." She flattened a narrow, wrinkled hand upon her chest. "I'm not going to die no more. Don't you, Carlos Cade." Shoes finished, she brightened. "Some cookies?"

"No."

With barely enough wind, she whistled as she laid out tomorrow's dress and underthings in the bedroom.

That night I itched. For something to do. I could smell fall, the inside of the earth. Crickets itched too. The grinding wouldn't stop. I walked. And walked. And walked. The hard part wasn't that Jill was gone. It was that she was there and not there at the same time. The night bloated up like something dead. The moon oozed through the sky.

On my way home from wherever I'd been, I found myself in front of Bryant, that sideshow of animal acts that called itself a junior high school. I worked a piece of cement loose from the sidewalk. I threw it at the wet window of the principal's office. The window broke with a noise like water. I ran.

That weekend I got high with some Indians downtown, beat up a kid in Reservoir Park because he knocked a little girl into the slippery slide, and read—probably *Ellery Queen Mystery Magazine,* whatever that's worth. I saw Hilda at dinner. She looked tired.

Work.

I went to work. Why? Shit. You tell me. If I didn't show, Arthur might get pissed and fire Mama. I was curious how much Arthur would deliver. And I remembered the bleached-out, blue-white eyes of my caseworker. He wore two school rings. "Work scores points," he said. Points. The worn-out, goddamn, pretend-you're-a-civilization game.

So Averell Bolten, a gray-bearded, singsongy guy no bigger than a boy, put me through my paces. Mowing grass mostly, moving sprinklers. "For a few more weeks," he said. "Then we winterize, lad. And rake them beautiful leaves. And rake some more."

My hands tingled and my ears still hummed from the mower when I climbed off the bus that night. The crickets whispered, "Car-los, Car-los." I was sore through the shoulders. I hadn't had a toke since lunch. But I bounced, grinned over chestfuls of cool, salt-sweet air. Jesus.

And with the top down, the stars like Roman candles, they kissed in his car, kissed with Lance leaning, pushing, trying to rise onto his knees, held too tightly by the wheel, Hilda moaning, rubbing her hands in circles on his back. "Oh," she said. "Ohhhh."

I slammed the screen door as hard as I could. Mama squealed in her sleep. Nothing else. Four cigarettes later I've nearly won at solitaire. Hilda opens the door and sighs. A smile.

"I saw," I said.

"So?"

"Lance all over you."

"You were all over Jill often enough."

"But Lance . . ."

"Is my business." Hissed. "What *I* want is *my* business." Sighed. "Carlie, don't be one of *those* brothers."

Hell, the next day I couldn't sleep through any classes. After algebra I saw him laughing with two basketball players in the hall. The five noisy minutes between classes would be enough if he'd just turn it off with the giants. He did. Said, "You guys be good, now."

Said, "Hey," when I squeezed his arm. He straightened the press of his sleeve as he waited, eyebrows raised. Girls turned to us, watched us in the corner as they passed— winked.

"You're slippery, Lance. Just so goddamn slippery."

"Yeah?"

"I know you. I *really* know you. Don't forget I really know you." I kept my voice down, my face kind. "Hilda doesn't. Leave her alone. Or I'll tell her."

He checked his watch. "Ancient history," he whispered. "We were kids. We said he fell. He *did* fall. Give it up. She'd believe me."

"What would Pep and Matt say?"

"Ask 'em." He smiled. He had asked them. "You'd be telling on yourself, Carlos. We might just say you did it." He patted my shoulder. "I've got to go."

"Wait," I said, my lips tight across my teeth. "Your mother."

His skin faded like I'd flipped a switch. He leaned against the window.

"You know," I said. "*I* know." He stared into the hall. "*You* pushed her."

"Jill's story?" A red stain spread on his white neck. "She said that? Jesus." He blinked. He blinked. "You won't tell that. Not even to get me. You'd involve your precious Jill."

The bell jolted both of us.

No potholes. No cracks. A new street. An old moon.

Flat-roofed, long houses of white stone and gold brick. Lawns brown, smooth as runways. Here and there a leafless stick staked where some insurance salesman, warehouse manager, or stock broker imagined a tree some day, and shade, and maybe even a hammock. Whose back yard rose into a goddamn mountain range. Shit.

Two weeks till Halloween and the breeze blew cold from the canyon above, with a marshy, dead-fish taste that had me itchy for a cigarette. Try to smoke through a nylon stocking. *Jesus Christ, hurry,* I thought. Moonlight wouldn't leave me alone. My shadow waved like a flag no matter where I stood. Just after two in the morning. I cut around the van and went out back.

I waited by the pool. I listened, watching for lights or anything in neighbor houses. The blue pool cover sagged with rain water and dark leaves. A silver rat floated in the leaves.

Our third job. The van and fifty percent of our take belonged to Earl Metts, an albino-looking guy, maybe five feet tall, who carried a .22 pistol and liked to be called Sugarman. You tell me. And forget what J.J. said. Sugarman managed this show. He worked on The Good Seed Nursery's planting crew. He took notes on anyone out of town while their yard was landscaped. Earl's "book." So far we'd pulled down close to six hundred bucks.

J.J. backed out the door with an amp and a turntable. "This big playroom downstairs," he whispered. "Check it out."

"Fuck this moonlight," I said.

Sugarman worked fast, piling every damn thing he could find in the middle of the floor: TV, typewriter, tape recorder, guitar, clock, candlesticks. My flashlight carved through two bedrooms. Lots of jewelry, a few okay clothes. And a workroom with too many tools.

Sugarman said, "Not too shabby."

Arms full, he started up the steps and the lights burst on. I dropped. A girl screamed. Screamed again. A big bearded guy in boxer shorts leaned in at the top of the stairs. A blond, eyes wide as her nipples, stood behind him. They'd been on the porch or something.

Veins thickened in the guy's neck. He said, "I called the cops."

Sugarman fired. A black hole unwound in red on the man's leg. He fell onto the stairs. My ears hurt. The girl screamed. Sugarman yelled, "Shut up, slut," and crouched beside the bearded guy, the pistol steady and close. The girl's red mouth rounded without noise now. Her eyes wanted to explode. I looked at her smooth stomach. I dove. The pistol fell. I grabbed it up. A gun, I thought. I can do anything.

I pointed the barrel at Sugarman's nose, my voice booming all over hell: "You're crazy. Let's split."

The bearded guy groaned as I went by. The girl slumped against the fridge. J.J. said, "Let's go. God."

Sugarman kept his head and drove slowly, shaking. From the back door, J.J. said, "Step on it, man. Drive. Push it. Punch this thing."

"Planes eat people, Mommy. They do. With ketchup."

For a moment the little girl held my hand. The window vibrated with takeoffs and landings. Then she ran to some other waiting stranger and squeezed *his* fingers.

Snow. White. Fog. White. Thick with dark shapes. The doors moaning. Late, her plane circled my head in fog. I was tired of looking at myself against the white, of remembering. Of coffee. I sat down. I smoked. Would the girl hold my hand again?

Jill's letters shrank that fall, down to two or three lonely sentences swearing love. We were twins, didn't I see? We *knew* each other. In purple ink, the last ones, tight, barbed purple lines. Four days ago she sent the flight number and time, saying, "We have to. No one will know." Tuesday night. Her father expected her Thursday afternoon. I would bring her back to the airport for him. Until then . . . Her face would not return.

I walked up one long pale corridor and down another. As empty and cold as the last two months.

Sugarman took it full force. Earl Metts turned twenty-nine two days before the trial. For twenty-nine his record was pretty goddamn impressive. All-star material. The cops thought so. Earl called us his "errand boys."

"A corrupter of youth," the prosecutor said. One freckled lady cried into a purple hanky. "A man to whom goodness is weakness. An evil man, who would have killed, whose instinct is to kill." Sugarman got ten years.

Because "the crime" took place in Ogden, outside his back yard, which made him look hard core, and because they dug up some stuff from an earlier number in his bedroom, and because he was not white and could not softshoe like Shirley Temple, J.J. went back to SIS, which he didn't seem to mind a hell of a lot.

My probation officer called me a "stupid ass." But the girl from the house, the daughter getting it on in the dark (whose face I kept finding in the airport that night), said I risked my life. She thanked me through tears in front of the whole court. Her boyfriend didn't. J.J. swore it was my first time out. Good old J.J. Nothing. I walked. I couldn't believe it.

Hilda drove me home in the Volvo. She chewed her silver nails. Through a heavy, dark rain.

When Mama finally got in, she said, "Oh, son, goodness."

I didn't eat. I smoked and drank coffee. The radio helped. Tomorrow at school no one would shake my hand. Even the teachers would forget.

The week before Thanksgiving, Lance and Hilda were royalty for the Junior Dance. "King and Queen," the caption on the front page of the *Leopard* said. They posed smiling beside a bug-eyed, ostrich-size papier-mâché turkey. I skipped the dance. I skipped most everything. School and work. School and work. Little Boy Bolten said, "That was a heroic thing you done." The last he mentioned it. Honest to God, I wanted to deck him.

Saturdays I detoured by the library on my way to Beehive. I checked out three books for the next week, adventure books usually, books about the West, ordinary jackoffs in tight spots. Try *The Big Sky* on sometime. And mysteries. I read them. That's all. I read them, showed my face at school, and worked.

Jill wrote, "I'm with you. You're with me."

Hooky would put me back on the Dust Trail in a minute. No, I'd check in at school tomorrow and the next day— and at work. Would Jill stay in the cabin? The car?

Now I heard, felt, stood, in the trembling air. A ghost on the runway, the plane barely existed in the cold and fog, red eyes blinking. I pressed my face against the glass. The girl said, "It's here. It's here."

One by one, owl-eyed, snow-flecked strangers stepped through the dark doorway, clothes let go then by the wind. "Honey!" "Daddy! Daddy!" "How's my princess?" "Where's my present?" "After Chicago, this is the tropics."

Jill—cheeks red as her turtleneck. She did not run. Flakes beaded on her blue beret, in the loose, soft curls at her neck. Curls. She stopped. Just out of reach. Her face flat, pinched, tight, held her features in, held in some feeling like a scream. I smiled. I couldn't move. I'd sweated over letters to another girl. Someone else's spider all those nights. She had dimes in her penny loafers. Orange butterflies of lipstick. "Hi," I said. "Hey."

And she rushed to me then, kissed me, stepped away, smiled. Kissed me. Careful not to touch again in this world of searching eyes, we walked. She wiped her tears. I wiped my mouth. We walked. We smoked the same cigarette.

She said, "Carlos, I'm never going back. I swear to God I'm not."

I said, "Okay."

She drove. Waited while I got her bags. Paler, thinner when I returned. Used her tongue and lips and hands. And I had her coat undone when some asshole bumped us with his door. "Pull over there, that empty corner."

"No," she said. She sighed and shook her hair. She turned the key. "I like wanting it so bad with you right here. God. I can't believe it. I want it our bed, our mountains."

Jesus.

The cabin windows steamed.

Even though I'd told Hilda—and had her swear not to tell Lance—even though Mama didn't give a good goddamn where I spent the night, I got Jill to take me home at five the next morning. Still dark. Caution. And I needed clothes, a bath, time.

I hold a pistol. I smell bullets. At the top of basement stairs, a girl, naked, tries to scream. Tries. At my feet, the guy she wants to save bleeds.

And what about Jill's hair, snow beaded in its curls? She promised.

The next night, on her back beneath the bearskin,

crying, Jill says, "And this spring they'll bus them in. Boys from this military school. They make us dance. They make us curtsy."

She rolls to me, squeezes me, kisses my shoulder. Her stomach still carries my name. It does. I am so stoned and warm I feel the cold edges of those letters as she pushes them against my thigh.

"There's something . . ." I finally said. "While you were gone, I . . . I got ticked at Lance over . . . Hilda and . . . everything."

A whisper: "Yeah?"

"And I told him what you said. Remember?" The quiet had never been quiet, not with the stream on fire like that, with the beams creaking like timbers in a pirate ship, not with our hearts thundering and thundering, the earth growing old, cracking, shrinking, rusting on its axis. Her hand tightened, relaxed. "He said . . ."

She inhaled into her voice, even, slow, quiet: "Don't worry. It's okay. We love each other. What could Lance say? What?"

"I just wanted . . . I broke my word. I get screwy. Hell, I don't know where I've been."

She held her breath. She turned away. "Carlos? I want to die now. I want us to kill ourselves. I'm serious. Let's have the most perfect time we can and then on . . . on New Year's just do it. We'll never have more than this. We won't. Let's promise, promise and not think about it. And then we'll just do it like nothing, like a kiss or a hug. Please." The bed began to shake. When it stopped, we listened. And we heard everything.

55 ——— YELLOW

Ginny said, "I hated this morning. I couldn't have stood the cat being gone. Yard sales are awful." We sat on orange plastic chairs with magazines in our laps. The laundromat windows were white with steam against the black outside. "They make your life seem like, like you're not even part of it—only your stuff."

A boy in swim trunks drew on the glass with his finger, made a small square with a cross in it—a window, or a present.

She said, "Let's just drive out of here on Friday when I'm through at work. Let's."

"I can't. I told you. I have business on Monday night. My last business. You go to the rodeo or something with Emma and Paula. The next morning we're gone."

"I'm coming with you. I won't be by myself. If this is such honest business, I can come. Carlos . . . We'll be honest with each other."

"Some things are tricky. I've got to think it through."

"We're together in this."

"That's right, we are. Believe me. That's why I need you to sign something." I put the card on her magazine, on a picture of Sally Ride, the astronaut, cradling a helmet in her arms. "Come on. I'm opening an account for you is all. Period."

"With what?"

"Nothing now. It's coming. Trust me. I'll put a cushion in here for you. That's all. This money's straight up."

"Keep it all in your own account."

"I might get flattened by a bus. You never know. Insurance."

The boy wrote DARTH in the steam. A lady in curlers folded flowered sheets.

"Listen, I'll tell you what. Read what I've written. We're partners now. Start tomorrow while I'm at work. I'm almost at the end."

"I don't want to be alone." Ginny crossed her arms and closed her eyes. Finally, she licked her lips. "We could try Minnesota. Emma says it's wilderness clear to Canada. She says . . ." Ginny shook her head. "Emma says the West's dead as . . ."

"The pioneers. You got it, Minnesota it is. Just sign."

"Or Florida," she said. "By the everglades."

"You bet. The card, Ginny, if you trust me."

"You killed the dog."

"Because I had to."

The Hickler's Market neon sign had been painted blue across the front, but architects' names were stenciled on the window, and ferns hung inside. A man with a mustache and granny glasses got into a LeCar and pulled away just as she arrived. No Caddie this time, a Volvo wagon, and Hilda looked smudged somehow, around the mouth, the eyes. The first lady of Utah showed up in jeans, a sport shirt, and tennis shoes. "Why here?" she asked, but she knew, and she half-smiled as she turned there on the sidewalk. "I drive by all the time, but I've never stopped."

I lit her cigarette. We smoked and walked. Hilda and I. Under small trees. Clean trees, clean houses—all small. Even the Arthurs' old place, all done up with striped awnings and potted bushes on the porch. Matt's, the shutters painted green. Bottoms' place with skylights on the roof, stained-glass windows. We had never left, that's what we knew, had gotten stuck somehow, and when she looked down the alley and saw our house was gone, that a garage with a boat inside stood in its place, she said, "Nobody would believe it anyway. It doesn't matter."

We walked out to the island and sat on the grass in the sun, no dogs, no sprinklers. College kids on ten speeds pedaled past. Heat, but not nearly so much as I remembered. Dandelions, bees, birds. She chewed a blade of grass, older only in her hands and eyes. I said, "Tomorrow's my last day at the car wash. I'm leaving next week. I don't know. It just seemed we should talk."

"Lance said you'd tell me lies."

"Why would I?"

"He says you're bitter, and it's eating you up."

"And you're not?"

"I'm homecoming queen. Why would I be bitter?"

"You know." I wanted to hold her hand.

"I can't change anything. Don't you try. Just don't. Leave Papa alone. Please."

Her eyes had thick black lines along the lids. "I'll trade," I said. "Leave Lance. That's what I wanted to tell you. Mrs. Governor or not, you shouldn't stick with him, Hilda. There're just some things—"

"He helped you long enough."

"Want to know why?"

"I know why. Christ, Carlos, what happened to us?" Now I held her hand. She pulled it away. She said, "Please."

A mail woman moved from house to house across the lawns, dogs barking behind doors. House to house. Gerry's house. Matt's. Pep's goddamn encampment of a house.

"I'm going to tell you some things that'll turn your head around. They're not lies. I'm so fucking tired of the goddamn lies. I'm going to tell you the truth. I want us to live the truth for a goddamn change."

"Carlos, you mean a lot to me. You do. I can't help you. You can't help me. I'm fine. I am fine. I have an appointment for lunch." She pulled in her legs, worked for a smile.

"I just want . . . what I want is to know you know, that

you see your life as it goddamn is. That's what I want."

"Don't shout." She stood. She said, "I hope it works out
for you. Then we'll get together for real."

"He's the one killed Greg Skink."

Her eyes were frightened now, her hands. "He said
you'd say that." She pried another cigarette from her pack.
"He said you . . . you're trying to squeeze him for money.
Greg Skink just fell, and I . . . I don't know why you'd do
this."

"He threw a rock and hit Skink on the head. Nothing.
An accident, but then Lance, Lance is the one . . ."

"That's not what happened." Smoke rushed from her
nose. "He fell. Why would everybody keep quiet?"

"And do you know what else?"

She stood back from me, head tilted, arms crossed, cigarette burning, eyes fixed on something in the sky. "Why
do this to me? Are you so jealous?"

"He pushed their mother from a cliff."

"He told me . . . He said you'd say *that*. Jesus Christ."
She's crying. "That came from Jill, didn't it? Jill was sick.
Do you hear me? Sad. She'd been to doctors. She was crazy.
Crazy! Are *you,* Carlos? God, maybe *you* need a doctor."
Her lips are shaking. "Leave Lance alone. Carlos, Carlos,
I love him. Leave us alone." Hilda coughs, coughs with her
eyes closed, and when it stops, she throws her cigarettes,
and runs. She does not look back. I lie back. I hear her
call, "Just leave us alone." Her car starts. I feel bugs in the
grass climbing onto me.

Even though I'd be through with the car wash that day,
the sunlight the next morning made things worse—too
yellow. The mountains. A flowered chair nobody bought.
Two round pillows. An empty room: just a pile of mostly
kitchen stuff off in one corner, and the old TV, up on

bricks, that nobody wanted for the fifty bucks Ginny asked.

The tape stopped, my pen capped, I smoked, smoldered holes along the empty lines of empty pages, and blew hazy rings around yellow mountains. Nothing.

I hadn't gone two steps. They cornered me by one of the pink trash barrels. Whippet licked his teeth. "Want you to fill in a few gaps for us."

"Looks like we got a killer, Cade," Dolores said.

Whippet said, "No question." My heart would not slow down.

The billboard woman was gone. A small Smokey the Bear stood with a shovel beneath a wide, coal-black rectangle now: THIS USED TO BE A FOREST.

"Congratulations," I said, staring at rooftops, at pigeons, at clouds.

"You don't seem surprised," Dolores said.

"I need more practice."

Aaron scowled from the icy window of his tropical hut. Five blonds, each hour-glassed, worked the pink bays, blue towels in hand. Shit. I would go out like the end of a Hollywood musical. The End.

Whippet said, "You know what we think? We think you're small potatoes. Be glad we think that. Be damn glad, Cade. What we figure is you happened into it. We know you were ringside at the fight. Let's say you just rode along the night they pinched the dog. Maybe you drove Ingus to Stonehenge. Somebody drove his car home. Possible. What matters to us is that you know more than we do. That matters a lot."

"Excuse me." Aaron spoke to the back of Dolores's craggy head. "I was wondering, gentlemen, when you might be finished with Mr. Cade." Good old Aaron. "This *is* his last day, and I did want him to help train the girls."

Dolores turned to Whippet. "Let's take this downtown."

Whippet said, "With a little luck we'll have him back by three or four." So they planned to have me back.

"Please," Aaron said. "This *is* his *last* day."

In the room of the green ceiling tiles, the box of a million holes, they wear coats, shiny green coats that came with the lead machete ties. Dolores sits beside me, backward on his chair—cowboy style. He is not a cowboy. He inflates his cheeks and breathes. Sitting sideways on the table across from me, his hand flat along the top of a black-and-white photograph, Whippet says, "Know him?"

"Nope." I keep my eyes calm on the picture of Danny's old man, his face creased and tired.

"Danny Ingus's father."

"I haven't seen him since junior high. Dead?"

"Upstairs healthy as you, Cade," Dolores says, "maybe healthier."

Whippet uncovers his crooked teeth. "He says he did it. We found somebody saw Nicks get slashed. Description fits. We found a knife. The old man hadn't even cleaned it— tossed under his bed." Whippet taps the photo. "We've got the deal down, Cade. Danny stole the dog Vice. Poor Danny got roughed up. Danny owed money. Danny blew Stone- henge. Stonehenge Faithful Anthony Nicks, born Noel Bonus, thumps Danny. Danny's old man gets even. What do you think?"

I had figured L.G. all along, which had been fine. "Can I smoke?" Whippet holds out one of his. A clear lighter with a tiny trout inside. The room smells of gasoline. I say, "I guess you've done your homework."

Whippet says, "You're in it. The dog. Maybe a joyride for the bombing. Straighten all this out now, last chance, we keep you clear." They bend in, lift their lips, get smiley.

"Ingus was a friend. He helped me land the car wash. Where I lived. Period. I got nothing to trade." Six more days. I would make it. But the old man in the picture? He didn't have to do what he did. And how about mine?

Cars idled four deep at each bay when the cops dropped me back at the Lucky Lady. The tall damp girls rolled their hips and smiled. Legs, long perfect legs. The world stank of Turtle Wax.

"Screw the cops," Aaron said. "They still hassling over the bomb and the Castro guy was murdered? Real live super detectives. *Do* you know anything?" A few drops had spattered his outfit—the white pants, the yellow and green Hawaiian shirt, the wide-brimmed Panama. His hair was braided with a red ribbon. He smoked an empty sequined cigarette holder. Bug-eyed. Shit. The Tycoon.

"I know I'm finished shining cars."

"Hey, I'm sorry to see you leave, Cade. Wow. I mean, is this something or what? You were here, Cade, in on it, an explorer of the possible. I wish you well. I sincerely do."

He pulled a fiver from the till and tucked it in my pocket. "For luck," he said, flicking the cigarette holder. "And because I hate to see you go. I do, man. But business is the name of this muchacho's life story. Give me your address and I'll get your last check in the mail end of next week."

"Next week?"

"Make it tomorrow. You're a good man, Cade. You are. I'd pay you now, but . . ."

"I'll be leaving town." I put my hand flat on his chest. "My money."

"Hey, stay cool. Take it easy. It's yours, man. You earned it. And hey, I almost owe you for your friend who dances, works the bar. I knew she was a pro. The lady can move.

We got to rapping the other day when she stopped. She was coming tomorrow to coach these chicks how to market their merchandise. Marketing's the battle, man. Then she heard you'd be amscray and changed her mind. Everybody loves Carlos. You see her, tell her I'm open to ideas. I'll pay." He signed my check with a big swirl. "I'll give you a free wash sometime. The cops didn't tell you anything, huh?"

I took the long way home, around City Creek, behind the Capitol all lit up. The dry smell of the hills. Sky—deep and . . . empty as the moon.

At the Safeway on West Temple, I found a poster in with all the ads for puppies and bake sales and babysitting. Tomorrow night my old man would be in Rose Park: "Awaiting His Return!" I ripped it up in the parking lot.

Like a toy, an MG Midget, top down, sat sideways in our yard. Moon sang, "Will you cook? Will you sew? Will you dance to the radio?" I smelled weed. Heard squealing, crazy laughter. Emma and Paula, their cowboy shirts fringed this time, stepped into the window.

"Well, here he is," Paula said.

"You sick, honey?" Ginny kissed my ear.

"Tired is all."

"Tired we can take care of," Emma shouted over the music, and she hurried toward the kitchen. "Food and drink's the doctor's orders." She shifted steamy pots. A red candle flickered in the center of my table, in a circle of blue Snoopy napkins and plates. Emma held up a glass. "To you, for your luck, laid off from a shitty job."

I asked Ginny, "Did you read it?"

"I will," she whispered. "I wanted to celebrate. We're going to be happy, Carlos Cade."

Paula and Emma ate . . . and ate . . . fried chicken, rolls, salad . . . and drank like whales, blue whales, walleyed queens of the sea. Ginny went easy except for laughing. She didn't smoke at all, while Emma and Paula and I damn near killed a lid and a little powder, too. "Next Monday night we blow this roof off again," I said.

"And your sister's married to the governor?" Paula said. "What a world."

The MG was barely down the drive before I took off all my clothes except my shoes and ran halfway up the mountain. I sat on warm rocks. But the dog had been warm even after it was dead. Crazy thinking. I stayed until Ginny called me from below. Ginny, calling to me.

56 ——— THE HAIR OF THE DOG

I can barely break loose of the black gravity in my head, but I push the pen all morning.

Out of work, almost finished with this record of what happened, I hear myself, the voice I've always heard, still talking. Who are these notebooks for? Lance will burn them. I'll have tapes. Will a newspaper buy them when the other money's gone? When Hilda's kids have kids, before the son of a bitch dies? For Ginny, I will take the money now, let him go. For Ginny. My back hurts. The tapes will keep him in line.

After thirty push-ups under the runt apple trees, I took a cold bath, washed my hair, pulled on a clean T-shirt and jeans, left Ginny a note:

> Running errands. Might be late.
> Just this once.
>
> Stay beautiful,

I put my notebooks in a garbage bag, four Spirals. I
pocketed the bullets and stashed the pistol under the driver's seat in the Polara. I waited to turn the key, looked
again at our house, our boulder, the brown mountains, the
lake thin as foil and floating off the ground.

"All right," I said, and fired her up.

After dropping twenty-five dollars in Bountiful on two
copies of my story, I had $93 of Danny's money left. My
back again. I bought a pint at the state store and drained
some in the glare and the heat on the freeway. I put the
copies in a locker at the bus station.

I smiled at the guard. My scalp itched. I smiled at the long
row of tellers, women ironed and curled in cages, counting
new money beyond glass doors. I tapped my cigarette on
the white sand of one of the lobby's heavy black ashtrays.
The elevator opened. The guard said, "Hello, Mr. Prescott." Mr. Prescott wore a thin, white suit with blue stripes.
On hold, I moved the phone to my other hand and turned
back to the street, watching girls in shorts.

"Carlos?" Lance said quietly, no clicking on the line.

"Problems?"

"No."

I checked the account number with him again. "I have
my notebooks under my arm. The note's close by. Money
isn't here in a half hour, I stroll up to the *Tribune*."

"Listen, it might take longer."

"You've got till three, then, that's forty-two minutes."

"Tell me about the note."

"Figure it out. You get the real McCoy, don't worry. I
want you to have it, carry it around for a while. Any copies
show up—and they won't—you say they're doctored. Hell,
you've got this taped, I give you trouble. Say it's all a crazy
man's blackmail scheme, the loony brother-in-law. Who's
going to say otherwise? But you don't want the bother. So

you take my notebooks, juicy stuff, and my three copies. I couldn't write 'em again. I'm through. You get Jill's note. You take the statement I'm going to sign about the lies I've made up about you. And you remember one hundred grand is a lot for me to gamble on."

"And something else, Carlos."

"The fine print."

"Don't break promises."

"The soft touch."

"Hey, I'm married to Hilda. You're family. Carlos, I love your sister."

"Somebody else had one. Don't forget. And a mother."

The notebooks beside me, the copies stashed in the Polara's trunk, I smoked on a shady bench and breathed bus exhaust on Main until three-thirty. This dead sparrow had maggots in the gutter. The *Tribune* time and temperature sign flashed: 96.

I could smell myself, sweat, whiskey, smoke. I would buy Ginny a ring with real diamonds.

The teller pecked my number into the computer. Her mouth opened. She had braces. I could not see her screen. She blinked. She pecked in my number again. She wrote on a pink bank slip: "$100,002." The paper did not shake in my hands. I took a thousand in cash.

"Gracias," I said.

"I'd like to open two accounts," I told the young woman reflected in the glass top of her desk in the middle of the bank. A tall man squeaked past on crutches. "For friends of mine."

I pushed the cards across the black glass. Her fingernails were gold. She swallowed and straightened her bangs. "They must be very good friends," she said. I laughed. And no one stared. And nobody cared but this woman right now.

"I guess so," I said. To be smart I put $88,500 in Ginny's

account. Five g's went in Stud's. Six thousand stayed in mine—five grand for Stud's second installment, a thousand for me, which was all Lance could weasel back, I figured, if he tried. I took $500 in cash and loaded up on temporary checks. We'd write with our new address.

The first thing on the street again, I did a little dance, spun and laughed. Shit. Nobody cared. I bought two burgers and a chocolate shake at Dee's with a fifty-dollar bill. Today was business. And so far, hell, business was great. This was the goddamn game most people called life.

Errand number one.

Number two. "I did it, Rose." Another booth, this one in ZC Mall, everywhere these boxes you can step inside to get ahold of somebody, boxes carved with initials and numbers, places to remember who you are and how you matter in the middle of the city where you grew up that doesn't know you from Joe Blow.

"Thirty g's," she said. "A lot to throw away."

"I didn't see a choice."

"Some dog, huh?"

"A dog to get us all buried."

"Can't nobody stop that."

A tiny blond kid in striped shorts tripped and let go of a green balloon. He cried as it floated up past the fountain, the balcony, clear to the ceiling of white light. I said, "Rose, you hang in there. You deserve a few breaks."

"Come see me, Cade."

"I'm leaving again. And . . . and in a couple of weeks, things work out, I'll send you some bread, huh?"

"I won't hold my breath."

"You're all right, Rose."

Number three. I told the saleswoman in Zales Jewelry that I was getting married next week. "Your first?" she asked.

Number four. The whiskey has loosened my arms. I am
too hot, but I see straight and I want them to know I know,
goddamn it. The afternoon crowd, trucks outside, plumb-
ers, electricians—repairmen. Motorcycles. Florida comes
right out when I send back my name. She has a red ribbon
in her hair. She wears this sleeveless yellow dress with no
belt and these tiny red shoes. She smiles, touches my arm,
leads me to the empty stools at the bar. Her eyes are bright
and she says, "Bring this guy a—"

"I'll pass," I say.

She nods to the bartender. "A root beer," she says, still
holding my arm with those thin ringed ringers. "Hey, I am
glad to see you. I went by that car wash and when I heard you
were going I got all nervous again. You remembered me."

"Should we go outside or somewhere else to talk?"

"No need. This is family—unless you're thinking more
than talk." She winks, sucks on the straw in the root beer.
The bartender sits under Phil Donahue on the TV at the
other end.

"I've thought about more than talk," I say as smooth as
you like, and she tilts her face. I take her hand. I squeeze
it. "I've thought of holding you underwater for maybe half
an hour for what you did to Danny, for what you damn
near did to me." Her fingers go stiff, but I don't let go.

"I want a cigarette. Carlos." She looks down the bar,
behind us, then whispers, "You think I killed him?"

"Nah, not your speed," I say. "Just poisoned his dog.
Trying to get him to blame me. Right?"

Her mouth opens, closes. Finally she says, "It was *you*
got Danny, wasn't it? You got scared. Now I see." She shuts
her eyes for a long time. I drop her hand. She stands,
straightens her hair. "I was his girl, Cade."

"You're everybody's girl."

"I'm not yours. *You're* poison. You are!" She is standing maybe five feet away. She leans at me, lips pulled up over her teeth. The bartender's beside me, repairmen gawking. I light a smoke. She spits. "No wonder everybody wants you gone."

I get to my feet. I smile all around. I say, "You're pretty, but you're dumb."

I walk out, and nobody comes after me, and I'm glad because I'm not sure what I'd do.

The poisoning? The goddamn poisoning. I will never know who turned against Danny first. I will never understand a goddamn thing.

Number five. I *would* get through my list. My old man's time was up. I tightened the cap on the damn-near empty pint, shoved it under the seat, and slid the pistol out. Loaded it. Slowly stuck it in my pants under my shirttail, and maybe this was too much for one day, but this couldn't wait. Not now. Too close—I bumped the Ford van next to me with the door of the Polara.

In the crowded parking lot a blind guy handed out leaflets for New Hope Bible College. "Life everlasting," he said. "Believe it. Everlasting life." White gravel threw off heat, glowed under floodlights aimed at a tall timber cross on a two-wheeled blue trailer behind him. Small black flies swirled around his smiling head.

Out front of the open double doors, where spotless, quiet people filed inside, one of those portable sign's white light bulbs blinked around black plastic mismatched letters:

THE MAsTer's CRUsaDE—welcOmE

An organ groaned into the rising darkness. I moved with the line into a long, high-ceilinged white room. The barrel pinched my gut. Who knew how the hell I smelled? The cross inside was silver, like an airplane propeller, and the pews, gray and rounded and pointed on the ends, could have been wings. Goddamn, Tiny Markem'd probably wear a pilot's outfit, Bernice a tight stewardess getup, and my old man? This was his last flight. Hell, maybe he'd already gone. But Bernice had a bright blue dress with a red belt. She worked the pedals and keys of the black organ to the rear of a wide platform under the cross. The pews were almost hot, they were so warm. The chalky air didn't move until two guys set up big fans on wheels at the back. The young guy next to me said, "That is a relief." He fiddled with his tie, combed his hair.

I tried to remember, to remember what my old man had done. What mattered more than money. He would hit the road tonight. I'd be calm. I'd hold the pistol against my old man's gut and nudge him to my car. I could make Wendover in two hours. If he came back, then, by God, I'd do what I did not ever want to do again, what I had meant to do reaching that razor around his neck that time.

The organ rose high over the grinding of the fans and fell. And the fans were nothing against the wild whisper that filled the place next. Tiny Markem's throaty carrying on: "And I saw a great white throne. And I saw the dead, small and great, stand before God. And the books were opened." Tiny stepped high in yellow pants and strutted the stage.

"Yes," the guy next to me said.

The woman on my other side put her hand on my leg. Against my sweaty stomach, would the pistol slide out when I stood? "Hallelujah," I said.

"And whosoever was not found written in the book," Tiny rasped, "was tossed into the lake of fire." The organ jumped in. Where was my old man?

Bernice sang "Onward Christian Soldiers." Everyone stood. Tiny stomped back and forth across the narrow stage. The fans hummed. Shit. My stomach. I took deep breaths until the noise stopped, until I saw my old man swaying in the back by Bernice. A damp white shirt. A shiny tie. He bowed his ugly head.

"March for Jesus," Tiny shouted, stomping again. The woman next to me sat down but grunted up once more when most everybody pounded with a foot. The building boomed.

"March for Jesus. March for Jesus," Tiny hollered. And they did, marched in place as he called, sweat running down their cheeks. My old man lifted his knees, too. "It is a long, dark, difficult road! March for Him! It is a road wild with demons! March on! Deadly with a darkness deeper than the darkest nightmare! March!" Tiny jumped from the stage. Bernice beat out a march, her back stiff, the pews emptied behind that short, curly headed maniac, and those hundreds marched in a long line around the white, white room. "March for Jesus! March for Jesus!" My old man marched in place beside Bernice. Two men fainted, were carried out. A woman shouted in a lunatic language. And a bald guy held her arm and called, "This is the path to righteousness. Do not desert the pilgrim with the news."

I was marching in the front when Tiny, soaked to the bones, bolted down the center aisle and sprang onto the stage, laughing. "Come forward," he said. "Give your hearts to Jesus. Come forward and be delivered to the spirit of God. Give your hearts to Jesus." And the pistol—shit, why did I bring the goddamn pistol?—all of a sudden leaped up over my belt. I grabbed it—just a touch—pushed it down, but my old man, my old man, goddamn him, must have seen. He jumped forward, elbowed Tiny aside, lifted his arms over his head, and bellowed down, "No!" He pointed. His lip shivered. His eyes swelled. The organ stopped. Tiny stayed back. The fans squealed. A woman said, "Help us, Jesus."

My old man leaned at me, his rotten teeth, his scar. He pointed again, threw his finger at my chest. "The beast," he said. "My own boy is possessed by the devil, I swear." Gasping. Hands grabbing at my back. "He's here to take me from the road. To take me away from God." My old man had tears on his craggy cheeks. "God is with us." He opened his arms, tossed back his head. "The devil must be cast out. Cast him out! Forever cast him out."

Florida had said, "You're poison."

The pistol stayed put, but it floated in my head back and forth over everyone, faces bleeding, screaming. I would shoot. I would shoot. But then, goddamn it, I lose. This wasn't my old man. "Cast the demon out," the pot-bellied, slobbering asshole who looked like my runaway father said. "Cast him out."

And this bruiser with a red ring swung at me. I clipped him quick alongside the head and ran, hobbled, did anything I could to keep the gun down.

Tiny shouted, "See how darkness flees!"

The blind man smoked a pipe. Those who'd fainted had Pepsis on the grass. Behind me three guys broke through the doors. "Hey!" They shook fists above their heads beside the cross.

No sirens. No lights. The road would not straighten, though, and I could barely hold the goddamn wheel. The whiskey ran out. I smoked.

The mistake, I said to myself, was the pistol. Guns took control. Next time I would control the goddamn gun. The mistake was trying it all in one day. The mistake, I said to myself, was starting to think I deserved anything in the first place. I laughed. My old man had seen his death in me at the front of that platform. How could he know I wouldn't be back? Maybe this was worse. Make him squirm and squirm and squirm. I would live. I'd seen his fear. Shown it to him. I wished my mother and Hilda could have seen it, too.

"You're cut," Ginny said. Her blue eyes dark. Her hair tangled.

"Not bad." I knelt beside her on the cushions on the floor, held her chin, kissed her cheek. "I tripped in some bushes at this guy I know's house."

"In a bar, you mean. God, your breath." She pulled away, tugged down her bikini top. "You said I wouldn't be alone."

"This was the last time. I promise. I tossed down a couple too many."

"You could have brought him here."

"He was too far gone. Kind of a jerk anyway."

She crossed her arms. "And you said I could start your life story."

"I had to take it. Make copies. One of my errands." I lit a cigarette in wind off the mountain.

Ginny squeezed my foot. "Carlos, can't we leave Friday, right after I finish work? Just split?"

"I have to wait," I said.

"Meet me someplace."

"If that's how you want it. I have some money for you."

"Carlos?"

"Tuesday we'll join up somewhere." My knuckles hurt where I'd slugged the guy. "Yeah." I took three hundred bucks from my wallet. "Yours," I said. "And this." I opened my hand around the ring. Her passbook was in my back pocket and, hell, I was all set to pull it out, but Ginny put her head down on her knees.

When she finally raised her eyes, she said, "You just don't get it, do you? What I want?"

"Sure I know. You . . . You don't get what I'm giving you." I slid the ring on, loose. "Have it sized down." She moved it to her index finger.

"I love you, Carlos." She took a long breath. "People's

lives get tied up together, and it matters. It does." I kissed her hair, her ears. She pushed me back, the air from the mountains pouring over us. "Please. I want to be quiet. God, I'd jump out of my skin." She narrowed her eyes, water edged along the lids. "Just don't leave me alone again. Don't leave me alone again and I'll stay. That's what I want. Okay?"

I needed it—that quick shot of whiskey the next morning. "The hair of the dog that bit you," Moon used to say. One shot to stop my forehead from cracking, to settle me down. I sat on the front steps. What was training now? I was through. Just the last little bit left. Ginny would start to read the notebooks tonight. She would know.

57 —— WIND

Cutoffs and flies. While the oil drains out of the Polara, I tip two Heinekens. I believe I stand for something. I light a smoke. I pour in gurgling quart after gurgling quart of Quaker State. The sun doesn't move. Just four more days. And Ginny will be home when?

The shadows turn. The mountain is empty. I will have a kid. I will walk my kid down streets with boats in the drive and moss in the trees. I will not worry. Her counter checks are on my notebooks on the table inside, wrapped in red paper with clowns.

I circle the house to an old gray stump, fifty roots twisting into baked red clay. I wonder why would anybody cut down a tree in this goddamn desert? I sit, watch the road, the shadows stretching over it, sweat, smoke. And wait. I turn fast again to check the slope, the bushes, the rocks. Nobody. Mr. Cat lies on the empty heap of an old ant mound and eats a robin, its breast open like a purse. Then I hear her motor.

"What took you tonight?"

"Took me? I dropped off the ring. And a couple of drinks at that D. B. Cooper club downtown."

"You and who else?"

"Emma and Paula, that's who else. To celebrate my job ending. Tomorrow's it." She pulls her open hands across her eyes. "Loskie, I want us to get out of here. That's what I want. I'm ready to read now."

"Here," I say. I hand her the present.

She opens the checks, drops them on the table, and says, "When it's all over, Carlos. Then I'll think about the money. You keep these. I just want to go—to go before we've changed so far our chance at this is lost."

She held the notebook pages flat on my table against the wind. Her hair twisted behind her. Propped on the porch, I smoked cigarette after cigarette between my yellow fingers. I stared at the lake, big and damn near green, one of the emptiest goddamn things on earth. Huge banners of dust twisted by.

When she sat by me, she said, "You didn't kill that boy Skink. That was something else." She pulled my head around and stared into my eyes. Her hair whipped between us. "Rose was married to *this* Danny?"

"Yeah."

"You know what happened to him, don't you?" Dust whooshed across the porch.

"I might. It doesn't involve me."

"Who else?"

"What?"

"Who else knows?"

"Don't worry."

She covered her eyes, her hair still swirling. "Your father," she said. "Your sister. What I can't believe, though, is this is the governor. This money from him, Loskie?"

"I told you that. The money is money." The wind jumped in one great gust so loud I could barely hear.

Ginny looked in my eyes. Then she put her arms around me. "Who's guilty is nobody," she said. She kissed me, long, trembling, and the house exploded with the next blast of air off the mountains, a door slamming, a blind falling to the floor.

Friday, first, I swept the red dirt off my table, across the floor into a heap in the corner.

I spoke all but the very end. Listened.

Got the note from the deposit box, xeroxed two copies at the library, put one copy back. Stud met me at the bank at closing time so there could be no double cross before our job. Stud laughed when the lady wrote his balance. I let him take five hundred out. I'd give him a check for the rest on Monday. I said, "My woman's going to ride along. It's okay. But let's keep the guns down." He hadn't shaved. I wondered.

Just back from the swimming pool doors behind South High, Ginny stood in the shade of a wall with a tall, skinny boy in glasses and striped shorts. I honked. The boy said something to Ginny, who held a green vase of yellow roses and a book with both arms. She said something back and he leaned to her and kissed her cheek. He opened the door, grinning. I heard traffic, the sound of a diving board snapping under a dive. The kid said, "Some car."

I said, "Thanks."

Ginny said to the kid, "You've got some car. I'm gonna miss it."

"Maybe we should have gotten rid of this one," I said as I pulled onto State. I smelled the roses.

"You didn't offer. Not enough room anyway," she said. "And you like this too much."

"Do all your kids kiss you."

"Today they did. I kissed them." She took off her shoes and closed her eyes. "Come on, Carlos. We're heading out. Don't let anything wreck it. Aren't they pretty?" She held up the flowers.

"I wish I'd thought to buy you flowers."

"You bought me a ring. Look." She lifted her right hand and laughed. "Now nothing can hurt me. I'll move it when we tie the knot."

"Who gave you the roses?"

"My boss."

"Guy you skinny dipped with?"

"As a matter of fact . . ."

"Jesus, Ginny."

"Jesus, Carlos, settle down. The other trainers gave me *this*." She tilted the book: *Rand McNally's Atlas of the World*. "We'll look all through it and pick a place. We'll pick and it will be perfect." I checked the rearview. Nobody. "I told them all I'd send postcards. I will. I want somebody to know where I am, that I'm happy."

"I'm just finding out about happy," I said. I fumbled out a smoke. "It takes a lot of forgetting, but if we forget, don't we goddamn disappear?"

"Carlos. Hey, your life's been this twisted thing. We'll straighten it out."

"With a knot?"

"Funny. Take me to dinner for starters—Chinese, and hot and spicy. I'm eight hundred bucks to the good."

"And then you'll read, read all there is to forget."

I put the notebooks on the table, where the checks are wrapped again. She carries the notebooks to the cushions on the floor. She reads on her stomach with her feet crossed over her while I do the dishes and watch lights soak up electricity across the valley.

Cigarette after cigarette. I climb the mountain. I hear a train. I start to pack. Four hours. I sweat in the fan in the dark. Her arm slides over me. "All of that's true?"

"There's one more part. The last thing."

"I can feel it," she says.

Five hours in the sack was all I could take, my heart out of kilter in my chest. Naked, her arms around her head, mumbling and tossing at times, Ginny slept. I fried an egg. The mountains crawled up from darkness. I smoked as I ate. I tapped my fingers, my toes.

I opened my newest notebook. I uncapped my pen next to it. Three cups of lukewarm, powdery goddamn coffee. I turned on the recorder, held the microphone. This was the last day—a place I thought I'd never go again. Today's would be quick. I shut the recorder off. I got the note from under the ice trays in the freezer. I unfolded it halfway. I smoked and listened to tiny birds in the coffee-colored grass.

58 —— THIN AIR

Sides warm and smooth, touching, we lie on our backs beneath a bearskin while the windows whiten. Our breath hardens in the cold air. We shower, holding each other, the lace of the water, the net of the water hotly tightening, tightening, until any second, one big splash and a miracle, we will combine, goddamn it. I know every curve and crease just hugging her like that.

Space heaters glowing in each corner, windows still milky over darkness, her cheeks like watercolor orange, we make the bed. We eat. Slowly. We move so fucking slowly. We do not talk. We smile. Sometimes I see that girl's silent mouth at the top of stairs. I want to talk, but I don't. I smile. I see Lance's cratered eyes staring down on the whole goddamn universe—and the sound: It's his laugh. No, it's the whole frozen wasted world, shrinking into ice, creaking.

We eat. Hotcakes, eggs bleeding yellow into thick syrup. Juice. So fresh I can never die. "Happy New Year," she says. Our glasses tinkle when they touch.

We wash the dishes, dry them, put them back. Turn the heaters down to low. Kiss. Kiss forgetting that we kiss. A cigarette. How much I'll miss cigarettes, I think. The bite at your gums, your tongue, your teeth. We flush the butts down the toilet.

"I'm ready," she says. She pulls on her furry boots. She zips her parka and tucks her hair into her beret. I feel her tits and squeeze between her legs.

"Ready for takeoff," I say.

"I'd like to leave a note." She slides a white, wrinkled envelope from her hip pocket. "My last will and testament," she says, her lips pale. "Ours." Typed on the envelope is DADDY. Who would I write? What would I say? The blue paper I take from the envelope will not stay still.

The New Year

Dear Daddy,
What a perfect day it is to turn the world inside out! To open myself to everything! There I will be—one clear thought, one life lived. I *have* lived. It is better to *end* a *life* than to slowly die. This way nothing dies. Not me. Not Carlos. Our feeling. What is in our hearts is exactly who we are—always. I hope you understand. You will, I know. You can see that Mother never died. Right next to me, Lance thought she would, but she's still just out there in the air. I hear her sometimes as

I fall asleep. Do you? Lance died. Someday you'll understand how it is I can be happy to end this note to
you and cross our little bridge a last time with a person
I love, with everything so crisp and cold. I am sorry
for you. If we are not blown up or badly burned, bury
us together under a black stone that says Death Is
Where You Find It.

Your daughter who loves,
Jill

I hold her face against mine. She leans the envelope
against a hurricane lamp.

Under all that snow, the cabin sinks into the ground.
The air shocks itself into our throats. The yellow Volvo is
white. We clean the windows in angel wings. First try, the
engine growls like a cat. She drives, mittens on the wheel.
A mile, no more. To the plowed, main road like an old
scab, dry and brittle through the tufted trees, the rolling,
clean, brand-new snow. The perfect snow. The last. We
climb white mountains. Up to Little Mountain, between
Emigration and Parley's canyons. The ridge where the road
peaks and dives. A week ago we looked before this snow.
Beyond the guardrail, the steep, brown mountain sloped,
sage and grass and dirt blood red.

A deer, a doe, unfolds from a drift, leaps over pavement,
slips on a silver slip of ice, straightens, tucks, springs
again—and is gone.

The sun is up, sharp, orange, thin clouds smoking, the
sky blue metal. STEEP INCLINE, NEXT 10 MILES says a bullet-
blistered sign resting on the snow. We park. No one passes
us. Two black birds grow heavy in the empty space beside
the mountain, the mountain smooth as skin, softer, almost
warm. The birds fall. Toward the hole. I taste syrup on my
tongue.

She leans to me, a mitten on each cheek. The tip of her

tongue. "I love you," she whispers. "There's more." My tongue thick with syrup.

"I love *you*," I say. But her face is dying already. So I cry to *show* her I love her. I touch her knee. Now she cries too.

"Okay," she says, looking forward then, into that diving, blinding emptiness of snow. She lowers the lever of the brake. In neutral, the engine still purring unafraid, we roll. I hate it that we are not the same person as I memorize her eyes, her cheeks, her ears.

"I love you," I say. Faster. The guardrail. The curve we will not make. She looks at *me* now, her eyes on fire. Honest to God flames. The birds dive. "Jill," I say. The last black flash of road. "Jill." Jesus. I throw my door open. "Jill!"

Snow. In my eyes, my mouth, my ears. Deep snow, powdered ice. I cannot stand. I roll. I sit, snow waist deep, and stare at the guardrail folded, ripped clean through its stripes to empty sky. I swim and twist and crawl and every goddamn thing to make the road. I run. I stand right there. The edge. Way the hell above the black bottom of the Volvo like a doorway in the snow.

Her wheels still turn.

59 ———— PIONEER DAY

Ginny closed the notebook. She tucked her legs inside her arms, the Spiral against her chest. With her eyes shut, she swallowed the last of her beer and pressed the can to her cheek. I flipped off the TV. Crickets. She dropped her cigarette into the can. She watched the string of smoke curl from the hole. "Did you really love her do you think?"

I leaned on the windowsill, moths beating our screens for our light over all the other million lights blinking down below. "We were . . . we were doubles or something. You read it."

"But you . . ."

"I loved her. Yeah, I loved her. But that part, that part . . . I was a kid."

"And you love me?"

"I told you."

"One rock hitting him just right," she said. "That's all it took to turn your life inside out. And we're leaving together to have a new life Monday night, no matter what?"

"Tuesday morning. Let me go alone."

"No, Carlos. No, I'm going." A plane roared over. "This *business,* it's Lance Arthur, isn't it?" Her sad eyes settled on mine.

"The last loose end. Just a private matter is all. Nothing to worry over."

She rolled onto her knees, her hands across her stomach, eyes still deeper. "You think he pushed their mother?"

"Yes. Jesus."

"Don't you . . . Don't you feel sorry?" She spread her arms.

"What?"

"I don't know." She stood. "I ache. I'm tired, Carlos. Real tired."

She worked her fingers slowly over my hair, held my face to her chest, where I could feel her heart. She whispered, "Good night." She kissed my forehead and dragged her feet into the darkness of the bedroom.

"Hey," I called. "Hey, tomorrow we study the atlas."

I carried that last Spiral down into the cool basement.

On a mountain road, I hear a car. Who's coming? I am alone, a boy alone in a storm, snow so heavy, falling so fast it will hide everything. The car cannot get through.

My car. Ginny idling down the canyon. The snow

stopped. I listened. She had whispered, "See ya." Off for a picnic with Paula and Emma. I moved my head to her pillow, to smell her. And I smelled her, and I smoked on my side in bed that morning, the day cloudy, the clouds these milky fish.

The notebooks were finished, my story over, nearly over, nearly begun. I would only keep one copy and the tapes, the voice. I scrambled three eggs and watched *Sunday Morning with Charles Kuralt*. A blind man without dark glasses had tried to solo-sail the Atlantic. He said, "I failed because of a dang radio malfunction." They cut to a redhead for Irish Spring soap. I did not eat my eggs. I'd pitch them to the cat.

Not in the window, the bushes, the tree. Not on the shed. The clouds trailed inky streaks of rain, but none reached the ground.

Mr. Cat's bowl was gone. So was his sack of food. Ginny's suitcase sat outside the door, though. On my table, the half-wrapped checks still collected mountain dust. In the basement, the notebooks, tapes, and pistol hadn't budged. The note was in the fridge, just right beneath the ice.

I sat on the counter while water boiled. I drank instant coffee on our boulder in mist. I smoked five, maybe six. Emma and Paula. What were their last names? They worked in the shoes at Sears. They lived in Sugarhouse. Together?

The clouds have fins. And Ginny waves, my windshield a reflection of dark clouds. She holds a bag of potato chips. She is stoned. We kiss. "Don't be mad," she says.

"What?"

"Mr. Cat. We couldn't take him. I gave him to them. A good home." Her hair is wet. If I don't follow through, deliver my stuff, will he have her hunted down?

"Ginny," I say, this cold just under my skin. I knot up.

She bites a potato chip that breaks in her hand. "I have to run an errand. Come with me."

"I don't want to be alone. I just don't."

"I know."

I left our house door open.

I took my last notebook—and copies of the rest. Ginny said, "This writing, it's time to let the past go."

"I want *it* to let go," I said. "That's what I want. I'm finished." I xeroxed the final chapters at a Skaggs. Ginny thumbed through magazines. I wrapped one copy of everything in brown paper, with a note.

> Don't read! Don't let anyone else! Please keep this in a safe place for me. I trust you.
>
> Carlos

I bought a padded envelope, pushed the works in, taped the fat thing shut, and addressed it to Moon in care of his record company in Nashville. He'd remember me. We walked it to the post office. Ginny kept her arm through mine. "In case the other gets lost," I said, and the stamp machine ticked out tiny flags. "I'll always have this."

"For what?"

"I don't know. Proof, I guess."

"Leave all that. You're a grown man. You don't need to prove anything."

"You're wrong."

"Live with it. Get over it."

The zip code book covered everyone. A warm drizzle. Church bells clanged. The roads were patched with water.

Over Main Street in Bountiful, the damp tucks of red, white, and blue cloth for the twenty-fourth looked like

skirts, skirt after skirt after skirt, knotted fast to one another
and tied up high.

Our drive is empty.

The mountains are barely there. A steamy mist slides
over them. Magpies flap out, glide in. Shout. Our nothing
shack sucks my tinny voice into its crooked walls. "Let's
figure out where." The lake stinks. The floor squeals. I
light a smoke. "Ginny."

I open the atlas on my table, but the table . . . Those
days are over.

I press myself against the screen, everything hot and
dark and glossy out. She pages through the atlas. "Water
is what I want. Lots of clean water." I stand behind her,
with one hand on her bare shoulder. We smoke and look
at Florida. She says, "I've never seen the ocean."

"You choose. We can always move."

"Run, you mean? I want to get fixed somewhere. Besides,
running gets expensive. God, I can't believe we don't
know."

"Then there'd be nothing to find out." I kiss her neck.
She stops on Minnesota.

"Look at all those lakes."

"Tough call between the two," I say. "Hot, cold. South,
north. No mountains."

"You want mountains?"

"You choose," I say.

"Calm down," she says. She takes my hands.

"Mountains are all I know. You choose."

She laughs. She laughs to do it, for us both to hear her
laugh, for us both to think this is fun, this choosing in the
dark a goddamn future. And so I laugh. She closes the
atlas, then flips it open and drops her finger. "How about
Ireland?" She grins.

"My car would never make it."

"Once more." She shuts the atlas and opens it and drops her finger again. "How about . . ." And now she narrows her eyes at me. "How about North Carolina? It's got ocean. And here, it's got mountains: the Great Smoky Mountains, the Stone Mountains, the Bald Mountains."

"My kid with an accent. Okay. We'll trust fate."

"I do," she says, but her head is down over the atlas and her fingers with the ring are tight around the back of her neck.

We went the next morning because I told Ginny they would be in it, that my business had to wait for this, because she said she couldn't stop thinking about the cat, that she couldn't sit still. "I've only seen the ones on TV," she said. I expected something to stop me, to end then, to make it clear we could not leave, as we rolled slowly down the canyon, our car packed, Ginny almost gone back to sleep. What had I forgotten? I popped another beer. She said, "If it's nice in North Carolina, I know, I'll have them send him on a plane."

The Skyline High School Marching Band. This girl in white boots and a tiny silver skirt bent her knees and tossed a baton twisting end over end up through the muggy air. A biplane towed a banner for Pioneer Days Rodeo through the dark sky behind the twirling baton. A drum roll. The baton fell past children leaning from office windows. The girl in the silver skirt dropped to one knee, caught the baton as though it never left, and spun it fast around her tan neck. Ginny said, "Amazing." The horns picked up again. Horses with deputies. Women in bonnets and long, checked dresses walking beside baby-faced men in broad black hats pulling noisy handcarts. A boy said, "Let's go home." A clown fell off a unicycle and his ass swelled up like a damn balloon.

Second South and Main. Right across from the bank. A

steamy pressure cooker. Sweat itched in my ears. I drank
Coke. I would be clear headed today of all days. I'd done
a few hits off a joint with my coffee sometime around dawn.
The beers. Period. That would be it. And here now he
would see me, see *me*, see *us*, that I was happy, see the
bank—keep it all straight. I'd left the pistol home. At first
I thought, just shoot him, Ginny would be better alone.
Like a movie. Walk out beside his car. But Ginny. And
Hilda. And I wanted it over. And I wasn't a killer. This
wasn't a movie. This went on. I tightened my arm around
Ginny's shoulder.

Horse shit sweetened the air. I smoked. An old fart with
dandruff moved away. A big crowd—six or seven deep
clear down Main, plenty with lawn chairs, binocs, and bags
of food. The dark street. Cops I'd never seen, in black.
The white floats. Women in white gowns waving white,
white gloves. A swan. Fat men in tasseled hats on motor-
bikes. The Salt Lake Kennel Club, twenty T-shirted, well-
fed, middle-aged dog lovers in formation, hand-signaling
their fluffed-up mutts to lie down, sit, and roll over. Clowns
in lousy suits, in wigs that didn't hide their hair, handed
out balloons, balloons printed UTAH POWER AND LIGHT. *Electricity.* The kiss of blue sparks.

"There," Ginny said on tiptoe. Beautiful in a light-blue
jacket, her hair swept up, Hilda perched over the backseat
of a shiny black Lincoln convertible above her two grinning
daughters, between Lance, in a white shirt, red suspenders,
and a bow tie, and my old man in a sweat-darkened shirt,
his hair combed. Lance and Hilda smiled, waved in big arcs
from side to side like wind-up toys in a goddamn dream.
My old man kept his hands between his legs, his eyes down.
A lady said, "She's gorgeous." A band played "Yellow Submarine." A black balloon floated away. I did step out.
"Hey!" I shouted. "Hey!" Ginny pulled at my arm.

The three turned. For just a snap the waving stopped.

My old man pointed, began to stand, but Hilda held him back. With both hands, Lance lobbed this spray of candy over the crowd. Which cheered. A clown said, "Excuse me, Bud," and edged me toward the curb. Tubas rumbled the air. And my old man swiveled—stared as the car moved on. Hilda's mouth opened. *She* waved to *me*. Lance waved with his left, waved with his right. A leggy blond wearing only a blue raincoat and rain hat waved beneath a two-story umbrella of salt. An umbrella of salt. Around the base, just outside the wheels, a stenciled line of blue letters read, WHEN IT RAINS IT POURS, over and over. The clouds were low.

Ginny said, "Let's get out of here."

60 ——— NEW RIVER

One step to go. To start again. And again. Things were planned. Safe. We would drive for Needmore, Peachland, New River.

She had not touched the checks, she wore the ring.

To me Stud said, "You look like somebody's been dead a couple of years." He said. "Hi, honey," to Ginny on the couch. His whiskers like iron filings, he still hadn't shaved. His bent hat dripped. He slapped it on his thigh, spattering water over the dry floor. He wore a tie-dyed strapped T-shirt with a hole in the back. He was on time.

"Have something to eat," Ginny said. Twinkies, tuna fish, bread, sausage, beer—along the counter. The fridge was clean, by God, off, its door open. The stove was spotless as that stove would ever get. The bathroom. Ginny busy last night, today. Doing it right. I'd packed food in garbage bags. The Polara was ready—my copy and the tapes under the spare in the trunk. With the help of two of Ginny's damn diet pills, I could have driven to hell and back.

"Come here a minute,' I said, and stepped onto the porch.

Water dripped from the roof. Stud wiped his mouth. "The woman's coming?"

"I told you. We're heading out right from there."

"Might be I'll take Bitsy off into a new life sometime, too." I showed him his check, and he tilted his head. "How do I know it's good?"

"You don't. But you've already got five and why would I quibble over another."

Stud dragged the toe of his boot through one of his muddy footprints. Then he looked out at the hazy valley. "Won't be any fireworks tonight," he said. " 'less *you* got some planned."

"We visit the governor's," I said. "You figured that. All you do is deliver a sack to me when I signal. Easy." I went over it.

"My pistol's in my truck," he said. "Storm ought to get people inside." And would Hilda and the kids still go?

Stud rubbed his forehead, glanced back in at Ginny. "Hey, I could use a sandwich?"

"It's a holiday," she said. "I'm off duty."

Stud threw down two slugs of Beam with his sausage, from a near-gone bottle he brought. "You know," he said, "some day we ought to pool our dough and start us a bar."

Ginny put on jeans and a shiny blouse. She said, "Are we going now?"

"You're cute," Stud said. He laughed.

I stuck the notebooks and the note in a grocery sack on the front seat of his truck, my pistol, too. The rain had let up, just a sprinkle now through a soup of green light. Ginny carried her shoes and the checks. My shoes squeaked. I got the bags of food.

I stared out over the lake one more time, and then I flipped the latch, threw the key in on the floor by the TV, and closed the door.

"Fifteen minutes," I said to Stud.

Ginny tossed the checks in back. She said, "I liked that little house." I released the brake and we coasted away.

Not fifty feet from the Governor's wrought-iron gate, the spotlighted flowerbeds, the stone house big as a hotel, ground-floor windows milky orange, we parked in front of Stud on "G." The drizzle smoked through streetlight at the corner. A limo glistened in the drive. Its plate said UTAH 1.

I cracked the window, flipped a cigarette through the rain. "Hang tight," I told Ginny. "Anything weird, you motor."

"Don't let there be anything weird. Just hurry."

"Won't be ten minutes."

Stud had a quart of Miller between his legs, his hat on my grocery sack beside him. Two minutes to go. Stud said, "My life's taken some crazy goddamn turns, Cade. Remember that cave and the snowstorm?"

"All right," I said, heating up, my skin damp all over, my clothes pulling as I shifted to check my watch again. "You know your part. Bring the stuff up. Period. No need to show off the pistol. Enjoy the rodeo."

"You're nuts. God, maybe I am. I'm trusting you, Cade."

"So long. This is nothing. Don't forget."

I knocked. Just once.

"This way," Lance said. He turned, walked slowly. Beneath a prismed chandelier, down a hall, across an ancient-looking, red, patterned rug, to the office at the end. A flag in each corner barely moved over floor vents in the air conditioning. Cool. I expected him to look down at me, but I looked down at him. Short. Not a wrinkle anywhere. He wore a yellow alligator shirt, a gold chain at the open neck, and crisp white pants. His watch beeped.

"Sit down."

"You *are* alone?"

"For fifteen minutes." He put his feet on the desk, laced his fingers. He smiled, the small scar on his freckled cheek rising. He held his ice blue eyes on mine. The walls were blue, speckled with stars. On a shelf, in a silver frame, Hilda smiled from a bed with a baby. Hilda skiing. Hilda in a gown. And over Lance hung that painting in this thick, carved, gold-painted frame, his mother, hers. Her eyes remembered me. "Cade . . ."

"Wait." I rushed from room to room, chest tight. Upstairs, too. Their bedroom with a canopy bed. Rachel's room, with clouds painted on the ceiling.

"All right," I said. "Sit there. Don't move. I'll get the stuff." And I noticed now the legal-looking paper underneath his folded hands. "A guy'll pass it to me and leave."

"Guy who knows nothing?"

"Not any of it."

Stud stepped out of the mist the second I waved. "Good man," I said. The sack was wet. I held out the check. "Get the hell away from here."

"This is big," Stud said. "Don't fall." He loped down the hazy drive past the limo to his truck.

Lance said, "So you're leaving? Where to?"

"Save it. My life is now officially my life again. I'm taking over."

"Fine, I just want you to sign a couple of things, what you suggested." He leaned out at me with a pen. He raised his eyebrows. "That's all I need."

"Right. Mr. Fair and Square. What about all the shit you've put me through? The dog thing. You pulled all the goddamn strings."

"Come on, Cade. Think. I knew you'd be at that fight. Some of my friends were there. Sure, I thought it wouldn't be bad to have you hightail it away again. That's it. The white dog was big money. You stepped in that on your own. I hear Ingus got what he deserved."

"Sure."

"You'd know."

I shifted the damp sack. Squeezed my eyes shut. Dropped the sack on a chair by the door. Forty minutes after. Five more. Squeezed my eyes shut again, but there he was. I pulled out the pistol. "Goddamn you."

Lance glanced at his watch. "Carlos . . . Think." He held out the pen. "You and your girlfriend motor away. The end."

"Right. You're lucky I didn't come to kill you, Lance. Goddamn you. You! Fuck, you with her painting over your desk."

"I loved my mother. She fell, Carlos."

"You loved no one."

Now Lance stood. "Cade, you came to make a delivery. Sign and get out of here."

The muscle of my heart would not relax. The pistol weighed nothing. "What I am, you made," I said.

"Sure." He laughed. "Sure. Starting with Skink, right? The great fairy tale. If you hadn't gotten all scared and told us to slide him down the hole, we wouldn't have."

"You threw the rock."

"I threw the rock," he said, "but we killed him, and you, no matter how long you try to believe otherwise, you son of a bitch, it was your begging, *your* bright idea to drop him down the hole. And Jill? You probably drove the car and jumped. How is it you have the note? Cade, I regret one hell of a lot, but number one I regret ever knowing you, ever helping you. If it hadn't been for my sister. If it weren't for yours . . ."

And I was the one sweating, soaked. Dripping on this goddamn fancy rug.

"You couldn't kill me, Carlos. Then where would your chickenshit life be? Let's not forget your sister. She's had enough. Sign this. We haven't long."

"What do you care if a guard sees me?"

"You cared. Remember?"

"I *was* with Jill right to the end."

"I don't want to know," he said. He pushed a pen across the desk. His eyes flickered to his watch.

"You think you're so fucking powerful." I got out the note, opened it. "Read this, goddamn it." But he would not lower his eyes. "You push your mother off—"

"I told you . . . Jill believed it. Sure, Jill believed . . . *She* even believed in *you*. Christ."

I lifted the pistol. He dropped back of the desk. And I fired. Hit the phone. And fired. The lady in the painting tore but would not fall. Would not fall, goddamn it.

An alarm exploded. Shrieked. Screamed. I ran into the hall. Behind me, Lance stood, a blue revolver in his fist, which did not flash. Did not fire. Did not burst through my hand, like a goddamn western—a bone snap, pain. I ran.

Out into the rain, the mist. Ghosts of smoke. I chucked the pistol into flowers. I ran to the Polara, the windows white, and I could see Ginny, Ginny staring. And when I grabbed the wet handle, the alarm died. I stood in the mist. I heard a siren. Far away. I tugged the handle. The door would not open. I rocked the car. And Ginny stared at me with her eyes melting in the fog. "Open the goddamn door, Ginny. Open the goddamn door." And she did.

She said, "You had a gun."

Streetlights raced with us. Two old couples dressed as pioneers stepped into the mist. Our tires screeched. Headlights. Hot. My chest would not rise far enough. Two blocks. Five blocks. Ten. I stopped. Turned. Saw nothing but rain, heard nothing but her breathing. I pushed my hand back through my hair, lit a smoke with the dash lighter. No sirens. She said, "Did you . . . Did you kill him?"

And I said, "No. I shot to . . . to show him . . . I showed him."

"It's us," she said. "That's all. Please?" The wipers cleared the rain. "I've got this child inside."

I said, "Ginny, the Governor . . ."

"This won't work," she said, sobbing. "I was going to save you." She jumped from the car and ran through the smoky drizzle alongside a bus, into a Mobil Station. No sirens. She pressed her small face against the gas station window. I got out. A pickup honked, sprayed me as it passed. I shouted, "Ginny!"

She stepped between stacks of oil and tires in the doorway then. Her yellow shape, a red horse flying above her head. "Ginny!"

She cupped her hands around her mouth. At first I couldn't hear. She wiped her eyes and called again: "It isn't yours!" A woman with a polka dot umbrella turned. No sirens, but cars were backing up. "Carlos, it's not yours!"

I slowly closed the door. The wipers cleared the glass. My lies and now hers. I knew a lie. I tightened my hands on the wheel. My stomach knotted. Cars were backing up. I made a sound from pain that no one heard, tossed the butt outside, and pressed the pedal to the floor. Ginny. Rain. Cold rain filling lakes high in the mountains. Rain sizzled from the tires as she waved. She waved. I swear. And I love her. I could have gone after her, but I didn't. I didn't, Ginny, did I, Ginny? This, all of this, is for you, and for a kid who is mine, I know it, and who is lucky, I know that, too, Ginny. I know that now, too.

ABOUT THE AUTHOR

Stephen Pett grew up in Salt Lake City and attended Colorado College. He is a graduate of the writing programs at Hollins College and the University of Utah, and is the author of *Pulpit of Bones,* a collection of poems. His fiction and poetry has been awarded numerous prizes, including First Place in the *Fiction Network* short fiction competition and the Iowa Arts Council Literature Award in fiction. He teaches at Iowa State University in Ames, Iowa, where he lives with his wife and two sons.

VINTAGE
CONTEMPORARIES

___ **The Mezzanine** by Nicholson Baker	$7.95	679-72576-8
___ **I Pass Like Night** by Jonathan Ames	$8.95	679-72857-0
___ **Love Always** by Ann Beattie	$5.95	394-74418-7
___ **The History of Luminous Motion** by Scott Bradfield	$8.95	679-72943-7
___ **First Love and Other Sorrows** by Harold Brodkey	$7.95	679-72075-8
___ **Stories in an Almost Classical Mode** by Harold Brodkey	$12.95	679-72431-1
___ **The Debut** by Anita Brookner	$6.95	679-72712-4
___ **Latecomers** by Anita Brookner	$8.95	679-72668-3
___ **Sleeping in Flame** by Jonathan Carroll	$8.95	679-72777-9
___ **Cathedral** by Raymond Carver	$7.95	679-72369-2
___ **Fires** by Raymond Carver	$7.95	679-72239-4
___ **What We Talk About When We Talk About Love**		
by Raymond Carver	$6.95	679-72305-6
___ **Where I'm Calling From** by Raymond Carver	$8.95	679-72231-9
___ **I Look Divine** by Christopher Coe	$5.95	394-75995-8
___ **Dancing Bear** by James Crumley	$6.95	394-72576-X
___ **The Last Good Kiss** by James Crumley	$6.95	394-75989-3
___ **One to Count Cadence** by James Crumley	$5.95	394-73559-5
___ **The Wrong Case** by James Crumley	$5.95	394-73558-7
___ **The Colorist** by Susan Daitch	$7.95	679-72492-3
___ **The Last Election** by Pete Davies	$6.95	394-74702-X
___ **Great Jones Street** by Don DeLillo	$7.95	679-72303-X
___ **The Names** by Don DeLillo	$7.95	679-72295-5
___ **Players** by Don DeLillo	$7.95	679-72293-9
___ **Ratner's Star** by Don DeLillo	$8.95	679-72292-0
___ **Running Dog** by Don DeLillo	$7.95	679-72294-7
___ **The Commitments** by Roddy Doyle	$6.95	679-72174-6
___ **Selected Stories** by Andre Dubus	$10.95	679-72533-4
___ **From Rockaway** by Jill Eisenstadt	$6.95	394-75761-0
___ **Platitudes** by Trey Ellis	$6.95	394-75439-5
___ **Days Between Stations** by Steve Erickson	$6.95	394-74685-6
___ **Rubicon Beach** by Steve Erickson	$6.95	394-75513-8
___ **A Fan's Notes** by Frederick Exley	$7.95	679-72076-6

VINTAGE
CONTEMPORARIES

VINTAGE
CONTEMPORARIES

___ **The Bushwhacked Piano** by Thomas McGuane	$7.95	394-72642-1
___ **Nobody's Angel** by Thomas McGuane	$7.95	394-74738-0
___ **Something to Be Desired** by Thomas McGuane	$4.95	394-73156-5
___ **To Skin a Cat** by Thomas McGuane	$5.95	394-75521-9
___ **Bright Lights, Big City** by Jay McInerney	$5.95	394-72641-3
___ **Ransom** by Jay McInerney	$5.95	394-74118-8
___ **Story of My Life** by Jay McInerney	$6.95	679-72257-2
___ **Mama Day** by Gloria Naylor	$8.95	679-72181-9
___ **The All-Girl Football Team** by Lewis Nordan	$5.95	394-75701-7
___ **Welcome to the Arrow-Catcher Fair** by Lewis Nordan	$6.95	679-72164-9
___ **River Dogs** by Robert Olmstead	$6.95	394-74684-8
___ **Soft Water** by Robert Olmstead	$6.95	394-75752-1
___ **Family Resemblances** by Lowry Pei	$6.95	394-75528-6
___ **Sirens** by Steve Pett	$8.95	394-75712-2
___ **Clea & Zeus Divorce** by Emily Prager	$6.95	394-75591-X
___ **A Visit From the Footbinder** by Emily Prager	$6.95	394-75592-8
___ **Mohawk** by Richard Russo	$8.95	679-72577-6
___ **The Risk Pool** by Richard Russo	$8.95	679-72334-X
___ **Rabbit Boss** by Thomas Sanchez	$8.95	679-72621-7
___ **Anywhere But Here** by Mona Simpson	$7.95	394-75559-6
___ **Carnival for the Gods** by Gladys Swan	$6.95	394-74330-X
___ **The Player** by Michael Tolkin	$7.95	679-72254-8
___ **Myra Breckinridge and Myron** by Gore Vidal	$8.95	394-75444-1
___ **The Car Thief** by Theodore Weesner	$6.95	394-74097-1
___ **Breaking and Entering** by Joy Williams	$6.95	394-75773-4
___ **Taking Care** by Joy Williams	$5.95	394-72912-9
___ **The Easter Parade** by Richard Yates	$8.95	679-72230-0
___ **Eleven Kinds of Loneliness** by Richard Yates	$8.95	679-72221-1
___ **Revolutionary Road** by Richard Yates	$8.95	679-72191-6

Now at your bookstore or call toll-free to order: 1-800-733-3000

(credit cards only).